THE RESTLESS SUPERMARKET

Ivan Vladislavić

LONDON · NEW YORK

First published in southern Africa in 2001 by David Philip Publishers
New edition in southern Africa published in 2012 by Umuzi, an
imprint of Random House Struik

First published this edition in 2014 by And Other Stories
London – New York
www.andotherstories.org

ISBN 9781908276322
eBook ISBN 9781908276339

A catalogue record for this book is available from the British Library.

for Luc de Graeve

The Restless Supermarket

Where can we always find happiness?
In the dictionary.

– Aubrey Tearle

The Café Europa

PART ONE

He reads the world, like a favourite volume, only to find beauties in it, or like an edition of some old work which he is preparing for the press, only to make emendations in it, and correct the errors that have inadvertently slipt in.

–William Hazlitt

A SALESMAN BUGGERING A PINK ELEPHANT (EXCUSE MY BULGARIAN). Not a sight one sees every day, even on the streets of Johannesburg – the Golden City as it were, Egoli as it are, to quote my pal Wessels, the last of the barnacles. As the century declines to a conclusion one has come to expect undignified behaviour as a matter of course, but this was an 'all-time low' (as the newspapers would put it). I see it before me now as if it were yesterday.

I say he was a salesman because of the pinstriped suit, the shirt-tails hanging out behind, the tie drooping on his chest like a slice of pizza. Old-fashioned associations on my part. He might just as well have been a popular star, or a lawyer with a passing interest in human rights, or the head of a syndicate for stealing motor cars. These days, the men in lounge suits are good-for-nothings more often than not, while the real businessmen are waltzing around in Bermuda shorts and espadrilles. Whoever he was, he had hold of the elephant on the pavement outside the Jumbo Liquor Market in Kotze Street, gripping its shocking pink buttocks in his paws and grinding his groin against its unyielding fibre-glass tail.

I stopped to stare. A lifetime of practice has turned me into one of the world's most shameless scrutineers.

The joker's eyes were screwed shut in rapture, but the elephant's were like saucers, with painted pupils as black as draughtsmen rattling in them. The beast's pointed ears stood on end like wistful wings and its trunk curled an outraged question mark over its little gasping mouth. Its eyes met mine without blinking.

'Hey, Arch! Check what Darryl's doing.' Spoken by another ill-suited entrepreneur fumbling for a wallet while the cashier rang up a carton of Camel cigarettes and a bottle of Red Heart rum.

The Jumbo Liquor Market, as its name suggests, is a 'convenience store' in the American mould. Sliding glass doors open directly onto the pavement so that the passing trade can totter in and out with a minimum of effort. From till to gutter in three easy steps. Arch came out to see what Darryl was up to. Arch, Darryl and the Third Man. A little triumvirate, unholy and unwise, but citizens nevertheless of the conurbation in which I find myself.

Bump and grind from the rear.

Arch said, 'Ag, stop it man Darr. You making your name tawty.' (Just who or what 'tawty' is, I cannot say: it's in none of the reference works and no one will enlighten me. Perhaps a South African counterpart of that scoundrel Mudd?)

Darr slumped down on the elephant's back and spoke passionately into one outflung ear: 'Suffer, baby, suffer.'

Snorts of laughter from Arch and the Third Man. What would *his* name be? Some monosyllabic chunk no doubt, some unfeeling stump like Gav or Ern or Gord. People were starting to gather. Shoppers from the supermarket on the next corner, drinkers from the verandah of the Chelsea Hotel across the way, the twilight children, drawn out in broad daylight by the spectacle, a couple of continental gentlemen in open-neck shirts. As representative a cross-section of conurbanites as you could wish to find.

Suffer, baby, suffer. It was the punchline of a Wessels joke, I'm sure, entertained reluctantly like all the rest. I never forget a punchline – but I'm damned if I can remember a joke. Except for that one about Rubber Dinghy Sithole. 'What's black and goes with the stream?' I've spoilt the effect by putting it back to front. It must be all of fifteen years since Erasmus at Posts and Telecommunications told it to me, around the time Rhodesia attained its majority, and for some reason it stuck. The pink elephant, I noticed, was chained to a parking meter, expired.

Right on cue, the Queen of Sheba staggered out of the alley between the Jumbo and Hypermeat. She had a throne there, a sponge-rubber armchair the colour of urine, upon which she sometimes reclined wearing a paper crown from a Christmas cracker and a robe of threadbare carpeting. She was drawn to Darr at once. As she gazed at him, she stuck a hand through the armhole of her dress and absent-mindedly rearranged her breasts. He huffed and puffed and oohed and aahed, and opened one eye to gauge the response of his growing audience.

Hypermeat was flogging half a dead sheep @ R12.95 a kilogram, and sirlion steaks @ R6.95 a cut. Doing a roaring trade, I suppose. 'Nice meat' said a blackboard, also chained to a parking meter, with ten minutes on the dial.

The Queen staggered closer. She smelt like the bottom of the barrel. Seeing that the rear end of the elephant was already occupied, she approached the front and tried to clamber up like a mahout. Darr kept thumping away. An 'ugly situation' all right, and bound to get uglier. Arch saw it coming. He took Darr by the arm and tried to drag him away, but was shrugged off. The Third Man, hurrying to Arch's assistance, dropped his wallet, and coins scattered across the pavement. The children swooped. I put my foot down on a one-rand coin and examined the little ones to see if there was a deserving case among them.

The Queen got a leg over the elephant's neck and sprang up, overbalanced, grabbed at an ear, which snapped off in her hands, and plunged over the other side. Her head struck the fender of the [Henry] Ford parked at the kerb. The car began to shriek; the Queen, God save her, was silent. Darryl came to a shuddering halt. A tiny peep, the sound a crib toy might make if you squeezed it, issued from the elephant's trunk.

'Meesta Ferreira! Meesta Ferreira! Pleece comb tew da frount!' the cashier said urgently into a microphone. Mr Ferreira's face appeared in a diamond of glass in the door at the back of the shop.

Enough. I kicked the coin down a stormwater drain and hurried on to the Café Europa. I had seen enough to know what would inevitably follow: *skop, skiet* and *donner,* and their corollaries, *snot* and *trane.* (These are Wesselisms for trouble and tears, and the fact that I stoop to them is a sign that better words have failed me.) Mr Ferreira arrives on the scene, thrusting out the managerial bulges of his pink blazer. Arch and Darr wrestle. The Queen bleeds unconsciously. Voices and fists are raised. The Queen comes round and begins to wail. Her courtiers creep out of their holes and try to console her by falling over her and tugging at her clothing. Speaking in indigenous tongues, roaring and cursing, laying on of hands and feet. Mr Ferreira enters into the spirit by taking out his revolver. The Third Man trots across the street, opens the door of a black sedan (one of those ubiquitous abbreviations that issue in an unbroken line from the Bayerische Motoren Werke) and reaches for something under the driver's seat. The owner of the stricken Ford comes running with a serviette tucked into his pullover, and examines the dented fender as if it is a wound in his own flesh. Multilingual sobbing. Four-letter words fly, the whole dashed alphabet. The air goes dark with obscenity, the leading players are obscured by it, the bystanders grow restless, Darryl is still darrylling away in the gloom, Arch is arching, the manager managing. And then warning shots, Your Honour, falling down.

In a word: chaos.

One Sunday morning not too long ago, on an overgrown plot in Prospect Road, I saw a body in the weeds, under a shroud of pages from the *Sunday Times*. I saw it from the window of my own flat, where I stood with a carton of long-life milk in my hand, and I could almost smell the pungent scent of the kakiebos crushed by its fall. It lay among the rusted pipes, blackened bricks and outcrops of old foundations that mark every bit of empty land in this city, as if a reef of disorder lay just below the surface, or a civilization had gone to ruin here before we ever arrived.

What do I mean by 'we'? Don't make me laugh.

*

Wessels was waiting for me as usual in the Café Europa. Properly: Martinus Theodosius Wessels – but I'm afraid I think of him as Empty. Empty Wessels make the most noise. Or in this case, *makes* the most noise. Appropriately, it grates the grammatical nerve-endings. Errors of number are Wessels's speciality.

'Yes yes, Mr Tearle,' he said through a jet of smoke. 'Hullo-ss.' Perhaps the sibilant centre of his own surname created this propensity for letting off steam. Before I could even sit down, he was rootling in my shopping-bag, trying to put me off my food. 'Salamis, hey. Sweating like a pig in there.'

Salamis? Rang a bell. I made a note to look it up.

'You'll never guess what I just saw.'

'Me first,' he said, 'I've got a major something to tell you.'

'So long as it's not a joke.'

'Uh-uh. Sit down, you making me nervous.'

'Take your foot off my chair.' The foot in question was encased in plaster of Paris. I'd known Wessels for several years, but I'd only recently made the acquaintance of this grisly extremity. The toes were squashed together like foetuses in a bottle, and there were lumps of plaster stuck to the hairs curling out of them. He made a performance of moving crutch and limb and dusting the plastic seat cover with a serviette.

Moçes appeared at my shoulder. Properly: Moses Someone-or-Other. I'd added the hammer and sickle because he was from Moçambique. A little joke between myself and my inner eye, entirely lost on the flapping ear.

'Have a dop,' said Wessels. He ordered himself a brandy.

I ordered my usual tea and specified separate bills. Wessels was obsessed with getting me drunk. Ditto himself, with more success. When he'd broken his ankle, falling down somewhere in a stupor, I asked him, 'Did it leak when you broke it?' But he didn't get it. He had the most fantastic excuse, though: said he'd hurt himself trying to effect a citizen's arrest on a cutpurse outside the Mini Cine.

(What sort of a name is that for a cinema? They might as well call it the Silly Billy. I won't be surprised if it goes out of business.)

'So what's the story?'

'The Café Europa,' waving his crutch recklessly, 'is closing down.'

'You're joking.' But I could see that for once he wasn't.

'At the end of the month, the doors will close on our little club for the last time. The end of an error.'

He mispronounces things deliberately to get under my skin. The last day of 1993 was less than a month away.

'Shame man,' Wessels went on. 'Tony told me this morning. I wished you was here to hear it with your own ears. Because you our main man and everythink.'

'God forbid.'

So the New Management was throwing in the towel. Properly: Anthony, pronounced ænθəni: for a reason I could never fathom. Popularly: Tony. But tony he wasn't, so I preferred to think of him as the New Management, which he was.

I called Moçes back. I said I would have a whiskey after all, with an 'e' please, deciding to indulge. Time was when you couldn't get anything stronger at the Café Europa than a double espresso. On high days and holidays, when grandchildren were born or horses came in, Mrs Mavrokordatos – the Old Management, although we never thought of her that way – might slip you an ouzo under the counter, in a thimble of a glass with a bunch of grapes and a twist of vine etched on it. That was before her own standards slipped in the direction of the shebeen.

'Did he say why?'

'Didn't have to. No customers, no profits. This kind of place isn't *in* any more.'

'What about Errol and Co? I thought the New Management was catering for them. Specifically.'

'Get real. They don't spend their bucks here. They shoot pool, they sit outside in the sun, they have a couple of pots. Half the time they don't even pay for those – it's cheaper to bring your own. I see them topping up their glasses with nips from the girls' bags. They think they clever, but I got experience in covert operations.'

'My eye.' He can hear a cork pop at fifty paces.

'I saw it coming. Three years ago already I told Mrs Mav changing with the times won't save us. We've had our chips.'

Wessels had taken to echoing me in the most infuriating manner. Still does. He swirls my sentiments around in his cavernous interior until they're completely out of shape and mixed up with his own, and then he booms them back at me, made discordant and disagreeable, and reeking of the ashtray. *I* was the one who said: Changing with the times is not for us. Staying the same is our forte. He never gave the matter a thought; he was too busy feeding his face and ogling the coloured girls, most of them young enough to be his daughters. To tell the truth, I was hardly surprised that the Café was closing down. I'd been predicting it for years.

'Our days are numbered.'

I'd said that too! And in my mind's eye, the numbered days were perfect spheres, like pool balls.

The pool room was through an archway. It was always dark in there, because the blinds were never opened, and when the fluorescent tubes over the tables glowed, the surrounding darkness thickened. Now Errol came suddenly into focus in the smoke-marbled light. He took a cloth from his pocket and drew his cue tenderly through it. The thing was his pride and joy. He'd tried to impress me once with the name of the manufacturer, but it meant nothing to me. He carried it in two parts, in a case lined with velvet, and would screw them together with the practised efficiency of an assassin.

Moçes brought my whiskey, John Jameson's on the rocks. Don't suppose that this semi-literate peasant appreciated the distinction between Scotch and the real thing: 'with an "e"' was shorthand, drummed into him with difficulty.

'To us!' said Wessels.

'Absent friends!' I regretted that afterwards, because it set his cogs whirring.

The whiskey made me sentimental. I don't like sentiment – it's one of the reasons I seldom indulge – but Wessels was waffling on about the good old days and I found myself looking around me with new eyes. Now that the existence of the place was threatened, I saw it in a new light. I would have to look at everything properly, preserve the details that the years had somehow failed to imprint on my mind.

Décor. Tables and chairs – travesties of their former selves since the reupholstering, but still affectingly receptive to the contours of the familiar human body. The espresso machine on the counter. Even the new fixtures

I had despised so much – the venetian blinds where I would have preferred to see the old brocade, the fake stained glass of the chapel where the one-armed bandits resided, the posters of football teams – all suddenly felt fragile. But not the television sets. There was a limit to everything.

The impending loss that grieved me most was Alibia, the painted city that covered an entire wall of the Café. I imagined workmen in overalls slapping polyvinyl acetate over our capital without a second thought. It should be moved to a new location, I decided: sawn up into blocks, numbered and packed, transported to safety, and reassembled. The Yanks were all for that sort of thing, carving up the world and recycling it as atmosphere. I don't know why I was thinking this way. After all, it was no Florentine fresco, it was of no historical significance, nothing important had ever happened in this room. There was no point in preserving any of it. It was merely – that phrase so beloved of the Lost and Found columns came into my head – 'of great sentimental value'.

'If these walls could speak, hey,' Wessels said as if he'd read my thoughts.

'If they could speak English, you mean.' Then I might have asked them: what is that stuff you're covered with? Apart from the one with the mural, the walls were papered, and the pattern had always bothered me. What did it represent? Rising damp? Autumn leaves? 'Besides, ears are common enough among walls, but mouths are rare.'

'Now that's above my fireplace,' said Wessels, and looked baffled.

'Never mind. I wonder what will open here when we're gone?'

'A whorehouse.' As if he knew for a fact. 'Or a disco.' He made Christmas lights with his fat fingers.

'So long as it's not another chicken outlet,' I said. 'We've got enough of those. Though why they should be called chicken outlets, I don't know. It sounds like the orifice through which a fowl passes an egg.'

'I know this tone of voice,' Wessels said, too familiarly by half. 'It's your letter-to-the-editor tone. We should write a letter to the *Star*. We haven't done that for ages. Hey, Mo-siss.'

He ordered another round, make that doubles, and I didn't protest. These were extraordinary circumstances.

'Dear Editor,' Wessels dictated, steepling his fingers and gazing up at the ceiling in what I understood to be a parody of my own attitude. 'It have come to my attention that Europa Caffy, last outpost of symbolization in the jungly flatland that go by the name of Hillbrow, most densely populated residential hairier in the southern hemisphere ...'

And growing denser by the day. More people and fewer motor vehicles. No one who could afford to drive a car wanted to come here any more.

I have never been able to hold my liquor, as they say, whereas Empty Wessels can hold a gallon (an ancient measure for liquids) in each leg without getting plastered. The walls have ears. I found myself going over the porous surface of Wessels's face as incredulously as I had just examined the wallpaper. Another crumbling ruin. His face sat like a lump of porridge on the cracked calyx of his old-fashioned suit with its ridiculously wide lapels. A drinker's nose, a real grog berry, with little sesamoid nodules in the wings of the nostrils. His features were all too big. You could say of him, without a hint of the figurative, that he was all ears. They were large and fleshy in the lobe and full of gristle, tufty in the middle, with tops like the curve of fat on a pork chop. It made sense to me that Empty Wessels should have these meaty handles attached to his head. Auditory meatus. To coin a false etymology.

Pitcher ~ pitchy ~ plague ~ plaguy. The whiskey beginning to talk. Then there was the hair. Also too big, obscenely thick for a man of his age, and worn in the ducktail style. The rear end of a bloody Muscovy. He dyes it black. Why does it vex me so?

'What's to become of us?' he was still dictating, mocking my accent. 'We part of the furniture around here.'

Speak for yourself. The whole of his person appears to be covered with the same stiff horsehair that sprouts from his ears. The way it sticks out of him, you could believe that he was stuffed with it. You wouldn't be surprised to see a shiny spring burst out of the fabric stretched over his belly.

'Those were the days. Yours faithfully.'

He has all the finesse of an ottoman, I thought. He had stopped speaking at last and was gazing at me over the spatulate ends of his fingers. You piece of wood. You wing-eared lounger. You stool. And then by anatomical association: You clot. You thrombus. 'Those were the days?' You have no idea what the days were. By the time you arrived on the scene, the days were no longer what they were supposed to be. That it should come to this. That I should end up with Wessels, of all people, up the creek in a leaky kayak. It was a bitter irony. I had often consoled myself that things were not as bad as they might have been, but now it came home to me that they were actually worse.

The same canoe coming and going (5): kayak.

Wessels called Moçes to turn up the volume on the television set. News from the Convention for a Democratic South Africa. For some time now, Wessels had been making a show of interest in national affairs. Oddly enough, I had a feeling he was trying to impress the waiters. CODESA this and CODESA that. The country was disappearing behind a cloud of acronyms. As for the décor at the 'World Trade Centre' – how could one expect proper political decisions to be made in those dreadful surroundings? The place looked like a brothel.

I excused myself.

Alcohol does not agree with me. It argues, it presents opposing viewpoints – like that Freek Robinson on the television. In the Gentlemen's room I scrutinized, as I always did, the peculiar geometrical pattern in the frosted glass of the window. In the beginning, it had reminded me of those abstract designs in nails and string that were thought so modern when I was starting out at Posts and Telecommunications. But then I'd begun to think of it as a hide stretched between stakes, the skin of some animal kept under glass.

I turned to the wall above the washbasin where the mirror was meant to be (I had seen it there myself as recently as the day before): four small holes and a faint outline of grime showed where it had been secured to the tiles. Someone had unscrewed it and carried it off. I couldn't believe it was gone. In the shiny tiles, my image wavered. I wet my fingers under the tap and ran them over what was left of my hair, then dried the bumpy top of my head with a wad of paper towels, staring down the pale ghost.

I took off my spectacles, huffed on them, dried them on my tie. Without my eye-glasses, the ghost in the wall disappeared entirely.

Alcohol spoke in the archaic, extravagant language it uses during our arguments. It said: This is your lucky day, spindleshanks. Nature has done you a favour by dimming your sight. And some petty thief, working hand in hand with natural forces, a marvellous example of symbiosis, has performed a greater service by carrying off the mirror, in which you might otherwise see yourself as you really are: not the distinguished figure you think you cut, not the debonair sea-captain, but a shabby deckhand, a figure of fun, a fogram. You and Wessels make a perfect pair, Wessels with his sprouty ears, you with your raisiny cranium and your fish-eyes.

When I got back to the table, Wessels was just leaving. He said he had to get home to feed the cat. That was rich. He wanted to get to the off-sales at the Senator before closing time.

That reminded me. 'I saw something amazing at the Jumbo Liquor Market when I was on my way over here. You know that mascot thing of theirs that they put out on the pavement, the elephant—'

'Dumbo.'

'Jumbo,' I corrected him.

'Dumbo, from the comics, the heffalump who could fly.'

'Never heard of him.'

'You mean you haven't read his books?'

'It didn't occur to me that he might be an author.'

'Sorry, Aubs-ss, got to run. We'll speak later.'

I had to call him back for his bill, which he was conveniently forgetting under the pot of sugar sachets. He paid up and hobbled out. Someone had written a message on the plaster cast and drawn an anatomical diagram. Obscene graffiti, I suppose.

When he had gone, I summoned Moçes to turn the sound down on the television. I was the only person watching, if you can call the idle apperception of an image on a screen 'watching': men in suits voicing opinions. Talking heads. Strictly, heads and shoulders. Moçes tapped the volume button with the end of a warped pool cue. Old Eveready used to make do with his forefinger, but these days people need 'equipment' for the simplest tasks. The set in the opposite corner went on murmuring. There was a different image on that screen: a football match. Alarmingly green lawn, cunningly mown into the MacLaren tartan. Arsenal 2, Urinal 1. A punchline, if I'm not mistaken. Half a dozen men (the Olé 'Enries, between you and me) were lounging in a semicircle of chairs below the set. The baize of an empty pool table, glimpsed through the archway, was the same acid green as the lighter squares on the football pitch. Errol and Co must have moved to another table, out of sight. I could hear the balls clicking together, like the building cracking its knuckles.

Why would a company that sold alcoholic beverages have a pink elephant as its mascot? It was supposedly a sign of extreme intoxication, even of delirium tremens. The *Pocket Oxford Dictionary* (the incomparable fourth edition, revised and reprinted with corrections in 1957, henceforth referred to as 'the *Pocket'*), which I happened to have stored in the place it was made for, was mum on the derivation, and I'd had no first-hand experience of such things, but the connotations were hardly attractive. Was it black humour? Or mere ignorance? Why not purple snakes? Could the elephant's name really be Dumbo? Lately, Wessels was always trying to trick me.

He would stow his nightcap under his pillow and hurry back for company. I wasn't in the mood. I wanted to be gone before he arrived.

Usually when I left the Café, I took a turn around Hillbrow, my daily constitutional, sometimes as far as the Fort, or even the Civic Theatre to watch the sun sink over Braamfontein. Our highveld sunsets are spectacularly garish, thanks to the quantities of mine dust and chemicals in the air. But this evening, I was drawn straight back to the opposite end of Kotze Street.

The one-eared elephant was behind bars, between the two cash desks, with his silver chain and padlock coiled like a serpent at his feet. He was looking out between the burglar bars with the same ecstatic expression frozen on his face. Dumbo? It was possible.

Sausages for a Greek island (7): Salamis. Ruled by Ajax, the king of detergents.

*

I was an old hand at the Café Europa, their most venerable patron, an incorrigible 'European'. Not a member though, never mind what Wessels said. We were never a club.

I am a proofreader by profession. When I retired half a dozen years ago, I came to live in a flat in Prospect Road on the edge of Hillbrow. Though my vocation had been a solitary one and I was used to my own company (never been married), I felt cooped up at home. The place was spacious enough and light, but my view of the skyline was all nickel and paste by night and factory roofs and television aerials by day. So I ventured out.

The public spaces in my neighbourhood were uninviting. The parks provided no seating arrangements. Where once there had been benches for whites only, now there were no benches at all to discourage loitering. The loiterers were quite happy to lie on the grass, but, needless to say, I was not. The park in Beatrice Street had a bench; but then it also had a reniform paddling pool that attracted the wrong sort of toddler. The public library was a morgue for dead romances. A series of children's drawings, hideous without exception, had been stuck on the walls in a misguided attempt to brighten the place up. There were no pavement cafés à la française. The weather was suitable, but not the social climate: the city fathers quite rightly did not want people baring their fangs in broad daylight, cluttering the thoroughfares, and giving the have-nots mistaken ideas about wealth and leisure.

After a week of fruitless wandering around the streets of Hillbrow, the happy day arrived when an escalator carried me up into the Café Europa on the first floor of Meissner's Building in Pretoria Street.

The ambience appealed at once. There was a hush in the din of traffic, a lull in the beat of the sunlight, with a melody tinkling through it like a brook. At the grand piano was a woman in a red evening dress, with a swirl of hair on a lacquered skewer. Even seated, she was tall and imposing. She was playing 'I Love Paris', which suited the establishment, if not the city and the season, down to a semiquaver. French doors gave onto a balcony, a sort of elevated pavement café with wrought-iron tables and chairs of bottle-green, shaded by striped umbrellas in the Cinzano livery, delicious monsters and rubber plants in pots. It was tempting to sit out of doors. On the other hand, it was so cool and quiet inside, with comfortable armchairs and sconces for reading by. At half a dozen tables, men of my generation, more or less, were playing backgammon or chess on inlaid boards, or reading newspapers with their folds pinched in wooden staves. Good idea: gave the news a bit of backbone. Another clutch of papers hung from hooks on a pillar, chafing their wings in the moted air.

I crossed the carpet, an autumnal layer as soft and yielding underfoot as oak leaves, past a glass counter where dainties were displayed in rows, like miniatures of the pianist's hairdo, and chose a little square table against the wall near the French doors, where I could have the best of both worlds: from inside, the ceiling fans circulated a muted hubbub of conversation in foreign tongues, piano music, the clack of dominoes, the smell of cigar smoke and ground coffee; while a breeze from outside carried in the hum of traffic and the scent of the Levant, thanks to the lamb on the rotisserie at the Haifa Hebrew Restaurant down below. The doors were set into a wall of plate glass, segmented by brocade curtains drawn into Corinthian columns, allowing a panoramic view of the buildings opposite. Between two of them, against a postcard of bright blue sky, the top of the Hillbrow Tower stuck up like an attachment for a vacuum cleaner. I had never been fond of it. But then I had never seen it from this perspective – gazing skywards is next to impossible with my bad neck – and I thought it made a touching contrast to the cast-iron Tours d'Eiffel in the balcony railing.

I sat down and opened my paper. I was accustomed to working in silence, and so the piano was unsettling at first, but I would discover in time that the right sort of background music supplies a very productive rhythm for browsing through telephone directories or hunting for literals in the classifieds. A fugue, well played, will facilitate the identification of anagrams, for example, while a march will ginger up a letter to the editor.

The waiter, an affable and fairly efficient old boy who introduced himself as Eveready, brought my tea in a civilized cup and saucer; the cup was spoilt somewhat by a picture of a coffee bean in a sombrero dancing the cachucha, but in these days of polystyrene, the lapse might be forgiven. The serviette was folded into an episcopal mitre. The sugar was in a pot (later one would find it in nasty little sachets, which were supposed to promote economy, and instead encouraged pilfering) and the pot was equipped with a genuine spoon (rather than a plastic spatula). An unobtrusive perspex sign, which now came to my attention, informed me that I was table No. 1, and this pleased me inordinately.

A European ambience. Prima. The least one would expect from an establishment that called itself the Café Europa. Importantly, it was ambience rather than atmosphere. You may find 'atmosphere' in fast-food restaurants, thick enough to cut with a plastic knife and obedient to the strictest laws, being the necessary by-product of gingham curtains and sepia-tinted photographs, tables shaped like kegs and lithographs of the Three Little Pigs. Atmosphere is an American commodity. And that is why the citizens of the Golden City covet it. They want to breathe deep-fried oxygen, they want to be part of the Space Age. Europeans prefer ambience, which cannot be pumped in overnight or sprayed on with an aerosol, but has to accrue over time.

*

My first impressions came back to me the day after I heard that the Café was closing. By noon, I found myself walking down to the Europa. I wanted to have the place to myself, before Wessels arrived sloshing over with inanities. I had been dwelling on everything that had happened to me there, on the old days and the old faces, as we think of them, when we mean the younger ones. I was surprised at how indistinct some of those faces had become, ghosts of their former selves. Platitudinously, your memories are a precious possession; they can't take them away from you, as Mevrouw Bonsma, our pianist, used to insist. I always wondered what she meant. Who were these robbers? And why should they want one's memories? They would want something of material value, surely, wristwatches, wallets, shoes …

I came to the Café more concerned than ever to get it clear in my head. I brought my notebook along for a change, in case I wished to make a few sketches or diagrams. I pictured the establishment as a set about to be struck. If only I could arrange it all in my mind, like a diligent stage manager, with every prop in place, perhaps the characters would troop on from the wings of memory and take a bow.

I was tempted to sit at No. 1, where I'd spent my very first hours at the Europa. But as I've already indicated, sentimentality irks me, especially the American variety, which is descended from the Irish. I sat instead at my usual place, the round table where Spilkin and I first shared our thoughts on the crossword puzzle, which had been the great love of his life until grosser affections supplanted it, and 'The Proofreader's Derby', which was and always will be mine. This table was No. 2. A signpost, a relic saved through my intervention, declared the fact (all the others had long since been filched, for reasons one can only guess at).

My eye was drawn to the city on the wall, to the walled city of Alibia, where I had roamed so often in my imagination.

In the foreground was a small harbour, with a profusion of fishing boats and yachts, and a curve of beach freckled with umbrellas. The palm-lined promenade cried out for women twirling parasols and old men nodding in Bath chairs with rugs over their knees. There were wharves and warehouses too, by no means quaint but necessarily somewhat Dickensian, and silos fat with grain, and tower cranes with their skinny shins in the water. Houses were heaped on the slopes behind, around narrow streets and squares. Despite the steepness of the terrain, there were canals thronged with barges, houseboats and gondolas. On one straight stretch of canal, evidently frozen over, one expected to see skaters in woollen caps racing to the tune of a barcarole. In the squares, there were outdoor cafés and neon signs advertising nightclubs; but in the windows of the houses up above, oil-lamps were burning. The baroque steeple of St Cloud's, intricately iced, measured itself against glazed office blocks of modest proportions, while in the east a clutch of onion domes had been harrowed from the black furrow of the horizon. A Slav would feel just as at home there as a Dutchman. It was a perfect alibi, a generous elsewhere in which the immigrant might find the landmarks he had left behind. I had seen pointed out St Peter's and St Paul's, the Aegean and the Baltic.

A receptionist at the German Consulate had shown us a bridge over the Neckar; and once an engineer from Mostar, then painting traffic signs for Roads and Works, had pinpointed the very house in which he had been born. His poor mother still lived there, with mortar-bombs raining down all around her.

What did Alibia mean to me? Certainly it was not 'home'. I am a true Johannesburger, because I was born within sight of the Hillbrow Tower, our very own Bow Bells – or so Spilkin used to say. Of course, this was long before the Johannes Gerhardus Strijdom Tower (properly) was built, but he said it had retrospective effect: had it been standing at the time of my birth, I would have seen it from my crib.

Alibia was close to my heart for a different reason, an egocentric one, I suppose: in the middle of the city, bulging above the skyline and overhung by a dirty brown cloud, was a hill whose bumpy summit looked auspiciously like the crown of my own head. My personal Golgotha.

I came into the world, as many do, with a healthy head of hair. In my case, it was black and enviably thick (but not a *thatch,* like Empty Wessels's). As a boy, I wore it with a parting in the middle, and as a young man, brushed straight back in the fashion of the day, which is how it stayed. In my prime, I cultivated a windswept appearance, with the tousle combed in and the loose ends held in place with oil. I fancied that this hairstyle reflected my character rather well: quick-witted and sporty, tidy but not without flair. However, as my hairline receded, which it began to do during my mid-twenties, I saw coming into view a skull to make a phrenologist's fingertips itch. It was singularly bumpy, roughly-hewn and battered-looking, with a pronounced mound right on top. The most dismaying revelation was a bluish blemish on the occipital plate, around three o'clock, which looked a bit like a raisin embedded in the sugared icing on a custard slice. My marchpane pate. Over the years, as the denuding of my head proceeded, several more of these partly submerged excrescences appeared. Another four to be precise: two more occipitals at eight and nine o'clock and a brace of cranials at twelve on the dot and half past five. But none was more disconcerting than the first. I went to see a dermatologist about it, a Dr Zinn, who was as bald as a coot himself, and he tugged on my forelock, then extant, and told me not to worry. Easier said than done. It was as surprising to me that I should be thinking inside this malformed and discoloured lump as it is to find white flesh inside a fractured coconut.

From much massaging with various preparations in an attempt to revivify the follicles, my fingertips had memorized every square inch – as we used to say then – of my scalp. The digits have a surprisingly long memory, no less enduring than the eyes. I knew my dome's shape exactly, and strange to say, it perfectly matched the hill that beetled over Alibia. Indeed, that hill might have been a study of my head, cast into relief against a permanent sunset, with the features below lost in a clown's ruff of staircases, closes and wynds.

'Yes yes.' The echo chamber slumped down in one chair and propped his plaster cast on another. Seeing the toes of Wessels that close to the table top made my stomach churn. 'Peace & luv' had been printed on the cast in red ink, next to a drawing of a bird. Glory be. The duv of peace, the pidgin. I averted my eyes.

'How's it?'

'Can't complain,' and so on. I don't know why I bother. One may as well speak to a plank.

Then a spar of sense sluiced out on the bilge water: 'I had a great idea.'

'You're moving back to Halfway House?'

'Serious. Let's have a party, before we close down here. A farewell.'

'What for?'

'To say fare thee well, what else? It'll be tough not seeing the guys any more.'

'I'll be only too pleased to see the back of this mob, if that's who you mean. I won't even grace them with a goodbye.' Errol and Co were lounging on the balcony. Goodbye wouldn't suit them, godless heathen that they were. They were always shouting chow-chow at one another like a bunch of jinricksha men.

'Not a goodbye bash,' he said brightly. 'A get-together, a reunion. We'll ask all the old faces.'

This was complex reasoning for Wessels – so early in the day too. I examined his nose, the surest barometer of his state of inebriation the night before. Strawberry this morning, a full three degrees – raspberry, ruddy, Rudolph – from the top of the scale. And out came the Paul Reveres. When he was really the worse for wear, it was Peter Stuyvesant. Perhaps he'd missed the bottlestore last night after all? Those old faces I had spent the night thinking about, those speechless heads with fading features, drifted through my mind.

'The old faces on their own might be awkward,' I said. 'You'd have to ask them to bring their old bodies along.'

'Serious Aub.'

'You could append it to the invitation, it's quite acceptable: BYOB.' Suitably baffled. I hate being called Aub.

'Wouldn't it be nice to see everyone again – Mevrouw Bonsma and them. Merlé. And Bogey – I wonder where he's at? Mrs Mav.'

'I honestly can't imagine that Mrs Mavrokordatos would want to come back here. It would rake up too many painful memories. It would break her heart to see what the place has become. To see what *we've* become.'

'Nothing wrong with us.'

'Not that her hands are clean. But in any case, we don't know where she is. We don't know where anyone is.'

'Tone's got Mrs Mav's number.'

So the New Management had finally turned into a monosyllable. He'd be an initial next and then he'd vanish altogether. 'What does Tone say about your plan?'

'He thinks it's a great idea to go out with a bang. You'll see. It'll be a jôl. I'll organize everything. You don't have to lift a finger, you can just pull in.'

A dʒɔl (from the Old Norse *jól,* a heathen festival) is a rowdy sort of Afrikaner party, accompanied by heavy drinking and smoking of marijuana. And 'pulling in' is one of the more popular vehicular metaphors for arriving unannounced.

'If it's all the same, I think I have a prior arrangement. Or will have any minute.'

I didn't like going out on New Year's Eve anyway. It had become far too dangerous, with flat-dwellers of colour using the occasion to heave unwanted furniture from their windows into the streets below. In fact, the entire 'festive season' had degenerated into a drunken street fight, and the wise lay low until it was all over.

'Anyway, you're invited. Now give us a page of your notebook.'

'No.'

'Don't be so snoop man.'

(Snoop? Put it on the list after 'tawty'.)

'I can't.' I showed him why: I number all the pages in advance, in the top right-hand corner, in ink, precisely to deter filchers. A tactic I learnt from Erasmus, whom I've mentioned before, my colleague at the Department of Posts and Telecommunications in the days of pen and paper.

*

During the course of my constitutional, I found the elephant's ear in the gutter at the top of Nugget Hill. The Queen of Sheba must have dropped it there; when the weather was good, the Pullinger Kop park served as her country seat. In the rosy light of sunset, the ear looked for all the world like a gigantic petal fallen from some impossible bloom. Closer inspection revealed treadmarks from tyres and shoes, gooey fingerprints, splashes of what might have been royal blood. Perhaps Her Majesty's minions had used the ear to stretcher her hither? Understandably, I was reluctant to touch this repulsive, disease-ridden thing, but I meant to drop in at the Jumbo Liquor Market the next morning to clear up the Dumbo question, and so I sacrificed a few pages from the classified section of my *Star* to wrap it in and bore it along with me.

As I was crossing Abel Road with my unsought trophy, a little preoccupied it's true, but as mindful of the traffic regulations as ever, a baker's delivery van, adorned with a painting of Atlas shouldering a crisply browned Planet Earth still steaming from the oven, careered around the corner and very nearly knocked me down. I am in good shape for a man of my age, pate excepted, and I was able to leap to safety. I had the presence of mind, even as I overbalanced on the kerb and plummeted to the pavement, to glance at the rear of the vehicle to note the registration number. And there on the bumper I saw, to my annoyance, a sign that read: 'How am I driving?'

Some bystanders came to my assistance, but I fended them off with elbows and epithets, equally sharp. They try to pick your pockets under cover of kindness. My fall had loosened the newspaper covering the ear, and people were staring. I rewrapped it as best I could, picked myself up, and hurried away. The mishap had disorientated me and I found myself going down Catherine Street, the way I had come. This was all too much. Unable to turn back without losing face, unwilling to stray from my accustomed path, I took refuge in the lounge at the Chelsea Hotel, and ordered a whisky to steady my nerves. They didn't have whiskey at all – which I should have taken as forewarning that the place had gone to the dogs.

No sooner had my drink arrived than a woman sidled into the chair opposite and commanded me to buy her one too. My astonished expression produced a gust of tittering from her friends at the next table. Ladies of the night, I would say. They all seemed to be wearing foundation garments on top of their daywear. I took out my notebook and jotted down a few points about the Atlas Bakery van while the episode was still fresh in my memory. The harlot did not go away. Instead, she started picking at the newspaper in which the ear was swaddled. I had to gulp my drink and leave. She made a crack in isiSotho or whatever, and the streetwalkers tee-heed in the same lingo.

It was growing dark. As I approached Abel Road for the second time that evening, the full horror of my narrow escape overwhelmed me and I broke out in a sweat. I shouldn't be surprised if the bolted drink also played a part. To think that I might have been lying in the roadway here right now, awaiting the ambulance or, God forbid, the mortuary van. Strangers rifling through my clothing, making a show of ascertaining my identity while lifting my small change, reading my notebook, leafing through my *Pocket* with their greasy fingers, scattering my bookmarks to the wind ... farceur ... feather ... fiat ... fleck ... flint ... I saw my life ebbing away. I saw my death, touch wood, as a precipitate efflux of vocabulary and idiom, the hoarded treasures of a lifetime spent in a minute, one immaculate vintage running into another, and the whole adulterated brew spilt on the dirty macadam of an unmemorable corner of a lawless conurbation. **Flow**: glide along as a stream; gush out, spring; (of blood) be spilt; (of wine) be poured out without stint (f. OE *flōwan,* unconnected with L *fluere:* flux). Unconnected. This city had a short memory. How many deaths might have occurred on this very spot and left no memorial? How many forgotten Abels had bled out their spirits at these crossroads, how many smooth-cheeked Cains were going about scot-free. And what would I have left behind, apart from these shop-soiled mortal remains? Invisible work. A pile of manuals and documents, obscure gazettes, directories and yearbooks, most of them out of print, which I had proofread well, and on which I had therefore left no visible trace. A negative achievement. 'The Proofreader's Derby', through which I had hoped to make a little mark, something of lasting value to which my name might be attached, lay incomplete in my desk drawer. Some second-hand furniture dealer would tip it into the rubbish skip in the alley behind his shop, along with my notes and cards and clippings, and the skip would be emptied into a landfill site and covered over with sand, and in the fullness of time another housing development would arise on the spot and bury it for ever. Hit and run! I saw myself lying there, sprawled across the elephant's ear, newsprint fluttering around me like the Prospect Road corpse, and some ambulance man, or paramedic as they style themselves nowadays, smelling the alcohol on my breath and making the obvious wisecrack. But could a corpse be said to have some-thing on its breath? The whisky was anachronistic anyway. If the bakery van had delivered me into the hands of the Great Compositor, I should never have stopped at the Chelsea to wet my whistle. I would have come up smelling not exactly of roses, but of Wilson's x x x mints. My generally impeccable sense of chronology had been quite disordered. And it was all Wessels's fault, talking about old faces and cartoon characters. He really was the bane of my life.

I didn't want to take the ear up in the lift with me; what if I bumped into that nosey Mrs Manashewitz? That's all I needed, to get half of Lenmar Mansions talking. So I left it in the care of Gideon, the nightwatchman, and he put it in the coal room in the parking garage overnight. Now that the thing had nearly cost me my life, I had more reason than ever to barter it for some useful information at the Jumbo Liquor Market.

*

Lenmar Mansions was built just after the war. It's a six-storey block, square and solid, made of bricks and mortar, as a building should be. I took a one-bedroomed flat on the top floor (the bachelors didn't suit me, despite my marital status). The minute I set foot in the place, I felt at ease. Spacious rooms, separated by proper walls and doors, parquet throughout, black and white tiles in the kitchen and bathroom. The south-facing lounge had large windows – there was no need for burglar-proofing so high up – and a small balcony.

In my researches, I discovered that the block had been built by the property tycoon Ronnie Lazerow, and named for his children Leonard and Marilyn. Portmanteau names of this kind have always been popular in Johannesburg. At one time, supposing the phenomenon might bear closer scrutiny, I started a list in my notebook.

Portmanteaus, residential: Lenmar Mansions … Milrita Heights … Norbeth East … Villa Ethelinda … Alanora Maisonettes …

But the sheer banality of the coinages exhausted my curiosity.

*

In the shiny glass doors of the Jumbo Liquor Market, with my black poly-thene rubbish bag over my shoulder, I appeared to myself for an instant as a sinister Santa Claus bearing gifts for the black Christmas everyone was threatening to visit upon us if they didn't get their own way at the

Convention for a Democratic South Africa, and this perception sent a malicious rush of sangfroid to my head. I deposited the bag on the cash desk. The cashier was the same young woman who had called out to Mr Ferreira, the manager, as the ritual ravishing of Jumbo/Dumbo reached its climax. I expected to be recognized – after all, I had played a prominent if unassuming part in that sordid drama – but the girl was clearly none too observant. Mrs Da Silva, as the badge on her lapel denoted her, seemed improbably young to be married, if you asked me, and inelegantly hirsute in the oxter.

'Ken I yelp yew, Sir?'

(I hope I've captured the accent. A phonetic transliteration – ken ai jelp ju: sɜ:? – would be better by far, but not everyone knows the language.)

'You may summon Mr Ferreira for me.' I glanced meaningfully at the elephant with its one ear cocked. 'You may say it is in connection with the corporate image.' If needs be, I can bandy the jargon about as well as the next man.

'Sorry, Sir, bud Meesta Ferreira yeece howt.'

Oh. 'Da Silva has absolutely nothing to do with the metallic element,' I said, conversationally, 'whose symbol in the periodic table is Ag, from the Latin *argentum;* whose properties are lustrous, malleable, ductile. What else? Precious. Well, that first and foremost.'

'Doughling, I yaven't god oll dye. Yew god empties in da beg?'

I unbagged the ear, liberating a gust of the anti-canine scent with which the plastic was impregnated. She still didn't seem to recognize me, but she was delighted to see the ear. She patted it with the convex ends of her manicured left hand. The nails on the other hand, I noticed, the one she used to punch the keys of the till, were half as long. In all likelihood the musculature on that arm would be more developed too.

'Where dod yew fine deece yeah?' she demanded.

I explained.

She spoke so fervently into the microphone sticking out of the till that it trembled like an antenna. 'Joaquim! Joaquim! Pleece comb tew da frount!'

Da Silva. As in sylvan. Forests and so on. Boscage. Woods. Five o'clock shadow on the upper lip, and not even teatime. Lipstick: cherry tomato.

Joaquim appeared from behind a ziggurat of boxed wine. Beaujolais in boxes. Whatever next. Whisky in tins? Instant ice – just add water and chill? Under Mrs Da Silva's direction, Joaquim tried the ear on the elephant, inserting the snapped-off metal strut like the stalk of a big autumn leaf into the hole in the elephant's head, and proving beyond a shadow of a doubt that it was indeed the missing part.

Mrs Da Silva clapped her lazy hand on her thigh, twice, and said, 'Tenk yew, tenk yew.'

Joaquim carried the ear into the storeroom at the rear.

Portuguese workforce: manuel labour.

A man in a suit, another pseudo-businessman, a Stan, a Vern, approached with a six-pack of Lion Lagers in his paw, and she excused herself to ring it up.

'Cheerio, Rosa,' he said.

'Yave a nace dye.'

Hypermeat was advertising lambada lamb sosaties, hottest prices in town. Little red and yellow flames flickered around the blistered letters.

'Ken I yelp yew still?'

'This elephant of yours interests me. I think I've seen him somewhere before.'

'Heece dere oll da time.'

'I mean I've seen an elephant like him somewhere else.'

'Oll hour brenches hev dem. Troyeville yas tew.'

'Wait a minute, it's coming back to me. It's Dumbo, isn't it? The little elephant who wanted to fly?'

'Ken be.'

Hopeless case.

'Yew wand somb kesh?' she said suddenly.

'For the ear? My dear Mrs Woods, I wouldn't dream of it. I was just doing my civic duty, as any decent person would.'

Before I could stop her, she had summoned Joaquim again, mumbled something to him – he must be a native of Moçambique, as he speaks the lingo – and in a trice he was pressing a bottle of Sedgwick's Old Brown Sherry into my hands. It was almost offensive.

'Could I have my bag, please?'

She spat on a working fingertip and dabbed up one of the yellow ones covered with pink elephants.

'That's one of yours,' I said firmly but politely. 'I'd prefer to have my own back, if it's all the same.'

Joaquim fetched my rubbish bag from the storeroom.

'*Obrigado*,' I said nonchalantly, wrapped the bottle of sherry in it and sauntered conveniently out onto the pavement, no wiser than when I had arrived. Old Brown Sherry. Cheapskates. Ships' kites. At least it wasn't Paarl Perlé, which was quite undrinkable, by all accounts, and smacked of bitter associations. I supposed it would do for cooking with.

I found one of Dumbo's literary efforts in the Central News Agency in Hillbrow, an autographed copy of *Dumbo and the Pachyderms from Alpha Centauri*. He was a brainchild, a brain*beast* of that Walter Disney, whose passion for furry animals was surely unhealthy. The family resemblance to the Liquor Market's mascot was striking. While I was paging, the shop manager came and stared at me over the erasers. Apparently I was acting suspiciously, and not for the first time. News to me. The rubbish bag was probably creating the wrong impression. I took out my *Oxford*. That made Management's eyebrows disappear. Ostrogoth ... overenthusiasm ... pagoda ... here we are: **pachyderm**. From the Greek *pakhus*, meaning thick, and *derma*, meaning skin.

'You may thank your lucky stars,' I informed Management, pocketing the *Pocket* again, 'that I am the last gentleman in Hillbrow, as honest as the day is long, and pachydermatous to boot. As for Henry Watson Fowler, the man's prejudice against polysyllabic humour did him no credit. No one's perfect.'

Departed, trumpeting (inwardly).

*

Wessels found me writing in my notebook, an Okay Bazaars (Hyperama) special with a blue cover and white spiral binding, good value for money. To my chagrin, he produced a notebook from his own pocket and rested it on his thigh. A child's scribbling block of cheap grey paper, feint ruled, with a chubby, bilingual little man called Mr Fatso/Mnr Vetsak on the cover. It was roughly the same size as mine, but also contrived to be a childish comment on it. He took out a pen, clicked the ballpoint in and out pensively, gazed up at a chandelier, and then made to write. No sooner had the pen touched paper than he let out a cry of frustration and had to wipe it clean on the lining of his jacket. I always write my rough copies with a pencil because it allows for erasure; I saw that Wessels, unable to lick the nib of the pen, but keen to emulate my technique in every particular, was licking the tip of his index finger between flourishes of the writing hand and surreptitiously using his tie as a blotter. The formation of each letter was accompanied by a sympathetic, schoolboyish contortion of facial muscles. That writing should be such a painful procedure! In anyone else, it might have been enough to thaw my frozen heart.

I introduced Mr Fatso/Mnr Vetsak to his brethren in my notebook – he fitted in between Mr Video and Mr Meat – and went on with my own work. Fortunately, I had finished my composition, in the requisite brief paragraphs, and was busy inking up a fair copy (which I would typewrite later that evening at home), and so I was able to put Wessels from my mind and concentrate on my penmanship.

When I had finished, I laid my notebook down on the table. The sight of a pen in Wessels's freckled fist in place of a reeking cigarette was compelling. But it was so obviously a ruse to implicate me in his plans for the Goodbye Bash – as I was determined to call it – that I resolved to make no comment. Soon he put down his pad too. He swizzled his brandy with his pen, then clipped it in the flap of his right ear.

No sign of Moçes. Perhaps he was out on the balcony, behind the venetian blinds, where Errol and Co were cackling and hooting. Probably sharing an illicit cocktail laced with amphetamines. Discipline among the waiters had broken down entirely under the influence of these hooligans.

'What you got there?'

'A letter to the editor of the *Star* about an unnerving experience I had yesterday, which I wanted to get off my chest.'

'We haven't had one of those for donkey's years-ss. Can I see?'

The man was a fount of amphibology. It was Café etiquette, in the old days, never to ask to read my communications until they were printed in the newspaper. Wessels's flouting of the rules, to which I had long thought myself inured, coupled now with his persistent invocation of the past, irritated me all over again. But having watched his version of writing, I was intrigued to see him reading as well, so I handed him the notebook, which he bore up towards his face at once like a toasted sandwich, as if he meant to take a bite out of it. As I expected: the thick lips moved to frame each word. Personally, I prefer reading silently, to myself. Reading belongs in the head, behind the eyes, not just under the breath, but inside the folds of the brain. I can tolerate reading out loud on occasion, if the words are enunciated clearly and the circumstances are fit. But this soundless movement of the lips is uncouth, like a cat twitching through a rutting dream.

7 December 1993

Dear Sir,

In a lifetime of accident-free motoring, I have been the owner of half a dozen passenger vehicles, including several purchased out of the box, but as a pensioner I am now reduced to travelling either by bus, an ordeal since the municipal prohibition on smoking is no longer enforced, or by shank's pony, ever the most reliable means of private transport, despite the hazards posed by 'muggers', excavations, hawkers, uneven paving-stones and reckless drivers.

Yesterday afternoon, I was crossing Abel Road in Hillbrow at the Catherine Street intersection when a delivery van in the service of the Atlas Bakery tore through a red robot and very nearly knocked me down.

As the rear bumper of the vehicle flashed before my eyes, I saw affixed to it a sign that read: 'How am I driving?' One might have assumed that the question was merely rhetorical. However, the telephone number appended made it clear that an answer was sought. I have a head for figures, thanks to my professional background, and so I was quick to memorize this number, along with the registration number, and several other details.

Immediately after the incident, I transcribed these details into the notebook I was carrying, and am enclosing a photostatic copy of the relevant page. The man in the street is not expected to have pen and paper to hand nowadays, I know, but then I have never resembled that mythical creature.

This morning, I dialled the telephone number of the Atlas Bakery and was put through to a Miss Papenfus, a superficially polite but intrinsically ineffectual young woman, who showed no interest whatsoever in the nimble undertones of her ostensibly flat-footed name.

Explaining the purpose of my call, I provided the registration number of the van and asked to speak to the driver concerned, but this request was refused. I was urged instead to address my complaint to the Director of Human Resources in writing, an offer I flatly rejected as being likely to end with my statement 'put on file' and duly forgotten. In any event, I am not a human resource, I am a member of the public, and I did not have a complaint, but an answer to a question.

Having failed to make a verbal report, an affidavit in the true sense of the word, I am now 'going public' through the channels of your newspaper.

'How am I driving?' You are driving atrociously. You are a menace on the road. A more urgent question might well be: 'Why am I driving?' And an honest answer should persuade you to seek a form of employment more suited to your temperament.

Yours faithfully,
A. Tearle
(Proofreader, retired)

Not one of my best, but adequate for a man who was out of practice.

Wessels, true to character, remarked on none of its qualities. After an elaborate show of thinking, which brought to mind the 'cog' in 'cogitation', he said: 'You checked all these facts and figures with those binoculars of yours? This ou must of been doing five miles an hour.'

'Bifocals, kilometres,' I said, leaving aside the finer points of grammar and usage for the time being. 'My eyesight is every bit as acute as your own.'

And I demonstrated by reading the signs that said 'Ladies' and 'Gentlemen' on the lavatory doors (facetiously, of course, I have absolutely nothing to prove to Wessels). That 'Gentlemen' in particular has always touched me. I stood up for it too, when its existence was threatened by the New Management's ethnic expedients 'Amadoda' and 'Abafazi'. Not that too many of the individuals, both scruffy and overly groomed, who crossed that threshold deserved the compliment, but it was the thought that counted. 'Gentlemen' was so much more encouraging than the 'Gents' one encountered everywhere else. Or the cute couplings of Adams and Eves, Jacks and Jills, Romeos and Juliets, Bonnies and Clydes, Guys and Dolls, Mickies and Minnies, and even, confusingly, Nuts and Bolts *(vide* 'nomenclature, cloakrooms' in the notebooks). Frequently illustrated with tailcoats and crinolines and other outward signs, increasingly archaic, of the distinctions between the sexes.

'Who's this guy Shanks, with the pony?'

'Old friend. Went to different schools together.'

'Didn't they teach you to write short and sweet? What's-his-face will cut this in half, if he gives it out at all.'

Unfortunately, he was right. This letter has been shortened – Ed. The letters editor was someone of the Wessels type, at home among the Gavs and Erns. He'd delete the half he didn't understand. Wouldn't even bother to use a pen: just hit a button and make it vanish.

'And what's the use of talking to the driver? He probably doesn't read the *Star*. Probably can't read!'

'Thanks for the constructive criticism.' I took back my notebook. Mr

Fatso/Mnr Vetsak puffed out his chest. Wessels wanted me to ask about his own literary efforts. I hid behind my newspaper.

'What you suppose I got here?'

'Invitation list. For the Goodbye Bash.'

'Reunion.'

'Have it your way.'

'You wanna see it?' And without waiting for a response, he shoved the pad under the bottom of my newspaper. I might have brushed it aside, but for the morbid fascination of Wessels's drunken handwriting. Across that grey parade-ground of paper staggered mutinous ranks of tipsy letters, incapable of standing up straight without the support of their neighbours, struggling vainly to keep their feet on the lines. Half a dozen had fallen flat on their faces, one or two had wobbled right off the page. The only upright character was the very first capital M, rooted to the spot by the blue ink-blot, like a plaster cast, in which its right leg was encased.

Mr M.T. Wessels
Mr Aubrie Tearle
Mevrou Anna Bonsma
Mr Dan Bogus—
Miss Merlé Graaff
Errol and Raylene
Vlooid en Nomsa
Bill and Pardner
Mrs Mav
Mrs Hay
Ernie and them (Harry, Eddie, Little Harry etc)
Carmelita and Pardner
Mr Everistus alius Eveready

One hardly knew where to start.

'Partner has a "t" in it,' I said. Boggled. 'A pardner is someone who trots along beside you on a bobtailed mare.'

'Have I missed anyone out?'

'Mnr Vetsak.'

'Ha, Aub. Jokes aside.'

'You've been very thorough. I see the bottle-washer's invited. You should ask him to bring the kitchen sink along.'

'I reckoned you wouldn't mind about Everistus. He was like family. And times have changed: if he pulled in here today, he could park off with us and have a fresh orange.'

First it was a club, now it's a family.

'How are you going to track everyone down?' I had a list of names and addresses he would have found very useful, but I wasn't going to help him with this nonsense.

'I've got my ways. My contacts.'

'What's become of Spilkin?'

'He was on first, but then I took him off again. I don't want to stand on anyone's feet.'

'I'd have thought Spilkin's name should lead all the rest, like Abou Ben Adhem. Not that he loved his fellow man, especially, but he had an eye for the ladies. Anyway, it's your party, invite who you please. Even the hooligans.'

Speak of the devil. Errol came sliding in from the balcony with Raylene in tow – or was it Maylene? they all sound like household cleaners to me – and then Floyd and Nomsa, who appears to wear wigs, and our very own Moçes bringing up the rear, with his waistcoat unbuttoned and his bowtie hanging down from one point of his collar. Errol pulled up a chair at our table – 'Please won't you join us,' I said – and flung himself over it like a discarded overall. Raylene or Maylene sat on the armrest and crossed her long right leg, not on her *own* knee but on Errol's! I couldn't quite see how it was done. She turned her face up to the fan, flushed, sweaty from the sun. They do seem to perspire rather a lot (although I remember reading somewhere that it's a sign of good health, except in the tropics). Floyd and Pardner went on into the kitchen. I believe Moçes was supplying them with drugs – or vice versa – although Wessels insisted he gave them food. Leftovers. They were undernourished, according to Wessels, who had developed an entirely misplaced social conscience. Undernourished! With those muscles?

'Howzit Wessie, Mr T, how the tawpies?' (I've recorded a few snippets of the argot over the months. A tɔːpiː is an elderly person – from their youthful perspective, more often than not someone in the prime of life. I suspect there's an element of the racial slur in it too. And 'Mr T', in case you were wondering, refers to me.) 'Dop?' Errol went on. 'Brandy or whatever the case may be?' His mouth hung open. Also characteristic. You'd think he was always hungry, like a baby bird or some sea-dweller browsing for plankton. Certainly, he was usually putting something in his mouth, a Chesterfield cigarette (when he scrounged 'smokes' from Wessels, he snapped off the filters before he lit them), or some Black Label beer straight from the bottle, or a luminous orange larva called a Cheesnak (sic). But it was more than hunger, it was lassitude, some slackness in his long dark face, in his whole lank body, as if the bones were too loosely jointed. Needed starch. The outsize clothing he favoured didn't help either. 'Slapgat' Wessels called it, and the vulgar Afrikanerism was apt.

'We was just wrapping about the closing-down jôl,' said Raylene/ Maylene, 'and Err had one of his bright ideas. He schemes we should get Hunky Dory to play. Like he's usually weekends only, but I reckon Tony could ask him to come on Thursday instead, specially for the party. For old time's sake.'

Err. Tony. Hunky Dory. They sounded more like conditions than human beings. But even Hunky Dory was a person. Tone had employed him as the resident musician. He played on Saturday nights only, but his equipment lay in the corner all week, like a junior electronics set, handfuls of gauges and dials, tangles of cable and wire, chromium tubing and grey insulation tape. 'Hunky Dory' hung on a string above the rostrum that passed as the stage, in glittering letters with ragged fringes of the kind usually reserved for Seasons Greetings, stirring gently in the breeze from the overhead fans.

I had once heard him manufacture 'music' on these 'instruments', to my regret.

'I would rather hear a tribe of cats quartered on a bandsaw, fortissimo and accelerando,' I quipped, 'than be subjected to Hocus Pocus and his engines.'

Errol's lip drooped. 'Come again?'

'Rock and roll gives me a headache.'

'Take a Grampa,' said Errol.

'You a funny old tawpy,' said Raylene/Maylene, and jogged her foot on Errol's knee. It was unnerving, as if they were one person, Siamese twins joined at the thigh, a single creature that didn't know whether it was Arthur or Martha. The impression was strengthened by the girl's muscular calf and rubber-toothed combat boot (Israeli army surplus, they claimed). To test the limits of my theory, Errol's right hand, which had been asleep on her hip with a cigarette smouldering between its fingers, awoke and began to creep over her bare midriff. It traced circles around her navel with the tip of an index finger and then dropped off again. The damp end of the cigarette slipped into the omphalic whorl in her flesh like a jack into a socket. The girl's belly rose and fell with her breathing, the cigarette fumed. It was perverse. It reminded me of something I had seen on television: a barber-shop quartet of ugly Mongolians, which turned out to be paunches with faces painted on them. Humor.

'What kind of music do you like smark, Mr T[earle]? Sakkie sakkie? Long arm?' She looked at my unbarbered crown. 'Classics?'

'Sherbet is good,' said Wessels. 'And Schoeman.'

'I'd have thought Brahms and Liszt were more in your line,' I countered.

'No really,' said the girl. 'What are you into?'

'Into? I'll tell you what I'm *out of*: the Talking Heads, the Simple Minds and the Exploding Pumpkins.'

That was bound to raise a laugh. Errol guffawed and slapped his better half's knee. I noticed, with a start, because I had never seen it before, the word 'Raylene' tattooed on his forearm in that mouldy verdigris so beloved of tattoo artists and meat inspectors. Perhaps he'd just had it done. It solved the identity crisis, anyway.

'How come you know this stuff?'

'He's a walking encyclopaedia,' said Errol. 'A seedy rom.' Don't ask me where they pick these things up.

'He makes a study of everythink,' said Wessels proudly.

A few more came back to me: 'Snoopy Doggy Dog. Prefabricated Sprouts. Animals.' Another guffaw. They might laugh, but they bought the records that made these jokers rich. The names were so ludicrous, you'd think the public was being challenged not to take them seriously. They might as well all call themselves The Charlatans and be done with it. I had a list of them in my notebook, which I was tempted to consult, but it was more telling to know them by heart. I'd made the list a few months before in the Look and Listen Record Bar, where I had gone to disprove Wessels's claim that there was a famous 'jazz' musician called Felonious Monk. As it turned out, I was right on a mere technicality – his name was *The*lonious – but I discovered something even more remarkable: his middle name was Sphere. Merle would have loved it. He was a rotund little figure too, a fully formed semibreve.

In the course of my researches, I wandered into the popular music section, and was soon as engrossed as one could be, given the din issuing from the loudspeakers ranged on all sides. The orchestras had the queerest names, fruit and vegetables, things like the Sweaty Lettuces and the Mango Grooves. By comparison, the 'Beatles' seemed rather innocuous, and felicitous too, when one recalled those neat young men in their suits and ties and their coleopterous hairdos. Michael and the Mechanics. Extraordinary. You never knew when such things might come in useful. I'd taken out my notebook to jot them down: absurd nomenclature, popular orchestras. (Absurd, from the Latin *surdus,* deaf, dull.) Pretty soon a sallow youth with a ponytail and a horsey set of teeth was hovering, looking over my shoulder, pretending that he could read. Probably thought I was acting suspiciously; by then, I was quite groggy from the noise as it was.

'Do you have any Status Quos?' I asked. Heard that one on the radio.

'Of course,' with a snort. I was surprised he didn't tap three times with his foot.

'Well I wouldn't listen to them if you paid me.'

Floyd and Nomsa came back from the kitchen with bottles of beer and a girl I hadn't seen before. There are more of them every day, and I confess that they all look rather alike to me. It's probably the colouring. The new girl struck me only because she seemed much too young to be drinking liquor. She had her fingers curled around the neck of a bottle like a child with a 'cooldrink'. A small hand glittering with plastic rings that might have come out of a lucky packet. Floyd was wearing a new playsuit with Donald Ducks on it: long shorts down to the knees and a matching shirt, many sizes too big for him. Not hand-me-downs, mind you, from an older brother: they all wore their clothes too big. Errol himself had an immense pair of trunks, in ecru canvas with red piping, of the sort that servants used to favour. The two of them looked like toddlers, very much enlarged. They even had oversized bootees on their feet, excessively padded baby shoes with their tongues lolling, but no laces. Quantities of silver buckles instead, which their clumsy fingers might manipulate more easily than bows. It would cost a fortune to bronze one of them.

These brawny, stubbled men in their rompers looked even stranger next to the girls, who were dressed for the beach, in stretchy pants and tops that were no more than singlets or brassières. Raylene's slim body was like a teenage boy's – a boy with a love for physical culture, I might add, for twirling Indian clubs or leaping over hurdles. Even the brown hairs on her arms were too thick and glossy for down. At least Nomsa had some flesh on her. Wessels was prodding that flesh now with a forefinger like a pestle. He had discovered a tattoo of a rose on her shoulder.

'It's a Bert Middler,' Nomsa explained. Whoever he is.

'No ways. More like a Naas Botha,' Wessels said. He was chafing away at the tattoo with a rubbery forefinger. 'Ask Mr T. He knows all about it.'

I'd been reading about rose cultivation in the paper a few weeks before: some rugby-lover had named a bloom after Botha, the fly-half.

I took refuge as usual behind the news.

Then Wessels wanted Nomsa to draw a replica of the rose on his plaster cast and they asked to borrow my pen. I refused. No ways, so to speak. They got one from Moçes instead. He was tiddly. Of no use as a waiter.

I should try to like them, I thought, despite their broken English. In fact, I should try to like them *for* that, I should find a place for them, not a soft spot, not in my heart, but a well-worn, callused spot, something pachydermatous and scarred, where their shrillness, their abrasiveness, their rough edges might be accommodated without tearing any tissue. I made resolutions to that effect. But they came to nothing, watching the girl Nomsa, a deracinated Xhosa as I recall, crouched over Wessels's plaster cast, with his stubby toes wriggling like newborn puppies, blindly delighted to be alive. The way she held the pen! It was worse than Wessels himself. You would have thought it was a vegetable peeler.

*

-rama suffix, commercial enterprises: Hyperama ... Meatarama ... Cupboard-a-rama ... Veg-a-rama ... Leatherama ... Motorama ... Computerama ...

*

Having once discovered the Café Europa, in the days before Wessels and Errol and everyone else, I made it my haunt. I steeped in its European ambience, in a mild dilution of pleasantly polite strangers, for half a year before I found companionship.

One afternoon, the stranger I would come to know as Spilkin entered the Café and sat at table No. 3, which was identical to mine, a small distance away and also ranged against Alibia. On the wall above that particular table was a sconce, which the muralist had cleverly appropriated as a beacon on one of the city's rounded hills. The cone of light that the beacon played upon the water – or rather upon the place where the water would have been if the sea in the foreground had spilled out over the wooden dado that hemmed it in like a breakwater – gave that quarter of the city a wartime air, a mood of siege quite at odds with the [George] Ferris wheel and the festive lights on the terraces at the Hotel Grande. The stranger shifted his chair and crossed his legs, so that the searchlight's beam, I imagined, would drop over his shoulder and illuminate the newspaper that he was about to prop against his knee.

He turned straight away to the page of the *Star* that carried the cartoons and puzzles, the chess problem, the bridge hand, the crossword. (Never played chess myself.) Then, cocking his head to one side, holding the paper at arm's length and squinting at it out of the corner of his eye, he began to tear a square out of the page. The action was so awkward and silly, and yet so familiar, that I felt a pang of sympathy for him, as one might for an old friend observed in an unguarded moment. This feeling was so intense that I had to examine him more carefully, smoothing vanishing cream into his wrinkled brow, putting curls back on his crown, trimming the exuberant eyebrows, to see if there was not some more youthful incarnation I would recognize, some immature pentimento. Proofreading him, if you like, for familiar flaws. He looked soft, small and mild, but inquisitive too, almost saucy, like a worldly cherub.

I had been doing the cryptic version of the *Star*'s two-speed crossword since my days as a junior proofreader in the Department of Posts and Telecommunications. For as long as I could remember, the cryptic clues had been printed above the grid and the straight ones below. Very sensible. All one had to do to obscure the straight clues, and thus remove the temptation to glance at them, was to fold the page in half. And it *was* a temptation. So long as the simple clues were visible, hovering on the periphery of vision, the eye was drawn to them, seeking the easy way out, despite the mind's attraction to the difficult problem. There was something wilful in the human eye that made it impossible to discipline. It *would* look. I had had the same problem in the old days when I reached the last page of a book. I would have to obscure the final paragraph with my hand or a bookmark to prevent my cheating eye from leaping to it at once. To think of coming all that way by the specified route, step by step, word by word, only to throw away whatever satisfaction there was to be gained, by skipping the last few paragraphs and arriving at the goal ahead of schedule. It was like taking a short cut in the last mile of a marathon.

I went further than most. The habit of years, the respect for rules and regulations, the dedication to matter in its proper order, front and back, that kept me reading steadily from A to B to 'The End', also made me read past it, through Appendices and Indices and Advertisements, through Bibliographies and Endnotes and Glossaries, until the endpapers loomed in their blank finality. And even then, nothing was more satisfying than to turn the final page of a tome, thinking that the race was run, and find a colophon, a 'finishing touch'. A meaningful fragment of the whole, put there to be read, but which no one, perhaps, had ever bothered to read, by which I mean to scan deliberately, to pass the eye over in full and conscious awareness of these particular shapes, impressed upon paper, now impressing themselves upon the retina and the cortex, and thus upon the soft surface of time itself.

About a year earlier, in the final months of my gainfully employed life, the editor of the puzzles page, as he was probably known, and almost certainly a new appointment, some wallah kicked upstairs at the behest of the nabobs of the tricameral parliament, had taken it upon himself to change the tried-and-tested format of the crossword. The two sets of clues, cryptic and straight, now appeared one below the other alongside the grid (with the straight ones on top!). The reasons for the change were never explained – they were always tinkering with the newspaper these days, moving things around, making them bigger or smaller or doing away with them altogether, in the scramble for what they called 'market share' – but the upshot was that one could no longer fold the paper to obscure the straight clues without folding the grid itself in half. Just one fleeting glance at the straight clues could take the difficult pleasure out of half a dozen cryptic ones. Even as one began to puzzle pleasantly over 'Races Thomas ran badly', the disobedient eye would leap with infuriating precision to 'Long-distance running races' in the straight column. It was dispiriting. The only solution was to remove the straight clues from eye-shot entirely by tearing them out, resisting all the while the desire to look at them: I had resorted to exactly the cock-eyed procedure the stranger was now performing, and my heart went out to him, alone as he was, and with no one to turn to.

I had kept to myself at the Café Europa in the beginning, but in time I did establish a nodding acquaintance with Mevrouw Bonsma, our pianist, and Mrs Mavrokordatos, our proprietor. To Mevrouw Bonsma I occasionally sent politely worded notes, requesting an old favourite. She knew everything. She was an immense reservoir of melodies, endlessly seeping, flowing one into the other, always brimming. It was a fullness I found a little disconcerting. I tried to trip her up a few times by asking for chestnuts such as 'The Isle of Capri' or 'Arrivederci Roma', but she played them all without missing a beat. I had hopes of making her open her leather portfolio, which she stowed in the cross-stitched seat of her stool every day, and which I assumed contained sheet music, although I had never seen her consult it. Finally, in a spirit of curiosity, for I am not in the habit of playing practical jokes, I made something up. Then Mevrouw approached my table and asked me to hum the beastly thing. I had to refuse. I had never hummed in my life, I told her, and certainly not for a pianist, and I saw no reason to start now.

My acquaintance with Mrs Mavrokordatos, circumscribed by the more dependable bounds of reciprocation between proprietor and customer (custom, like costume, from the ME and OF *custume,* from the Latin *consuetudo),* was both more formal and more at ease. It was through the kind offices of Mrs Mavrokordatos that I found a neater, less bothersome solution to my dilemma with the crossword than the wretched ripping I had been reduced to. When I arrived at the Café in the afternoon, I would hand her the newspaper and she would snip out the straight clues with a pair of scissors, giving me the little patch of newsprint, considerately folded clue-side-in, to store in my wallet. This arrangement had a couple of advantages, in addition to the embarrassment it spared me. If there was some important information on the reverse side of the page, some damaged article I would only discover later that evening or the next morning when I was trawling for typographical errors, I could easily restore the excision, snug as a jigsaw piece. This very thing happened on more than one occasion. And in the unlikely event of my not being able to complete the puzzle, I could consult the straight clues. In my opinion, it was better to finish the puzzle with the aid of the simple clues than not to finish it at all. This proved to be one of the matters on which Spilkin and I held diametrically opposed views. (Dress sense was another. Not to mention … no, let me not mention it.) It wasn't that we differed on the status of the straight clues themselves: in his book, as in mine, the straight clues were for simple minds. But we did not attach the same importance to completion, to finalization. He was quite happy (although it very seldom came to this) to leave a puzzle unfinished; whereas I could not get to sleep at night if a clue eluded me.

The stranger Spilkin, a person whose name I did not even know, finished tearing, crumpled the scrap into a ball and tossed it into the ashtray, where it immediately began to unfold, blossoming like a desert bloom in a time-phase film. He smoothed the page flat, propped it on his knee in the beam of the searchlight and took a pen from his pocket. It was a beautiful pen, a fountain pen with a marbled barrel, a Waterman I would have said (and I would have been right). The sort of pen advertising copywriters liked to call a 'writing instrument'. This pen, reclining elegantly on the soft cushion of his forefinger, with its nib as sleek as a ballet slipper, made me proof him more thoroughly, from the open-neck shirt down to the white slip-ons. His clothes were pastel and sporty, casual but expensive; they would have been perfectly at home on the greens, under a blue sky, but looked flashy in this dim brown interior.

He began to fill out the clues with remarkable facility.

How long would it take him? Half an hour was considered 'good'. I consulted my records: that day's puzzle had taken me twenty-three minutes to solve. Now that my notebook lay open on the table, on the inlaid chequerboard I'd always fondly wished might be transformed one day into a crossword grid, I suddenly resolved to take up the matter of the inconvenient new format of the clues with the editor of the *Star*. I had been putting it off for months, but watching Spilkin's contortions had made me aware that the problem was not just my own. A whole community of people were being inconvenienced by some lowly editorial whim. I took up the cudgels on their behalf.

The letter was a good one.

18 July 1987

Dear Sir,

Until recently, the cryptic and the straight clues to your two-speed crossword puzzle appeared above and below the grid respectively, and appropriately so. This enabled the proponents of the higher method to obscure the evidence of the lower by the simple expedient of folding the page in half.

Since the two sets of clues now appear alongside the grid, this procedure is no longer possible. Your puzzles editor can verify this in an instant.

Some of your readers may be accustomed to a diet of chalk and cheese, but my constitution will not bear it. This new format will improve neither your circulation nor mine. I urge you to revert to the time-honoured one.

Yours faithfully, etcetera

The letters editor thought my letter had merit too, for he published it in this shortened version. One never takes excision lightly, but at least the blade was true. (The present incumbent, by contrast, uses a rusty hacksaw or the blunderbuss of the delete button.) The casualties? A mot on origami that I had been in two minds about all along – 'your puzzles editor, *unless he be an expert in origami, the Japanese art of folding paper into decorative shapes and figures*'; and a postscript suggesting that the type used for the clues be increased from 10 point to 12. '*The eyesight of many of our citizens, especially the senior ones,*' I wrote, '*is more likely to be so-so than 20-20, I should imagine.'* Dispatched to File 13, now restored to their rightful place.

So engrossed was I in the composition of this letter that I forgot to stop the clock, and when I glanced his way again, the man at No. 3 had turned to the business pages and was doodling on the lists of share prices. Then Mrs Mavrokordatos came in and greeted him warmly – Ronald, I thought she called him – welcoming him back and saying she had missed him, and he said he was delighted to be back, he had missed her too. His voice was small and mild too, if a little nasal, and his grammar seemed presentable. I gathered from what passed between them that he was a former customer, recently retired like myself, that he had been away for some time on the south coast of Natal (KwaZulu-Natal, as he called it, quite properly) staying with a son, but that the arrangement had not 'panned out'.

'I'm not cut out for living in a granny flat,' he said, and they both laughed. 'But tell me, who's that?'

For a moment I thought he was referring to me – I had just risen to leave – but he meant Mevrouw Bonsma. She was playing 'Never on Sunday', which served me rather well as an exit march.

When I returned to the Café a few days later, and then at regular intervals thereafter, I found him sitting at the same table, under the light, 'ensconced' as I thought of it. A creature of habit. Good for him. (How wrong one can be about people.) Habit maketh the manners and all the rest that maketh the man. Predictable behaviour is what makes people tolerable, and obviates a risky reliance on goodwill and other misnomers. Every day he turned to the crossword, painstakingly removed the straight clues, and went on with the puzzle. So I had the opportunity to measure his skill against my own after all. I discovered that he was a very good crossword solver indeed. Almost superhuman. He usually finished the puzzle in under fifteen minutes! At least, I assumed that he finished it, although I could not tell at that distance.

Proofreaders (one may retire from the post but not the profession) generally have suspicious minds and long memories. The *Reader's Digest,* to which I subscribed in the days when my word power still needed improving, once published an anecdote (if you'll pardon the contradiction in terms, etymologically speaking) in the 'Life's Like That' feature, about a commuter, a mediocre crossword puzzler, who watched enviously every evening for many months as a fellow-traveller completed the cryptic puzzle in ten minutes flat. Until one day the master left his paper behind him in the train compartment when he disembarked, and the other, taking it up to marvel, discovered that the grid was filled with nonsense that bore no relation to the clues. Looking at the slim gold strap of Spilkin's watch and the chubby fingers of his hands (surgeons and cardsharps have long thin fingers only in films), I became convinced that he was up to the same trick. One afternoon, when he left the paper unattended for a moment to visit the Gentlemen's room, I actually rose and approached his table, meaning to snatch a glance at the puzzle, but he reappeared in a trice and nearly caught me red-handed. I avoided an embarrassing situation only by stooping to tie a shoelace. It was time to put a stop to this ridiculous behaviour.

It so happened that my letter on the new crossword format had been published that day and I now saw that it would provide the perfect excuse for making his acquaintance – and a rather impressive introduction, too.

Once he had returned to his puzzle, I opened my newspaper to the letters page and prepared to accost him. But my opening gambit – 'Your troubles are over, Mr …?' – died on my lips. My impending approach had transmitted itself to him as a receptivity to communication, for as I opened my mouth he cocked his head, rested the end of the fountain pen against his greying temple, and asked:

'Clam for a solitary sailor?'

For a moment I was utterly nonplussed. The idiom, the rakish air, the slightly nautical plimsolls he was sporting that day, the voice which was rummier than the one he used with Eveready and Mrs Mavrokordatos, all of this took me aback. Was he making an indecent proposal? It was unthinkable. While I blanched, he snapped his fingers – an accomplishment I have never been able to master, even with the application of lubricating spittle to the relevant forefinger and opposable thumb – and exclaimed:

'Abalone!'

Click. I clattered through my newspaper and scanned the clues. There it was: fifteen down.

'Three across: Mabel out for a stroll? Five-letter word,' I countered. And before he had time to reply, supplied the answer myself: 'Amble.'

And so, swapping clues and offering tips, we began to hold a conversation.

He said he was a Spilkin. I knew the name: a dozen or so in the Johannesburg directory, with concentrations in Melrose and Cyrildene. Spilkin. It suited him, this combination of soft and sharp, lip and bodkin, wet flesh and dry glass. He said he was a retired optician.

'By a stroke of luck,' I said, 'you have met the only person in the Café Europa who knows the difference between an optician and an optometrist.'

'And an ophthalmologist?'

Easy as pie, I said. I could even spell it. Apophthegm and phthisical too, which were in the same orthographical league. I was a retired proofreader, I said, by way of explanation, and my name was Tearle. (Just the surname, to match his 'Spilkin'. To tell the truth, deep down where the roots of language coil about the bones, I have never really felt like an Aubrey. Meaning a ruler of elves. Never had the slightest ambition in that direction. As for Aub, the inevitable diminutive – it's nearly as bad as Sphere.)

'How do you spell it?' he asked.

Well really. 'o-p-h-'

'I mean Tearle.'

'Oh. With two e's.'

'Spilkin has two i's. Which was a distinct advantage in my chosen profession. I trust that having two e's didn't harm yours?'

'Not at all.'

The details of that first conversation escape me now (this reconstructed sample is more or less representative), but we spoke, naturally enough, about optometry and proofreading, and the link between them: the eye. We discovered that we had much in common. I described, in lyrical fashion, the passage of the eye along a line of print; and he explained, with technical precision, the neurological fireworks and muscular gymnastics that made that movement possible. He admired my spectacles – horn-rims thirty years old and not to be bought for love or money – and gave a remarkably accurate account of my astigmatism and my lazy left by glancing through the lenses. This introduced a note of friendly competition. I recited seven verses of lemmata from the M section of the *Concise Oxford Dictionary* (my beloved fourth edition of 1951, reprinted with revised Addenda in 1956, boon companion of my heyday, well fingered and thumbed): Mauser ~ mazard ~ mazarine ~ measles … measly ~ medal ~ medallion ~ medium … medlar ~ melancholy ~ mélange ~ memento … memoir ~ menses ~ Menshevik ~ mercury … mercy ~ mesdames ~ meseems ~ metal … metallic ~ meteoric ~ meteorite ~ metropolitan … -metry ~ microscope ~ microscopic ~ mighty … He chimed in with the standard eye chart (the one devised by Professor Snellen) and an undergraduate mnemonic for recalling it: **E**ggheads **f**rom **P**aris, **t**he **o**melet **z**one, and so on. If only I'd had that by heart when I went before the Medical Board! I wrote it down in my notebook. Then we produced a facsimile chart on the back of an advertising flyer from the newspaper and made several suggestions for improving it. I felt, for instance, that an 's' might be more useful on line 2 than an 'o', so that the mnemonic might read '**E**lephants **f**ind **P**retoria **t**he **s**uperior **z**oo'. We became quite light-hearted and boisterous. He secured the chart to a screw on the sconce to test my eyes and I passed with flying colours, having memorized the mnemonic while I transcribed it. 'Thanks to you,' I said, 'I will never fail an eye test again.'

'You could always ask them to turn it upside down.'

And that reminded me of the crossword. I showed him my letter and he was delighted with it.

A few days later, the *Star* published a brace of readers' letters supporting my views about the new format, from J. Serebro of Wendywood and 'Also Miffed' of Germiston. The puzzles editor surrendered, the old format was restored. Tearle and Tradition had prevailed.

Spilkin had Mevrouw Bonsma play the theme from *The Longest Day* in my honour.

*

The 'spilkin': a crucial spillikin, in a game of that name, the retrieval of which renders a whole nest of others more immediately accessible.

By analogy: the key word in a crossword puzzle, whose vowels and consonants provide the newels and rails for whole flights of solutions.

And hence: a crucial aspect of any problem.

*

Passing down Kotze Street on my way to the Café, I found Dumbo at the end of his tether again, still minus an ear. I'd have thought Management would be anxious to restore their corpulent corporate image to its proper state. Surely it would be bad for business having this elephantine amputee loitering on the doorstep? I almost went in to put my case, but that Rosa was on duty, moustachioed and prickly, and no doubt itching to cross my palm with another bottle of plonk.

Hypermeat had a special on half a lambkin. Heads or tails? Baa or Baa? A black sheep of the two-legged variety pressed a handbill on me: Hillbrow Hyperpawn was buying old coins, jewellery, watches. Any old iron? Endless irony. The shop was in Kapteijn Street, with piles of cheap loot in its dusty window. I had made a few purchases there myself, years back, when it was still Bernstein's Second Time Lucky. Slightly shop-soiled goods and antiques, direct from the factory to the public.

Another new butchery: Hack's Meat Superette. Something new every week. Men's outfitters folding up and chicken grillers hatching. Why this obsession with poultry? Was it a tribal thing? A cook in a tissue-paper toque and a grease-proof inquisitor's gown flicked a cigarette butt into my path, and rows of skewered carcases, cranked round by a machine behind fat-spattered glass, applauded with flippery wings. And what were these? Charred bits and pieces, cartilaginous lumps, new species of offal. There were new varieties of dirt on the pavements too. Sticky black scabs on the cement flags, blotches, bumps, nodules that cleaved to the soles of my brogues. More of them all the time, like some skin disease. What is this stuff? Where on earth is it coming from? You never saw it falling from the sky or spilt by a human hand. It seemed to be *striking through* from beneath, like some subcutaneous festering. A less fastidious man than myself, a man more accustomed to taking specimens, an indigent geologist, say, a botanist, a pathologist, might have made a study of it to determine its origins. Animal or vegetable? Outside the Pink Cadillac, which only opened its doors after dark, a heap of children, messily corked, theatrically ragged, like urchin extras from a production of *Oliver,* slept in black and white. A photograph from the archive of atrocities: a heap of corpses, with their big feet jutting out of blackened clothing, filthy as chimney sweeps. Perhaps they were pavement sweeps, responsible for spreading the dirt under the pretext of mopping it up.

Two portraits of Steffi Graf, the ladies' tennis champion, ringed round by garlands of last year's Weinacht tinsel (or was it this year's tinsel, ahead of its time?), presided over the Wurstbude. In the first, she was preparing to serve. She was improbably, impeccably muscled, undoubtedly well-fed, a living tribute to scientific nutrition. The fake coals in the grilling machine cast a healthy pink glow over her wintergreened calves. In the second picture, she was holding up a trophy, a silver platter ideal for a sucking-pig, on the centre court at Wimbledon.

Herr Toppelmann, Kurt, the proprietor, put my Bratwurst and two rolls on a plate, tonged out a goose-pimpled dill pickle, dabbed mustard and patted butter. Everyone else got a cardboard tray, but I had argued for the plate on medical grounds – my dysfunctional duodenum (entirely spurious, I might add) – and he'd conceded. I also got my sausage whole, rather than lopped into segments by the ingenious stainless-steel, counter-top guillotine, as the advertising to the trade might have put it. Most of the regulars went for the Currywurst, which meant that their sausage segments were smothered in tomato sauce and dusted with curry powder. They speared up the segments with two toothpicks, dispensed from a little drum like a schoolroom pencil sharpener. It could be done with one toothpick, to tell the truth, but those in the know found that two afforded a certain Germanic stability. I would have none of it. I told Herr Toppelmann I wanted a Bratwurst, whole, on a plate, and a knife and fork to eat it with, I don't need my food cut up for me like a child.

I had to drag in the duodenum again, and the high blood pressure, when in truth I have the constitution of a man half my age, because there were principles involved, of linguistics and cuisine. Currywurst? It was ersatz, a jerry-built portmanteau if ever I heard one. I had denounced it the very first time I came in here, this having been the express purpose of my visit, but he refused to remove it from the menu. I vowed never to eat one. For the same principled reason, I avoided the pickle-barrel tables on the pavement outside: they were tacky, in the senses popular on both sides of the Atlantic, they smacked of fast food, grubby little hands that might tug at one's flannels and spoil one's appetite. I stood at the counter instead, where I could listen to Herr Toppelmann conversing in German with regulars of that persuasion, or, when the place was empty, hold a brief conversation with him myself in English and watch the sausages squirming.

This afternoon the place was empty, so I told him the news: the Café Europa was closing down. He took it very well.

'Also I,' he said in his charming English, 'am closing down.'

'No.'

'Ja. I go home to Germany.'

Typical. But I sympathized, too. 'I can't say I blame you. Who would want to live under a black government?'

'No, no, that is most unfair, you do not understand. I go home because my father in Frankfurt is sick. In the kidney.'

'Ah. A Frankfurter. I might have guessed.'

'I am most happy to be governed by the black man. Black persons and I are coming along strongly together.'

Indeed. The scarlet women of the Quirinale Hotel. Ever willing to put a crease in the Senf, if not quite to cut it. I was in here, eating a sausage, when the Berlin Wall came down. What was it Herr Toppelmann had said then? Communism is kaput in Germany, but here is just starting, it will come very bad. (His English had improved over the years.) The forcemeat philosopher. A rush of irritation, as quick and queasying as a spurt of saliva in the mouth, as he jabbed my Bratwurst with a fork and it spewed grease onto the grille. Bloody Germans. From Germany out *und so weiter.* Hungarians, Italians, Scots. Immigrants. Foul-weather friends. Slobodan would be hurrying back to where he came from too, no doubt, Wessels would search for him in vain ... although he was so much at home here, living off the fat of the land. I felt fat too, schmaltzy and bloated. Stuffed with change, like a piggy bank or a parking meter. The mustard got into my cold sore and burned. I left half the Bratwurst on the plate and crossed the street. The wurst is still to come, I thought, in my Toppelmann twang. Nein, nein, the wurst is behind us. The opposite pavement was crowded with curio-sellers and their wares, wooden animals and idols shamelessly displaying their private parts. I was tempted to march through these hordes like some maddened Gulliver, trampling them underfoot. I escalated, like tensions in the Middle East, like the incidence of armed robbery on the Reef, and issued into the Café where, for the first time in many a long month, my eye was caught by the silver trophy gathering dust among the bottles. I'd been meaning to take it down and give it a good going over with Brasso. The brave little figure, tiptoe on the summit, clad in nothing but a wisp of lacy tarnishing, brought a lump to my throat. The proofreader's cup, the floating trophy for 'The Proofreader's Derby'.

'How ya doin'?' said Tone.

'How am I doing? If I was the frivolous sort, my managerial friend, I should affix a sign asking that question to the seat of my pants. And a telephone number.' Then, resorting to sign language, tapping my larynx with the edge of my hand, 'I'm up to here.' Perhaps it wasn't a lump after all, but a bolus of change, half-digested, sour, swimming in bile, bumping against my epiglottis. My little tongue.

'I know what you mean,' said Tone. 'I'm also gatvol. But you've got to take the punch. Have a drink, man, it'll make you feel better.'

Everything will stay the same. Everything will change. A football match was on one screen, and Joseph Slovo, the communist kingpin, on the other. Day or night, rain or shine, in some corner of a foreign field, someone was playing football. While in Kempton Park, at the World Trade Centre, they were levelling the playing fields and shifting the goalposts. As if the negoti-haters, as you-know-who used to call them, were nothing but glorified groundsmen.

My mouth was still burning, but my throat was dry. Perhaps I needed a drop of the damp after all. Moçes was lurking behind a potted palm, its fronds stirring gently in a breeze off the Bay of Alibia, dallying with some young woman, didn't look like kitchen staff, too dolled up, lips as red as paint. Helen of Troyeville, or some Carmen from the Quirinale, the sort Herr Toppelmann came along with. Moçes was so enamoured of her, I practically had to stand on my chair to attract his attention. I started the lecture on service, abridged, but I really didn't have the energy, and he looked so down in the mouth, I felt it necessary to be conciliatory.

'Who's the girl?'

'She's my nephew.'

'Ha! You mean she's your niece.' Needs the talk on customer relations.

'No, sir. She's my nephew.'

'Is she your brother's daughter? Yes? Then she's your *niece*.'

Looks baffled. Then deliberately: 'She's my nephew.'

For crying in a bucket. Whiskey, pronto. The nephew stilted out in her high heels.

Errol, on his way to the Gentlemen's room in a hurry: 'Hoezit bra. Checking out the chocolates?'

I wouldn't eat what Tone calls a pastry if he gave them away. As for 'bra', I had voiced my objection to the term repeatedly, which only made them use it more.

I took out my files, but before I could set to work, Wessels wobbled in and started waving Mr Fatso/Mnr Vetsak under my nose. 'I've nearly got everyone,' he smirked, as if the party were no more than a confidence trick, and ran a smoke-stained forefinger down a row of ticks. 'Even Merlé, see? Still dossing out in Illovo with her daughter, who might be able to bring her. No promises at this stage. Mevrou Bonsma's still at the Dorchester, but it's becoming a bit rough. She's got a school now. Only ones I can't find is Everistus, who's gone off to his rondavel in the hills for a week or so.

Someone died. But I left a message. You know he's grafting at Bradlows. And Spilkin and Pardner, natch, who's back in Joeys but lying low.'

Lying low? Like Apaches. Apache here, Apache there (punchlines, Wessels). Something to do with beards.

'What you got there? Looks familiar.'

I closed the file on his finger. He knew exactly what it was, but he was the last person I felt like discussing it with. It was a selection from the fardel of notes and jottings and clippings and scribbled-upon typescripts that represented the raw material of 'The Proofreader's Derby'. This unfinished business had chafed at my peace of mind for too long. I had made a bargain with myself: if I finished 'The Proofreader's Derby' before the end of the month, I would take it with me to the Goodbye Bash and present it to the sceptics – I might even make photostatic copies, one for each to bear away as a souvenir. If not, I would stay home, and a plague on all their townhouses!

*

13 December 1993

Dear Sir,

An able-bodied man might wear a T-shirt, though why he would choose to, when proper shirts with buttons and collars are freely available, is a mystery to me.

But what manner of monster would fit into a 't-shirt' of the style advertised in your newspaper on 11 December (Hyperama Festive Season Bonanza)? A one-armed bandit, I suppose, some twisted wreck of a human being, the sort who would live in an a-frame house made entirely of i-beams …

Would the sub-editors care to explain?

Yours faithfully, etcetera

*

In the first weeks of my acquaintance with Spilkin, I always arrived at the Café Europa to find him already there, seated at one of the little tables against the wall. And I always sat down at the other, with the big round one in between, as if each encounter was the first between people who had never met before. We seemed to be participating in the primary activity that the café as a social institution made possible: being on one's own in the company of congenial strangers. Another stranger, looking on, might have thought that our conversation had a cultured quality about it as well, carried on at intervals from a seemly distance while we each went about our own business, revolving around niceties of expression and quibbles of logic, anagrammatical teasers, aqueous humours, questions of craft, specifications of lenses and lemmata, headwords, grades of graphite, presbyopia and strabismus, occasionally politics – this was before change beset us and made the subject so tiresome. I say, Tearle, you don't happen to have a pen-wiper handy? Why not use a serviette, Spilkin? Capital idea. Spilkin this and Tearle that. It all helped to cultivate a sort of formal bonhomie between us, the polite and companionable ease that someone who had never been in an officers' mess might expect to enjoy there.

But happening to arrive one day at the same time, we fell into conversation on the escalator, and happy as I was with our arrangement, it seemed absurd to part and sit at separate tables. We should sit at the round table, obviously, we should meet one another halfway; but we both hesitated, with our hands on the backs of our chairs.

'Alfresco, perhaps?' Spilkin said, nodding towards the balcony.

'"Fresco" is a relative term, Spilkin.' He brought out a slightly haughty tone in me, which I was rather pleased about. 'Sit out there and you'll be breathing exhaust fumes in the rush hour, which is about to start. Every twenty minutes or so, the upper deck of the Braamfontein bus will slide into view and the passengers will gaze at you through the railings as if you're a beast in a cage. Say a chimpanzee from Sierra Leone in the Jardin des Plantes.' This flourish was prompted by the little Eiffels (I have never been abroad).

I could see he was impressed, but he continued to gaze around the room as if a better option might suggest itself. I had other bolts in my quiver – the wind will scatter my papers to the four corners of the block, the sun will blister my pate, the occupants of the flats above will drop the ash of their cigarettes upon me – but I aimed at a more subtle target in the gloomier depths of the room: 'Over there?'

He voiced the obvious objection: 'Too close to the W[ater] C[loset].'

The spot where we already found ourselves now became defined as a reasonable compromise between two unsuitable extremes, and by common consent, we sat down at the round table (it was No. 2) facing one another, with Alibia to my right and his left. A sudden chill shook me, as if a seaward breeze had lifted a handful of pins and needles off the white beach in front of the casino and flung them in my face. He opened the *Tonight!* section to the crossword and folded it in half with a casual flick, which I had to interpret as a gesture of gratitude. I opened my briefcase – only a fool or a drug dealer would carry a briefcase through the streets of Hillbrow today, but it was a common enough occurrence then – and unpacked my equipment, laying each piece in its position, which was as rigidly preordained as a place-setting: notebook, pencil (Faber-Castell 2B), sharpener, eraser, dictionary *(Concise Oxford,* fourth edition, *opere citato,* under the worthy editorship of Henry and Frank Fowler, faithfully revised by a certain McIntosh, proofreaders inexplicably unacknowledged, as usual), lever-arch research file, punch, scissors, Sellotape, index cards.

I opened the file and the notebook. I sharpened the pencil into the ashtray and returned it to its spot.

It has always been my practice before setting to work, to limber up with a few minutes of basic lexicology, stretching the verbal tendons, if you like, to guard against injury, and so I opened the dictionary at my marker. Since my retirement I had been working my way steadily through the *Concise,* a leisurely passage, no more than a column a day, lingering over words. Let's see. **Chew, Chianti, chiaroscuro. Chiasmus** – *I cannot dig, to beg I am ashamed.* **Chibol. Chibouk.** Chibouque may have been better. **Chicanery**: from the Persian for 'polo-stick'. As far as **chime**. Which comes from the same root as 'cymbal'. Might make a fine graaff (a lexical backflip). When I was nicely warmed up, it was time for a bit of lexical fartlek (to use that unfortunate term, from the Swiss *fart*, speed, and *lek,* play): I opened the dictionary at random and put my finger down on **Candlemas**: feast of purification. I went to **feast**, quickly, and then rambled through the entry at my leisure. A large or sumptuous meal. Partake of a feast, eat or drink sumptuously. From the Latin *festus,* joyous. Obviously the same root as festival ... I sprinted for that entry, via fertile ~ feudal ~ fictile ... too far ... back to festival. Here we are, **festival**, from the med. Latin *festivalis,* as festive. **Festive** ... from *festum,* as feast. Bingo. Back to **fictile**. Made of earth or clay by a potter; of pottery. From the Latin *fictilis,* f. *fingere, fict* – fashion. Quick dash to **fashion** (farthingale ~ fasces ~ no sign of fartlek) and stroll through *factio,* f. *facere, fact* – do, make. Must remember to check 'finger'. But first sprint to **fiction**. Yes, of course, as fictile. An invented idea or statement, an imaginary thing. A conventionally accepted falsehood. Back to **facile**: easily achieved but of little value. Of speech, writing etc., fluent, ready, glib. From the Latin *facilis,* f. *facere* – do. Take a breather. I turned to my notebook.

'If you don't mind my asking, Tearle,' Spilkin said, as I'd hoped he might, 'what are you up to?'

I had been dying to tell someone about 'The Proofreader's Derby' (although I wasn't thinking of it in those terms yet). I was wrapped up in it then, rapt, passionately intent. And Spilkin and I would have to get to know one another, now that we were sharing a table.

'I'm working on my System of Records.'

'Gee-gees?'

'Proofreading.'

That would have stopped many men in their tracks, but Spilkin, give him his due, was a sharp one: 'Your life's work?'

I'd never thought of it that way, but he was spot on. The story of my life. I nodded.

'Tell me about it then.'

'Well, in this file here, which is just one of several dozen, are the fruits of a long career – I won't say a distinguished one, in the ordinary sense of the word, but certainly respectable. My documentation, my papers. You'll see that many of them are clippings of one sort or another, from newspapers mainly, but also magazines and journals, and books. Those are the photostatic copies, mind you, or the handwritten quotations; I would never be so barbarous (from the Greek *barbaros,* foreign) as to tear a page from a book. And then also gazettes, programmes, handbills, posters, wedding invitations, menus. I've got some unusual things, collector's items. This here is a label from a tin: "Pot' o' Gold petit poise." Now I'm busy transcribing the important parts of these documents into this notebook here – also one of many, twenty-six to be precise, one for each letter of the alphabet – in a form that allows for easy reference without losing the essence. I never had the time to collate all this raw material while I was employed, although I was gathering diligently for thirty years and more, and so I'm devoting my retirement to the task. Keeping the grey matter supple, too. They say it's as important as taking care of the body, you know.'

'Who's that?'

'Excuse me?'

'Everyone's always pointing fingers at "them". "They" said this and "they" did that. Who do you mean exactly?'

'Who do you mean by "everyone"?' I countered.

'People in general.'

'Well, that's who I mean by "they".'

'No, it's not.'

'What are you driving at?'

'Americans. That's who you mean. Yanks. Specifically Californians. Jane Fonda and Sylvester Stallone.'

'Who?'

'They're the ones who're sprouting this stuff about the mind and the body as if it was all their idea, as if it didn't go back to the Greeks!' Mrs Mavrokordatos's ear pinkened. 'The gymnasium, a noble institution founded for the social good, issues in the naked commercialism of Jim's Gym.'

I must have looked nonplussed, because he laughed out loud and said:

'Cheer up, Tearle. Just a bit of verbal sparring, just pulling your leg, good for the circulation, didn't mean to distract you from your story. So, what are the important parts of these documents you were talking about?'

In retrospect, this episode strikes me as rather unkind, revealing a streak of nastiness in Spilkin I would have been wise to acknowledge. But if I looked flushed and flummoxed then, it was not that I had taken offence, nor even that I found the sparring strenuous, but a simple expression of pleased astonishment that we appeared to understand each other so well. I went on happily.

'They're examples. Various kinds of things. Literals, misspellings, inversions, anacolutha, haplographies and dittographies, which are really two aspects of the same blindness. There's a fine line between proofreading and editing, they say, although the proofreader worth his salt will know exactly where it is. Homonyms (dog, dog). Homophones (some, sum). Puns. You would be surprised how many typographical errors are the result of unconscious identifications. The odd apocope.'

'You mean mistakes.'

'No, I mean corrigenda: things to be corrected, especially in a printed book. From the Latin. Not the same as "mistakes" at all, once you know the ins and outs. People make mistakes. Their fingers slip, their concentration lapses. And what they leave behind are not mistakes, but corrigenda.'

He was looking at me a little sceptically. 'Enlighten me. An example. I'm slow on the uptake.' Which he was not.

I assembled a typical triad: a cutting from the file, an index card from the box and an alphabetical entry in the notebook, and turned them all towards Spilkin.

'Here's one I've already processed – see the red cross? This was one of my first finds. I came across it in the *Pretoria News* of 7 January 1956. An article on poultry farming. Corrigenda in the press were relatively few and far between then and I was new at the game, so I was especially pleased to capture it.'

He examined the clipping. The headline read: Feathers Fly As Poultry Farmers Meet. The corrigendum was in the third paragraph: 'Mr Goosen refused to anser questions about the price of eggs.' Spilkin chuckled when he got there, to show that he had spotted it.

'I collected corrigenda haphazardly for a good fifteen years, by which time I had quite a pile of them, even allowing for the relative scarcity of material. Four or five files' worth, I should think. In the early seventies, I made my first attempt to establish order by developing a catalogue. You see that I transferred the relevant word – in this instance, "anser" – onto an index card. This number here records the location of the original document in the files – the N means "newspaper clipping". And this T in the corner stands for "typographical error".

'Unfortunately, I never had more time than my annual leave and the occasional long weekend to devote to the system, and so I was never able to catch up. Also, the volume of corrigenda in printed matter of all kinds increased steadily over the years, and so the collected material gradually outstripped the index system. By the time I retired, the Records had grown to occupy more than a dozen files, and no more than a third had been catalogued.

'I'm ashamed to say that it was only then, when I turned my full and undivided attention to the system, that I perceived its inadequacy. The essence was escaping me. The stress in proofreading must fall at least as strongly on the reading as on the proof: one might contemplate a single word and comprehend it, but one could hardly be said to be "reading" it. Proofreading as a skill only comes into its own at the level of the sequence, in the order of motion; a solitary word, set firmly in space, is beyond its purview. The eye has to move. The proofreader is a tightrope artist, managing the difficult tension between momentum and inertia, story and stock, sentence and word. As soon as he becomes too engrossed in the sense of what he's reading, he loses sight of the unitary word; on the other hand, the failure to register sense at some level, however rarefied, will lead to harrowing technical misjudgements. If he is to survive this hazardous passage without falling, he must find the still moving point between the excitement of the chase and the rapture of possession.

'To cut a long story short: I am revising the entire system, documents and catalogue alike, by providing fuller versions of the corrigenda, preserving the context of each one, arranged alphabetically in these notebooks. Returning to our example, you see the new version here, in the form: "anser/answer: Mr Goosen refused to anser questions about the price of eggs." First the example, then the correct form. From the thing to be corrected, to the corrected thing. And note that this more complete version contains the germ of an explanation for the typist's error – deeply buried as it may be – in the relationship between "anser" and "goose".

'The task remains daunting. I've got this mass of documents, growing larger by the day, as standards of correctness decline. Then perhaps a quarter or a fifth of the material – the proportion continues to shrink in relation to the mass – is referenced on these cards. I could simply throw the cards away, except that they help me to relocate the original corrigenda: over the years, many that seemed blindingly obvious when I first identified them have blended back into the printed background – like a bird in the bush, which vanishes as soon as you take your eye off it – and without an index card, it can take me hours of proofing and reproofing to drive them out into the open again. And then finally, I have these notebooks, growing steadily fuller, and matters of internal organization to think about. But in the end, I hope to arrive at a unified system.'

(If I had known then what would become of my System of Records, I might have abandoned the project entirely. And if I had looked into Spilkin's heart ...)

'It's a beautiful system,' he said, casting his merry eyes upon me, eyes that seemed more than usually wet. I had touched him, I thought. 'What are its beauties, specifically? Breadth, depth, one is tempted to say length. It's ambitious, one might almost say grandiose. The beauty of error. It gives me goose-flesh.'

'Thank you, Spilkin. I hoped you would understand.'

'So, what are you going to do with it?'

'I beg your pardon?'

'You're going to put it to some use, I should think.'

'Must it be useful?'

'Not necessarily. But it seems like a lot of effort to go to for no good reason.'

'It's no effort at all. I enjoy it, I find it very rewarding.'

I had some thoughts on my hobby-horse's utility: one of my initial aims had been to determine *species* of error, and to assist in eliminating them. But Spilkin's question betrayed an uncharacteristic crudeness, as if he were talking about a crowbar or a mallet, and so I kept my thoughts to myself, and the matter was left unresolved.

Be that as it may, Spilkin took to the task like a duck to water. He was an avid newspaper reader himself, and soon he was dredging up some gems, which he generously passed on to me. He was at ease in the murkier depths of the classifieds, areas of print even I found it difficult to venture into – 221. Miscellaneous Sales 235. Poultry/ Livestock 300. Bands/Discos 413. Hairdressers/Barbers 950. Senior Citizens – and he had the stomach for 107. Deaths, which is more than I can say for myself (duodenum or no duodenum). In my heyday, I'd made a few memorable finds in those funereal quarters – 'knowing you enriched our livers' ... 'Loved by al, missed by many' ... 'I will always remember your simile' – but lately I'd grown afraid of coming across someone I knew. There were too many familiar names, and just looking at them made my teeth ache. This aversion was a shame, because the quality of those particular pages deteriorated spectacularly as time went by: apparently the people employed to answer the telephones in the Classified Department were no longer required to speak English.

There was another reason: a surfeit of heroism. Too many exemplary demises, milk-fed and arum-scented, too many equable departures for glory. Nine out of ten people died peacefully. Did no one die kicking and screaming any more, cursing God and the sawbones? They all seemed to struggle with such good grace against cruel misfortune. One miserable death acknowledged, one long season of pointless suffering faced with bitterness and resentment, would have been a breath of fresh air.

*

In later years, the death notices became so consumed by corrigenda that I was able to venture back into that territory from time to time. The rot reached such unnatural proportions that it began to subvert the purpose of the service itself, and the whole enterprise acquired the tone of a macabre joke. One could imagine the unhappy surprise of those left behind when they came to clip their remembrances.

Maggots, death notices: Till we meat again ... Our heart felt thanks ... Safe in God's cave ... The father figure of refrigerator services ... Pissed away after a long illness ...

*

Spilkin and I began to meet at the Café nearly every day, circumstances permitting. Before making his acquaintance, I had fallen into the habit of arriving in the mid-afternoon, to pre-empt the stream of after-work regulars and improve my chances of securing my favourite table (I had not been pushy enough to ask Mrs Mavrokordatos to reserve it for me); now I found, by empirical experiment, that no matter how early I arrived, Spilkin had beaten me to it, and no matter how late I left, Spilkin would outstay me. On the single occasion that I stayed till midnight and the closing, he contrived to dawdle so that he would be the last through the door. All his waking hours were passed at the Europa. He took lunch and supper there – outlandish platters of moussaka and shish kebabs, spaghetti Bolognese and Vienna schnitzel, Strammer Maxes and Croque Monsieurs. In those days, my own eating habits were more conservative than they are today, and in any event, dining out constantly was beyond my means. I deduced that Spilkin was rather better off than myself – no doubt there is money to be made in spectacles and prudent investment. Why he should have such an antipathy to being in his own home, I do not know. He had a room in the Flamingo, a residential hotel in Edith Cavell Street, but I never set foot in it. The laws of propriety, which propriety prevented us from ever discussing, had declared our private lives, the lives we led once we left the Café, strictly out of bounds.

As I've said, I was on comfortably proper terms with Mrs Mavrokordatos, although our relationship was not without its personal touches. She had begun to take in the *Star,* for instance, and kept it behind the counter in its own binder so that I should have first crack at it. But with Spilkin she behaved differently, almost as if she were his housekeeper or, their ages notwithstanding, his mother. She was always plying him with complimentary titbits – Italian kisses (as I believe they're called), almond-flavoured amaretti sprinkled with angelica, oily dolmades, little tumblers of resinous retsina.

Once I said to her: 'You should charge him rent for that chair.'

And he piped up: 'She should pay me for sitting here. Thanks to me, she can say in all honesty that this place is never empty.' There were always people coming and going, men mainly, clustering around tables where card games were in progress, drifting off into corners for quieter conversations, talking over their shoulders to 'contacts' at the next table, hailing newcomers by sending up smoke signals from their cigars. The recent arrivals from abroad spoke more loudly than the others, and offered cigarettes from garishly coloured packets, which were inhaled like the fair weather of home. Those who were leaving looked distant and bored, and wore too much gold jewellery. They came and they went. But Spilkin was a fixture.

'There are limits – or there should be,' I said. 'No offence, Mrs Mavrokordatos, you know how fond I am of this establishment, but I'm beginning to think that Spilkin here is an extremist, beneath his moderate exterior.'

I resisted the urge to follow his example, to seek out company earlier in the day, to pop in at all hours. I have never been the sort of person who pops in anywhere. I could no more pop in than I could knock about or toddle along. It's not my way. I disciplined myself to leave my flat no earlier than three in the afternoon and to return at a decent hour. Routine is the foundation of happiness. A proofreader needs a clear head and a sharp eye. All my life it had been lights out at ten on the dot, and I saw no reason to make rash changes now. My routine gave me more than enough time for doing the crossword, reading the newspaper, writing the odd letter to the editor, conversing with my friend, and of course working on my System of Records, the meaty main course for which all these other activities were mere appetizers. In this way, several satisfying months went by.

Spilkin was a ladies' man. Did I mind, he enquired one day, if Mevrouw Bonsma joined us, just this once?

'Mevrouw' because it did not seem right to call her 'Bonsma', in accordance with our usual practice – the house style, as I thought of it – and because Spilkin had got it into his head that she was Dutch. He said he could not look at her without being reminded of poffertjes (which turned out to be sugar-coated fritters, much eaten in the Low Countries). For my part, I found that she put me in mind of windswept dykes and wheels of cheese. But I went along with his suggestion. I am not easily swayed, but I was perhaps a little too much under his influence at the time.

'Tell us about Rotterdam,' said Spilkin, 'and your triumphs as a soloist with the Philharmonic.'

Mevrouw Bonsma disengaged her long teeth with a click and patted his arm with a hand as red and square as a stevedore's (it is with pianists as it is with surgeons and cardsharps). 'You know very well, Spilkijn,' – he had introduced himself thus and she seemed to think it was a diminutive – 'that I was born and bred in Rustenburg.' Despite all her efforts to modulate it and make it lilt, her voice hissed and crackled like an old gramophone record.

'A lady of your accomplishments? Impossible.'

'I am just a farm girl at heart. Sincerely, I have never even been in an aeroplane.'

'Mevrouw!' Pursing his lips, giving the exotic diphthong the shape of a grape, then swallowing it whole like a tickled schoolboy. If he made 'Mevrouw Bonsma' sound as sweet and juicy as a fruit, she made 'Spilkin' into an acute little instrument for winkling the stubborn flesh from its shell. Bodkin, kilderkin, cannikin, sooterkin. Was it my imagination or was there a trace of a Dutch accent like a dusting of cinnamon on her flat vowels? Perhaps she was putting it on, under suggestion.

The banter continued while she powdered her face. Pancake, she explained, for the lights. Light, actually: a sixty-watt globe in a bluebell shade, dipping its head over the keyboard. 'Once an artiste, always an artiste. But I have no illusions, life has stripped me of them, one by one. People used to sit up and take notice when I played. Now I am "background music", that's all.' The skin of her neck had the texture of crêpe. She enamelled her lips and went bravely back to work.

'So, what do you think?'

I had had the opportunity to examine Mevrouw Bonsma closely over the months, but I had not drawn many conclusions from the exercise. She was highly strung, but that was fitting. And she thought too much about what other people thought of her. Taking pride in one's appearance is nothing less than good manners, but she was overly concerned with trifles. An occupational hazard, perhaps. While one of her raw-boned hands bickered away at the keys, the other was always wandering to the nape of her neck, fumbling for a label, checking whether her jersey was on the right way round. I saw that she did not have the feet of a pianist either. Her big plates of meat, tilted on the wineglass heels of slippers made of silver chain-mail, pumped the pedals, while her hands rolled over the keys, setting up a pale vibrato in the flesh of her upper arms. She looked like a navvy driving some shiny piece of earth-moving equipment. Five-letter word: spade. Or: piano. Incongruously, the music itself was a soft, insistent outpouring, like drizzle on the roof, or the tinkling of a wind-chime, to which one grows so accustomed, one only hears it when it falls silent. 'A charming woman.'

'You like her?'

'Well enough.' I did too, although we were not friends as such. There was something heroic in her efforts to be light, to keep her bulk afloat on such a thin stream of sound. Her fingertips touched the keys with exquisite delicacy, defying gravity, skipping like a flurry of raindrops across the surface of a pond, producing ever more intricate Venn diagrams of interlocking ripples.

Spilkin and I sat up straighter than usual, while she paddled through 'Swanee River'.

'Her name,' Spilkin whispered, 'is Suzanna, but I promised not to tell.

She enjoys being Mevrouwed. Bit of a snob, never mind the country-girl stuff.'

Total snob, in reverse, to a degree (6). National serviceman in a boa (6). New edition of Bosman (6).

When she rolled without missing a beat into 'Red Sails in the Sunset', we gave her a round of applause, which found a few polite echoes at the other tables – or it may have been draughtsmen clacking over their foes. She showed us her grateful yellowed ivories.

'Just this once' was no more than a manner of speaking. Mevrouw Bonsma acquired a permanent place at our table. She would join us between shifts at the piano, to moisten her throat with the mug of tea or rock shandy to which her contract entitled her. She laughed voraciously at Spilkin's jokes, as if she were crushing rusks between her molars, and left fading echoes of her laughing mouth on the rim of her teacup and the ends of her satin-tipped cigarettes.

Once had been a tolerable novelty; but being in her company constantly aggravated me. The sheer bulk of her was an imposition. When she sat down at the table, I felt myself rise momentarily in my own chair, as if the room had subsided in her vicinity. She loomed over us like a dam wall, which had seemed sturdy enough when observed from a safe distance, but appeared to be crumbling away now that we squatted, like a pair of truant schoolboys, in the damp shade at its foot. I felt as if I was *on the shores of Mevrouw Bonsma*. The phrase rang in my head, trying to fit itself to the tune of 'Loch Lomond' or 'On Top of Old Smokey', without success. Always, it was Rotterdam I saw. Such a watery fecundity! What if she burst? I would be washed away like a stick of balsa on a flood of evergreens. Even when she went back to the piano, the threat remained. She had elbowed her way out of the background to which she belonged, and could no longer be ignored. When she played, we had to listen. Her personal favourites bubbled along perkily, flats tumbling like little propellers, sharps concealed like lures in soft lumps of melody. The special requests, hauled up from the abysmal deeps, could be positively sodden. More than once I felt as if I was drowning.

It was impossible to discuss my fears with Spilkin. I could not be sure what he thought of Mevrouw Bonsma. He seemed to like her a great deal. But then he also treated her as if she were a fool. He thought nothing of speaking about her in the third person, while she sat nodding pleasantly, fingering the ugly beauty spot stuck like a pastille of salted licorice to the corner of her mouth.

As an act of self-preservation, to save myself from being swept away, I began to tell her about my System of Records. 'Over my head,' she protested, 'Greek to me. I'm no good with words.' But she was impressed with me, I could tell, she thought I was frightfully clever, and so I kept pressing my clippings on her and reading her extracts from the notebooks. At other times, it was lexical gymnastics, flashy routines full of pikes and rolls and tearles with a twist, moves I could execute in my sleep. '**Medley**, Mevrouw,' I would say. 'Heterogeneous mixture. See meddle. **Meddle**, busy oneself unduly. And **mêlée**. Same root in "mix" – from the Latin *misceo.*' Then again: 'Do you see, Mevrouw,' I would say. '**Wormwood**. From the OE *wormod, wermod,* after worm, wood: cf vermouth. And **vermouth**. From the G. *Wermut,* wormwood. That's what we call a backflip. Let me show you how it works here in the dictionary.' And sometimes, when both of us were exhausted, I would fall back on frenzied bouts of lexical fartlek. 'Here we are: **absinth**. A shrubby plant, *Artemisia absinthium,* or its essence. Also called "wormwood". Hence a liqueur flavoured with wormwood. Are you still with me? **Artemisia**. Any of various plants, including sagebrush and wormwood, f. ME, f. L., f. G. plant sacred to Artemis. **Artemis**. G. Myth. The virgin goddess of the hunt and the moon. **Sagebrush** perhaps? f. L. *salvia,* the healing plant, from *salvus,* healthy, safe. **Salvation**!' And so on. She would bite her bottom lip with her ragged incisors and gaze at me anxiously. I had the distinct impression that she admired me, an impression I had not gained from a member of the fairer sex (to stretch a point) for quite some time, and it flattered my vanity, I suppose, or what few shreds of it remained. I couldn't help myself: I began to take pleasure in making her clap one of her big red hands to her mouth in astonishment and delight.

My behaviour was uncharacteristic; obviously, it lacked the decorum people associate with me. And it appeared to infect Spilkin too. Lapsing out of character, just as I had done, he began to tell jokes. Have you heard the one about? he was always asking. Mevrouw Bonsma, who did not have a funny bone in her body, declared that he was the wittiest man alive. Under this onslaught, shoals of old punchlines came adrift in my head and slewed about, looking for jokes to attach themselves to. Knock knock. Who's there? Ja. Ja who? Boo. Boo who? To get to the other side. And one to hold the light bulb. Because it feels so good when I stop. What was that Indian's name again? Said the Texan. Said the Irishman. Said the Jew. Clutter and disorder. I found myself plucking index cards out of box-files like some door-to-door salesman in a cartoon, an ugly little man with Dagwood Bumstead shoes and a daft hairstyle. Spilkin told another joke, something off-colour, lime-green, puce.

What was this attack of nerves all about? To speak for myself, I found the lack of discrimination in Mevrouw Bonsma's dim interior alarming. A great jumble of music had been poured into her, like leftovers into an olla podrida, and it bubbled out in an indiscriminate broth. I am a repository too; but in me, everything has its place. In me, things are filed, whereas she was merely filled.

I imagined that Spilkin, with his fine sense of discrimination, felt the same. When Mevrouw Bonsma sat at our table, we burbled away desperately, as if trying to mend a crack in her foundation. When she returned to her piano, we sat in depleted silence, with our backs stiff and our fists clenched on our knees, while our newspapers lay unread on the table before us. When I went home exhausted, Spilkin was still clamped to the table under the sconce, like a floodlit statue.

Later it occurred to me that if Spilkin had felt the same anxieties as I did, he would have responded with a recitation of the eye chart or some favourite prescriptions, a mortar of solid sense, rather than this sludge of inane jokes. In the light of his subsequent behaviour, I came to believe, strange as it may seem, that he was competing with me for her favours. In which case *he* had infected *me!*

Then Mevrouw Bonsma, bless her chapped heels, announced that she had invited Merle and Benny to join us for afternoon tea.

More people! I was mortified. But as it happened, the newcomer – because there was only one – was just what was needed to restore our equilibrium.

*

Benny turned out to be a Pekingese, a canine knick-knack, disproportionately fierce. Benito, I called her afterwards: Il Puce, The Fleabag. In those days, animals were not allowed into the Europa, and so she spent her first visit to the Café tethered to a downpipe next to the door, nipping at the heels of patrons as they came and went. She had a go at my turn-ups, but I made her see sense with the business end of a brogue. They say that people grow to resemble their pets, or choose pets that resemble them. Merle was small, full of bounce, with round wet eyes and limp grey hair in a bob. She was already settled at our table, in the company of Spilkin and Mevrouw Bonsma, thankfully not in my chair. I hardly had time to sit before she declared, matter-of-factly, 'You must be A. Tearle.'

'I am *the* Tearle,' I replied, 'the definite article.'

'I've seen your letters to the editor. Suzanna shows them to me.'

'Good.' How about that.

'I liked that one about the rubbish bins, very acute. How did it go again?' She tucked one flap of her hair behind her ear, as if to hear me better.

'You mean the one about the lack of?' I paused for effect, and then recited from memory: 'One appreciates that the removal of the rubbish bins from our streets is part of a strategy to thwart the murderous ambitions of terrorists. But with littering now reaching unprecedented heights, one cannot but fear that the litter problem itself has become a time bomb waiting to explode.'

'That was well put.'

'Thank you.'

'I've heard all about your System of Records too, from Suzanna, who professes not to understand what you're up to. Sounds fascinating.'

'Thank you.' This enthusiasm was quite disarming.

'Have you got them in your bag?'

'A good sample.'

'So, what does it stand for – the A?' With a sharp forefinger, she traced the letter in the monogram embossed on my leather briefcase, and then tucked back another flap of hair to expose a second delicate and expectant ear.

'Aubrey.' *Sotto voce,* but Spilkin's theatrical eyebrows twitched. 'However, we don't hold with first names. You can call me Tearle.'

'Poppycock.' From the Dutch *pappekak.* The sort of mush that would agglomerate in Mevrouw Bonsma's dental sluices. 'I'll do nothing of the sort. I am not a public schoolboy. It's pernicious, this bandying about of surnames. Even the press has fallen into the habit. Thatcher said this and Reagan did that. As if people are no longer entitled to the common courtesies. As long as I have a say in the matter, I shall be Mrs Graaff to the world at large and Merle to my friends.'

As it happened, I agreed with her on the neglect of honorifics in the public sphere. But with Spilkin and Tearle it was quite another matter. Before I could begin to explain, she rattled on. 'Pleased to meet you, Aubrey.' She gave my hand a hard squeeze. A metacarpal twinged. 'As for you, Myron, Suzanna's told me all about you too.'

Oh my! He didn't look one bit like a Myron.

'If you don't mind,' said Mevrouw Bonsma, 'I'd prefer to be called Mevrouw Bonsma.' And simpered hugely, showing a smear of lipstick on a crooked tooth, like blood drawn from her own lip. There was certainly some Dutch influence in her dentition.

Merle observed her down a turned-up nose. It would be hard and dry, that nose, pressing into one's cheek. 'My dear, I couldn't. You've been Suzanna for far too long. It's … set.'

Eveready was hovering. She ordered hot chocolate, although she'd been invited for tea. Then she swept her eyes over the room. 'So this is where you've been hiding out.'

Really. I wouldn't put it that way.

'What's this?' She fluttered a hand at the mural and looked at me.

'It's nowhere in particular. Or rather anywhere in general. It's a composite.' Not Erewhon, but Erewhyna. Alibia. Did the name come to me on the spur of the moment?

'Looks French. I would say Nice. Met a Dr Plesance there once, on the promenade. A chessplayer, rheumatic, but very good-natured and fun to be with. Back in a tick. Just want to speak to that woman about Benny.'

'I regret to inform you that her dear little dog,' said Mevrouw Bonsma, 'is unable to join us.'

'Right of admission reserved,' said Spilkin. 'No quadrupeds allowed.'

Merle made for the counter, and soon Mrs Mavrokordatos was frothing a porringer with warm milk from the espresso machine. A momentary lapse of taste on her part, harbinger of a general collapse still shrouded in the mists of the future. 'If she must cater for our four-legged friends,' I said, 'let them have separate crockery.'

'I knew you'd get along famously,' said Mevrouw Bonsma. 'She's good with words, like the two of you. She was a schoolteacher in her younger days, before her marriage. And at various other times, a librarian in the Reference Library and an office manager. She knows the Dewey Decimal System backwards.'

There is dew on the terraced lawns of the Hotel Grande, where Merle goes walking before dinner. It is the dew that makes her kick off her shoes and it is her bare feet and the wet hem of her gown that make her the talk of Alibia. When she catches a chill, Dr Plesance has remedies, all of which he has tried out on himself while performing voluntary service during various epidemics. So the ambulance returns empty to the hospital on the hill and Merle is carried on a chaise into the doctor's parlour.

Merle came back. 'That woman has the most extraordinary name.'

'Mavrokordatos,' said Spilkin.

'Large-hearted,' I said. 'From the Greek *makros,* long, large, and the Latin *cordis,* heart.'

She appraised me with a quirk of a smile around her mouth.

'Only joking,' I added, just to be on the safe side.

Then she opened a handbag as large and black as a doctor's, fished out a tube of artificial sweeteners and spilled half a dozen into her mug. She put on a pair of spectacles and blinked experimentally at the room. They were cat's-eye frames, with diamanté glittering in their canthi, and they made her look astonished. Astonishing? Both. From the depths of the bag, she produced a big flat box.

'Anyone for Trivial Pursuit?'

*

Merle came again the next day. This time the black bag offered up, along with half a packet of ginger snaps, to which Mrs Mavrokordatos turned a blind eye, the *Better Baby Book of Names for Boys*. The bag was an armamentarium. In the right hands, the terms it contained, considered as tools for categorizing and classifying, might get the better of any disorder.

'Let's see, Aubrey ... Aubrey ... here we are. From the German *Alberich*, ruler of elves. You must be the elf then? Only joking, Myron. Famous Aubreys: John Aubrey, author of *Brief Lives*. Just the one, I'm afraid, it's not very common. And even that's a stretch, being a surname.'

I knew the meaning of my own name perfectly well, but there was no stopping her once she got going.

'And Myron. Greek: *muron*. Sweet oil, perfume, hence "something delightful" – that's in quotes. Famous Myrons – this is more like it – Myron, Greek sculptor, known for his *Discobolus*. Myron Cohen, Jewish-American humorist, known for his *You Don't Have to be Jewish*. Of course not. And Myron the Myrmidon, cartoon character, known for his battles in intergalactic space. In order of merit, descending.'

On her next visit, Merle brought a packet of McVitie's Jaffa cakes and a chart depicting the human skeleton. She unrolled it on the table and secured the corners with salt and pepper cellars. Then she had Mevrouw Bonsma hold out her hands, as if she was addressing an invisible piano, and tapped off on them, with a knitting needle brought solely for that purpose, the phalanges, metacarpals and carpals, and, advancing the length of one arm, the radius and ulna, the humerus, the clavicula. I was able to chime in then with an apposite onions, as the handspring of lexical gymnastics is called – clavicle *and* clavichord, from the Latin *clavis,* key – and halt the pointer's progress to other parts of our pianist's anatomy. Not that there was anything unseemly in the display, but people may have jumped to the wrong conclusions.

Merle and Mevrouw Bonsma were old friends. They both lived in the Dorchester, at the bottom end of Twist Street, one of those establishments that housed whole floors of widows. Grannies a gogo, as Spilkin said. The two women had met up when Merle moved to the hotel after the death of her husband Douglas, but they had known one another for years. Mevrouw Bonsma, it turned out, had worked as a typist during the lean times when she could not find work as a musician, and was once employed by an insurance house where Merle kept the company library. She was the most elegant typist Merle had ever come across; her hands on the keyboard were almost lyrical.

It was Merle who showed me that there was more to Mevrouw Bonsma than met the ear.

'If you think she's "leaking indiscriminately",' said Merle, 'you haven't been listening properly, that's all. She never plays anything without good reason. She's like a weathervane, turning with the wind; open your ears and you'll learn something about the air you're breathing, the cross-currents you're borne along by. She responds to the climate in a room, and she can change it too, as easily as opening a window.'

I had noticed from the very beginning a certain affinity between the music Mevrouw Bonsma played and the activities I was engaged in – the reliable rhythms of a waltz, for instance, suited lexical gymnastics down to a T – but Merle convinced me that such congruence was more than a happy accident. There was often a subtle interplay between the room and the music, as if Mevrouw Bonsma were a medium, communicating the moods of the patrons to the keyboard, turning them into music, and channelling them back, to bolster or subvert. When there was an argument brewing, voices raised, a fist thumping a table, she would find the dissonant chords to accompany it. And just as often, by a quiet counter-argument of interlinked melodies, she would smooth the ruffled feathers and cool the heated blood, and restore the company to an even temper.

Sometimes she seemed almost clairaudient. I made a note of the occasion when she began to play the uncharacteristically rowdy theme tune from *Zorba the Greek*. And who should come bounding through the door not a minute later but Mrs Mavrokordatos's brother, who went by that name – or something very like it – and answered to that character. I had only seen him in the Café once, and it afterwards transpired that he had just stepped off an aeroplane from Athens after an absence of many months. Instead of greeting his sister with a conventional embrace, he began to kick up his heels to the music in a traditional dance of homecoming. He might have broken the crockery, if it wasn't for the wall-to-wall carpeting.

Not all of Mevrouw Bonsma's musical accompaniments were as dramatic as this. Often they were simply little chains of association, reminiscent, some of them, of an untaxing session of lexical fartlek. But even these connections were usually invisible to me, inaudible, below my threshold of hearing (not that there's anything wrong with my ears). Merle, who was more educated than myself musically, made it all as clear as day, by an effortless and unassuming laying on of labels and drawing of distinctions.

I saw that I had misjudged Mevrouw Bonsma. She had a system, albeit one founded as much on intuition as on ratiocination; and there is nothing I admire more than a system. Enclosed in her hardy flesh was a sensitive, highly developed creature – and not struggling to get out, far from it, quite content to be there. Was refinement not precisely an appreciation of those qualities that were hard to see, that always lay hidden beneath the surface, where a superficial eye would fail to appreciate them? As usual the poor Americans had it all wrong; the real thing could not be grasped in a fist or quaffed in a few greedy gulps. It had to be found, more often than not, after vigorous effort. Under the benign influence of this understanding – which, I hardly need add, had an immediate appeal for a proofreader – the threat Mevrouw Bonsma had once posed was dispelled, and soon seemed inconceivable to me. Spilkin's joke-telling subsided too, as suddenly as it had developed – an even more merciful reversal. So I finally accepted her into our company. When her shift was over, she would join us to talk or play games, and I came to enjoy her companionship almost as much as Spilkin's and Merle's. She seemed smaller, now that her contents were properly secured.

Merle, by contrast, was at home in our midst from the outset. Suddenly there were four of us. I have never been the most sociable of men, but I found her company unusually convivial. She was an organizer and perhaps we needed organizing, having nearly lost our sense of ourselves. She liked board games and cards, which neither Spilkin nor I had a taste for, but we played along because she was a good talker and had a quick mind. She tried to teach us bridge, and we bumbled through a few games of that. More often it was General Knowledge, always with a musical category for the benefit of Mevrouw Bonsma. Sometimes Merle insisted on giving her clues, *humpty-dumpty-dum,* so that she would not lag too far behind. Merle usually won. It was all in good spirit.

A month or two after the advent of Merle, influenza kept me abed for a few days. When I returned to the Café – to a salubrious air from 'The Happy Huntsman' – she said she was delighted to see me. 'I wanted to come in search, because I thought you might be ill. But Myron wouldn't tell me where you stayed. It wasn't the same without you. We've become quite a little circle, haven't we?'

'Not that,' Spilkin admonished her.

She was taken aback. 'I'd call us a circle. Wouldn't you, Aubrey?'

I wasn't sure. Probably. But before I could make up my mind, Spilkin said: 'It's a question of arithmetic – or is it geometry? Two people cannot be a circle. Two is a couple, a pair, a brace. Three is a crowd only in idiom. Primarily three is a triangle. Four will always be a square – or two pairs.' Was that a meaningful glance at Mevrouw Bonsma, who was pulling up her chair beside his? 'But five …? Now my head and my heart tell me that *five* might be a circle. Only a specialist would see a pentagon. It's a good thing there are just the four of us. A circle is a dangerous thing.'

'Viz, it has no end,' said the Bonsma cheesily.

'What do you say, Tearle?'

'I'm with you, Spilkin.'

He was right. Ever since Merle's arrival, we had settled down very comfortably. The four of us made for solid geometry. We were bricks, regular good fellows. Four-square was the term that came to my mind. Four squares too, I'd no objection to that: four of a kind, four equals, coevals, discriminating human beings, adults with compatible systems of thought and feeling, gathered around a table to amuse themselves, to pass the time pleasantly in conversation, in listening to music, in reading and other pursuits that broadened the mind. I might have wished that the table itself was square rather than round, to underpin our quadrilaterality, our state of balance, but how could I have guessed what lay ahead when Spilkin and I first made the choice?

Which isn't to say that Merle did not have some peculiar ideas. Here was a woman who turned first to the last page of a book and read that to see whether she felt like tackling the whole thing. It was abnormal. When she suggested that the four of us go to the symphony to celebrate Mevrouw Bonsma's fifty-eighth, I followed Spilkin's lead and made short shrift of the idea. There was no point in throwing the rules and regulations overboard.

So the two of them went on their own.

*

Proofreading, properly done, is an art. It demands great reserves of skill, experience and application. It is also a responsibility; and while not all responsibilities are onerous, never mind what the newspapers say, this one deserves the adjective. Only when an eye has scrutinized every word in a text may it truly be said to have been read. And the fact is that more often than not, the only eye that looks at every word and at the spaces in between them, at the folios, the running heads, every last entry in an index, every full stop and comma, every hyphen and parenthesis – the only eye that does all these things belongs neither to the author, nor the editor, nor even the most assiduous reader, but to the proofreader. The proofreader is a trailblazer and a minesweeper. The readers who follow him may take any path with confidence, may go down any passage and cross any border, and never lose their bearings.

Getting things right is not just a matter of form (although that is important enough in itself), but of necessity. Dotting one i might be regarded as a mere punctilio, and failing to do so dismissed as a trifle. But all the dots left off all the i's accumulate, they build up, they pack together like a cloud over a field of stubbly iotas. Soon there is a haze of them in every hollow, and the finer distinctions begin to evade us. In the end, the veil of uncertainty grows so thick that everything is obscured. As for the crosses left off the t's, who do you suppose shall bear them?

It is one of the ironies of the art that the better it is practised, the fewer traces of it remain. The world remembers a handful of proofreading blunders – the Breeches Bible, the Printers' Bible, the Unrighteous Bible of 1652 (see Ebenezer Cobham Brewer's *Dictionary of Phrase and Fable*, at **Bible**) and a few ghost words in the dictionaries – gravy, abacot, Dord. But the world knows nothing of the successes.

Standards of proofreading have been declining steadily since the nineteen-sixties, when the permissive attitude to life first gained ground, and so have standards of morality, conduct in public life, personal hygiene and medical care, the standard of living, and so on. All these are symptoms of a more general malaise. Decline with a capital D. Perhaps it goes back to the War. While I myself was working in the field, I did not have time to devote to proselytizing; I had my own garden to tend. Once retired, I began to pursue that most genteel form of activism, the letter to the editor. Nevertheless, I had always felt that the solution to the problem of declining standards lay with the individual, in the revivification of outmoded notions of personal responsibility, and so I turned from tending my garden to 'cleaning up my own backyard', as the expression goes (in point of fact, I don't have a backyard at all). I am no Dictionary-thumper and I try to be tactful, but my patience was often tested. Take the Haifa débâcle.

The speciality of the Haifa Hebrew Restaurant was not, as one might have expected, traditional delicacies such as smoked salmon or gefilte fish (chopped fish mixed with crumbs, eggs and seasonings), which I had come across before on hotel menus, but things called *schwarmas,* composed primarily of grilled lamb. A special device had been installed for their manufacture. The lamb, piled up into a tower on an electric spit, was suffered to gyrate crazily before red-hot elements, while a singed onion and a deflating tomato, skewered at the top of the tower, dribbled their juices down its length. (These juices, dispelled in aromatic vapour, often made mouths water in the Café Europa up above.) I had peered into the smoky interior of the restaurant several times in passing and mistaken the translucent orb at the top for a sheep's eye: the discovery that it was something more palatable was the immediate reward of my first venture across the threshold. A sign picked out in plastic lettering on an illuminated glass panel of Mediterranean blue informed the paying public that the lamb now rotating would be served in a so-called *pita,* with *tehini,* which sounded merely laughable, or *humus,* which sounded truly nauseating. It was that infelicitous 'humus', glimpsed from the doorway a few days earlier, which had brought me here in defiance of the threat of bomb blasts that hung in those days over fast-food establishments. I have no special knowledge of the Hebrew tongue, but I had done my homework in the greatest school of all, the *Oxford English Dictionary,* and came equipped for battle. Although this was a professional visit, I did not want to appear ill-mannered, and so I ordered one of the schwarmas, and while the chef was carving my portion with a machete, introduced myself to the manager, a certain Shlomo.

'Forgive me if I speak frankly,' I said after the pleasantries, 'but you do not want to put "humus" on the mutton.'

'Hey? What you?' and so forth.

'"Humus" is in the ground. Decomposing vegetable matter in the soil. Leaves, peelings, biodegradable stuff. What you want is "hummus". Two m's.'

'Two humus fifty cent extra,' said Shlomo, whose intellectual apparatus really did seem to be in slow motion, going to talk with his lady friend at the other end of the counter.

I pursued him with the dictionary. The seventh edition of the *Concise* was the first to record 'hummus' and I had brought it along purposely to show him the entry. 'Look – two m's. Em-em.'

'English not so good,' he said with a sympathetic grin, which made me suspect that he was referring to mine! Then I noticed the derivation: from the Turkish *humus*. An awkward moment. A version with one m could only cloud the issue. I put the dictionary away and resorted to some schoolboy dactylology and the mouthing of duo and tuo and twain, hoping to hit on something that would approximate the Hebrew. 'Bi, bi,' I said.

'Bye-bye,' chirruped the lady friend and pointed at my head with her Craven A. Some days before, I had scratched my salient excrescence – cranial, high noon – on an overhanging branch at Pullinger Kop, and it was still inflamed. I retired self-consciously to a dimmer corner of the counter.

To my surprise, the schwarma was quite tasty, and the double helping of hummus did no harm – in fact, I have preferred it that way ever since. Instead of the customary plate, there was an ingenious little aluminium stand like a letter-rack for propping the schwarma in, and as the pita itself was rather like an envelope of unleavened bread with enclosures of lettuce and lamb, it suited very well. I resolved there and then to become more cosmopolitan in my eating habits, even as I set about the big 'clean-up'.

Alas, all my attempts to alert the shopkeepers of Hillbrow to the errors of their ways met with the same inarticulate incomprehension I had encountered at the Haifa. After half an hour of fruitless argumentation, the manager of the Restless Supermarket – he had introduced himself as Stan, although the badge on his lapel clearly said Stelios – showed me into his little office, a mezzanine cubicle with pegboard walls and gunmetal furniture. In the top drawer of the desk I saw lying a stapler, a bottle of Liquid Paper (God help us), and a revolver. When I had seen the stationery, he pushed the drawer shut with his thigh and offered me a drink, which I accepted out of politeness. He said:

'My friend, we ollaways open. You come any day, twenty-four hour.'

'I accept that, Stelios (if I may). But my point is that "restless" doesn't mean that you never rest. Don't you see? It means, and I quote, never still, fidgety.'

'But we ollaways busy, never close.'

'You'd be even busier if you'd just listen to me, man. The name "Restless Supermarket", it creates the wrong impression. One thinks of mess, of groceries jumbled together, of groceries jumbling *themselves* together, of wilful chaos. Is that what you want?'

He looked disbelievingly at the shelves on the closed-circuit television, where sturdy towers of Bourneville cocoa and orderly ranks of tinned fruit and washing powder mutely supported my argument, and said, 'My friend, you come two o'clock, you come three o'clock, I'm talking a.m., I got fresh rolls.'

'That's another thing, that sign on the bakery wall that says: "All our food is fresh and clean." Clean food? I'm sorry, it doesn't make sense.'

After ten minutes of this, he opened the drawer again.

Then there was the time I ventured down Nugget Hill to the Casablanca Roadhouse, no easy walk with my knees, to point out the unwitting obscenity that shoddy neon calligraphy had produced in FLICK LIGHTS FOR SERVICE. They wouldn't hear a word of it. Fuck you too, they said quite amiably. Not having a car made my mission doubly difficult: the waiter kept asking what had become of my 'wheels' and pretending to attach the tray to my forearm. I had to eat a Dagwood Bumstead for my pains, the speciality of the house, served at a very uncomfortable picnic table with a round of dill pickle adhering to the *outside* of the wax-paper wrapping. It was one culinary adventure that did not bear repeating, although it repeated itself of its own accord, ad nauseam.

And then there were the 'wanton dumplings' at the Majestic Tasty Chinese Take Away, which I wouldn't touch with a disposable chopstick, and the unfortunate messages in the fortune biscuits.

Not all my efforts at reform, nor even my most telling ones, had to do with commercial signage or catering. Once Spilkin complained so bitterly about the typographical errors in a book he had just purchased that I was persuaded to look into it myself. I hadn't read a novel in twenty years, and one glance at the contents of *The Unhappy Millionaire* showed the wisdom of abstention: it was the story of an American Midas whose life had been ruined by his immeasurable riches. On the other hand, it seemed that I had been neglecting an exceptionally rich field for my System of Records. I found a spelling mistake on the title-page and a dittography in the first line. There were five obvious corrigenda on the first page alone. Some professionals regard one proofreading error in five pages as an acceptable norm; I myself think that one should aim for perfection and let the norms take care of themselves. Spilkin was reluctant to demand a refund from the bookseller, and so I took matters into my own hands.

The publishing house was a well-known English one with branches, or perhaps one should say tentacles, all over the world. I decided to make an example of them. I spent the next week proofreading this corny farrago, meticulously as you please, and then mailed it to their head office in London, surface mail. Was it any wonder, my covering letter said, that this millionaire was unhappy, finding himself in such a shabbily produced publication? They were welcome to share my work with their editorial department as a lesson in how it should be done.

Such a high-minded gesture, made at my own expense, would be easy to ridicule. But my new friends at the Café Europa, not excepting Mevrouw Bonsma in her placid way, seemed to understand what was at stake.

Schwarma, incidentally, from the Hebrew for 'lamb'. I had imagined, rather fancifully, that there might be some connection with 'schwa', the character rendered as ə in phonetic transcription and derived from the Hebrew word for 'empty'. The lexical world was overpopulated with scrawny, open-mouthed schwas, like hordes of hungry little pitas waiting for their stomachs to be filled.

*

The fame of my System of Records, if not their function exactly, had gone before them, and Merle wished to make their acquaintance almost as soon as she had made mine. For someone of her classificatory acumen and experience, it was quite self-evident how the Records worked, but

I could see from the word 'go' that she wanted to make more of them than I had. From the pocket of her cardigan she produced a rubber thimble for her forefinger and fluttered through my index cards with practised ease, making girlish exclamations of delight. I remember she also leafed through the files of clippings, removing some that caught her eye and piling them face down on the arm of her chair. Then she turned one over in the afternoon sunlight slanting from the balcony windows, and laid it flat on the palm of her hand as gently as if it had been a feather or a pressed flower. It was an advertisement for Stirling's *Hardy Perennails.* What might that lackadaisical florilegium contain? Voilets, dandeloins, hiacynths, anenomes. She laid the clipping face up on the table, turned over another, laid them side by side, shuffled them together, turned over a third, piled all three in one order and then another, as if she was trying to discover the rules of an unknown game; later, I came to associate that flick of her wrist with solitaire, which she sometimes played when the Café was full and noisy, turning the cards over expectantly, rediscovering order in the soothing congruences of chance.

The green fingers and thumbs of Mevrouw Bonsma interleaved a catalogue of floral riches: daffodils, heart's-ease and phlox, meadowsweet and lady's smocks.

When she was finished, Merle laid two clippings side by side. One was marked with a red cross, which meant that it had already been processed. I might have looked up the distinguishing corrigendum in my index in a matter of minutes. But evidently she had no interest in that, for she pointed to the photographs, which happened to show two women, and said, 'Look, they could be sisters!' I examined their faces closely. They looked nothing alike. With a laugh, she pointed out the family resemblance tucked away in the captions: Frau Schneider and Mrs Sartorius.

Merle was a great keeper of lists, as I am. But more than that, she was a lover of names. She had dozens of reference books on the origins of Christian names for boys and girls, surnames, nicknames, eponyms. Merle: from the Latin *merulus* via the Old French, meaning blackbird, of all things; and Graaff: from the German *Graf,* earl. She had lists of so-called 'aptronyms' that she had compiled herself, and curious theories about nominative determinism. Her memory was a trove of oddities, involving characters real and imaginary. Many people know that *Three Men in a Boat* was written by Jerome K. Jerome. But she knew what the K. stood for. And many know Dr Jekyll and Mr Hyde, and the warring qualities each embodied. But she knew that one was Henry to his friends, and the other Edward. She knew that Patrice Lumumba's middle name was Emergy. That Ali Baba had a brother Cassim (not nearly as famous, but treacherous as a snake). And she once told me, without batting an eyelid, that Judy Garland had been born Frances Gumm, which surprised me no end.

After I'd introduced her to the System of Records, she started bringing in her reference books and lists to show me. There issued from the black bag in rapid succession (I was keeping track in my notebook) anatomical charts of the alimentary canal, the musculature, the endocrine (but thankfully not the reproductive) system; atlases; posters showing the flags of the world and butchers' cuts for beef and mutton; a compendium of the internationally accepted rules for sports and games; a board for snakes and ladders, and another for Ludo ('I play Ludo!' Mevrouw Bonsma tautologized); lists of weights and measures; handy reckoners; books on the international standard road signs, origami, first aid, national cuisines, bibliography (the last by a person called Bibliotheker); the book of postal codes (the 1972 edition, in which I myself had taken a hand); and the *Reader's Digest Book of the Car.* In this way, I supposed, she was expressing her gratitude for my having introduced her to the Records, and I was grateful in turn; I found many of her books interesting and turned up some first-rate corrigenda in them.

But Spilkin cast another light on things. He said she was trying to get to know me. 'That is what people do,' he said, 'they share their interests. Isn't that just what you and I did when we met?'

'But this isn't the same at all.'

Fact is, the more Merle and I 'shared our interests', the more I realized how different they were. My Records had a serious practical purpose:

nothing as meanly instrumental as Spilkin had once implied, but a sincere wish to document, so allowing for comparison and improvement. Above all, they were *exempla*. Lexical gymnastics, although they had a recreational dimension, were aimed at maintaining the highest levels of skill and fitness and therefore at improving the quality of the Records. Even in my more frivolous pursuits, such as crosswording, I sought completion, while at the same time enriching my vocabulary and deepening my philological understanding. I never lost sight of my main purpose, which was to hold up examples of order and disorder, and thus contribute to the great task of maintaining order where it already existed and restoring it where it had been disrupted.

Merle's lists were no more than pretexts for games. She was always inventing, always trying to create something new, seeking entertainment. But fantasizing, simply for the sake of it, had never struck me as a constructive way to pass the time. When I said so, she had the temerity to call me 'dry'.

'It's not dryness. It's rigour.'

'Of the mortis variety.'

'That's rigor,' I said, to put her in her place. 'We're not in the Land of the Free and Easy. You won't catch me in Noah Webster's leaky ark. Onions is my man, for fullness, and the Brothers Fowler for concision. I mean Henry and Frank.'

'There, it's the worst case of dryness I've ever encountered. But just you leave it to me. We'll get the sap flowing in no time.'

Fun and games. One quietish evening – card games in progress at a few tables, conversation at others, Spilkin perched on a stool at the piano to watch the strings rippling like water over a weir – Merle piped up: 'Want to play Wellington in plimsolls?'

'Is that like playing Hamlet in tights?'

'It's a game. You have to think of eponyms and their progenitors and put them together. Like Wellington and Plimsoll. That was the first one I came up with.'

'Tell me the rules.'

'There aren't any. They're just amusing combinations – I could have made Plimsoll in wellingtons too, but that's not so funny. Mind you, they shouldn't *have* to be funny.'

I really was at a loss. When she scooped up my *Concise*, without so much as a by-your-leave, I didn't even think to protest. She tossed aside my bookmarks and began to leaf.

Then she said: 'Wellington in bluchers. That's nice, they were both brass hats. Old Blücher's lost his umlaut, I see. Pity. They're like a couple of eyes for laces. Blücher in wellies, on the other hand, or rather foot, is an historical impossibility. But we don't want to get bogged down in footwear.'

As I've said, games hold the barest interest for me at the best of times. But games without rules? Then again, there might be some etymological capital to be gained. I called for another example.

She blew on her tea, stirring up a little tempest, said pensively, 'Mae West in a macintosh,' and then laughed so uproariously that Spilkin came over to see what he was missing. Mevrouw Bonsma let him have a ditty for his trip across the room. He had to stop at a couple of tables along the way to exchange a friendly word or two – as if he were the manager rather than Mrs Mavrokordatos – and that gave Merle a chance to sip and ponder.

I racked my brain for eponyms. But my moisture content was lower then than it is now, although I am a good few years older and brittler in the bone, as you would expect. All that would come into my mind was Boycott! Boycott! Boycott! The newspapers were full of it.

Spilkin took to it like a bufflehead to water. 'No bloomers in the jacuzzi. By order.' It came out of him just like that.

'Leotards are fine,' Merle countered.

Watching the pair of them giggling like teenagers, I couldn't help thinking that the joke was on me. I tried to laugh along in self-defence, but my face was stuck. It had gone all stiff around the mouth, as if my risorii had seized up, and I tried massaging them from the inside with my tongue.

'What a long face,' Merle said. She had taken off her spectacles and her eyes were streaming, making furrows down her powdered cheeks. I have always found the notion of laughing until one cries repugnant.

One wants to preserve the boundaries between emotions, I think, or they lose their value.

'Sandwich ...' Spilkin began.

'This has gone far enough.'

'... with sideburns!'

'Not allowed.'

'Stop being so silly.'

'A bit of silliness never harmed anyone – except a stuffy old cardigan like you.'

Monsoons of laughter. Enough. I marched out and didn't slacken my pace until I had shut my own front door behind me. To think that she would speak to me like that. Stuffy? Sinuses were clear. Lungs as capacious as ever. I've never smoked – a dirty habit for an untidy mind – and always walked. I went out onto the balcony to breathe some night air. The lights of the city stretched away to the south. No diamonds and velvet here, but wampum and brushed nylon. Strings of cheap yellow beads showed where the motorways ran, while those blocks of tawdry marcasite, marred by empty sockets, were the South Western Townships ('Soweto'), or so Gideon, the Lenmar's nightwatchman, assured me. The black holes belonged to the mines. Some people thought the most cosmopolitan touch on our skyline was the Hillbrow Tower: the flats that offered a view of it were actually more expensive. When I was flat-hunting, the caretaker at Milrita Heights had presented it as a feature, flinging back the curtains in the lounge with a theatrical gesture to show the smooth grey shaft plunging past the window. How was she to know I found it vulgar? Like an enormous parking meter. I'd settled for a place on the south side of Lenmar Mansions, with a view of the southern suburbs.

I went back inside and sat down at the dining-room table, where my notebooks were piled. The tips of my fingers felt dry. I had to keep licking them to turn the pages. Was I as dry as all that? A bent old stick, a twig, a broken reed. Perhaps Merle was right: I had no sense of fun. What were all these facts for? I had lists of every description: street names, buildings, shops, taxis, T-shirt slogans, books, sandwiches, orchestras, species of violence. I even had lists of lists. Here was my list of portmanteaus for residential blocks: Lenmar, Milrita, Norbeth, Ethelinda. It was clear enough what it captured. But what had I hoped it would *reveal*? Merle might turn the whole thing into a game. Test your knowledge of the city: match the constituent part in Column A (Len) with its mate in Column B (Mar). I would never have thought of that. Was setting an example enough? Or did one also have to enjoy oneself? Perhaps it was time I cultivated the sense of fun I seemed to be lacking.

When I arrived at the Café the next day, I had in my briefcase a notebook containing a peace offering. It was one of my lists. 'Mr' prefix, commercial enterprises. I showed it to Merle and Spilkin at once.

Spilkin's eyes glittered. 'Mr Bathroom, Mr Cupboard, Mr Juice ... Mr Propshaft ... Mr Spare Parts! Who are these people, Tearle? Friends of yours? Or family?'

'Businesses. Culled from the telephone directories when I was employed by Posts and Telecommunications. I thought you might find the phenomenon interesting.'

'I do.'

'As I recall, the mania was started by a Mr X-haust, as they chose to spell it, back in the seventies. There was a logo too: a little man in overalls with a stethoscope around his neck for auscultating the Wankel engine.' The eponym, skilfully inserted into the flow of the conversation, went unremarked. 'Dr Exhaust, then, strictly speaking.'

'Perhaps he was a surgeon.'

'Mr X-haust,' said Merle. 'It's quaintly polite. If he got into the newspapers these days, they'd call him plain old X-haust.'

'Well, it struck me as odd at the time. As if the title alone rendered the enterprise reliable. Not Bertie X-haust, or X-haust and Co, but Mr X-haust. An exhaust man of the old school, someone you could trust to tinker with your manifold.'

'It's better than Uncle,' said Spilkin.

'You've got an uncle in the furniture business.'

'Or "Oom", which one also comes across.'

'The extraordinary thing is how it caught on. The next year there were half a dozen copycats in the directory: Mr Frosty – an ice-cream maker – Mr Ladder, Mr Plastic, Mr Sweets. And more and more every year – a full column within five editions. Then a couple of Doctors, a brace of Sirs – Sir Juice and Sir Rubble – and even a Missus or two. I haven't updated my list for a while, but it shouldn't surprise me if they ran to a page by now.'

Eveready brought us the 1987 directory from behind the counter.

'More than a page,' Merle said. 'They should form an organization.'

'A union.'

'A support group. Mr Furniture would be chairman.'

'Chairperson,' Spilkin corrected her. 'And I propose Mr Cash and Carry for Treasurer.'

'What about this Mr Spare Parts …'

'He could do the catering.'

'A resurrection man,' I should have said, 'or a muti murderer.' One could joke about such things in those days, people saw the funny side of it, and understood that one meant no harm. But I just sat there with a mouth full of false teeth. Frosty ~ fugleman ~ fugle ~ fumigate. The wrong associations. Anyway, I could hardly have got a word in edgeways. They went at it hammer and tongs, just as I'd hoped they might, for a good twenty minutes. Unashamedly light-hearted fun. When Mevrouw Bonsma joined us, Spilkin dubbed her Mrs Tuning Fork and she was tickled. Then Merle said I was in the Book too, and pointed to Mr Crusty. A jest, but wounding nevertheless, given the unavoidable connotations of 'dryness'. Crusty: irritable, curt, says the *Concise*. Also crust-like, hard – a veiled reference, perhaps, to my excrescences. It was then, in an attempt to crack off my crustiness with levity, that I suggested we boil the last half-hour's shenanigans down into something for the *Reader's Digest*, under the rubric of 'Towards More Picturesque Speech' or 'Life's Like That'. They pooh-poohed the idea (to be picturesque for a moment).

But when Merle went to the Ladies' room, Spilkin leant over – Mrs Mavrokordatos had ouzoed him again, to judge by his liquorish, little-boy breath – and whispered in my ear, 'You were made for each other: Mr and Mrs Dictionary.'

*

From that day forward, I vowed to adopt a more relaxed approach towards social intercourse and to take the whole idea of fun more seriously. And I sustained that effort, through thick and thin, in one way or another, until the curtain – and everything else – fell on the Goodbye Bash.

I initiated several games along the lines of 'Wellington in plimsolls'. I tracked down cryptic clues for Spilkin in the papers and made up some of my own, most memorably the classics 'Sautéd poet' (8) and 'female cannibal' (3-5). Anecdotes of the more tasteful kind, which were occasionally to be found on the wireless, I transcribed into my notebook and brought out at opportune moments. I tried to be lighter, moister and less crusty, like a good soufflé. Once or twice, I ventured to clap along with Mevrouw Bonsma's cheerier medleys.

In those golden days of the Café Europa, which were then beginning, I might have gone too far. My imagination was awakening from a long slumber, like some Rip van Winkel, and was bound to overreach as it stretched its limbs in a new world. (The comparison is unsuited in some ways, as my sleeping habits have always been perfectly normal, and I've never been married, much less henpecked, but it can stand.) Looking back, I would say that the handclapping was certainly a mistake. I also delivered a few witticisms that might have been better suppressed, although it was never my intention to wound, as some would claim afterwards. But my most immoderate indiscretion was a practical joke, a form of wit I had always considered the lowest, fathoms below sarcasm (which strikes me as perfectly acceptable in a red-blooded fray).

All four of us were at the table one afternoon when Spilkin started the crossword. He was milling around, struggling to find the first indispensable 'spilkin', as even the most proficient puzzlers sometimes do, and Merle said, 'Need a hand there?'

'It's a tricky one. I'll get it going in a minute.'

'It can't be that hard.' Merle was not a crossword puzzler herself – she said the people who compiled them had all the fun – and she was just pulling his leg. But her teasing prodded some sense of fun in me, or perhaps it was a cunning streak that I mistook for that etiolated sense.

I said, 'He exaggerates how difficult it is, to make you admire him. The *Star*'s crossword is laughably simple. The cryptic clues would pass for straight clues in any normally endowed society. Intellectually speaking.'

'Bosh,' said Spilkin, 'it takes you hours.'

'Because I stretch it out to prolong the pleasure. I could do it in ten minutes flat if I wanted to – but what's the point of rushing?'

'I'd like to see you get it out faster than me.'

'Sounds like a challenge, Aubrey.'

'Name your weapons.'

He waggled the Waterman. Perfect. Eveready brought my copy of the newspaper from behind the counter. I extracted the *Tonight!* section, turned to the puzzle and folded the straight clues under. Sharpened my pencil and poised it. Nodded to Merle to start the clock.

'One across,' I said. 'Poetry serves badly.' And paused for a finely judged second. 'Verses.' I spoke it out loud and wrote it in. Spilkin followed suit. 'Two across: Safely wired near the dangerous part.' One thousand and one, one thousand and two. 'Earthed.' Wrote that in. 'One down: Muddled reports etc looking back. Retrospect.'

Now that I had the attention of the table I fell silent, except for making popping sounds with my lips and palatal clicks with the tip of my tongue. It was an extraordinary performance, even if I say so myself, for someone to whom the very notion of putting on a show was anathema. The timing was masterly. I let as much as twenty seconds slip by between certain clues and then, just when they thought I had stalled, rattled off three in as much time again. I had the whole thing out in six and a half minutes, including a magnanimous minute of grace allowing Spilkin – who had given up his own efforts to gaze at me, envious and amazed – a shot at the last clue.

I felt sorry for him, eventually, and nearly revealed the deception: I had just done the puzzle for the second time that day. My first effort, discarded in the waiting room at the General Hospital, where I'd gone for my blood pressure pills – and my Valia, for the nerves – had taken the better part of an hour.

In the years that followed, I sometimes surprised Spilkin watching me as I did the crossword at my usual pace, gazing out of the window between clues, sipping my tea. The expression on his face was slightly hurt and exasperated, as if I was patronizing him. I nearly confessed more than once. Now I'm pleased I didn't.

As for the appropriate balance between gravity and levity in my deal-ings with the world, I am happy to say that it was restored in due course, when my acquaintances of those far-off days were scattered to the winds. Composure is everything. In the end, I was not so much a Rip van Winkel, who was immoderate and foolish after all, but a Derrick van Bummel. You remember, the schoolmaster in the same tale – dapper, learned, undaunted by 'the most gigantic word in the dictionary'. One can even forgive him his drawling aloud from the newspaper, seeing that his companions were unqualified to do it for themselves.

*

If I had had my way (or a better start in life, if you'd rather), I would have been a proofreader of dictionaries. Lexicographical proofreading is the ultimate test of skill, application and nerve.

A proofreader worth his salt grieves over an error, no matter how small, in a printed work of any kind, from a chewing-gum wrapper ('Did you know that the jodphur originated in India?' – Ripley's Believe It Or Not) to a Bible ('Printers have persecuted me without a cause' – Psalm 119, verse 161). Every error matters, not least because admitting even one into respectable company opens the door to countless others. Everyone welcome! the cry goes up, and the portals are flung wide. Only by striving constantly for perfection, and regretting every failure to achieve it, can the hordes be kept at bay.

However, errors once made should be acknowledged and understood, and their implications distinguished from one another. The repercussions of an error are nearly always bounded by the context in which it occurs. In certain exceptional spheres, such as pharmaceutical packaging, apparently minor errors may have fatal consequences. In the more mundane healthy climate, most errors on the part of the proofreader, committed in a spirit of honest endeavour rather than laxity and laissez-faire, are like ripples on a pond: disturbing but contained, and eventually finite. An error in the pages of a novel, for instance, may be compounded by reproduction, sometimes tens of thousands of times. Yet despite this wasteful abundance, the error itself seldom transcends the covers between which it is caught like a slow-moving insect, unless through the agency of an ill-tutored student, or a civilian foolish enough to seek instruction in these quarters. The good proofreader, the craftsman in pursuit of perfection, seeking to uphold standards but failing honestly, acknowledges the flaw, the place where the eye blinked and the hand slipped, and accords it its proper, proportionate place. Then he turns his attention to the work at hand.

Some say that an error of the right kind in the right place, something not too ugly, something truly devious, an error that demonstrates by its elusiveness how easily we might all slip into error ourselves, might have a purpose, perhaps even a beauty, of its own. One beggar at the banquet, they contend, cleverly disguised as a righteous burgher, discovered looting the cheeseboard and unmasked, will make the rest of the company savour their fine liqueurs more appreciatively. I myself find this conceit specious – as if a fly in the ointment improved it – although I grant that it might have some validity in a certain kind of publication, say, a coffee-table book or a hand-printed caprice. An error in that neck of the woods is hardly the end of the world.

But a proofreading error in a dictionary is invariably catastrophic.

Such an error is sent out into the world to multiply. It inveigles itself into the hearts of a trusting public. It works its mischief, like an odourless poison or a magistrate's moustache, under the very nose of authority. It is exuberant and prolific. It has the capacity to generate its misleading progeny in an infinite number of places. It may introduce errors where none existed before, and unteach the best-learned lessons. It may settle down in respectable company and become naturalized as a citizen of good standing, until not even the most discriminating neighbour knows its shady past. The Great Cham himself gave us several bastards born on the wrong side of the galleys.

So it is easy to see why the dictionary should be the foremost test of proofreading skill, the Everest of proofreading, the Qomolongma, as a contracting Sherpa (7) might style it. Sadly, I was never able to plant my blue pennant on this summit.

After dictionaries, I would say that certain kinds of reference work present the greatest challenges: maps, calendars, timetables, technical manuals, logarithmic charts, diagnostic cyclopaedias, operating instructions, recipe books, telephone directories. And I was fortunate enough to make the last-mentioned field my own for two decades and more.

Erasmus of the Department once told me that some very authoritative authors did not regard publications such as these as proper books. In the opinion of these gentlemen, and Charles Lamb was mentioned by name, almanacs and guidebooks are 'non-books' – *biblia abiblia,* they spitefully put it. I wouldn't know about that. When someone says, 'Are you in the Book?' which book do they have in mind – *Essays of Elia?* Even the Bible, that perennial best seller, needs qualifying as the Good Book; but the Book, plain and simple, is the telephone directory, and that's all there is to it.

The demands of the telephone directory are different to those of the dictionary, of course. The emphasis falls less on first principles and final appeals than on service and convenience. Here, the errors the proofreader commits may be ranked according to the degree of inconvenience that results. On this scale, misspelling a surname but maintaining its alphabetical position is the least of blunders. People are understandably particular about the orthography of their personal names, especially those in which doubled consonants or optional concluding vowels create many variants: 'with one t' (or two) and 'with an e' (or without) are most commonly specified. But the fact is that only the most forgetful ever need look up their own telephone numbers in the directory, and people are as lax about the spelling of others' names as they are finical about their own, and so the chances of causing offence are negligible. An error in the address is more bothersome; it may lead to misdirected mail, or turn an outing into a wild-goose chase. But again, few people consult the directory to obtain addresses. Placing a name out of alphabetical order is rather more serious: the user of the directory might not be able to find the number he is seeking. But the gravest error a proofreader can commit is undoubtedly a wrong number. It is inconvenient for the user, who is unable to reach the party he seeks; and it is annoying for the subscriber, who does not receive his calls; but for the third party whose number has been given by mistake, and who therefore receives all the misdirected calls, it can be a nuisance beyond enduring. Should this innocent bystander be a private citizen, and the directory entry falsely advertising his number a commercial enterprise, the volume of wrong numbers may be such that the victim has no choice but to sacrifice his own number, effectively rendering himself invisible.

The proofreading of numbers is a taxing business, requiring the highest levels of concentration. Needless to say, I was rather good at it. Not infrequently, I was seconded to assist in difficult operations involving other directories. But the one task that always gave me grey hairs, in the days when their colour still concerned me more than their number, was the proofreading of the emergency telephone numbers. I give them here to show that I have not lost my touch entirely, and also because one can never be too careful these days. Please note that they are for the Greater Johannesburg area only.

- ☞ Flying Squad 10111
- ☞ Ambulance 999
- ☞ Fire Brigade 624-2800
- ☞ Hospital 488-4911
- ☞ Poison Information Centre 642-2417
- ☞ Water 403-3226
- ☞ Electricity 080011-1550
- ☞ Gas 726-3138

*

As a young man, I briefly entertained the ambition to wield the blue pencil. There have been some fine editors, even of novels, and a handful who are virtually illustrious. Saxe Commins of Random House, whose famous blue staff could strike poetic bubbly from the most prosaic rock. Pascal Covici, midwife and manservant to John Steinbeck. Maxwell Perkins of Scribners, topiarist of the verdant shrubbery of Thomas Wolfe's imagination. All Americans, you'll note, adept at bathing themselves in limelight.

But there has never been a *famous* proofreader. God forbid. If one should ever pretend to an exalted position, treat him with circumspection. He is undoubtedly a charlatan.

I became a proofreader; there was hardly a choice involved. Proofreaders are born, and made, in the back rooms.

As for being a fabulist, nothing was further from my mind. There are more than enough of those. In any event, invention never interested me. I had no wish to add to the great bloated mass of the given; I wished to take something away from it. To be not a contributor, but a subtractor. The impulse was alembical. Possibly even alchemical; over the years, my attention shifted more and more from the perfected product to the parings, the shavings, the dross. In the end, I was only happy when I was up to my elbows in rejectamenta. Mr Crusty was the wrong label; Mr Spare Parts might have suited me. Some people found the idea unpleasant. Merle would not let me rest.

'You know Aubrey, when I see you sweating over this system of yours, it makes me sad.'

This was a new one. The Records always made her giggle like a schoolgirl.

'How's that?'

'What's going to become of it? It's all very well us amusing ourselves with it, but it would be nice if it had some broader application, if more people could somehow … use it.'

For a moment I thought she was going to stoop to that ghastly American 'utilize', but 'use' was bad enough. Spilkin had said something similar: What are you going to *do* with it? What is it *for*? This was rich, coming from the fun-and-games specialists, the hedonists. They were up to something.

'My Records have a use, thank you very much. I've said it a thousand times: it's a system of exempla. Each of these entries is a stitch in time, my dear.' Dear was daring.

'But who'll be interested in it in this unwieldy form? It's raw material, really, it's all odds and sods. You should work it up into something longer, something people could read.' She was turning some of my clippings over, sizing them up shrewdly, as if imagining ways of tacking them together with a storyline. 'Paragraphs and things, threaded together. The cobbling would be fun.'

Fun. That more familiar three-letter word warned me what was really behind all this. But a train of thought was already puffing down my one-track mind. I had recognized long before that my exempla needed to be embodied in sentences in order to capture the proofreader's true function and inculcate his habits of mind. Perhaps I hadn't gone far enough. If sentences were good, why shouldn't paragraphs be better? One of the great problems of proofreading was precisely the tension between momentum and inertia. The story was a horse that wished to bolt, and the unwary or unpractised proofreader might find himself thrown and dragged behind its flashing hooves.

But the wicked Bibles and lying dictionaries cautioned me.

'It's possible, a story of some kind, with all my corrigenda, my "things to be corrected" woven into it. But where will I put the correct versions, my "things corrected"? Weaving them in too will be an impossible task. It will spoil the story.'

'Leave them out. Make it more interesting for whoever reads it. That will be the fun of it, as always: inventing order. Not extracting it, mind you, like a lemon-squeezer, but creating it.'

'Leave them out! What if it falls into the wrong hands? Some story full of contrived errors could wreak havoc among the impressionable.' A ticklish sensation crept over my skull at the thought: the follicles puckering, trying to make the vanished hair stand on end.

'Forgive me,' said Merle, 'but isn't this exactly what you spend your life doing – hunting for errors? Why deny others the pleasure?'

'My corrigenda are accidents of carelessness or ignorance, designated as such, and held up for scrutiny. The perpetrators had no evil intent. What you are proposing would be premeditated. And in such fatal concentrations. It scares me. In any event, I'm a professional.'

'It won't be for greenhorns.' She seized my writing hand, with the pencil still in it, and squeezed it till it hurt. Thankfully it wasn't my left hand, my thumbing hand as I think of it: the bones of that, and the thumb-bones in particular, have been weakened by a lifetime of thumbing through. 'It will be for the amateur, in the best sense of the word, for those who are already in the know – or like to think they are. It will preach to the converted and renew their faith. It will be sent to try them. It will be a test of skill for the whole clan of proofreaders – prospective, practising and pensioned-off. It will further the aims of your noble profession.'

And with that, 'The Proofreader's Derby' – although I still hadn't dubbed it that – was born.

*

When I think of those times now (casting some shadows from my mind), they are dappled with daylight sifted through the north-facing windows of the Café Europa. Like gold dust blown in off the dumps. My golden days, caesar salad days, days of whiskey and roses. All in all, a moisturizing season, with the sap rising in dusty veins and the juices in the grey matter trickling.

Four people around a table. A round table. No. 2. We got to know one another a little, and to like one another to the same modest extent. There was not much depth to our association. I acknowledge it freely. I can scarcely recall a conversation now that could not be plumbed with a teaspoon or a swizzlestick, depending on one's preference. But it was stable, reliable, secure – qualities some of us only came to appreciate fully after we had been overwhelmed by flimsy, crooked things. In my day, solidity was a virtue. Yet all around, the cry goes up for transparency, as if the capacity to be seen through were laudable, as if a house were better made of glass than stone.

The Records grew in leaps and bounds. There were now four people clipping items from newspapers and magazines, jotting down scraps from shop windows or advertising flyers. None of them had my practised eye, of course, but Spilkin came up with some gems. Even Mevrouw Bonsma made some well-meaning contributions from sheet music and knitting patterns – notably that old chestnut, 'knit one, pearl one'. Soon I was spending half an hour a day cataloguing the new acquisitions.

Every other waking moment was devoted to transforming the System of Records into the Proofreader's Test.

I am an accomplished composer of letters to the press, as I hope I have demonstrated, and an expert curator of lists, ditto. But the Test was a new departure for me. I came to regard it as in essence fanciful. I had very little experience as a consumer of fancies and none whatsoever as a producer, but that is exactly what seemed to be required. Although my 'raw material', as Merle encouraged me to think of it – the phrase never ceased to remind me of *meat* – had all been culled from published, or at the least, public sources, I was now required to place the elements into entirely new and undeniably imaginary relationships with one another. Imaginary relationships ... I was like a man who, never having held a needle between his fingers, is given some mismatched offcuts, a fistful of gauds and ribbons, a few skeins of thread, and commanded to make himself a suit of clothes.

I took my cue from Merle, laying sentences side by side, building up paragraphs incrementally, nudging those into groups or 'fascicles', as I called them, allowing the Test to shape itself anyhow. I found that this patchworking obliged me to begin inventing as well. When a sentence wasn't quite the right shape, I had to lop off a bit here or add on a bit there, cutting my cloth to suit the pattern – not *my* pattern, but its own. This was fancy, pure and simple, and so antithetical to my usual way of working, which consists of a precise and considered re-establishment of the disturbed order, that I frequently lost my nerve and wished to throw the whole project over. I forged myself a golden rule: the corrigenda themselves, the tesserae that formed the substance of the Test, could not be invented. The plaster (and

I did seem to require quite a bit of it) mattered less. I took comfort in the thought that the laws that governed my seemingly random activities were bound to become apparent as I went along. In other words, I trusted that this detour through the thickets of invention would bring me back, wiser and happier, to the manicured lawns of the given.

For quite some time now, I have been inclined, looking back, to think that this is exactly what happened. But just lately, new doubts have beset me. Perhaps I shall never walk in that garden again?

Merle became my inspiration. I tried out sentences on her occasionally, as they took shape, but I always baulked at a paragraph. And naturally the finished material was kept from the others. Mevrouw Bonsma was relieved, I think. Spilkin, on the other hand, was always looking over my shoulder and winking so deliberately you'd have thought he was trying to demonstrate the musculature of the eye. It got to the point where I had to carry my confidential papers with me to the Gentlemen's room to answer the call of nature.

As the months passed, the Test's purpose became clearer to me, even if the laws of its composition did not. I began to see it as the centrepiece of an event, a championship if you like. When the Test was finished, and I had no inkling when that might be, it would be *administered*. There would be entrants, and they would pay a fee, and the one with the best results would receive a prize. A dictionary might be apt; say the seventh edition of the *Concise* – something newly revised would appeal to the youngsters – paid for out of the entry monies. I would have to decide on the winner myself. Merle's notion that the Test be allowed to enter the world without correction was indefensible. I would prepare a corrected version, and hold it back until such time as the Test had been administered, so that everyone might have the 'fun' that meant so much to them. But then the corrected version would be made available too, as an antidote and an objective corroboration of my adjudication. If the inaugural event had to be delayed, well, so be it. It was essential, at any rate, that I myself adjudicate, that I retain control at least in the beginning. Later on, should the event become too popular for one person to manage, I might consider employing an administrator. Start small, I told myself. But how small was that? How many people would be interested in entering a proofreading competition? It would depend, among other things, on how well it was publicized. Would one advertise in the papers? What if people responded in 'droves', as the drudges put it? Who would foot the bill for a venue and for duplicating copies of the Test itself? Then again, if the entry fees were fixed at the right level, the whole undertaking might become profitable and eke out my pension. While these thoughts went round in my head, the Test continued to grow, and with it, my grand plans for the inaugural competition. Think big, I told myself. Instead of a dozen boozy subeditors cooped up in the ping-pong room at the Hillbrow Recreation Centre, why not the cream of the publishing world, possibly a few international figures – hardly celebrities, but prominent people, a Hugh Blythorne, a Dr Kate Babcock (if she was still with us) – all comfortably settled in the Selborne Hall? Competing not for a used copy of Peter Mark Roget's *Thesaurus,* but for the *Oxford English Dictionary* in twenty volumes. The Proofreader of the Year Competition. The Aubrey Tearle Proofreader of the Year Competition. The First Annual etcetera.

I wrote in turn, and at mounting expense, to the Publishers' Association, the larger publishing houses, the Printers' Association, the larger printing houses, the smaller publishers and printers, the chains of bookshops, my former employers at Posts and Telecommunications, setting out the details of my project and requesting a meeting to discuss sponsorship. Disgracefully, I had not a single reply. Then I sent an abridged version of my letter to the *Star.*

17 May 1988

Dear Sir,

The late edition of your newspaper of 10 May asks: 'How real is the threat of Muslin fundamentalism?' In my view, it threatens the very fabric of society.

I am a retired proofreader with forty years' practical experience involving a wide range of publications, notably telephone directories. In the course of my career, I came to believe that a standardized Test of proofreading ability would go a long way towards ensuring that qualified personnel are employed and standards maintained in this all-important but undervalued department.

I have devoted the years of my retirement to devising such a Test, drawing on Records kept during a lifetime of work, and this undertaking is now nearing completion. Besides its obvious value as a means of grading our own abilities, the Test may have wider applications in commerce and entertainment, which would serve to publicize the profession and draw young school-leavers into its ranks.

I am approaching your newspaper first because you fly the blue peter of the profession from your masthead, so to speak, in the Greater Johannesburg area. (Many of my letters, including several on orthographical subjects, have been published in your columns, and so we are not strangers to one another.) I would be happy to discuss the ways in which you might become involved in my venture at your convenience. A representative extract from the Test, an 'appetizer', will be forwarded on request.

Yours faithfully, etcetera

Breaking with tradition, I let Merle and Spilkin read the letter before I mailed it. Spilkin had me change 'practical' to 'hands-on', 'our own' to 'in-house' and 'first' to 'up-front'. He said this prepositional largesse would show that I was clued up on current usage. Merle had me change 'at your convenience' to 'as soon as possible' – 'Or they'll think you want to meet them in the lavatory.' I made the changes against my better judgement, which is why I present the original here, without meaning to suggest that it would have provoked a more satisfactory response than the tardy one I duly received.

10 June 1988

Dear Mr Tearl,

Thank you for your letter of the 17th inst.

I regret to inforn you that we do not have vacancies for subs at this moment in time. However, we have placed your letter on file and you will be notified if a position opens up in the near future.

Computer literacy and a familiarity with Quark will be a big plus factor.

Yours faithfully,
Mr J.B. de Beer
(Personnel Manager)

Even as it confirmed my worst fears about declining standards, this dismissive missive brought me down to earth. I was a man of sober habits, and the first draughts of invention had gone straight to my head.

On Spilkin's advice I turned, somewhat chastened, to Mrs Mavrokordatos. She immediately placed her establishment at my disposal for the inaugural championship. I had never intended to broach the question of sponsorship or exploit the special privileges I enjoyed as a regular customer, but to my delight she herself proposed a finger supper, for organizers and competitors, a simple spread that took my own conservative tastes into account: cubes of sweetmilk cheese on Salty Cracks, sandwiches in triangles, hard-boiled eggs. I was grateful. But I also made the point that I had become more adventurous in my eating habits over time. With Merle's encouragement, my public-service proofreading had evolved into a field study of national cuisines, and I no longer thought of Mrs Mavrokordatos's menu as a dyspeptic hotchpotch. I was dipping into it myself occasionally. A couple of dolmades and other delicacies, served up with a pinch of Attic salt, would therefore not go amiss at our event. Delighted in turn.

'Mavrokordatos' was singularly apt: she had a heart the size of a barn.

(I must say I'm pleased she wasn't a Mavrokephalos, of whom there are several in the Book, chiefly in the Emmarentia area.)

The name for my championship came to me soon after: 'The Proof-reader's Derby.' I liked the connotations: laurels contested fiercely in a sporting spirit and a homely setting.

*

I acquired the trophy – and I'm not ashamed to admit it – at Bernstein's Second Time Lucky. Electroplated nickel silver, black with tarnish, and 'Bernie' gave it to me for a song, or I should not have managed. It was a magnificent specimen, a loving cup, all of three feet tall from the scuffed green baize on the bottom of the Bakelite drum to the slim fingertip of the figurine on the lid, a little woman *en pointe,* with one arm trailing behind her like a lame wing and the other gesturing heavenwards. More suited perhaps to holding the diaphanous shell of a reading-lamp, or to perching on the radiator of a vintage car, like a goddess on the entablature of a Roman temple, than to turning somersaults and doing backflips. The balancing-beam at a stretch. For she was a gymnast of the old school and suitably, if featurelessly, naked.

Two tins of Brasso (the Silvo isn't nearly as good) later, I bore the trophy to the Café in a laundry bag. Caused quite a stir when I set it up on the table. 'Ladies and gentlemen: the floating trophy for "The Proofreader's Derby".'

'Breathtaking,' said Spilkin. I had set the trophy down so that the engraving on the bowl was facing Merle, but he had an unerring eye for what he wasn't supposed to see, as if years of gazing through optical instruments had taught him to see round corners. He hooked a little finger into one of the handles and turned the cup towards him. 'Transvaal Gymnastics Union. Senior Ladies – Overall Champion.'

'Bernie says it could be ground off. But it would cost more than the trophy's worth.'

'Keep it. It adds character. You can always put "National Proofreading Champion" or whatever on the other side. "Donated by Aubrey Tearle."'

'That's what I thought. More or less.' There was the link with lexical gymnastics too, but not everyone would see that.

'What's this?' Spilkin had spotted the row of little holes at regular intervals around the drum. It had been encircled by thumbnail shields of silver engraved with the names of the winners, but I had clipped off the rivets with a pair of pliers the night before. The shields, still filigreed with oxide, were in a Gee's Linctus tin in my pocket and now I tipped them out on the table top.

Lily, Rose, Myrtle. How had names so fragrant become so stale? Was it because girls were no longer named after flowers but chemical compounds, vitamins, large muscle groups?

Spilkin spread them out, and then chose one and drew it towards him with a godlike forefinger. 'Daphne Willis ~ 1928.' Whether it was that the gesture awakened in the bones of his hands some memory of all the games that had been played at this table, or that the shields spread out on the inlaid chequerboard were like tokens in a board game, or that the backgammon draughtsmen clicking on a neighbouring table sounded a familiar rhythm, he sensed an opportunity for play. 'Willis. A learner among wilis.'

'Which Willie refers?' Mevrouw Bonsma asked, deflating into a chair.

'*Villi,* Mevrouw. The ghosts of girls abandoned by their lovers.'

'Basta! Thank you, Tearle.' She hummed an air from Puccini and performed a *pas seul* with two sturdy fingers.

Spilkin stirred the shields thoughtfully, unintentionally upstaging Mevrouw Bonsma. 'You try one, Merle.'

'You're good with names,' I put in.

'What a lovely name. Almost an echo.'

'That's close.' I looked over her shoulder. 'She has left in a confusing echo. Five letters.'

'Chloe,' said Spilkin like a shot.

'Chloe Mulrooney, to be precise, 1933.'

'Biscuits?'

'Wouldn't it be nice if there was a Dymphna.' Merle might have been turning over her own fragile girlhood in her fingers.

Erica. I care for her. Easy as pie.

'My turn.'

'Aubrey! What's wrong with your finger?'

'Brasso.' It was black to the second joint. 'I was up half the night cleaning this thing.'

'Don't go native on us, Tearle.'

'You can't walk around like that. People will think … I'm not sure what they'll think.'

'They'll think he's got a finger in the wrong pie,' said Spilkin. 'Mulrooney. Or mulberry.'

Macaroony. Macaroni. Merle was unpacking her handbag. Spilkin raked the shields over to his side of the table as if he had won them fair and square. A pair of bluntnosed scissors, made for the nursery. A season ticket for the bus. Where did she go by bus? She had a daughter in the northern suburbs somewhere, Illovo or thereabouts, and grandchildren she sometimes babysat. Jason (the leader of the Argonauts) and Kerry (a county in the Republic of Ireland). A packet of Romany Creams. A book of horoscopes. A cardboard box full of Johnson and Johnson earbuds: little blue and white dumb-bells. Tissues. And now finally what she was looking for: a bottle of acetone. She tipped some of it onto a pad of tissue paper and dabbed at my finger. It made no difference whatsoever. But it was so long since anyone had touched me tenderly that it brought a lump to my throat. What the rhinopharyngealists might call a tracheal clonus.

At Merle's suggestion, Mrs Mavrokordatos put the trophy on a shelf behind the counter, in pride of place above the coffee cups, where it was to remain in anticipation of the joyous day when I would present it to the first deserving winner. It was a shame I wouldn't be able to compete myself, but there seemed to be no way around it.

*

In its own way, governed by its own laws, 'The Proofreader's Derby' kept growing. Although I spent a good part of each day at home and each evening at the Europa working on it, I was no nearer finishing. As fast as I eliminated entries from the System of Records, new ones took their place. Standards were slipping. Where once one had been obliged to scour the world minutely for eligible corrigenda, now every printed surface was flyblown with them. My research assistants heaped fuel on the fire.

On top of all this, as I left the Café one night, I carelessly let fall from my file a page containing the following fascicle:

In the small hours of that bitter morning, Fluxman stood sleepless at the window of his penhouse, looking down on Alibia. Tutivillus Heights was the city's only skyscarper – in Alibia, the top of a six-story block will brush the brow of heaven – and it made him feel immensely alert and far-seeing, and utterly detached from the earth. His eyes wandered from rooftop to rooftop, from street to street. He felt it. The building was swaying, a motion so gentle it would have escaped the notice of all but the most perceptive observer. It was not soothing at all; it filled him with foreboding. Then he recalled who he was and what he stood for. He erased his frowning mistgivings from the glass before him with an eraser shaped like an egg, but they came back again and again.

Eveready, it emerged afterwards, retrieved the page from under a table and passed it on to Spilkin, who thus had the good fortune of becoming the first person to lay eyes on a sustained passage of 'The Proofreader's Derby' (even Merle had tasted no more than a line or two). Out of context, it was not at its best; I dare say it was like a scrap of canvas hacked from the frame with a pocket knife – and I give it here precisely to demonstrate that fact. But Spilkin seemed to understand perfectly. The following evening, I found the missing page on a plate by my chair, spindled and clasped by a serviette ring, along with a note in Spilkin's sharply focused hand.

My dear Tearle,

What a luck to enter the world of your imagination at last, even if it was through the back door, where there is no sign to reserve the right of admission. The whole thing breathes and sweats and so on. You should be in no great hurry to finish: the longer you spend on it the better, I think. It was very exciting looking for 'corrigenda'. You'll make a proofreader of me yet. You might even start a craze. I found

Line 2: 'penhouse' for *penthouse*
Line 3: 'skyscarper' for *skyscraper*
Line 10: 'mistgivings' for *misgivings*

You must let me know how I faired.

Sincerely,
Spilkin

I was disappointed to see that he'd missed 'story' for *storey*. But he hadn't done too badly.

Then that 'faired' grabbed my attention. Automatically, my mind performed a flawless backflip from Spilkin to spillikin – one of the wooden or ivory slips thrown in a heap in the game of *spillikins* to be removed each without disturbing the rest – and then reeled off-balance into spell-I-can, into spell-I-can't. I'd expected more of him.

Or was he having me on?

*

'No great hurry' ... hasty advice on Spilkin's part, hastily accepted on mine. Five years had slipped by since then, and I was still trying to finish 'The Proofreader's Derby'. Why did Empty Wessels have to start this Goodbye Bash business and go raking up the past? There was so much of it too, a mountain of bygones. And the bit that was mine, the bit I had to show was so paltry, a scant barrowload. Has my whole life come down to a pile of papers, I asked myself, and those riddled with corrigenda? Would I have to say, looking back, not 'It was all one big mistake,' but 'It was an endless succession of little mistakes'? More than I care to remember, let alone to correct. There might be some saving grace in a great mistake, boldly made – but in an unbroken line of piffling errors?

I was losing faith, or had already lost it. God knows, the past few years have given me cause.

The TO LET signs had gone up in the windows of the Café Europa. The Bash loomed. I had promised myself that I would finish 'The Proofreader's Derby' before then, by hook or by crook; that when the doors finally closed on the Café Europa, I would also close the book on this chapter of my life. I might even make something of the occasion, a little ceremony, a brief speech. But now I felt like taking my papers – files full of clippings, boxes of index cards, notebooks, typescripts of fascicles, the lot – and throwing them over the fence into the open plot in Prospect Road, scattering them among the green clumps of weeds where the body had lain that Sunday morning, obscured by the news, in the shadow of the sign that said No Dumping – By Order. Dumping was the done thing, to judge by the piles of rubbish already left there, another inexplicable mania. Perhaps the Queen of Sheba or one of her consorts, whose rotten kingdom this was, would find my disjecta membra *useful* to kindle fire when they cooked their tripe and tubers, to cover themselves at night when they slept like the dead, to wipe their illiterate backsides when they did their business.

Filled with despair, I packed every last scrap of paper connected with 'The Proofreader's Derby' into two enormous grey-paper shopping-bags with handles of gallows hemp and the ignominious stars and stripes all over them – two of the matching set of three that was Moçes' unexpected gift to me the Christmas before – and went out into the street. I could hardly carry the blinking things. The nightwatchman Gideon offered to lend me a hand, and I had to give him the abridged version of my talk on his responsibilities, which were to open and shut the door for the tenants of Lenmar Mansions and to guard their fixed and moveable assets, indeed to frustrate the relentless efforts of criminals to transform the one kind into the other. What was fixed anyway? There were people, deprived creatures without garages, who resorted to chaining their cars to trees at night to secure them against car thieves. But that faith in growing, rooted things was misplaced: there were tree thieves as well, preying on the municipal flora. As fast as the Parks Department planted trees and shrubs on traffic islands and freeway embankments, thieves dug them up and carried them off, either to replant them in their own gardens or to resell them. Another species of thief stole manhole covers and sold them to scrap-metal dealers. Yet others specialized in bus-stop benches and kerbstones, street signs and fences, water pipes and electricity cables, milestones and monumental masonry. Material for building shacks. Entire houses had been stolen by these cannibals, even schools and factories.

People stole supermarket trolleys too, for their own intrinsic worth, or to transport their stolen goods in. And one of these trolleys was lying abandoned on the corner of O'Reilly and Fife. I had dragged the shopping-bags this far, but my bad elbow was beginning to act up. I dumped the bags in the trolley and righted it.

As I progressed along O'Reilly Road, pushing the trolley containing what Spilkin – so long ago now – had encouraged me to think of as my life's work, I caught my breath and came to a more sober assessment of my situation: I, Aubrey Tearle, Proofreader Emeritus, was walking through the streets in broad daylight, in command of a stolen supermarket trolley. What was happening to me? What would become of me? If anyone enquired after the trolley's provenance, I would say I was simply returning it to its lawful owners, the Checkers Corporation, the Okay Bazaars, Pick and Pay. The performance of my civic duty. That purpose had been at the back of my mind all along, and now took its proper place at the front. As for the trolley's contents, culled from a thousand public fora but now indisputably private property ... My precious papers! I had rushed out with the express intention of dumping them, but that was unthinkable. If someone tried to take them from me, I would defend them with my life. How horribly likely it was that I would be waylaid. It was years since I had ventured out with anything more substantial than the *Pocket* and a notebook. I should turn back. But that would make it harder to explain the trolley, if needs be. I must go on. And what if it rained? Then I would amount to nothing more than soggy paper, slimy and illegibly grey. I would boil down to: papier mâché. Moulded paper pulp made into solid objects. From the French for chewed paper. Chewed paper! Beset by ferocious doubts, by snaggle-toothed second and third thoughts, I pressed on into the concrete jungle.

Dumbo was on duty, chained in habitual servitude to a parking meter. Another misplaced source of security. I had seen meters beheaded, expiring in the gutters, or on kerbs spattered with five-cent pieces. Surprise, surprise: the missing ear was back. I stopped to examine the surgery. Someone had done a neat job with the welding torch – but the effect was odd ... unhinged ... untoward. Then it struck me why: the ear was not just back – it was back to front! Nincompoops. From the Latin *non compos mentis*, 'no mental compost' (Wessels). I was reminded of Noodler in *Peter Pan*. Naming all the pirates was Merle's game. Captain Jas Hook, Bill Jukes, Skylights, Smee, I forget the others. My favourite was Gentleman Starkey – once an usher in a school. And hers was Noodler, whose hands were fixed on backwards. The only truly tragic figure in pantomime, she said.

Someone had better tell them. I steered my trolley into the shop, but a figure as broad as a nightclub bouncer rose to block my passage. It was Joaquim, he who had pressed the hooch upon me when I had brought back the ear. Rosa peered anxiously over his shoulder, mustachios aquiver. I addressed myself to her, but he flapped his hands in my face, as if to dispel an odour. What would they call it? ... a 'pong'. These people. I had to shout to be heard.

'Wad dozy wunt, Quim?' she asked. 'Wad? Wad?'

Quim *(noun, coarse slang)* said, enunciated I should say, as if translating my words into an infinitely superior foreign tongue, 'He sigh his yeah is beck tew frount.'

I could have blown my top, my lobes were liquefying, a magma of vitriol and vituperation boiled out of my spinal column, pressed up against my crusty dome – but I caught sight of myself in a mirrored pillar, like an Aborigine scribbled all over with Vat 69 and Castle Dumpies, R8.99 per dozen, in shoewhite on grey skin. I had espied myself there before, from time to time, but never in such a state of extremity. My hair was standing to attention in clumps, ragtag bands of desperate bristles whose company had been routed. My shirt was hanging out, and one tail of it was damp. My staring eyes, replete with scrutinizing, were afloat in my bifocals like melted cubes in the icy bottoms of shot-glasses. And then the trolley … I was stooped over it like a geriatric in a walking frame. I looked like a tramp – worse, like a hobo, one of the bag ladies and gentlemen, the collectors of old iron and empties, the perpetual window-shoppers, pushing their stolen trolleys through the streets as if the city were no more than a vast parking lot for supermarkets. These scavengers had turned the trolley into a symbol of want rather than plenty. Had I become one of them? I barely recognized myself.

But the light of recognition was dawning in Mrs Da Silva's calculating eyes. Mention of the ear had jogged her memory. Before she could foist another bottle of Old Brown Ruin on me, I retreated. Down the length of Kotze Street, up and down kerbs at five robots, never mind the disabled, and not a soul would meet my eye.

The security guard at the Okay Bazaars, that merely satisfactory retailer, took his employer's property into grateful, white-gloved hands: the gloves were a relic of the days of bomb threats, when they were meant to make more palatable the notion of a stranger's hands upon one's person. Frisking, they called it, as if there was pleasure to be had in being fondled by 'Mickey' Mouse paws, as if it were *fun* – and it probably was for some, it takes all kinds, and more's the pity: a limited range of tried-and-tested kinds would simplify things immensely. It is with the wider world as it is with washing powders. I'd written a perspicuous letter or two on that very subject, carbon copies of which were adding their eloquent ounces to the shopping-bags as I lugged them across the road and up the escalator. An idolmonger from north of the border, one of the precursors of that entire race of Queequegs with which our pavements are now thronged, offered to lend a hand, but I wasn't born yesterday and made shift.

My entrance created quite a stir. Tony and a crony actually forsook a poker game to establish what was in the bags. Paperwork, I said. That is all we know, and all we need to know.

The trek across town had upset me. I was a bundle of nerves, to tell the truth. What had possessed me? As much to celebrate having come through the streets unscathed as to settle my stomach, I ordered a whiskey, washed down one of my Valia, and fell to. Had to make the best of a Wessels-free environment. And despite the shaky start to the day, I made steady progress: by lunchtime I had ten fascicles of 'The Proofreader's Derby' shipshape. In the bag, which is to say, out of the bag and in the book. A Strammer Max for lunch, in memoriam, the last surviving item of the original menu, from the heyday of Mrs Mavrokordatos. Strammer Max: a stout Bavarian ploughman. One of Moçes' many cousins, recently appointed as Chief Cook and Bottlequaffer, didn't make too bad a hash of it, either. The afternoon held out the promise of another ten fascicles.

But it was not to be.

I was still mopping up the cooking juices in the continental manner when Errol burst in with a duffel bag slung over one shoulder and a bulky object wrapped in an army greatcoat in his arms. A corpse, was my first startled thought. And why not? Some poor pedestrian to be disposed of, some victim of senseless violence gone stiff as a board. The empty arms of the coat waved for help, and an ashtray went flying as Errol hurried across the room. Then, as he passed through the archway into the pool room, one end of the package struck the wall with a clang. Must be stolen property after all, I thought, a parking meter or a lamp standard. That Tone should allow these petty criminals to fence their booty under his roof … it was unconscionable.

(I'd taken a good look at the Prospect Road corpse through my opera glasses: black male, fortyish, fifteen stone. But the next day the *Star* said it was a *white* man, burnt to a char.)

Errol's buddies had been loafing in the shadows all morning in a state of inebriation, but his arrival was greeted by a lively uproar. Half the customers, the waiters, even Tone himself pressed through the archway to gape. So much raucous laughter and obscene banter ensued that there was simply no going on with my work.

I scrutinized and took stock. Errol and Floyd were down on the floor behind the pool tables, where the shadows were thickest, writhing in a tangle of arms and legs. The greatcoat sprawled in a pathetic attitude across the green baize, empty and abject, light blazing down on it, and the thought that it must belong to some human being the boys were now trying to overpower or violate forced its way back into my mind. Dim faces studded with shiny teeth came and went in the glare and gloom like portraits on rocking walls. Demonic laughter. I advanced to intervene. But then Floyd scampered clear and vanished, as if through a trapdoor, and Errol stood up alone behind the central table. He raised one end of the object they had been wrestling over – my relief that it was an object after all was short-lived – and rested it against his crotch. The end of a cylinder of some kind, perhaps a broken pipe … a traffic light? Surely not! He bent over and wrapped both his arms around the pipe. Then he hauled it up, swivelling his hips as he did so, and slowly, in obscene mimicry of a gigantic male member, tumescent, from the Latin *tumere,* swell, the Hillbrow Tower rose into the light.

My cry of protest was drowned out by drunken hooting and gleeful applause. Thrusting, lurching from step to step, Errol advanced upon Raylene, who fled shrieking in make-believe terror to the other side of the room. He turned his attention to the new girl, the youngster who still looked like a child to me, never mind the combat boots. She was too awestruck to do anything but gaze at him. He staggered towards her, phallus towering. Would no one defend her honour?

'Where did you get that?' My voice was indignant and authoritative. I knew perfectly well where he'd 'found' it: recognized it at once.

'In his pants!'

'It followed him home.'

'It's stolen property. Stolen from decent people with charity in their hearts. Not to mention your poor countrymen afflicted with tuberculosis. I've a good mind to call the police.'

Titters and jeers. Let them, I thought, as Errol butted the air with the broken tower. 'You have no sense of responsibility. In fact, you have an overdeveloped sense of irresponsibility. There's a destructive streak in you. Vandals, that's what you are, it's the sack of Rome all over again.'

'A sack of what?'

'Not that kind of sack, you blockhead, it's from the ...' And then the derivation slipped unaccountably from my mind. The drama of it! Silence had fallen. A circle of dim faces, gazing now at me, now at the hooligan with the tower jutting from his loins. I became aware of the dictionary clasped in my right hand: I must have taken it up intuitively, like a sword. By a stroke of good fortune it was not my precious *Pocket,* but the eighth edition of the *Concise,* published in 1990, carried to the Café that morning in one of the shopping-bags. An altogether weightier tome, somewhat too replete with Yankee-Doodlisms for its own good. What a shame I hadn't brought along the *Shorter,* which I could still heft like a man half my age on a good day. All the same, I must have looked like a prophet in a den of iniquity. Like Moses – the original, with the serpent rather than the sickle in his bosom – come down off the mountain, clutching his tablets. I opened the dictionary. Verses of lemmata whirled in a sortilege of sorts – rub ~ rudder ~ ruddle ~ rule ... ruler ~ run ~ run ~ runcinate – and as it sometimes happens, once in a thousand consultations, it fell open at the very page I sought – saccharin ~ sacring. Perhaps in this heightened atmosphere my fingers had been guided by some extrasensory urgency, as my eyes now were, to **sack**^{2}. (Of victorious army or its commander) plunder, give over to plunder (a captured town etc.). (Of burglar etc.) carry off valuable contents of. From the French in the phrase *mettre à sac,* put to sack. From the Italian *sacco* sack^1. My eye performed a backward roll to **sack**^{1}: large usually oblong bag for storing and conveying goods, usually open at one end and made of coarse flax or hemp. A jog would bring me to **hessian**, strong coarse cloth of hemp or jute, of Hesse in Germany. Foreign geography: Venetian blinds. Angostura bitters. Gin. But this was neither the time nor the place for the finer points. I focused again. Put to the sack: put in the sack. It was that literal. I opened my mouth to speak into the silence – and who knows what the effects would have been? These were surely moments in which lives might have been changed. But just then Wessels burst in, hopping on his good foot and waving his crutch, and with a swashbuckling 'Bonsai!', brought the crutch crashing down on the tower. Errol swung away, the end of the tower (where the revolving nightclub used to be) smashed into the neon tubes of the overhead light, and the room went dark in a shower of breaking glass.

In the rush for the exit that followed, I was knocked sideways, and heaven only knows what injuries I might have sustained had not Moçes, of all people, caught me up in his arms, as he had seen it done on television, practically shielding me with his own body, and marshalled me to safety. It was just as well I was wearing a chain on my glasses. When I found myself at my table again, I felt like some storm-tossed craft back at its moorings.

In a while, a semblance of order was restored. Tony marched around with his hands on his hips, detailing the costs of fluorescent tubes and the resurfacing of pool tables, while Moçes was set to dabbing up the splinters with cotton wool dipped in cane spirits (a home remedy from Tony's mother). Wessels sat down and stuck his grog blossom in my papers: 'What you liaising there?' I gave him what for. Who did he think he was, undermining my authority in front of these hooligans, and then carrying on as if nothing had happened? Sulkily, he produced the Mr Fatso/Mnr Vetsak pad and began to go through his invitation list, muttering names under his breath and ticking them off extravagantly.

'The Proofreader's Derby' could not hold my attention. My eyes kept wandering to Alibia, and I saw myself there, in a houndstooth overcoat, bending my steps to a fogbound wynd. My coat was the very opposite of Errol's, which looked as if it was made of flea-bitten underfelt, and gave you the urge to smother him under the nearest carpet. The heels of my brogues resounded like hammerblows on the cobbles, my breath puffed out in chubby bales of mist, my scarf waved behind me on an icy breeze, as if borne up by a cleverly concealed armature. In an even narrower close, I was drawn to a lighted window. Tucking a coat-cuff into my palm I wiped a hole in the rimed glass and peered through. I looked in on the Café Europa. At myself, in an inglenook, raising a toby jug brimming with porter to drink some congenial stranger's health. And in a corner, sipping shrub: Merle.

Wessels interrupted this reverie to draw to my attention an article in the *Star*. Vandals strike at Miniland. As if I didn't know. 'For the second time in three months, vandals' – my word exactly – 'went on the rampage at Santarama Miniland, the miniature village that raises funds to fight the spread of TB, hurling entire buildings into the harbour and turning the Carlton Centre upside down.'

These days, the newspapers contained so little one might believe in. But here was an indisputable fact. The city belonged to these Goliaths now, the country belonged to them. I saw them stretched out on the runways at Jan Smuts, with their heads propped on the terminal buildings, taking a smoke break, going slow. Flagpoles and street lights were no more than toothpicks in their fists, which they were always raising. I saw them marching down into the Big Hole of Kimberley, with the cables of the bucket winches tangled about their ankles, crunching underfoot the little miners who had flocked to build the new South Africa. I saw them striding up to the Union Buildings, two terraces at a time, in their big running shoes with the tongues hanging out. Shout! said their T-shirts. No! said their trousers. Bang! Bang! Action! Noise!

That useless letters editor at the *Star* had still not seen fit to publish my letter of 7 December, concerning my close shave with an Atlas Bakery van.

Later that afternoon, Errol and Floyd slunk out with their booty. Floyd, the stouter of the two, had the tower under his arm, swathed in the greatcoat again. I couldn't help thinking of resurrection men, the descendants of those infamous Williams, Burke and Hare, stalking my city in the wall, and I held my peace. But Errol in passing patted his duffel bag with his long fingers and said: 'The sack of Johannesburg.' One of his sleepy, soft-lidded eyes closed and opened in a parody of a wink. What Spilkin would have called a nictitation. What does he have in there? The Botanical Gardens?

The Supreme Court? The War Memorial? Zoo Lake? Then again, why should it be landmarks he's carrying off? Why not a jumble of street corners and parking garages – let's say the north-east corner of Tudhope Avenue and Barnato Street in Berea, or the south-west corner of Rissik and Bree – paving-stones and bus-stop benches – say the bus stop in Louis Botha, opposite the Victory Theatre in Orange Grove, where you might wait all day for a smoke-filled double-decker to take you to the city – trees – the avenue of oaks in King George Street on the western edge of Joubert Park – why not municipal swimming pools, parks, skylines, lobbies, doorways, vistas – say the view from the gardens of the Civic Centre, from the first bench to the right of the path that slopes down to Loveday Street, looking along Jorissen into the sunset …

After a while, I turned my attention to the sack of Tearle, the *sacks*. I couldn't possibly drag them through the streets again. I had Moçes summon me a taxi, one of Rose's, a compulsory treat. Moçes carried my bags down for me – a 'madala', he said, shouldn't have to stoop – and I felt moved to give him a small gratuity. He offered to wait with me at the kerbside, until the taxi came, to shoo away the artless dodgers who had gathered like mosquitoes, but I didn't think it was necessary.

I shall lift up mine eyes. At least the Hillbrow Tower was still there, the real thing I mean, ugly as it is. It was a shame one couldn't go up there any more. Dinner dancing, and so on. Cheek to cheek, with the world at one's feet. Or if not the world, at least the most densely populated residential area in the southern hemisphere. And there was Wessels, leaning on the Eiffels of the balcony railing and smoking a Peter Stuyvesant, moored, I should say, like a blimp in a cloud of blue smoke above that echoing Parisian scene, looking *down* on me, with me at *his* feet. I fancied I could see his crooked teeth glinting. That I should have ended up with Empty Wessels, whom I had never even liked. It was a bitter irony. How could I have foreseen such an outcome, in the gold-flecked afternoons of my past, how imagined that I would become a stranger in my home away from home, beset on all sides by change and dissolution? Or imagined: a pink elephant with its ear on backwards standing on a street corner, as if it were the most natural thing in the world, a dead body lying in an empty plot on a Sunday morning, burnt beyond recognition, a man of advanced years bearing what is left of his life in two paper shopping-bags. Then, as now, the television was full of experts, little people standing on tiptoe, touting their 'scenarios' of the future. As if tomorrow could be scripted. As if one might have expected to see the hammer and sickle trampled underfoot on Red Square and hoisted on the steps of the Union Buildings. The inconceivable times of our lives!

But I'm getting ahead of myself.

*

Bogey came to us in a cement-grey suit of communistic cut. It was single-breasted and ill-proportioned for his squat frame: too broad in the shoulder, too wide in the lapel, too long in the drop. The jacket pockets were shaped like shovels and the legs of the trousers were thick and round as traffic bollards. What material it was made of I couldn't say, something Victorian, approaching sackcloth. A black patent-leather hat. In this case, the material was plain, but the shape was puzzling. Not enough altitude to be alpine. More like a trilby that had had the spirit knocked out of it.

'Trilby O'Ferrall,' Merle said in answer to my question. 'Miss.'

'Slobodan Boguslavić,' said the concrete-clad one underneath the hat, conjuring a fleshy hand from the end of his sleeve. He sounded as if his mouth was full of olives. 'Dan for short.'

'Why not Slob?' said Spilkin, shaking the hand.

'Or Zog,' I put in nimbly. 'There's a name I always fancied.'

'Thank you very much,' said Bogey. And with that, he more or less exhausted his conversational English. We discovered later that his words of introduction had been taught to him by a Swissair hostess on the flight from Zürich.

After he had shaken hands with Merle and me, and pressed his lips to Mevrouw Bonsma's knuckles, with an elaborate pantomime of applause and gestures towards the piano, he reached for a chair at an adjoining table and drew it up between Spilkin and Mevrouw Bonsma. There was a moment of resistance, in which they both held their positions, while the arm of Bogey's chair nudged insistently against Spilkin's. I glowered at him, and saw nothing but the crown of his hat, deeply creased and puckered like a toothless mouth. It reminded me of a whelp mumbling for the teat. More and more in those days, as 'The Proofreader's Derby' continued to disturb my mental equilibrium, I was seeing things, thinking oddities, making morbid associations that would once have seemed quite mad to me. Nudge, nudge. Then Mevrouw Bonsma moved anticlockwise and bumped into me, and Spilkin moved clockwise and bumped into Merle, and then Merle and I, like elements in a physics experiment, with no option despite our specific gravity but to transmit the momentum, both moved and bumped into one another, and moved back and bumped into the others, and so on, until in this convulsive fashion, clutching our cushions to our backsides, moving furniture and fundament together, the five of us finally came to rest with equal spaces between our chairs.

'There,' said Spilkin, 'order has been restored.'

Choosing to ignore the fact, of which he must have been keenly aware, that what had been restored was an entirely different order. In a minute of unseemly shuffling and pardon-begging, a quaternion of equals had been transformed irrevocably into a circle. What was it Spilkin had said about the pentagon? How I regretted then my failure to insist upon a wiser seating arrangement at the outset. A square table, at which each person had a side, clearly demarcated, would have exposed how undesirable this shapeless new arrangement was. Might have deterred it altogether. But a round table was so accommodating, made it seem so matter-of-course. A stranger walking into the Café at that moment might have thought that the five of us had been sitting there all our lives.

When he had made himself comfortable, Bogey unbuttoned the jacket of his suit, revealing a comical pot belly and a candy-striped shirt with an immense collar. He transferred his hat from his head to his left knee. His hair was thickly pomaded and swept back from the forehead; an indentation like a plimsoll line encircled his head where the hat had pressed. The extraordinary thing about the pomade, from an etymological point of view, was that it smelt of apples. I caught a whiff and it turned my stomach. As for the skull, Johann Friedrich Blumenbach would have loved it. For the moment, he produced his passport and showed us the syllables of his name, thickly sliced, like one of the sausages I had recently discovered at the Wurstbude in the course of researching the cuisines of the world. Bɔguːslaːviːtʃ.

The rest of the evening was a sequence of absurd charades about the newcomer and his history, with a Magyar soundtrack courtesy of Mevrouw Bonsma. *Istanbul was Constantinople, now it's Istanbul …* Trust Merle to proffer an atlas, on which he was able to point out his island of origin in the Adriatic, a place devoid of vowels, and then to describe in a dotted line of greasy fingerprints left floating in his wake like oil slicks on the surface of the paper, his passage to our shores, while Spilkin said, 'Ja, ja,' as if he had confessed to being a German. Bogey seemed extraordinarily interested in the keys to the maps, the tuffets for prairies, the puffs of green popcorn for rainforests, the sutures for railway lines. In the middle of this performance, he changed seats with Spilkin, so that he and Merle could look at the new world from the same vantage point. Then they pored over the tidal charts at the front of her diary, as a month of crescent moons waxed and waned under his fingernails, and fumbled their way through lists of public holidays and the months of the year. I would have gone home then, had she not taken his rude forefinger and used it as a pointer to pick out the syllables: January. February. March.

'April, May … June, July,' Spilkin hummed. A folk song.

Regretfully, there was no 'Slobodan' in the *Better Baby* onomasticon.

I waited until well past my bedtime for him to take his leave, so that I might speak plainly, but he did not go. It was more consideration than he deserved, seeing that he didn't understand a word we were saying. Finally I said to Merle: 'You've done your good turn. But don't encourage him too much. We don't want this to become a habit.'

'Why do you say that?' She sounded genuinely surprised.

'It won't be comfortable with him around. He's uncouth. And not much of a conversationalist.'

'Well of course not, he doesn't speak the language.'

'Exactly. He won't be able to keep up his end. Our discussions will be lopsided. You'll have to get it across to him that he's not welcome here.'

'I'll do no such thing.'

'I don't mind him coming to the Café, you know, he's a welcome new splash against our famous cosmopolitan background. But I'd rather not have him at my table. He could join us again one day when he's picked up a few words of English.'

'Aubrey, how could you! He's just a stranger in a strange city, looking for a bit of company. And he seems like a nice person.'

'Nice?' I looked to Spilkin for support, but he pulled a mouth. 'Alliaceous is more like it.'

'Who?'

'Oniony-garlicky. From the Latin *allium*. I feel like I'm downwind of a saveloy, something full of hickory smoke and paprika. Look at his hands. He's altogether too sausagey, of finger and breath.' He smelt of change, to tell the truth, but I did not say so.

'Of all the unkind things,' said Merle.

'I regret that you have now taken the cake,' said Mevrouw Bonsma.

Whereupon the four-flushing topic of conversation, who had been gazing from one of us to the other with an eager smile on his face, doffed the shiny hat from his knee. The kneecap was like a skull embedded in cement.

We could have called him Boguslavić, by analogy with Tearle and Spilkin. It was not that difficult to master, especially when you saw it written down. I made a spirited defence of the principle, but to no avail. He himself badly wanted to be 'Dan', but an English label would not stick to such greasy goods. In the end, we called him Bogey. He would tell people – once he'd acquired the language – that it was because of his resemblance to Humphrey Bogart. When he leant on the piano, he said, with the brim of his hat aslant and the ceiling fan flicking shadows over his stubble, you would swear you were in Casablanca.

I would tell people to look it up in the *Oxford*. Bogey, noun, 'an awkward thing or circumstance'. Or even, forgive the vulgarity, '*slang,* a piece of dried nasal mucus'.

*

The winds of change smelt, thanks to Bogey, like an osso bucco – a shin of veal containing marrowbones stewed in wine with vegetables. But the fact is, I needed no olfactory clues to the way the winds were blowing. The eye, sharp as ever, had it before the nose.

An era was ending. And without sounding my own cornetto, I think I can say that I saw it coming before anyone else in the Café Europa, and possibly in the whole of Hillbrow (although I wouldn't lay claim to more territory than that).

A large part of my working life had been devoted to the proofreading of telephone directories, and specifically the Johannesburg Book. Quite apart from the technical challenges of the task, which I've already described, although they're probably beyond the layman, there were unique insights to be gained into the city and the ways of its inhabitants. Initially, in my apprenticeship, I was struck by the obvious oddities: the Cook who lived in Baker Street, the Towers of Brixton, the Blairs of Blairgowrie, the Blacks of Blackheath. The Heaths, too. No Gowries, mind you, praise be. I compiled a few amusing lists along these lines, passing fancies. But as my eye matured, I began to notice subtler things, submerged reefs beneath the placid surface, patterns that only came into focus when one had squinted until one's eyes watered. I noticed, for example, a preponderance of Baums and Blooms in Cyrildene; and likewise of Pintos and Pinheiros in Rosettenville; and of Le Roux in Linmeyer. Fully eleven per cent of the Van Rensburgs in the Book of 1973 had settled in Florida, whereas eight per cent of the Smiths, of whom there were more than four hundred, were in Kensington. By contrast, there were only three Schlapoberskys, and they were all in Oaklands. A small mercy, some might say. Don't suppose that

I was obsessed with ethnic groups – the concentration of medical men in Hurlingham, for instance, struck me with equal force – but it is in the nature of surnames to conceal age, status and sex, and reveal race.

With experience, my perceptions sharpened further, and I began to notice not just the patterns within directories, but the changes from one directory to the next, the slight shifts in emphasis and secret movements that only a comparison over time would uncover. I could tell that business was booming in Cleveland and dying out in Jeppestown, thanks to the new motorway. Without ever setting foot in Jules Street, I saw that it was becoming the used-car centre of the city. I saw that the head offices of the big businesses – the manufacturers, the insurance houses, the retailers, and their touts in the advertising agencies – were moving from the city centre to Rosebank and Sandton. I saw new suburbs rise from the veld – Lonehill, Mondeor, Amoroso – and old ones fall into decay – Doornfontein, Bertrams, Vrededorp – and then rise again, occasionally, in a flurry of restaurants and antique shops. Sometimes I saw the tracks of vast processes, generations on the march from poverty to wealth, *Völkerwanderungs,* exoduses, archaeological flows – and then I wished that I had turned my attention to directories as a younger man and kept comprehensive records.

In the twilight of my career, some intriguing trends became apparent in the Book, signs of the momentous changes that lay in store for the city and the country, glimmering between the lines, if one had eyes to see them, even before they became visible in the world.

Take the influx of Moodleys and Naidoos into Mayfair. I had been a proofreader of telephone directories long enough to have observed the steady relocation of these very surnames from Fordsburg and Pageview to Lenasia (or from Frdsbrg and Pgvw to Lns, as the crude abbreviations foisted upon us had it). The fact that they were flowing back into the city fascinated me. There were more of them every year. And it soon became clear, to this latterday Canute, that the tide would not be turned. An historic migration was afoot, comparable to the great scattering of the tribes before Chaka, the King of the Zulus.

In the years after my retirement, I kept up with the life of the Book, although my interest became rather more sociological than philological. There were some remarkable developments, notably the growing number of Hi's, Ho's and Fats in the Bedfordview area, an influx of -ićs and -wiczs and -ovas into all areas, including my own, and an inexplicable outbreak of MacGillicuddies in Orchards. But the most striking of all seemed less of a trend than an aberration. I was browsing one evening when I came across a Merope with a Hillbrow address. 'M' was then the fastest-growing section, thanks to the burgeoning numbers of African subscribers, but naturally one expected all these Mamabolas and Mathebulas and Masemolas to be in Mdwlnds and Mbpne and other far-flung places. This one was in Hillbrow. The 642- prefix corroborated it. I went at once to my desk and dialled the number. A child answered, a daughter of Africa, and while the little one was summoning her daddy, I put the receiver down.

The next morning found me loitering in the lobby at the High Point Centre, where Mr Merope apparently made his home. At first, the office-bound traffic was all white, as one would have expected. But by mid-morning, I had seen emerge from the lifts not one or two but half a dozen men who might have been he, black men wearing business suits and toting briefcases, trying and failing to look like chauffeurs or watchmen, and half as many black women besides, trying more successfully to pass as domestic servants.

Silently, while we slept, the tide was darkening. When I said so to Merle at the Café later that same day, she pointed out that Merope was one of the Pleiades, 'somewhat dimmer than the rest' from having married a mortal, and made light of my story. 'Must be a Greek,' she said. 'What was the initial?'

'V.'

'Vasilas. That seals it.'

I didn't mention the telephone call, for fear of seeming duplicitous.

It was not my imagination: there were more and more people of colour in Hillbrow. And it was obvious to me that they were living in our midst.

Were the authorities turning a blind eye? When I raised the question with our caretaker Mrs Manashewitz, I discovered that the law was being circumvented by the registration of residential contracts for these outsiders in the names of white proxies. It took years before this situation became public knowledge, and letters about the 'greying' of Hillbrow began to appear in the newspapers – grey was misleading; the effect might be grey only from a great distance, as in a photograph taken from a satellite, whereas from close up it was more like salt and pepper – but by then, it was too late. Having diagnosed the cause of the problems of overcrowding and littering and so on when they were just beginning, I did nothing to alert the authorities. These were the golden days, as I've said, and my mind was occupied with other matters. Then, too, the law-abiding tenants of Lenmar Mansions were fortunate that Mrs Manashewitz, who like myself would have been a great champion of freedom of movement in an ideal world, was disinclined to break the law.

It was just a matter of time before these people felt free to wander about outside, and then to poke their noses into every doorway. Why should the Café Europa be spared?

One evening, a woman rose from a table in one of the shadowier corners and went towards the Ladies' room. As she passed under the chandelier, I saw a gleam of crimson lipstick and a glimmer of ebony skin (not that I'm especially familiar, to tell the truth, with that heavy hard dark wood used for furniture). No one else seemed to notice. Merle was playing patience, Spilkin had his eyes shut and was tapping out the rhythm of 'The Girl from Ipanema' on the arm of his chair (Mevrouw Bonsma's inimitable version). I went to fetch *The Times* from its hook, and scuffed my feet between the tables until she emerged from the Ladies with her lips newly glossed and her hair fluffed up. Indigenous, no doubt about it. I was quite shaken. She returned to her table, where another shadowy figure was waiting. A casual circuit of the room, as if I was just stretching my legs, took me past the two of them and revealed the unsurprising fact that the companion was a man, a bit of a bruiser, possibly an Italian.

'What's biting you?' Merle asked, when I had resumed my seat. And then tried to soften the expression by turning it into a lesson in colloquial speech for Bogey.

I pointed out the clandestine liaison.

'Perhaps Mrs Mav has applied for international status?'

I couldn't remember exactly what that was, or whether it might still be applicable in these lawless times, whatever it was, something about foreign Africans and the number of lavatories, but I could hardly concentrate with Merle slapping my knee and telling me to stop staring. Later, I recalled that assignations across the colour bar were no longer illegal, strictly speaking. What people did behind closed doors was probably no business of mine. But when they made a public spectacle of themselves, did I have to look the other way?

As it turned out, averting the eyes, if not turning a blind one, was the order of the day. See no evil, etcetera. Other black women appeared in the Café. Always women, in the beginning, on the arms of sallow-skinned men wearing gold jewellery and open-neck shirts. Continentals and Slavs, men with overstuffed wallets and easy habits, consumers of espressos from tiny cups which they held in their signet-ringed fingers like the crockery from doll's houses.

Mrs Mavrokordatos had her nose in her books and her eye on the bottom line.

'You're starting to attract a different sort of clientele,' I said to her one day.

'You mean blacks?'

'They're ladies of the night, in case you haven't noticed.'

'And what if they are? The men have money and like to spend it, and I want them to spend it in here. Don't pull such big eyes, Mr Tearle. I need the business. You have to change with the times or you get left behind.'

Big eyes? Was it just a way of speaking, or a dig at my bifocals? All the better to scrutinize you with, I should have said.

I went back to my chair and surveyed the clusters at the tables with new eyes. The men were leaning in, they had clumps of hair at their necks where the shirt collars gaped, they had small buttons on the vamps of their shoes and thickly jointed watch-straps like astronauts. The dark women had fleshy shoulders, upholstery puckers of skin in their armpits, and glaringly red lips, which made their mouths seem even larger than they were. So large that the rest of their features looked somehow devoured. Black women. There would be black men too, one of these days, sleek and tufty, here and there.

You have to change with the times or you get left behind. And if you're left behind, is that such a bad thing? Is the past such a terrible place to be?

*

Bogey did not go away. He came back as often as he pleased – to practise his English, he said. Merle took a schoolmistressy interest in his progress. To give him his due, he was a fast learner. His head proved to be stuffed with odds and ends of American, scraps of motion pictures and hits and commercials just waiting to be used. He fitted his 'balonies' and 'gee-whizzes' and 'gimme-a-breaks' into conversation like a child trying to master an educational toy intended for a more advanced age group. Once, he referred to Mevrouw Bonsma as a 'broad'. You would think a Sauer Street nib-licker had emptied the Balaam Basket down his throat.

Predictably, it did not end with Bogey either. He had opened up a crack in our society with his chocklike person, and other strangers squeezed through it and made themselves at home. We welcomed them with open arms, we were so accommodating. We were no longer a foursome but a circle, and it is in the nature of a circle to widen irreversibly, like a ripple, while pretending to remain itself. But I knew better, I saw precisely what we were becoming, and I charted the evolutionary decline stage by stage. We were a sextet, and then briefly a septet, and then, God help us, an ogdoad. Ugly words for unpretty polygons and battered circles; each mutation heralded by the shuffling of chairs, as if we were dogs in search of new places to settle. It shouldn't surprise anyone that necks were craned from other quarters. The lesser patrons patronizing us!

Many of these newcomers were men like Bogey. They had ridiculous names, like Grog and Bleb, which I vowed never to utter. Just as I vowed never to answer to their flatulent 'Aubreys'. They were argumentative and obstinate. They sat at our table crackling their yellow newspapers like stage lightning and thundering among the crockery with their fists. They were obsessed with communism, both its demise in the old countries and its apparent resurrection in the new. Whenever Eveready came near, they tried to draw him into discussion about the Congress of South African Trade Unions, to call a spade a spade. Their great love was 'talking politics'. Our ways did not cut much ice with them.

In my eyes, what bound them together most tellingly was their putrid spelling. I overheard one of them in the Central News Agency trying to locate the works of Bulgakov, with which I was familiar in my youth. B-L-U-G-O-V- They couldn't even spell correctly in their mother tongues!

Broken English is no longer a drawback in the business world. Bogey went into import-export, commodity unspecified. He spent a great deal of money on clothes. His first and proudest purchase was a leather jacket from the Oriental Plaza. The garment was clearly some sort of Mohammedan practical joke. It was made entirely of offcuts, hundreds of patches of different colours, mainly if not exclusively imitation, and none larger than a playing card. A joker, I should say, or a knave.

'Neat, no?' he asked like a matinee secret agent.

'Neat, no,' I replied. 'You look like something swept out of an abattoir.' The overall impression was of a bale of bloodied hides, with one rudimentary cephalon still attached. It was the meaty colour of him too, and the Bovrilish substance he had taken to smearing on his head in place of the home country's pomade.

What was it again in the perfume factory? Something lost. (One of Wessels's cracks.) Pull yourself together, Pedro. (Mine.)

Bogey showed me the lining of his jacket, as enragingly red as a matador's cape. Then the label, which was sewn on the *outside* at the back, between the shoulder blades. Leatherama. I added it to my -rama list, below Cupboard-a-rama and Veg-a-rama. Merle said I was cruel. But even she had to laugh when he appeared a few days later in a pair of sunglasses with 'Glarebusters' printed across the lenses. My scorn he mistook for concern that the trade name obscured his vision, and he would not be quiet until

I had looked through them and confirmed, out loud for all to hear, that one could see right through the words from the other side. 'You see, I no see,' he kept declaiming. And then, when I had them on my nose, plunging the place into darkness, he went on in tones of childlike wonder, as if there were some witchcraft involved, '*You* no see, *I* see.'

This liking for things with their labels on the outside is degenerate. What sort of person willingly turns himself into an unsalaried sandwich-man? A walking 'salami on wry' (Sonja's Delicatessen). And pays for the privilege?

But despite my better judgement, I found myself making allowances for him. He was enchanted with being a consumer. No, it was more than that, for we are all consumers, willy-nilly, even the less materialistic of us, like myself. He, however, was a consumerist. His passion was not mere consumption, but consumerism. He regarded it with religious awe and defended it with the zeal of a convert. And coming from a country in which the opportunity to practise his faith had been so cruelly curtailed, who could blame him?

I saw him window-shopping in Pretoria Street one evening as I left the Café, and followed at a distance. He was waddling along with his hands behind his back, pigeon-toed, short-legged, bobbing his head from side to side, sweating in the butchered jacket. The blind trilby had been driven from his head by a straw Tyrolean with a guinea-fowl feather in the band. All in all, he looked like some odd bird that had strayed off course.

He stopped outside the Ambassador and looked into the glass-fronted display cases at photographs of revellers disporting themselves in the hotel's discotheque. Shamelessly under the weather, most of them. Went on to Exclusive Books, where the latest blockbuster by the author of *The Unhappy Millionaire* had been given a whole window to itself. Went on again past Freeman and Marks, the outfitters, High Point Lock and Key, Papoutsi (from the Greek *papoutsus,* shoe) the shoe shop, past the Daelite (that is, Daylight) Pharmacy, past the trestle-table of knives and holsters at the top of the steps to the High Point Centre, tarried in front of Diplomat Luggage Specialists. He gazed through the iron mesh at the carry-alls and tote bags, some of them quite possibly relatives of his poor jacket. 'Window-shopping.' What a shabby word, concealing a rash of thwarted desire beneath a cloak of respectability. As if it were no more than a pleasant pastime. The expression on his face was curious and greedy, inquisitive and acquisitive. Avis, avid. Could there be some connection? I reached for my *Pocket*.

But he was on the move again, down the stairs past the hanging gardens of High Point, to the automatic photograph booth. He drew the curtain and I watched his feet sticking out below, facing west, and then north, and then south. He was having himself photographed, full-face and in profile, like a felon. And now east! From behind! Then I understood why: for the label. I hurried away before he should see me.

After several months, Bogey and his comrades discovered Benjamin Goldberg's, the world's largest 'liquor supermarket', and his faith in consumption found a shrine. He would ferry the new arrivals from Eastern Europe out there – more and more of them, as time went by – to introduce them to the mysterious abundance of the new world. Weekly pilgrimages were made. Sometimes they went merely to browse in the bottle-lined aisles, absorbing the atmosphere osmotically through their swarthy skins; more often, they returned with primitive forms of alcohol that the sober-minded could never have imagined and could scarcely pronounce, wines and brandies made from macerated fruits, beers as black as pitch, luminous vintages in oddly-shaped bottles with small animals suspended in them, liqueurs named after the leaders of obscure reformations, spirits so volatile the smokers had to stub out their cigarettes before the stoppers were drawn for fear of igniting a conflagration. They were always forcing their firewaters upon us, to win approval and friendship, when these were not freely given. Mrs Mavrokordatos let them keep their bottles behind the counter.

When the Bogeymen had had a few too many, which was often, one had to mind one's tongue in their company. A single word – and not just the obvious tear-jerkers like 'mother' and 'home', but innocents like 'football' or 'sausage' – would make them weep inconsolably or break glasses in their fists. Mrs Mavrokordatos, more fool her, paid for the breakages from her own pocket. And Mevrouw Bonsma would chip in as well. They were just boys, she said, far away from home, as if that justified their Bohemian excesses.

All the others, even Spilkin, found this hooliganism picturesque. When I dissented, the old accusations of 'dryness' resurfaced.

'Any fool can see,' I had occasion to remark, 'that the problem is not dryness but wetness, a certain soaked quality, a sousedness.' Soٰuséd, I styled it, pointedly, by analogy with curséd.

*

Not all the newcomers were Bogeymen and Bohemians, although they were all Philistines. As the circle widened, so did the cracks, and some peculiar creatures came floating through. There was a Mrs Hay, for example, a clairvoyant adept at performing her own facelifts, by gathering up the slack and securing it to her skull along the hairline and behind the ears with tabs of sticking plaster, in different ways every week, so that she always looked subtly unfamiliar. For me she predicted a long and happy life, bless her, in the bottom of a cup of Joko made with a tea bag (a *round* tea bag, which flavoured more in the steeping than the square kind, the advertising insisted, but portended less in the dregs). Then there was a McAllister who had worked for the municipality reading meters, until he fell into a French drain and broke his hip. He was prone to quoting Rabbie Burns at us, especially 'To a Mouse'; and very often prone full stop, from a surfeit of usquebaugh. Jimbo, we called him, just a vowel removed from a pink elephant. And there was Wessels, who struck me at first only because he said 'Hull-ohs' when he arrived and 'Chow-chow' when he departed.

Wessels. Of all people! Riddled with plurality, liverish, toothy, thatched, thick as two short planks.

I missed the days of intimate quadrilaterality. But I would be lying if I said that I was not sucked into the maelstrom of our growing circularity.

All these new acquaintances had one happy advantage for me at least, one 'spin-off' – the perfectly apt Americanese, implying as it does that something is going round in circles rather too quickly and throwing off consequences like sparks. I had never before in my life been exposed to so much misuse and malapropism, so much sheer barbarism. I had stumbled upon a windfall in the least likely place. Even as I struggled to concentrate in the mounting babble, I began to keep lists of these bad apples for incorporation into 'The Proofreader's Derby'. It wouldn't take long before the newest of the newcomers, in sub-standard English of one variety or another – we had ceased to attract the better sort of person – would stick a nose into my business and ask: 'What are you scribbling in that notebook of yours?'

'Oh, it's just something you said.' And I'd put the book quickly in my pocket, with a deliberately dusty chuckle. 'Nothing important.'

Then they would insist, indefatigably, until at last I relented: 'Don't say I didn't warn you … You see, a moment ago you said: "My cousin's a computer boff." Well, it's not "boff" – it's "buff". Or "boffin". But never "boff" or "buffin", which I've also heard more than once.'

And from there it was a short step to telling them all about 'The Proofreader's Derby', and a whole lot of other things besides. My 'topics' (Merle). Things they didn't necessarily want to hear. Not one in ten had the foggiest idea what I meant; but they were impressed with me anyway, and proud to be part of my research. It was the index cards that did it, and the lever-arch files with the granite finish.

As far as my letters to the press were concerned, I believe the admiration was sincere. I had long since learnt to lay the newspaper down on the table in such a way that Merle would realize one of my letters had been published, and share it with the others. None of them in all that time ever earned the distinction, although several followed my example and tried their hand at it. What thrilled them most was seeing my name in print. 'A. Tearle,' they would mutter, turning it over in their mouths like so much melanzano or what-have-you, savouring the unexpected taste of it, while the living embodiment sat before them, sipping a tea, twirling a pencil. 'A. Tearle.' I served as a basic English lesson.

Once, when I'd included a covering note to explain a complicated layout and unthinkingly appended my full name, the editor took it upon himself to add it to my letter. As if that wasn't bad enough, the imbecile rendered it *Audrey* Tearle. I hoped no one would notice, but the fool with the echolalia did, illiterate as he was, and started cracking jokes about 'Little Audrey'. He was full of jokes. It reminded me of the mania for joke-telling that had seized Spilkin when Mevrouw Bonsma first settled among us, and I prayed it was just a 'phase' this one was going through, a nervous habit perhaps, brought on by the strain of being in more sophisticated company than he was accustomed to. But the condition proved to be chronic.

'Who is that dolt?' I asked Merle, when he had gone to the Gentlemen's room, which he did at regular intervals, seeing that Mrs Mavrokordatos was plying him with beer.

'Wessels,' she said. 'Martinus Theodosius Wessels.'

Perhaps that was when 'Empty' first occurred to me.

*

For two whole weeks, Mevrouw Bonsma poured out nothing but dirges, long draughts of 'Galway Bay' and 'The Mountains of Mourne' that had the Bohemians weeping as if they were Irishmen themselves, which they very nearly were. I said it was homesickness; the Wessels character insisted it was 'dronkverdriet' (d(r)ɔŋkfɜːd(r)it). We pleaded for jollier melodies – 'Loch Lomond' was a favourite with McAllister, I recall, to restore the geographical balance – but Mevrouw would not comply.

'I remain your humble servant, but I cannot. I feel so sad, and so does the piano. It hurts here.' She stroked a tender spot on the keyboard and sucked a föhn off the Alibian Alps through the gaps in her teeth.

'I feel it too,' said Merle. 'I feel it in my bones. Something terrible is about to happen.'

'What do you say, Mrs Hay?'

Our clairvoyant just hitched up a region of her fallen face with her thumb and kept silent.

Whether or not the tragedy had been foretold in bone and ivory, it came to pass. Mrs Mavrokordatos acquired for the Café Europa two television sets. They were hoisted aloft on pivoting platforms attached to the walls, one over the door to the kitchen and the other over Mevrouw Bonsma's head. Once again, I had to alert our proprietress to the perils of the course she was pursuing.

'This will bring in the wrong crowd.'

'You mean blacks?'

People had Africans on the brain.

'I mean television watchers. "Viewers" as they want to be called. And sports enthusiasts in particular, *fanatics* of hockey, cricket, and especially football.'

I was right. The television sets brought in a lot of noisy immigrants from Glasgow and Manchester and Leeds, whose greatest joy was to watch the football teams from their old home towns, turnipy manikins with bulging legs and rosy cheeks, rushing around on lawns of the unnatural lushness usually reserved for botanical gardens. The clubs had the quaintest names, Rangers and Hearts, Tottenham Hotspurs and Crystal Palace. Occasionally there were local fixtures too, played by teams out of the Christmas pantomime, such as the Chiefs and the Pirates. I half expected poor old Noodler to take the pitch. One of the players, by the name of Khumalo, claimed to be a doctor. Probably struck off the roll for misconduct. The football fanatics were all diminutives: Robby and Freddy, Bobby and Teddy, a whole dynasty of Harries. Clientele, Mrs Mavrokordatos insisted, so long as their money is good. The phrase that came to my mind was 'paying customers'. When they gave the attendance figures at sports stadia, that was the term they always used, as if there were bound to be gatecrashers and cheats too, who should not be counted.

After the sports fanatics, came a variety of others: spinsters addicted to situation comedies, bachelors with a passion for news or weather reports, devotees of the quiz show or the courtroom drama.

As I'd anticipated, Mevrouw Bonsma's reign was drawing to a close. Soon she was confined to a single shift between five o'clock and half past six, a period known with cavalier disregard for accuracy on every count as the 'Happy Hour'. By arrangement with the proprietor of the Haifa, a noticeboard spangled with chalky Hebrew Magen Dovids was secured to the railings at the bottom of the escalator in the street outside, with a photograph of Mevrouw Bonsma signed 'Yours, Suzanna' sellotaped to it under plastic, as if she were a piece of cheap merchandise – a disposable watch or an overripe melon. I tried to get up a petition to have more of Mevrouw Bonsma and less of the television sets, but no one would sign it, apart from the old squares, and even they thought it was a losing battle.

It wasn't long before the television sets were being left on even while Mevrouw Bonsma played. At five to five every day, as she settled herself at the piano, Eveready climbed up on a chair and turned the volume down, so that those with the urge could follow the silent sequence of events that flickered there.

One evening, a brief part of one evening, stands out in my mind now as a turning point. Not *the* turning point, not the spilkin that unlocks the whole puzzle, but a key nevertheless, as significant as the discovery of a Merope in High Point.

I had been detained that day at the General Hospital, queuing interminably for my pills, and darkness was falling by the time I alighted from my bus in Edith Cavell Street. Meissner's Building rode at anchor in the traffic like an ocean-going liner. I remember glancing up at the windows of the Europa, aglow between the columns of brocade, and feeling a comforting sense of anticipation. It was winter and I was looking forward to the heaters and, dare I say it, the warmth of human fellowship.

But as I stepped onto the escalator, there was a commotion on the first floor. A drunkard, a young black man in a shiny suit, appeared at the top of the escalator, and with an unprintable curse, hurled himself down it. The stairs were going in the other direction, bearing him back ceaselessly to the top, where they should soon have deposited him in the mechanical course of events. But he applied himself to the task of plunging downwards with such maniacal energy that he managed to make headway and bore slowly down upon me.

He seemed oblivious of me. As if I was invisible. There was nothing I could do, a man of my age, not exactly frail but necessarily careful, what with the blood pressure and the spastic colon (which pains me all the more acutely, thanks to my vocation); I could hardly be expected to flee. I did take a few precautionary steps backwards down the moving stairs, to no avail. I rose relentlessly.

A nightmare. Imagine: me, Aubrey Tearle, stepping calmly backwards, while rising swiftly and effortlessly into the air; and him, the nameless ruffian, panting and crying out in a fury of exertion, while sinking by painful degrees. Herr Toppelmann once had a clock whose hands sped backwards, trying in vain to erase the motto printed across its face: *Manchmal geht alles verkehrt* – which Toppelmann did into English as 'On several occasions, everything is going wrong' – and it alarmed me in quite the same way. Could there be a more disquieting concept, one more filled with dreadful fascination, than 'anticlockwise'.

We converged, and despite the fact that he was the one doing the foolish thing, the machinery cast me as the aggressor. I gripped the moving handrails, jutted out my jaw in the shape of a cowcatcher, braced myself, and we collided with a thump and were swept up to the landing, all his efforts cancelled out in a headlong moment. I found myself immersed in his smell, which I recognized as an adulterated version of my own: Shield for Sportsmen. Improbably, for I had expected us to end up in a heap, with bruises and broken bones, he stumbled backwards and sprawled supine on the floor, and I took two steps along the length of his body, just as if he had been a log across a stream, stepping once on his belly and once on his chest, and then found solid ground beyond him. It was just as well for him, I thought, that I was wearing my Hush Puppies rather than my brogues.

He scrambled to his feet. I expected him to set upon me, but my expectations were disappointed. His face was contorted with laughter. 'Be cool, my bra!' he sang out, and launched himself again, neither onto the up escalator nor the down, but onto the narrow metal ledge between the two, and plunged shrieking downwards to the street. This ledge was very much like a slide in a children's playground, except that it was studded with sharp little projections put there expressly to deter such pranks.

Against my better judgement, I found myself sinking again, even as my blood pressure rose, expecting to find him gushing vital fluids at the bottom, exsanguinating himself through lacerated arteries of calf and thigh. He had indeed ripped one leg of his trousers from turn-up to waistband, but otherwise he was completely unscathed. This miraculous escape seemed to tickle him. Waggling an exposed buttock, cursing good-naturedly, he went away down Pretoria Street.

For the second time in a minute I escalated, like death on the roads, like train violence. A tatter of tartan underpants fluttered on a spike. What was it he had called me? His *bra*? How odd. It was the first time I had come across that bit of argot – but it would not be the last.

The excitement was not yet over: the doors of the Café Europa were locked against me! A pang, an actual physical pain, not in my heart, which would have been worrying enough, but in my side, shot through me. It was probably a stitch brought on by all the exertion, but at the time, it felt like a stab of betrayal. Abandoned. I remembered how the Europa had opened its arms to me when first I came here. Now this cold shoulder.

I put my hand to the glass, and brought my face close, as if I was gazing into the promised land.

It was a busy night and nearly every table was occupied. Here and there a few dissenters were chatting or reading, but the overwhelming majority were watching the television sets. Half of them were staring in one direction and half in the other, and although I knew that they might be focused on the same image, to me they epitomized the idea of divided attention. They were so intent, I almost saw the trajectory of each gaze, solid as a beam; and yet together they made a confused thatch, like a jumble of immense pick-up sticks criss-crossing the room, piled to the ceiling.

Bogey and a pal were at the gaming machines, recently installed in a little cubicle separated from the rest of us by glass panes. I had warned Mrs Mavrokordatos about the one-armed bandits too: they'll bring in the able-bodied variety. And the vice squad. But she just scoffed at the idea. It wasn't even gambling, she said, they were playing for free games, with tokens. Did she think I was blind? That I wouldn't see her passing Bogey a cheque under the counter? What was the isolation ward for?

Then my eye wandered over to Table 2. There was Merle, scratching around in the bottomless bag. Spilkin. A Harry and a Willy – the Spaniards, I called them, in spite of their nationality, because of their penchant for singing Olé Olé Olé during football matches. Arsenal fanatics they were. A woman I did not know. Wessels asprawl. All looking at the screen above Mevrouw Bonsma's head.

I looked too.

The screen was stuffed with little television sets, a whole brood of miniatures, as if the thing had spawned. I was not much of a 'viewer', but I recognized the programme. Tellyfun Quiz. It was a favourite in the Café and, I gathered, in the country at large, and so I had been subjected to it several times. Telly. The word turned my stomach. Loo, brolly, iffy, butty, bumf. A degenerate vocabulary descended from the nursery. Words without spines, the flabby offspring of a population of milksops. 'Telly' was bad enough on its own, but squatting on 'fun' like a slug on a cowpat, it was repulsive.

The rules of the game had always eluded me. The contestants were made to clamber about on staircases and guess what was inside the television sets scattered on the landings. The hosts, as they were known, asked them questions, while the screens flashed Booby! Booby! Booby! There were two hosts, a gnome with the haunted eyes of a morphine addict and a body like a jam doughnut, so rotund he needed braces for his trousers; and a slender young woman, strictly speaking a hostess, with a bob of blonde hair. She was much the more presentable of the two, the very image of Merle in her younger days, I imagined. If only she would keep her mouth shut. Instead, she was nagging the contestants to switch on their television sets. Here it came now, in a wit-curdling simper … *Turn on the telly!*

Lip-reading is a useful skill to acquire, especially in these days of shoddy enunciation, but it can be a burden too. Although I looked away from the screen, I could not help seeing half a dozen patrons mouthing the catchphrase. How irritating it must be for Mevrouw Bonsma. Her beehive stuck up from behind the piano, her glistening eyes, which should have been staring wistfully into her own heart, were staring instead at – the other television set! She was tinkling away, as if she were accompanying a silent film, tellytinkling. Fortepiano! Back in time! Anticlockwise!

I looked to Spilkin to see if he was still the same man, to see whether his grey hairs had turned black overnight. And there lay the key to the episode. Spilkin was the spilkin, as it should be. He looked back at me with an expression so lacking in sympathy it made me shudder, as if he had never clapped eyes on me before. And then one by one, the other gazes trembled and fell away from the screen.

I must have looked a fright, with my nose pressed to the glass and my spectacles misted over.

Spilkin jiggled an eyebrow and Eveready came to open up. It was he who had tossed the drunkard out and locked the door behind him. He was quite proud of the fact.

'He thinks it is a shebeen,' he said.

An Irish term, naturalized.

*

Vocabulary, milksop: iffy … butty … whiffy … naff … dishy … dinky … fab …

*

'It was like Little Hans and the dyke,' Spilkin laughed, 'with Eveready and Mevrouw Bonsma in the leading roles.'

'What do you mean?'

'Come, come,' he said with a salacious gesture. 'Must I draw you a picture?'

'I don't believe you, that's all. Mevrouw hasn't said a word. And there are sanctions against forcing yourself on a lady.'

'No force required. Go ahead and ask her.'

I suspected that it was all a tasteless joke; the 'solitary sailor' tone rang a distant bell. Nevertheless, I said I would take the matter up with Eveready; if there was an ounce of truth in it, he would find himself endorsed out, or whatever the expression was.

Then Spilkin admitted that he was just pulling my leg.

*

One of the benefits of television, Mrs Mavrokordatos said, was that it was educational. It brought you news. Personally, I didn't see the connection. New information, fresh events reported, streamed from the set at specified times each day, gathering and subsiding in the official channels to a rhythm as pacific as an ocean roar. Just now and then, like a bottle on the tide, something out of the ordinary came bobbing along, and then one could pay attention if one chose.

One evening, I was working on 'The Proofreader's Derby', fine-tuning a fascicle about Fluxman's encounter with a 'mugger', when a hush fell over the Café Europa and all eyes turned to the screens. Our State President appeared there, looking gloomy, and announced his retirement.

I felt sorry for him. He assured us that he was in perfect health, but I know high blood pressure when I see it.

'Poor old sod's losing his faculties,' Spilkin quipped.

'Just like the University of the Witwatersrand.' I'd read in that day's *Star* that the Russian Department was closing down.

'What's the P.W. stand for?' asked an Eddy, recently arrived from Birmingham.

Merle enlightened him: Pieter Willem. But Wessels had other ideas. He said it stood for Poor William.

When I got up to leave a little later, this same Wessels stumbled after me. He wanted to walk me home.

'Forget it. It's miles out of your way.'

'Ah, come on Aubs, man, I need the exercise. It'll get the circulation going.'

I had the impression he was mimicking me. Perhaps he'd heard me extolling the virtues of an active lifestyle? Shirty blighter. Stamping his feet and beating his chest with his hands as if he was on fire. He should have been wearing a coat instead of this leaf-green suit, with lapels like the fronds of some tropical plant and a flap in the back of the jacket wide enough to admit a cat. The last thing I needed was for him to find out where I lived. I went in the opposite direction to throw him off the scent.

All the way down Twist Street, he railed against the world in terms I would rather not repeat. He kept calling me 'Aubs', as if he was seeing double – but I suppose it was better than 'Churl', which was how he rendered my surname. I had to nudge him every few paces like a tugboat to keep him on the pavement, or I dare say he might have met his death under the wheels of a bus.

On the corner of Esselen Street, he stopped and stared across the intersection. He was trying to decipher the placard tied to a pole there. It was perfectly clear to me: WHY PW QUIT. Shrugging off my restraining hand, he went lumbering across the street, souvenir hunting, I thought. Just as he gained the opposite kerb, a man who had lain hidden in the shadows of a nearby bus shelter suddenly sat up on the bench. One of our growing army of indigents, muffled in greatcoat and balaclava.

Wessels stopped dead and gazed at this apparition. Then he cried out: 'Peewee! What's the problem, my old china?'

He made such a racket that concerned faces appeared between the gingham curtains in the windows of the Porterhouse. The Porterhouse! As if a pot of porter had ever been drawn in that dump. As if one in a hundred of their penny-pinching patrons even knew what porter was! I had a good mind to go in and give the manager a blast, but Wessels had fallen on his knees and was trying to kiss the hem of the vagrant's coat. The other gazed back through bleary eyes.

'Speak to me, Peewee,' Wessels implored. 'Or have the kaffertjies got your tongue?'

I ought to have left him there to degrade himself, but sheer irritation drove me to his rescue. The vagrant was white, or had been before liquor and the elements savaged his complexion. Not that it made a blind bit of difference. Summoning reserves of strength I scarcely knew I possessed, I dragged Wessels away.

'Don't worry, Aubs,' he reassured me. 'I'll stand by you, man, even though I'm farming backwards.'

Duty done, I left him on the corner of Wolmarans Street, clinging to a traffic light, with his tie folded over his shoulder and his trousers falling down, garishly enamelled in red and amber and green like a cheap china ornament for the bar counter.

*

Spilkin took a shine to Wessels. I never could account for it, despite everything.

Just what Wessels had done with his life before then was anybody's guess. He claimed to have been an 'agent', a game ranger, a member of the armed forces, a *lid.* Although this last was merely the Afrikaans for 'member', it struck me as apposite: he was stopperish, corky, a brother of the bung. He had a photograph of himself in uniform, but anyone could see by the toggle and braid that it was strictly fancy dress. A chauffeur or a commissionaire.

The photograph went around the circle a couple of times, and it had a surprising effect on Spilkin. 'Take a look,' he confided quietly, 'this really gets to me: the way the cap presses down the tops of his ears. Pathetic, in its way, but endearing too.'

'Must have been going to a party.'

'He says he was on active service. He has stories about Magnus Malan and Constand Viljoen. He says he has "contacts" in high places.'

'I'm amazed you're taken in by him. That nonsense about being the General's batman. Generals don't even have batmen, except in those comic-books he reads about the War, where the Germans go around shouting "Achtung!" all the time. He must have been a driver ... an ambulance driver! The St John's Brigade. It's as plain as the nose on my face.'

To tell the truth, I myself had felt an unwelcome pang of sympathy for Wessels, with his ears sticking out like the tips of a wing collar.

But he soon put paid to such feelings. He simply did not understand the rules of conduct in force at the Café Europa. Despite the new blood, we still observed certain proprieties. There was an unwritten law, for example, that we did not tolerate hawkers and other itinerants. Encourage them now, we used to say, and in next to no time, the streets will be crawling with beggars. But Wessels was above the law. First it was peaches from a snotty-nosed little Asiatic, then a painted wooden budgerigar, a *good cockatoo* from a dope fiend – he was in a clammy sweat and running a fever – and a wrought-iron pot-plant stand from a poor white. When he bought a rose in cellophane from a débutante, ridiculously overpriced, and fobbed it off on Merle, I thought it was time to speak out.

He twisted everything around. He said my 'outburst', which was really no more than a mild reprimand, was 'petty jealousy'. He began to tease me.

'Got the hots for old Merlé?' Smirking in the shadow of his lascivious quiff, as if he was talking about a beast in heat, a leghorn or an Aberdeen Angus. And this while Merle was at the table! The way he pronounced her name only made it worse; I had set him right several times, but he insisted that it rhymed with Perlé. As in *Paarl* Perlé.

'Mer-*lay*! Ter-*lay*!' he began to chant. The rhyme (properly pronounced) had occurred to me too, but I would never have expressed it. It was like something out of a rhyming dictionary.

'What are we up to now, Martinus?' Merle said in her sweet way, and smiled to conceal her embarrassment.

'Mer-*lay*! Ter-*lay*!' It still resounds in my head, across the years.

I was prepared to cast a positive light on the Eddie-Come-Latelies and their crude ways, and especially on the faults of ignorance. Bogey had started out saying 'Merlie', but then he was a foreigner and he only needed correcting once. Wessels was incorrigible. If anything, being amended only spurred him on. That Wessels should cleave to me, like a limpet to a bass, like a leech to a calf ... stick to rather than part from (6).

In the end, those two arch-offenders, Empty and Bogey, the guileful and the gauche, drew Merle into their mischief. I came upon them one afternoon, conspiring together. I saw in a flash that they were up to no good.

It was on this very day that I first noticed the hill in the mural, the one shaped like my head, Arthur's Seat or the Mount of Olives, depending on your nationality. Possibly even one of the hills of Rome – although Rome, as Wessels once informed me, was not built on a Sunday (we were arguing about restrictions on the trading hours of bottlestores). I've already confessed that the oddest ideas were popping into my head as

'The Proofreader's Derby' took its toll on my mental health. I tried to find the connections afterwards; they had their heads together, whispering, and they sprang apart as I approached. I had a startling impression of Wessels's hair, sleekly crouched over his brutal thoughts like some marsh-dweller on its eggs. I sat down, in an awkward silence. My eyes turned to the streets of Alibia, roaming from quays lapped by a dirty vinaigrette of engine-oil and brine, along cobbled ways past factories and boarding houses, to the staircases of the hills, and to one hill in particular, thrusting up through a greasy thundercloud (the residue of Bogey's hairdo, which he would rest against the wall, although Mrs Mavrokordatos had asked him not to).

A shadow, which matched the hill in every particular, although it was marginally smaller, lay upon the painted surface; and turning slightly, I saw that it was the shadow of my own head. At one special angle – if I gazed into the corner where Mrs Mavrokordatos sat behind her till, keeping watch over the dainties and a growing array of bottles – the silhouettes were identical. Why had I never noticed it before? The source of the shadow was a spotlight above Mevrouw Bonsma's piano, recently installed in place of the bluebell lamp to make her more visible, even as she became less audible. Perhaps it had been adjusted lately, perhaps I had never sat in exactly this spot before, and a unique combination of variables had produced a unique optical effect. Spilkin would be in a position to explain the physics of it; but he was absent without leave. I waggled my head, so that the shadow elongated and contracted, again and again, returning always to the point at which its shape echoed the hill's perfectly.

Eveready at my elbow, plucking the sleeve of my blazer to get my attention. I had 'wandered off', as they say, which was not like me. Tea, to calm the nerves.

'As I was saying,' Wessels was saying, although he had not been speaking at all, 'you don't wanna get dirty. Wear a jean or overalls.'

The discomfort welled up again.

'And don't forget your torches.'

I feigned indifference. But later on, I contrived to leave the Café at the same time as Merle and, concealing my bad temper, quizzed her about the mystery.

'Tinus is planning a little outing for next Saturday,' she said.

'Who? Oh, him. Where to?'

'The zoo.'

'Of all the hare-brained—'

'Keep your voice down, Aubrey. We're going to see the animals. People do it all the time. It'll be great fun.'

She knew as well as I did that we frowned on extramural socializing. One had to protect one's privacy. This Wessels character, for whom everyone felt sorry, seemed determined to turn everything upside down. Perhaps he was trying to push me out of the polygon?

'Who else is going?'

'Just Tinus and Bogey and me so far. There's place for one more. We were going to ask you.'

'What about Spilkin?'

'He's busy, bad luck for him. We're trying out Bogey's car.'

'His car!'

'He's bought himself a Mazda.'

'I thought he was broke.'

'He has business interests that bring in a little.'

'Can he drive? They drive on the right over there.'

'He's got his learner's.'

'I should have been kept abreast.'

That made her giggle like a schoolgirl. I was reminded of Wessels and his childish rhymes. And then I became aware of Merle's bosom, which had never impressed itself upon me so insistently before, and of my embarrassing head. This playground atmosphere was becoming intolerable.

In the weeks that followed, I worried that someone else would notice the resemblance between my head and the hill, and make me the butt of a joke. I thought about changing seats. I thought about withdrawing from the Café entirely. But more than ever, I began to see Alibia as my territory, which it was up to me to defend. Afterwards, when one of the others cast a shadow on my head-shaped hill, my capital, it was as if they were *inside* my head. My head was in the city, a part of it, as solid as the earth beneath my feet. And Wessels and the others were in my head, flitting through it like migrant workers without the proper papers, as insubstantial as shadows.

*

The Zoological Gardens were even more trying than I'd anticipated.

We went at night. The authorities had instituted special night tours to allow for the viewing of nocturnal animals. Learn more about hyenas, bats, civets and owls, the pamphlet said. Bring your own torch. Prying into the lairs of innocent creatures? It did not strike me as edifying, and I thought of staying away. But then I imagined Merle surrounded by animals like Wessels and Bogey.

Predictably, the Mazda was a jalopy. On the rear bumper was a sticker that read: Don't look at my tits. I had come across this bit of smut before, emblazoned across the front of a harlot's T-shirt. Distasteful as it was, one saw the logic: it gave lechers like Wessels an excuse to gaze at the breasts in question. But its import in relation to a motor car was obscure.

Bogey was scarcely competent behind the wheel. To make matters worse, he'd brought one of the Bogeymen along, a slab of gristle called Zbignieuw. Merle had to sit in front, next to the driver, who perched himself on a copy of the *Reader's Digest Book of the Car*. That left Wessels, Zbignieuw and me to cram into the back, which was already cluttered with empty bottles and dirty laundry. I refused to ride bodkin. I'd be squashed to a pulp. In the end, Zbignieuw piled in first and Wessels and I had to squeeze into the unoccupied margins. Just my luck to be on the driver's side, where I could smell the back of Bogey's head, wafted to me on the breeze like the aroma of a Sunday roast. As I'd feared, he was wearing the leather jacket. It was bound to incense the beasts.

The start of the tour was tiresome but innocuous. We ranged ourselves upon trailers, along with the other paying guests – two dozen of us all told, mainly mommies, daddies and little ones – and a tractor dragged us about from cage to cage. Those who had heeded the advice to bring their torches were able to rouse the nocturnals from their slumbers (evidently they were prone to unnatural behaviour) by shining the beams in their faces, while our guide, a nasal young woman dressed for a safari, provided us with useful information about their habits and habitats. I busied myself proofreading the little notices appended to each cage and maintaining an appearance of enjoying myself. I wouldn't have them calling me a stick in the mud.

When we had finished eyeballing the owls, an encounter that should have signalled the end of our tour, our guide announced that there was a treat in store for us. Whispering excitedly, we were conveyed to a cage concealed in a grove of trees in a distant corner of the gardens, and encouraged to winkle out the creature contained therein. Something vicious, to judge by the thickness of the bars, and the moat and railings that kept us at a distance.

Fingers of light probed between the bars. What was that? A table and chairs! A premonitory shiver passed through our party. A television set? A painting suspended in thin air. A kettle. The torch-beams slipped from object to object, settled on a bed in one corner of the cage, where something lay sleeping under blankets. After a while, the blankets were tossed back and a face appeared. Everyone twittered.

I turned my attention to the signpost: 'Homo Sapiens. Mammal. Typical male (1.75 m, 76 kg). Omnivorous, omnipotent, omnipresent. Hunts profligately, including its own kind. Considered the most dangerous and destructive of all species ...' Profligately. That was good.

The man in the cage sat up on the edge of his bed and gazed back at us with an expression compounded of suspicion, belligerence and boredom. I recognized the look: it was the same one we had seen on the faces of a dozen other animals in the past hour or two. Very cleverly captured. He must be an actor.

Abruptly, he lost all interest in us and stood up. Underpants, thank heavens. The members of our party, Merle not excepted, were engrossed, nudging one another and leering, like schoolchildren studying the reproductive system, as he crossed to the other side of the cage and opened the door of a refrigerator. An eerie, artificial light fell upon his body. Our guide seemed to be training the beam of her torch upon his loins.

The human animal – the term the guide urged us to use when we addressed our questions to her – removed a bottle from the refrigerator, slammed the door shut and went to sit in a chair. He switched on a lamp, took up a remote-control device and pressed a button. The television set started to life in the other corner of the cage. He stared at the screen and drank from the bottle.

While the others asked jokey questions – what does it eat? where does it relieve itself? does it talk? – I had time to examine my own feelings. I felt – what would capture it – threatened? No, that was too reminiscent of 'endangered'. Certainly not merely affronted. I felt – I had to stop myself from quaking – that we were *in mortal danger.* We were on the verge of extinction, I realized, and the fact seemed chillingly explicit. But what did I really mean? Who were 'we'? The human race? People of good sense and common decency? The ragtag remnants of the Café Europa? Was it a royal 'we'?

These were hardly the circumstances in which to consider such questions; in any event, while I was musing, scientific enquiry had turned, as it invariably does when the wrong minds engage in it, to mockery. There was something about the human animal's disdain for us, the lack of a reciprocal interest to compensate for our own morbid curiosity, that was extremely provocative. Predictably, Wessels, who had never shown much self-control, was among the first provoked – although Merle assured me afterwards that he was not entirely to blame for what followed. She said a child had tossed a pebble at the animal to attract his attention. He ignored us. A little fusillade of twigs and sucking sweets rained down on him. A coin struck him on the shoulder, but still he gazed blankly ahead.

It was Wessels who flicked a cigarette end through the bars. The reaction was explosive. The man leapt up, brandishing a club that had been hidden behind the chair, and hurled himself at us. He struck the bars a mighty blow, so violently that we started back in fright. A single metallic note resounded into the night. I wish Mevrouw Bonsma had been there to capture that sound precisely. All I can say is that it was deep, sonorous, and filled with rage.

The note subsided, calando, into a stunned silence.

Then a cackling and cawing arose in the cages all around and rippled outwards. At the same time, one of the children in our party, perhaps the one who had started it all, began to cry, which made the adults laugh. Merle giggled, the Bogeymen chattered like apes. I hesitate to say it, but only I fell back in shame, while the cacophony of grunts and cries rolled out over the treetops, and the man in the cage, switching off the television set and then the lamp, went back to bed.

'Good Lord, Aubrey,' Merle said, when we were enduring the campfire coffee and buttermilk rusks that concluded the tour and came with the price of the ticket, 'you look like you've seen a ghost. You mustn't overdo it.'

'I'm not much of a night owl,' I might have said.

'You know what would hit the spot?' Wessels said. 'A slice of Mrs Mav's balaclava.'

It was my fault, teaching him 'baclava'. To stop him calling it shredded wheat.

Merle insisted that Zbignieuw sit in front on the way home. In the car she touched my hand, and declared it as rough as sandpaper. 'You're so dry, I could write on you.'

'Dermatographic, you mean?' Always wanted to drop that into a conversation.

'You need moisturizing,' she said, and produced from her bag a bottle of Vaseline Intensive Care.

*

12 October 1989

Dear Sir,

Allow me to respond to your article of 10 October entitled 'Beastly nature on public display', in which you applaud the exhibition of a 'human animal' in a cage at the Zoological Gardens.

This spectacle, well intentioned though it may be, does nothing but harm.

It upsets the true animals. On the night of our visit, we found the nocturnals sleeping, while the diurnals paced their enclosures in insomniac despair or tossed about on their pallets counting sheep.

It degrades the visitor. What message are we sending to our young people? That they are no better than apes? Whereas this 'human habitat' was equipped with all the modern conveniences, such as a refrigerator and a television set, there was no sign of a book. It might have been an idea to include some reading matter as part of the 'natural world'.

It augments the tide of exhibitionism, which is one of the evils of our day.

It damages race relations. Was it wise to choose a black man? Apart from the question of just what sort of man might be regarded as 'typical' of the species, this display provides easy ammunition for South Africa's extremist critics abroad.

Sincerely, etcetera

*

It was around this time that Mrs Mavrokordatos got the idea of staying open all night. A 24-hour service! You'd think we were the Restless Supermarket, I told her, or the Zoological Gardens. And I warned her of the consequences. Indigents will be coming in to find shelter, dozing off in our chairs and slobbering on the upholstery.

Eveready can go round waking them up, she said.

The new regimen threw everything out of kilter. Proper dining hours went by the board. In place of square meals such as breakfast and lunch came bastardized forms of dining, like the so-called brunch, which was neither fish nor fowl, and the buffet, named after the battering the well-mannered could expect to receive in the scrummage for unequal portions.

The menu was always out of date. I had long since acquired a taste for

Vienna schnitzel and Parma ham, but these old standards slipped from view. On any day of the week, the kitchen was liable to throw up an entirely new range of dishes, nouvelle cuisines that did not agree with me any more than I agreed with them. Savoury tarts, for instance, which the unsavoury ones demanded for the sake of their waistlines; only to change their minds the next day and insist on 'fatcakes' stuffed with mincemeat, and acidulous stews for macerating stiff porridges. Chicken reared its ugly head. 'Supply must meet demand,' Mrs Mavrokordatos said, and Mevrouw Bonsma assented.

To keep up my strength, I turned once again to the international restaurants of Hillbrow, combining these visits when I could with public-service proofreading. I remember crossing spoons with a waiter in a so-called Pizzaghetti Factory one evening. 'Pizzaghetti? Factory? It's the nadir of poor taste. And "farinaceous" is stretching a point. I would say "farraginous". From the Latin *far,* corn. Are you with me? You should serve this stuff in a nosebag.'

Milksop ran for the manager.

Never fear, I gave them both a talking-to about their macaronic menu, and especially the 'Quattro Stagione', which was nothing more than a 'Four Seasons' in plain English, the garden-variety winter, spring, summer and autumn. I wanted to know which of the seasons was represented by which of the ingredients. They didn't have a clue. *I* had to tell *them!*

'The way I see it, the ham is autumn leaves. The mushrooms, the dead wood of winter. The olives are the ripe fruits of summer. But why artichokes? Not nearly vernal enough. I would have had little budding capers. I've been tempted to cut a caper myself when spring comes. Never succumbed, mind you.'

Do you suppose they understood a word I said?

No more than Fräulein Schrenke, proprietress of the Potato Kitchen, when I pointed out that a conspicuous lack of ambience was ruining her business. 'You need to colour these bare walls with an artwork or two. Something to warm the place up a bit.'

'Like what?'

I did not usually have such information at my fingertips, but I had spent the morning in the library doing some research, and so I was able to flourish a shortlist. 'Perhaps the "Battle between Carnival and Lent" by Pieter Bruegel. Or Adriaan van Ostade's "A Room with Many Figures". Or even – the simplest ideas are often the best – "The Potato Eaters".'

'Hungarians?'

'Hollanders, I suppose.'

I put a photostatic reproduction of the work down on the counter. Made at my own expense. My pick of the three was the Van Ostade, but the Van Gogh also had something of Alibia in it. It might have been a wayside eatery on one of those Alibian country roads that bends away from the sea into the hinterland.

'Die Kartoffelesser. Where should I buy such a thing, Mr Tearle?'

'Who said anything about buying? You'll employ someone to make a copy for you, faithful in all the essentials. This wall here is crying out for a fresco.'

'I am not an associate of artists.'

'I know just the person. A fräulein like yourself, an art student, whom Mrs Mavrokordatos engaged to do some decorating at the Café Europa.'

Using nothing but brushes and tubes, this person, who was much given to paint-spattered dungarees, had transformed the windows of the cubicle containing the one-armed bandits into something resembling stained glass. On closer examination, her tableaux proved to be depictions of bloody carnage and mindless vandalism. They disgusted me at first, but in time I came to appreciate their efficacy. In the door to the 'chapel' – a door that shut itself with the aplomb of a commissionaire, thanks to a spring-loaded elbow – was a lozenge of glass that had escaped the artist's attentions. I could never look through that clear pane, at the men and women attached to the machines inside, the air around them aswirl with smoke, without being reminded of a gas chamber. Throw in Bogey and Zbignieuw and their ilk, and the effect was uncannily lifelike. It was better by far to gaze through the fake stained glass, to fit one's eye to a block of blue sky above a blazing cottage or to a patch of grass beside the bloodied smock of a ravaged peasant, and view the world through a glaze of unreality.

'I have the young lady's telephone number here in my notebook.'

But Fräulein Schrenke was blunt. 'It is a Fata Morgana,' she said. 'My business is going downstream. Black people are eating porridge more than potatoes. I cannot spend money on nonsenses.'

The Fräulein's assistant, a youngster with shell-shock and eczema, banged a polystyrene casket down on the counter. 'Need some tools?'

I gathered he meant a knife and fork.

I have always liked the Germans. I admire their discipline. Which made the collapse of order in their fatherland all the more shocking. I was passing a lot of time with Herr Toppelmann in those days. As I've mentioned, I was in the Wurstbude, eating a Bratwurst off my personalized crockery, when the Berlin Wall came tumbling down.

'It is well,' Herr Toppelmann said, 'now Europe is again one.' And he made a pretzel of index and middle fingers to demonstrate the union.

I supposed he was right. I was as glad as anyone to see the Iron Curtain fall. But hadn't the East always been a source of conflict and corruption in Europe? Wasn't there a crooked line between that infamous Bosnian Gavrilo Princip and the Slobodan Boguslavićes of the world? A line drawn in blood and therefore indelible. One hoped this German business didn't lead to a licentious collapsing of borders everywhere. There was never a shortage of volunteers to wield the sledgehammer. People were so delighted to see things fall down, to see the boundaries effaced and the monuments toppled, and to greet every fall with wild jubilation. In our own towns and cities, in every little Jericho on the veld, the mobs were on the march, exercising their God-given right to go in procession through the streets. When you scrutinized it properly, it was more like prancing. Lifting up their knees like a bunch of Mother Browns. 'Long leave! Long leave!' Nothing must continue, everything must change. Great gouts of change came sluicing out of the television set, to make up for the petty trickle from the one-armed bandits. Mevrouw Bonsma breathed deeply and played on, but she sank nonetheless beneath the polluted airwaves.

What did I think of all this? Herr Toppelmann wanted to know.

Frankly?

But of course.

Frankly, I found it struthious. That's s-t-r-u-t-h-i-o-u-s. Of or like an ostrich, of the ostrich tribe. From the Latin *struthio.* From the Greek *strouthos,* sparrow. Out of proportion, but there you are.

The dust had hardly settled in Germany before the rubble of the Berlin Wall was up for sale. One of Bogey's country cousins arrived with a piece of it in his luggage, a bit of brick and a layer of paint-smeared plaster. Muggins had paid fifteen marks for it, according to the cardboard container, which also had a picture purporting to show that the paint was a scrap of the garish babble with which the entire wall had been coated. The Western side, that is. It reminded me of the old scouting trick: you could always find your bearings by determining which side of the tree trunk had gathered moss.

Bogey was all for launching the product on the 'domestic market'. He had picked up the phrase at the Small Business Development Corporation (which he had begun to frequent almost as religiously as Benjamin Goldberg's), and he said he would find his 'capital' there too. When I pointed out that shipping rubble from Europe could prove costly, he said he wasn't that stupid. Half of Johannesburg was in ruins. He would scavenge his merchandise at the Civic Theatre.

Half a city (6): Berlin? Beirut? Joburg.

*

One day, as I was passing along Kotze Street, three palm trees hove in sight, proceeding sedately through the lunch-hour traffic. Nothing surprised me any more, and I strolled on for a closer look as if it were the most ordinary thing in the world. Each tree had a lorry to itself. They were imposing specimens, fully grown, their roots bound up in hessian like enormous potted ferns. I deduced that they were en route to the Civic Theatre, which was then being renovated; although the construction work was far from complete, the landscape gardeners were already at it, and

I had been monitoring their progress during my daily constitutionals. I followed the convoy to the construction site.

Today the place depressed me. This endless cycle of building and demolition, this ceaseless production of rubble. Was this the end of civilization? While the trees were being unloaded, I went to view the shattered masonry that Bogey had threatened to market. And it was then that I remembered the flagstones. Near the grand entrance, Johannesburg's Civic Theatre had boasted a little memorial terrace, modelled on the famous original outside Grauman's Chinese Theatre in Hollywood. Here, visiting stars of stage and screen and local celebrities alike had left impressions of their hands and feet (and other parts of the anatomy when these were famous) in squares of wet cement. Second-rate buffoons mostly, worthless even before they washed up on these shores, but with a few old troupers among them, like Danny Kaye and Sidney James. What had become of their memorials? The place where they should have been was covered with rubble and rusted scaffolding.

The junior official dozing in the prefabricated hut marked 'Site Manager' did not have the faintest idea what I was talking about, and left me to hunt about alone under boards and buttresses. After a while, a curious labourer approached. I was able to convey the object of my quest to him by pressing my palms into a bank of muddy earth and scratching my name on it with a nail. He kindly fetched me an ill-named 'hard hat' from somewhere, and with that bit of protection rattling against my skull, I was guided into the half-built interior of the theatre. In a corner smelling of wet cement, under a sheet of blue plastic, I rediscovered the missing evidence, stacked up in blocks. My guide heaved one of them into the light for me. It was Max Bygraves. A personal favourite. I put my hands into the impressions of his and, strangely enough, they were a perfect fit.

Perhaps our first language was a dialogue with the earth in prints of hoof and paw? It is always affecting when a part of one's own body becomes a measure of the world. The inch assumes its proper importance in the length of a thumb joint. The measures that matter most are not metres or yards, but hands and feet. Not to mention heads (thinking of my head and the hill).

Merle, who was rather well travelled, had been to Grauman's. Her most vivid recollection of the place, she once said, was that all the stars had the daintiest extremities imaginable. The stilettos had left behind breathless little exclamation marks, as if the earth was surprised to find such sublime beings abroad upon her surface. The tourists went about trying to force their walking shoes into the tracks left by their idols – but none of them fitted. Ugly sisters! Clodhoppers!

Just then a terrible racket started up outside. Glancing out through a ragged hole in the wall, I saw palm trees gesticulating on the horizon, and imagined for a bizarre moment that I had been transformed, with horrible injustice, into a tourist in America. But it was just our newly transplanted windbreak attracting attention. Vegetable décor, animate atmosphere. The workers were tamping down the earth around the boles with pneumatic hammers. Strips of instant lawn were piled up like rolled carpets, ready to be laid. In a week or two, the ill-informed would swear that the palms had grown to maturity on this very spot.

*

Into the crumbling order of the Café Europa, Spilkin introduced a lady friend. Darlene. I took her for one of the escorts, as they apparently preferred to be known, an increasingly brazen coterie of whores who drummed up custom under our roof. Even when she joined our table, I assumed that she was just another hanger-on and that Spilkin's interest in her, like my own, was sociological. But at the end of the evening, when I rose to leave, I suddenly noticed his hand on her thigh. It was a shock, believe me. Like spotting an error on the final proofs – a comma, say, where there should have been a full stop – just as the printer's devil stuffed them into his satchel. It gave me such a turn, I nearly regurgitated my dinner.

I had the good sense to keep my objections to the liaison, such as they were, to myself. Times were changing and one never knew what would happen next. But in the days to come, I made a point of appraising this Darlene with my old eye for detail: I marked the chipped nail polish, the bruised eyeshadow, the great buckles as trusty as a steeplejack's on the straps of her brassière, the bent pins holding together the frames of her sunglasses. None of it up to scratch. I didn't like her colour either. One isn't supposed to say so, but I'm past caring. Coffee finds favour in some quarters, but this was insipid. Less melanin in it than a cup of Milo. Great-grandfather on the mother's side came from Madras, I discovered later, and it showed in her features. A touch of the tarboosh, I said to Merle, but she wasn't amused.

Naturally, there was more to it than her colour. She was *coarse,* in a raw state, unrefined. She was one of those people who consider it amusing to sneak up behind you and clap their hands over your eyes – never mind the greasy fingerprints they leave all over your lenses – and you're supposed to guess who the culprit is. I would not play the game, even though I recognized her at once by her smell: sweat, perfume and cigarette smoke. Always an unsettling combination.

She was barely literate. She kept saying pri-horrity and cre-hative, negoti-hation and reconcili-hation. Some of it was almost Dickensian. 'I's allus paid on the werry last Vens'day arternoon of the munt,' she'd say, and you'd swear some gin-shop red-herring vendor was standing before you rather than a bank teller. She developed a passion for pasticchio nuts. She ordered expressos and blonk da blonks as if they were going out of fashion. And she never shut up for a minute.

I began to mine her, like all the others, for misuse. Considerately, when Spilkin wasn't around. But she would go and tell him, pleased as punch, that she was going to be *in my book.* He pretended to be proud of her, but that snout of his was out of joint.

Nevertheless, he chose to show me a 'love letter' she had written him on the back of a postcard from the Durban aquarium. Darling My, it began dyslectically. I had the foresight to reconstruct it for my notebook.

Darling My,

Having a wonderfull time here in Durbs. The family is all fine. But I can't stop thinking about you, Sweetie. Its just a natural phenomena. C U soon.

PS please pay the phone bill, I forgot!!!

Chow for now,
Your darling Darlene

The telephone account was included. An address in Bezuidenhout Valley. I returned the card and the account to their envelope, and Spilkin put it away in a folder. He had some other papers there, which he rummaged through, and for a moment I thought he was going to inflict his reply upon me too. I could just imagine: My fuliginous darling, my sooty beauty, my dirty sweep. But he thought better of it.

Her letter was the last straw. He found it charmingly innocent and endearing, but I was mortified. It was so tasteless. Not just the fact that she was taking advantage again, but the babyish hand, the tone, the excess of exclamation marks. It changed my opinion of Spilkin irrevocably. The forgivable weaknesses, the hairline cracks that had been there all along, suddenly yawned wide to swallow my good estimation of him. But I couldn't help thinking that her coarseness had rubbed off on him, that close association had roughened him up, and so I refused to give in.

I raised my concerns with him tactfully. Could he really afford the little wax-paper packets of nuts he was required to bring her every other day, as if she were a squirrel? Wasn't it possible that she was using him? Couldn't he see that they had different standards of behaviour, different systems of pronunciation, different grazing habits? (I never said a word about her colour.)

But none of it did any good. He was blind to her flaws, and my observations merely annoyed him. I knew from experience how an error that was glaringly obvious to everyone else could continue to evade the best of proofreaders. He would look past it again and again.

Spilkin and I ended up shouting at one another more than once, thanks to her sheer stupidity. Memorably when she tore half my crossword out of the newspaper on the back of a recipe for pickled fish. It reminded me, ironically, of something Spilkin used to say when we still saw eye to eye: 'There was always a crossword between us, Tearle, but never a cross word.'

Spilkin across and Darlene down. Darlene across and Spilkin down? I still haven't found the words.

*

Our Eveready was a waiter of the old school, trained in the beachfront hotels of Durban by a Hindu master. In his spare time, he had a church of his own, with headquarters at his kraal in Zululand, and he was the archbishop. He did not like bacon, although he would serve it up grudgingly. But he resolutely refused to tender alcohol. It was against the commandments of his church, which he himself had brought down from the top of a mine-dump on the East Rand. Seeing that the sale of alcoholic beverages made up a growing proportion of the Café's earnings, it was not long before Eveready's conscientious abstention proved inconvenient to Mrs Mavrokordatos.

Then there was a raid by the Hillbrow police, all the bottles on the premises were confiscated, and Eveready abruptly left Mrs Mavrokordatos's employ. She said he had taken early retirement. But Wessels, who witnessed the sorry scene, said the poor fellow had been dismissed, protesting his innocence to the last, on suspicion of having tipped off the police about our proprietress's liquor sales. After that, some of the policemen who had conducted the raid would pop in occasionally, and chat with Mrs Mavrokordatos in a corner, or drop a few coins in the fruit machines. Wessels recognized some of them from his days on the force, but did not let on because they were working undercover. Quote unquote.

Eveready's replacement was a native of Soweto. Name of Vest. Waistcoat, I dubbed him. He had none of his predecessor's antipathy to alcohol. The more people drank, he told me, the more likely they were to make mistakes with their money or drop their change. He was a bad apple all right. Standards of service went into immediate decline. The waiters were always searching under the tables for some drunkard's pennies – when they weren't watching television, that is.

The standards plumbed new depths (long since superseded) on the day Nelson 'The Madiba' Mandela was released from prison. You couldn't get a pot of tea for love or money, because the waiters would not be dragged away from the screen. The kitchen staff, including several we had never seen before, trooped through in their aprons and shower-caps, and created quite a carnival atmosphere. The whole business went on for hours; it must have been four o'clock before he finally showed his face, and I had a feeling they'd been delaying deliberately, playing to the gallery. Now you see him, now you don't. Some of the resident courtesans had been lifting their elbows all day, and when they finally clapped eyes on him, they began to weep, from sheer relief. Darlene, too. You never heard such a racket. Ululation and whatnot. Everyone wanted to get in on the act. Then they all stood to attention, waiters, cooks, bottle-washers, baggages, with their curled-up fists in the air, and sang the plaintive gobbledygook of their anthem. Vest had his pen in his fist and his order book under his arm. You could have waited till doomsday without attracting a waiter's attention. In the end, Mrs Mavrokordatos had to fetch me a pot of tea herself, like a common serving girl. By which time I needed something stronger to steady my nerves.

*

First impressions? I was pleased to see that The Madiba was just another old party with spectacles, like myself, although he had rather more hair than was seemly. That aside, he was straight as a ruler, smart as a pin, not unreasonably black. The prison authorities had given him a finely tailored suit to step out in – but they might have spent the money more profitably on an eye test. **D**ip **e**ach **f**rog, **p**our **o**ver **t**he **e**gg **c**ustard, and so on. He could hardly see with the spectacles he had, even after his wife had huffed on the lenses as if she meant to make a meal of them. They kept sliding down on his nose when he tried to read his speech.

'Needs a new prescription,' Spilkin said. 'Myopic.'

I wrote a letter about it afterwards to the *Star,* starting with the etymology: from the Greek *muops (muo* shut + *ops* eye). Shut-eye. Then a little joke about needing forty winks. Presented my credentials as something of an expert on eyewear. Thought of giving Spilkin a nod, decided against. Didn't deserve it. Took the opportunity to comment on the lack of vision displayed by Mr Etcetera during his first speech to the masses. Behind my jocular tone was a serious point. The Madiba had been out of circulation, so to speak, for nearly thirty years. He could scarcely have a clear-sighted view of world affairs. How much more important, then, that further obstacles not be put in his way. Surely people realized that the lack of appropriate lenses might lead to serious errors of judgement; a single word misread – 'suspicious' for 'auspicious', say, or 'congenital' for 'congenial', or 'treasonable' for 'reasonable' – might plunge the country into crisis. As it was, there were several elementary grammatical errors in the speech (which I was pleased to correct for the benefit of the newspaper's readers).

My letter came back unread: I could tell by the crispness of the folds in the paper that it had not received due consideration. That short-sighted letters editor had decided criticism was premature. It was the first sign that people like us would no longer have a say.

Why were standards falling fastest in those areas where examples should be set – in the public service, in the press, in broadcasting? It was thanks to shoddy pronunciation that I misapprehended The Madiba's name. Spilkin had to set me right: not Conrad Mandela, but *Comrade*. And then he went and told the story to everyone who would listen. Darlene, who would have been well-advised to keep her trap shut, said it was amazing how the very people who thought they knew everything about the world knew nothing about their own country. 'You whites,' she said, and it struck me as odd, with Spilkin sitting there as large as life.

*

The most beautiful and mysterious of all the proofreader's charms is the delete mark: ℘.

Its origins are obscure. Debra Nitsch traces it back to the scribes and clerks, which is not inconceivable. But she is surely being whimsical when she sees in the mark the little gilded halo, complete with handle, found in engravings of medieval morality plays. And her story about the snuffer is pure conjecture.

Fleischer and Toyk are marginally better. Mervyn Toyk, as befits a son of the South-West, puts his money on the lasso. Helmut Fleischer sees half a percentage sign, and comments drily that it always summons up a missing something – 'or rather a missing nothing'.

I myself plump for nothing, plain and simple. Make it nothing, the mark insists. Plunge it in this white hole, where it will vanish for ever. Paint it the colour of this little swatch: paper-white on paper-white. Through this soap-bubble loop, this circus-lion hoop, this insatiable and unshuttable maw, an endless quantity of bad copy has passed and been voided. Spoilt material, repetitious and dull verbiage, misplaced stops, misspellings, solecisms, anacolutha. Throw them in, sear them, make them hop. Keep our country beautiful. Imagine, if you can, the mountain of delenda purged from the galleys of the world. Who would build on such a landfill?

*

Our accompanist fell silent. For three days, the piano stood in the corner as if Mevrouw Bonsma, bless her, had been packed away inside it on a bed of dry ice and crumpled sheet music. Then the removal men, not the brawny louts one would have preferred, but a cadaverous gang of body snatchers, came and carried it away. Urchins brandishing ceremonial bottles of glue made a guard of honour at the bottom of the escalator, but the piano would not fit through the front door. It went instead through the kitchen, like a deep-freeze, and out of the service entrance into the alley at the back of Meissner's Building.

Once Spilkin went looking for Mevrouw Bonsma to invite her for tea. But our humble servant, whom she remained, sent word that she could not face the Café 'in her private capacity'. He came back in a mood and would not speak to me for a week, as if the absence of harmony were my fault.

Without the tacking thread of her melodies, things felt disconnected and out of sorts. The television did not help. In place of Mevrouw Bonsma, we had music video films. The Balaam Box again: scraps from the cutting-room floor strung together in no discernible order. It was enough to make your hair curl. As it was, the so-called artists had the daftest hairdos. I recall one in particular, as bald as a stone except for a little pile of greasy brown curls like a dog's dropping on the crown of his head. Claimed to be a doctor – a dentist, Darlene said – but a veterinarian was more likely.

My fear had been that my nerves were dying back, like the branches of an old tree in winter. I had flattered myself that I was the pachydermatous one, Fowler be damned. But perhaps it was the very opposite. Was my skin not too thin, parched to a wash of lime-white over my bones, with the nerve-endings jangling in the noisy air, raw as the root hairs of an uptorn plant? Was the skin of the world not thickening, growing hard with calluses? Even Spilkin, with Darlene at his knee, clapping her hands delightedly every time they solved one of the straight clues on the two-speed puzzle, had grown deaf to the bedlam around him.

*

The new order? The new *disorder* is more like it. Mrs Mavrokordatos was right: television was educational. It taught the geography of conflict. In time, every lost soul with a goggle-box would know the way to Bosnia and Baghdad.

And it taught the grammar of neglect. These were ungrammatical years. Could no one speak English properly any more? And would the solecists be the very ones who insisted on speaking the most? Suddenly everybody was talking to everybody else. Talks about talks. About talks about talks. And so unidiomatically on. I had the impression that no one understood a word anyone else said. I stopped watching. Lip-reading would no longer suffice. After Spilkin left, there was no one to see to my eyes. And, of course, his charts were always custom-made. I tried the eye clinic at the hospital once, but I had the chart down pat.

The circle unravelled. Some invisible hand had found a loose thread, and tugged at it constantly. I kept a list of departures and destinations in my notebook, or I'm sure I should have lost track. I might have made this list available to Empty Wessels when he started planning the Goodbye Bash. But why should I stir that pot of mischief? Even the latecomers drifted off eventually, and I added them to the bottom of the list – until the exercise began to bore me. In the end, I was left with the Slob and Wessels. And then the Slob slouched away too – going home, he said, to fight in the war of independence, which I didn't believe for a second – and one fine morning, it was just Wessels and me. Hopefully, I put his name on the list, but he refused to go.

It became a labour of Hercules to sustain my interest in 'The Proofreader's Derby'. Not from a lack of material, of which there was a superabundance, but from a fatalistic certainty that it would do no good. Nonetheless, I persevered. Wessels was always taunting me that I would never finish it; and after a while, the urge to frustrate this ill-natured prediction was practically all that kept me going.

From time to time, I managed a letter to the press. There was a particularly fine one on the absence of rubbish bins in the conurbation – the poor were stealing them, I'd heard, for brewing beer and doing the laundry. I won't give the letter here, but it made an excellent companion piece to one from years before on the same subject – only then, the absence of bins had been put down to the war against terrorism. There was also a broadside on standard pronunciation, which I fired off the day after we finally saw the back of Darlene (with Spilkin in tow). Showed considerable sensitivity on my part, I thought – the very quality that Merle, of all people, declared I lacked. A Parthian shot over her cardiganed shoulder.

'Where are you off to?' I asked Spilkin.

'We'll be aestivating at the coast, in some ravaged urban area or other.'

Smart Alec. It took me a week to figure it out. I left it off my list of destinations on purpose and sent a spineless question mark traipsing after him.

*

'You never told us you had a daughter! Or have you been hiding a young wife away from us all these years?' There was a picture of this 'relative' of mine in the sports section, Wessels said. Tilde Tearle. A very athletic young woman, a marathon runner, who always found the energy to smile as she crossed the finishing line in yet another test of endurance.

How had she come by such a beautiful name? I wondered. Perhaps her mother was Spanish.

When I made enquiries, she turned out to be a Tilda. Short for Matilda, I presume, and nothing diacritical about it. I might have known it was too good to be true.

*

The theme of Merle's valedictory address was *fault-finding*. 'You're always picking nits, Tearle,' she said. She had never called me 'Tearle' before and I was touched, but she spoilt it by adding, 'You're like a dog with a bone, worrying and gnawing, trying to find the weak spot in everything you get your teeth into.'

'It's my training.'

'But it upsets people so.'

'An occupational hazard.'

'You'll do what you have to do.' (As if she was talking to an old dog about new tricks.) 'But I can't help thinking you're a bit of a round peg in a square hole here. You don't fit in. You should go somewhere else, somewhere you belong. What's the point of rattling about?' (I puzzled over that *round* peg afterwards. Was it a slip of the tongue? Or did she mean that I was out of shape?) 'If you really must stay to the bitter end, at least you could try not to make the people around you unhappy. Find a little compassion in that hard heart of yours.' (Hard. Bitter. Dry. Variations on a theme.) 'Look on the bright side. Open up. Try talking to people properly, instead of playing these silly games.'

What, I might have asked, had become of the much-vaunted idea of fun? And if she was such an optimist, why was she abandoning ship? I'd have given long odds it was the dirt on the streets, the noise, the creeping decay. And I shouldn't be surprised if she found the liaison between Spilkin and Darlene distasteful too. But I wasn't going to pry.

She gave me her telephone number and said I should 'call'. Yoo-hoo.

Not blinking likely. I did try to give her a peck on the cheek and dealt her instead a nasty blow on the nose with the frame of my spectacles.

She became tearful. I remember she opened her bag, which smelt of Zoo biscuits and Gee's Linctus, and found a handkerchief. While she dabbed at her eyes, I considered the monogram. DG. That would be the late lamented Douglas. He seemed fascinating to me all of a sudden. I should have liked to know more about him. Did he have a moustache? Was he a golfer? What did he do for a living? But I could not pursue this line of questioning because Il Puce was panting foully in my face. She had been carried in especially to make her farewells.

'Say goodbye to Benny.'

I had to shake the dogsbody by the paw.

'Keep in touch!'

And that was that.

With Merle gone, I should have been able to concentrate on my work. I'd always enjoyed her company too much (I don't mind saying that I'd grown fond of her), and I welcomed the opportunity to find my own way again. But I had lost interest in 'The Proofreader's Derby', the circumstances just weren't conducive, I was listing on the tide of change, going under, and it was all I could do to send off the occasional letter to the editor, desperate notes that smelt tipsy from having been shut up in the sticky gourd of Wessels's company, and got short shrift.

Some time after Merle left, I came across Withering in the paper, I mean William, the botanist, the one who worked on the foxglove, and I had a mind to write to her about it. I looked up her address in the Book. Imagine my chagrin to find it listed as Slvmnte. I thought she'd gone to roost with the bad eggs of Illovo. But Slvmnte? Where the dckns was that?

My eye roved over the next page or two: Lnehll. Hlfwy Hse. Where Wessels was thinking of retiring to. Qllrna. Sdrrd. Vgnvw. Properly Veganview. Overlooking the fruit and vegetable market, I'll warrant.

Where were the vowels? Was this what the drudges meant by 'vowelence'? The city had been shot full of holes. It was turning into the sort of place a Boguslavić would feel at home in.

*

The story remains to be told of the losing battle Erasmus and I fought to keep the Book free of abbreviations. Bones with the marrow sucked out of them. 'Leave out an "a" here and an "e" there,' Erasmus warned the bigwigs at Posts and Telecommunications, 'and you'll be leaving out half the alphabet in the end.' And he was right. Someone should find out the meaning of Brnnda and Rwltch, Slvmnte and Wst Prgs, and publish a list for use in emergencies.

*

Mrs Mavrokordatos, our oracle, told me to be happy in my misery and apologized about the *Star*. Subscription cancelled.

The next morning, there was a sign on the door: Under New Management.

'They should hang one of those on the Houses of Parliament,' I told Wessels.

That unstable epoch. Every day brought a new departure, and every other day a new arrival. There was so much coming and going, one could not always tell them apart.

The New Management called itself Anthony. A manager? That dog in a manger (7)? Before you could whistle, he'd taken out the porcelain urinals and installed industrial troughs made of stainless steel, more fit for hospital laundries and army messes than a café. You'd think he was expecting a corrosive new strain of urine. Handfuls of solid disinfectant were always disintegrating in these troughs, and I made it my business, when I answered the call of nature, to shift the pellets aside hydraulically so that they would not clog the drainage pipes. He wanted to rename the cloakrooms, he already had the little signs – *Amadoda* and *Abafazi* – but I wouldn't stand for it. 'How on earth will people know which is which?' I said. 'We'll be Ladies and Gentlemen here, thank you very much, so long as even one decent person remains among us.'

God forbid a stone should be left unturned. The New Management embarked upon its alterations, knocking down walls and blinding windows. I had the devil's own job saving Alibia. He would have sloshed some

Portuguese colour scheme all over it. Our beautiful brocade ended up in the alley, and then on the backs of the Queen of Sheba and her entourage. I arrived one morning to find the door bolted against me: Closed for renovations. That'll be the day! I banged until he let me in. Place was frightfully full of brick dust, but I took up my post regardless.

In the new room through the archway, workmen were running wiring through plastic conduits and smoothing plaster with trowels. Wessels said that the New Management was putting in a [Candido] Jacuzzi, place was becoming a fully-fledged bordello, but I could see by the light fittings what was in store. Our numbered days flew apart, rushed to the four corners of a flat world, disappeared down holes.

'Snooker, origins unknown,' I told the New Management, 'although one might speculate. In my day, snooker saloons were not frequented by gentlemen, who preferred billiards, from the French *billette,* diminutive of *bille,* a tree trunk. But I grant that a certain old-world charm has attached itself to the pastime over the years, what with bowties and embroidered waistcoats. And one does need an eye. In short, I'm prepared to put up with snooker tables.'

'Not snooker, man, pool.'

'Pool! That's a different ball game altogether. Snooker by numbers. They trick the balls up with digits, for those who are incapable of remembering the value of a colour. That will attract the wrong crowd.'

Which it did. A sort of gang. The doors had hardly opened on the re-fashioned Café Europa when Errol and Co 'rolled up' and 'parked off', as if they were motor vehicles.

The first thing I noticed about them was their footwear. The boys were shod in tennis shoes with treads like tractors and oversized sandals with soles like the pontoons on a seaplane. The girls, on the other hand, went in for military surplus.

'Bovver boots,' Wessels said, when I drew his attention to them.

'Bother.' He also says Smiff. He had a friend of that name in the force, another *lid,* a Captain Keef Smiff.

'Bovver,' he insisted. 'That's what they calls them.'

The man's ineducable. You'd think he was one of the lost generation the television's always rabbiting on about.

The other thing one could not fail to notice about Errol and Co was that they were daubed all over with writing: slogans, labels, tattoos. I had made allowances for Bogey's declamatory clothing because he came from a deprived society, where opportunities for expressing oneself were few and far between. But what excuse could one make for this lot?

I'd been keeping a list of such things for decades, and trying to search out trends – the names of American colleges, the faces of popular stars, obscene humour – but the practice had become so anarchic, it defied understanding. Most of the slogans were nonsensical. Blue! for example, on a yellow shirt. Aqua. Factory. Sweat. Big shirts with 'Big Shirt' printed across them in 72 point Garamond. Baseball caps with 'Boy' written on them. Africans do not like being referred to as 'Boy', and so I supposed this to be a provocative gesture. But when the girls wore the caps, I wasn't sure what to think. Is Raylene one of these newfangled 'gender-blenders'?

They tried to push me around in the beginning, but I stood up to them. I was never afraid of bullies, as Erasmus at Posts and Telecommunications could testify. I could always get the better of them with words: their nursery language didn't stand a chance.

'I'll evaginate you, you over-inflated little windsock,' I remember saying to Errol the day he tried to occupy table No. 2, whose little perspex signboard now seemed to state, with obvious pathos, that it was a table for two: Wessels and me.

'He chaffs you a cunt,' Mbongeni said. This one's claim to fame was the enormous knitted tea cosy he wore upon his head in place of a cap. Stuffed full of hair, unshorn for decades. A religious observance.

'No man, he said you a "windgat".'

'You twit. You've got less gorm than a block of wood.'

Sheepish laughter. My barbs had struck mutton under their woolly hides. And they respected me for it.

'He's insulting you,' said the girl called Nomsa.

'I'll add injury to insult in a minute. If I were ten years younger, or twenty for that matter, I'd give you an astragalus sandwich.'

'I don't smark aspragalus,' said Errol.

'Ag, loss the old tawpy. He doesn't know what goes for what.'

And they shambled away to the pool table.

Erasmus, who has been in my thoughts lately, had a conceit about snooker, which influenced my own understanding of the game. The white ball, he said, did all the thinking. It was always pushing the other balls around, especially the red ones, which were not worth much, and making them do things they would not otherwise have done. Yet the most important ball on the table was the black one, which just sat there all day, waiting to get potted.

I would have shared this with Errol and Co, but it was too grandiose an analogy for pool. I elaborated another instead; it is possible to play the perfect game of pool, to 'clear the table', as they say, but it is seldom done because two things get in the way: chance and human error. And it is just the same with proofreading. I never got round to sharing this idea with them either, I never really broke the ice. If I had, all the nastiness that followed might have been averted.

As for Wessels, he was always too busy watching the proceedings at the Convention for a Democratic South Africa to talk. It was all a bit above his fireplace, he said, but he liked to keep in touch with developments, to be part of history in the making. Giving himself airs.

'I hear they're thrashing out the future,' I told him. 'And I'm behind them all the way. They should not spare the rod.'

I could see them beating one another senseless with their olive branches.

'Just a sec, Aubs-ss. I'm watching this.'

Joseph Slovo dancing. A man of his age. And in the *Oxford,* too.

I have a high regard for furniture and its place in the scheme of things. But the negotiators, as the talkers were called, were obsessed with it. Specifically with the table. With the comings and goings around it – no one cared a fig for its shape – with coming to it, sitting around it, laying things upon it, leaving it in a huff. They had a thing about the chair too: occupying it, addressing it, rotating it. And then the window! I made a vow: if one more person opens a window of opportunity, I'll heave a brick through it.

The New Management, not to be outdone, started tinkering with the furnishings. Our décor declined relentlessly. Pictures of footballers were tacked to the walls. Oilskin tablecloths were flung over the chequerboards: half the chessmen had been stolen and no one played any more. The chairs were covered in a garish new material and a layer of plastic. Plastic upholstery. The New Management defended it on economic grounds, but it was indecent. I still recall the sucking sound the backs of Nomsa's thighs made on the plastic when she crossed and uncrossed her legs. It was like the smacking of lips. I was compelled to stare at her scarlet mouth, while the word 'labia' resounded in my head, with that 'b' smack in the middle of it, tight-lipped and pressing.

'This place won't last,' I said to myself. And to Wessels as well. And he parroted back at me, through that sticky beak, those fly-paper lips, where a word was always stuck, waving its feelers: 'This place won't last.'

When the news got out that the Café Europa was closing down, no one was less surprised than I.

*

One day, I overheard Floyd teaching Nomsa the mysteries of chess with the stragglers from that fighting army. 'This is a lighthouse,' he said, 'and it ducks both ways. And this is a horse and it's just a lightie.'

*

It was neither the black Christmas the trade unions had promised us, nor the white one of Bing Crosby's dreams. Our Christmas-tide was grey.

*

On Boxing Day, Wessels was quizzing me, in his sly way, about my plans for New Year's Eve. What would I be doing? he wanted to know. Dinner-dancing at the Ambassador? I would be at the Goodbye Bash, I replied warily, like everyone else. He corrected me: the Goodbye Bash wasn't on

Friday, which was the last day of the year, but the evening before. 'We all got better things to do on Old Year's. Hunky's got a gig at the Dev ...'

Was he trying to trick me? They'd said all along the Café was closing down at the end of the month. I could not have been mistaken. But the New Management confirmed it: the Bash was on Thursday. Friday night he would be tucking into a 'slap-up graze' at the Clay Oven.

To tell the truth, I was relieved. The rowdiness always reached a crescendo on New Year's Eve, when I would be more than pleased to stay indoors. On the other hand, I now had one day less in which to finish 'The Proofreader's Derby'.

*

The corrective surgery had not been entirely successful. Dumbo's ear was now facing in the right direction, but flying at half mast. He was looking a little down in the mouth, under that crooked trunk. While Wessels hobbled on into the shop, I paused on the pavement to commiserate.

I hadn't wanted to go shopping at all, never mind at the Jumbo Liquor Market. Rosie Woods might cause a scene. 'Let's walk over to Solomon Kramer's in Yeoville. They've got as fine an array of bottles as you could hope to find, to judge by the window display. Or take a bus out to Benjamin Goldberg's and see the attraction for ourselves ...'

But Wessels insisted. The booze for the Goodbye Bash had to come from the Jumbo. Something about the free ice. In Hebcoolers. Heb? From the Greek *hepta,* seven. Refrigeration seven days a week. Or short for Hebrew?

'The New Management's got plenty of alcohol anyway. Why should we buy more?'

'Bring your own booze. It was your idea.'

'Where from!'

'We'll just get a few special things. I'm sure Tone'll chip in with some mix.'

I peered over the curvature of the ear, trying to gauge the mood of Rosie. Just my luck: the Queen of Sheba, nodding unremarked in the shadows of the doorway to Hypermeat, roused herself at the sight of me and shuffled out into the sunlight. She had lost most of her clothing, and what remained was sackcloth and ashes. Head bound up in a citrus pocket. Grubby brassière. Hessian boots. My worst nightmare lurched into motion: she began groping at Dumbo's rear. Was it starting all over again? Would we be treated to the Queen's impression of Darryl darrylling? I could see her scrambling up on the invalid's back, overbalancing, grabbing for the tender ear. It might well have happened. But before she could get a leg over, Quim dashed out of the shop and began lashing her alliteratively with a quirt. New acquisition. Sent her packing to a decent distance.

I emerged from cover and hailed my rescuer. My idea was to clarify the matter of his origins – 'He also talks pork and cheese,' Wessels had said, 'probably a cousin of Moçes' – but he was in no mood for conversation. He marched back into the shop, and when Rosie raised her muscular button-punching arm like a boom to let him in, I slipped in too. Fired off an *'Obrigado'* just to shake her up a bit. What in God's name had she been spraying in her armpits? Doom?

Wessels was blundering around like a bull in a china shop. I could imagine him moseying along Kotze Street, waving his crutch at the throng as if he were trying to part the Red Sea, with your humble servant, A. Tearle, following in his wake, as laden down as a Bactrian camel.

He handed me the plastic basket and began sniffing out purchases with the end of his crutch. Mainstay. Klipdrift. Störtebeker Apfelschnaps. Little plastic sachets of whisky and gin. Count Pushkin. Lord Nelson. Coffin varnish. I thought he would want Paarl Perlé just to wound me, but instead it was Fifth Avenue Cold Duck.

'Champagne,' he said.

'In inverted commas.'

*

I was up all night, typing out the fair foul copy of 'The Proofreader's Derby'.

When I sat down to work, there spilled from one of the files an index card, on which I had written, all those years ago: National Proofreading

Champion. And in smaller letters: Floating Trophy presented by A. Tearle. The words I had meant to have engraved on the trophy. I propped the good intention against the glass of the window and it kept me going in the wee hours.

Somewhere near dawn, I was gazing through the window at the lights of the south spread out to the horizon, when I became aware of my reflection in the glass, my cheeks stubbled, my nose throbbing, my excrescences, occipital and cranial, pulsating, my hair crying out to be cut, rampant, quaquaversal, awry.

I laboured on. Then at last, as the sun cast its bloodshot eye over the penultimate day of the year, I was done. For the first time in years, I felt at peace with myself and the world.

The Proofreader's Derby _(CORRECTED)

PART TWO

For Merle Graaff

The power of attaching an interest to the most trifling or painful pursuits is one of the greatest happinesses of our nature.

– *William Hazlitt*

FLUXMAN WAS LYING AWAKE IN HIS BED, LEAFING THROUGH THE coming day's work in his mind, when water began to run beyond his window. It was not the patter of a garden sprinkler on a lawn or the spurt of a hose in a bucket, the usual suburban backdrop to his Saturday mornings. It was a river rushing in a gorge, breakers rolling against a shore. But it began as abruptly as if an enormous tap had been opened wide. He clenched his fists beneath the blankets and held his breath, listening, expecting the worst. He thought he heard people crying out, footsteps pounding on his stoep, the rasping of rushes against the hull of a wicker basket.

After a while, he stuck out his head and looked around. Everything in place. Slippers in alphabetical order on the carpet, papers drawn up in open file on the desk, curtains closed tight. Then his eyes widened to admit the watery play of light behind the brocade. He sat up in bed and tried to decipher this wash of colour and sound. Gingerly, he dipped a foot in the shallow pile of the carpet. Wall-to-wall had been known to hover, trembling over the abyss, long after the earth below had fallen away. Seemed solid enough. He stuffed his feet into the sheepskin slippers and went over to the window. He could sense the fluid pressure of water on the other side, and he paused, with his fingers brushing the edges of the two curtains where they met, afraid for the drowned world he might find beyond the glass. Then he took a deep breath and flung the curtains open.

My gardening days are over, he thought.

Where his front lawn had been – just last night, as he shut the window before bed, he'd reminded himself that it needed mowing – lay a vast reach of mud-brown water, fringed to the left by bulrushes and the right by palms, and dammed up in the distance ahead by a sheer cement quay topped by a metal railing. There were several small islands scattered around, mounds of foliage trimmed with beach sand. The scene was idyllic, if somewhat contrived, and oddly familiar. Fluxman was sure he had seen it before somewhere on his travels, but for the life of him, he could not say where. He scrutinized it carefully from front to back. The water was lapping at his house: beneath the window-sill, small waves spilled over onto the slasto paving of his stoep. In the shallows, his letter box stuck out above the surface, with the newspaper wedged in its throat; further out, the roof of the carport showed where his driveway had been. Beyond that, where the water deepened, the curved brackets of the street lights mimicked the necks of the wading birds he saw stilting among the rushes.

People appeared on the quay, rushing up and down, shouting noiselessly and pointing with agitated gestures into the water below. The object of their attention came into sight, floating out from behind an island: a young girl, bedraggled and half-drowned, clinging to a spar of wood and paddling weakly against the dirty current.

Fluxman had resolved long ago not to busy himself with the affairs of the world, especially not through sleight of hand – but this was an emergency, and he reached instinctively for his blue pencil.

Before he could wield it, however, there was a commotion in the rushes. A small head with a glazed eye peered over the horizon, as if an enormous seabird had poked its head out of its nest to look around, and floated closer, revealing the sleek curve of a neck, the ominous fork of a wishbone. Then the rushes yielded before the thrusting breast, and a duck-billed pedalboat came crashing through the greenery and surged into open water. Although it was shaped like a Muscovy, it reminded Fluxman of a letter from the Greek alphabet: a plump, inflatable delta.

There were two men in the boat, a middle-aged one in a straw hat and a younger one who might have been his son, both pedalling away furiously. Head held high, parting the waves with its fibreglass sternum, the duck made quickly for the girl. The watchers on the quay clustered at the railing, waving with their caps, urging the rescuers on. The waves in the wake unrolled like scrolls of beaten metal.

Now Fluxman remembered where he had seen all this before: it was the Wetland Ramble from the Zoological Gardens. He had wandered there once, with Ms Georgina Hole.

The duck bore down on the girl, then slewed to a halt and settled in the water. The younger man scrambled into the prow, where he might reach a helping hand down over an upswept wing. His companion, pedalling gently to hold the boat steady against the current, took up a canary-yellow camera and began to film the operation. A copybook rescue, Fluxman thought. He could imagine the gratitude in the girl's eyes. Would she weep as her saviour hauled her aboard, streaming fresh water and wreathed with hyacinth? Would she cling to him as if she would never let him go? Would she fall in love with him, would she make him fall in love with her, fulfilling their destiny in the happy ending? Or would she overdo it, playing to the camera and weeping on cue, making him lose sympathy with her?

The hand of the rescuer closed around the girl's wrist. A close-up was called for. Any cameraman worth his salt would capture it. Let his strong fingers slip on her goose-pimpled skin, let the grasp be almost broken, the girl be almost lost, before he drew her safely in ...

At that moment, the duck lurched forward in the water.

Here we go again, Fluxman said to himself. Will nothing ever run smoothly again? Can nothing go on steadily to its conclusion? Must it always be one crude disruption after another?

The man kneeling in the prow teetered. The one with the camera stuck resolutely to his task. The duck twitched again, as if it had flexed its wings to fly only to find them useless, and both men went tumbling. Then something immense bore up from below, ramming into the bird, tilting its tail feathers up into the air and driving its head below the water. A buckled undercarriage of rods and paddles churned the sky to froth. A mouth opened, the mouth of a hippopotamus, with weeds and splintered fibreglass between its teeth; the black rock of its back shuddered and sluiced water, sank again below the surface. A momentary calm. Then the rock rose irresistibly for a second time and threw the bird over on its side. The men fell into the water. The wounded duck subsided and began to circle around the compass point of its own broken neck, while the watchers clawed up the stones beneath their feet and hurled them over the edge to drive off the monster. Once the water had settled, the older of the two rescuers could be seen clinging to a broken wing, with the straw hat jammed down over his eyes. There was no sign of the other. The girl was gone as well.

The rush of water, the roaring that had woken Fluxman that morning, continued unabated. He scanned the surface, looking as much for the source of this sound as for signs of survivors. Just beyond the carport, a stream of bubbles was boiling to the surface. Burst mains. Was the water level rising?

What difference did it make? Let the catastrophe go on without him.

Tucking his pencil behind his ear, he turned away from the window and drew on his dressing-gown. He went from room to room in his house. Everything seemed to be in order. He scrutinized it all in passing, to make sure it stayed that way, as he worked his passage to the kitchen. Enough excitement for one day; he needed toast, and coffee, and quiet columns of print. He looked through the window into the backyard. That also seemed to be under control. A slight agitation in the swimming-pool water, perhaps, a sympathetic stirring, an excess of bubbles.

He switched on the kettle, and its hiss soon drowned out the faint cries skipping shorewards over the lake outside.

*

Breakfast had no bulk without the newspaper. Fluxman dusted the crumbs off his plate into the sink and ran the tap to wash them away. Suddenly, he remembered the long-handled net for skimming leaves from the pool, lying in its brackets against the garage wall. It might just reach the letter box. He fetched the net and carried it through the house.

The breath of the wetlands enveloped him as he opened the front door. The water had stopped running and the silence smelt sour. On the far shore, the capsized Muscovy had been grappled to the quay. A man in leather shorts and an alpine hat was preparing to abseil down.

Fluxman weighed the net in his hand and measured the gap with his eye.

He was still pondering his next step, when something stirred in the shallows and a body floated to the surface. For God's sake! Would it never end? A filthy swell as green as soup ran over the slasto and swirled around his feet. He recoiled, but could not bring himself to withdraw. The body was floating face down in the water. He snared it with the net and dragged it in, until it bumped against the stoep, rising and falling with the wrack. He took a grip on one of the body's rubber handles, felt the distasteful fret of it against his palm, waited for the swell to rise, and heaved it onto the slasto.

He was prepared for savaged flesh, for puncture holes and lacerations, but not for the chaos that met his practised eye, the jumble of sprockets and yellow vinyl and rubbery connective tissue, the ooze of blood and lubricating gels, the tangle of wiring beaded with solder. He rolled the bobber over, shuddering at the touch of gizzard flesh and bristles, the crab apple of the eye, the broken springs, the oily feathers, the webbed fingers, the shattered lenses, the sockets filled with ground glass and riverweeds. Beyond repair, he thought desperately. A cacophony of categories, a jumble of kinds, an elemental disorder, wanton and fatal. With the soggy end of his slipper, he thrust the body back into the water and watched it drift away. Beyond repair! Not once in all his long career had such an unholy perception entered his mind. His heart sank sickeningly and he willed it back into place with a cry. He felt peculiarly loose and disconnected. He gazed in alarm at the backs of his hands, at the palms and the wrists, at his arms, his chest, his thighs. Even as he was proofreading himself, he was walking back into the house, his knees and ankles buckling and squeaking like dislocated hinges. He shut the door behind him, stuffing newsprint into the crack beneath it, and walked again, leaving a trail of slimy footprints on the parquet – from the right foot only, like a one-legged man – to his study.

For an hour he sat at his desk, gazing at his papers without seeing them, turning things over in his mind. Several times he picked up the jar of buttons he used as a paperweight and absently stirred the contents with his forefinger. Then he took down the last official street guide to Alibia and opened it to Astra Vista, where he lived. He put his finger down on his neighbourhood. The error glared out at him. Where once there had been neat and orderly rows of houses just like his own, there was the Zoological Gardens. Or a chunk of it anyway. Gar … the map said. Gar. The rest seemed to have been left behind on the other side of the city. He paged to the place in the book where the Zoo was supposed to be, and found it occupied by several blocks of Astra Vista. His old neighbours the Armstrongs, from Number 93 across the way, had come off badly: in its new position, their front door opened onto the elephants' enclosure. What else had been carelessly left behind in the relocation? The penguin house, several rows of cages belonging to the smaller primates, aviaries. Parrots, parrots.

He should speak to Munnery. He picked up the telephone, but there was no dialling tone. Was he too late? Had Munnery finally been wiped off the map? He dared not think it. Through the window, he saw the telephone line from his roof slanting down into the water like an anchor chain. There was no time to lose; he had vacillated far too long as it was. He must go to Munnery at once. He fetched his rucksack from behind the bathroom door and began to pack: maps, spare pencils, sharpeners, the Phone Book, an apple or two, a packet of trail mix, a bag of pistachio nuts, a month's supply of notepads, a torch, a flask of fresh water, a loaf of rye bread. He donned khakis and boots.

When he was finished, he gave his house the once-over, swiftly and thoroughly, focusing so intensely, his head began to throb. Then he took his alpenstock from the stand at the door and went out into the disjointed city.

*

The golf course at the Royal Alibian Country Club had once been the pride of the sporting gentry, but there was not much left of it now: spite and neglect had scattered most of the links to the four corners of the city. On any outing, one was bound to stumble across a bit of it somewhere, and so Fluxman was hardly surprised when the service lane behind his house gave onto one of the more scenic sections of the front nine. Rather, he was delighted. He was not a sportsman himself (although he was often taken for one, with his youthful physique and fine head of hair), but he liked to walk, and in the old days, when the Alibian landscape was more set in its ways, he had always resented the hold the sports clubs had on the city's scenic parkland. The RACC had been the main culprit. It was one of the rare delights of the new disorder, he reasoned now, that he should find the property of the Royal, the long dog-leg fairway of the fourth, to be precise, seen and envied so often on the television during the Alibian Open, flung down here in his own backyard. It was pleasing for this reason too: another bit of the Royal, the celebrated eighteenth no less, had wound up at Munnery's place, which was his destination, and it would be an auspicious symmetry to begin and end his journey on the course.

He set off down the fairway with an unaccustomed spring in his step, swinging his alpenstock at the sprinkling of copper-bottomed pots and pans he espied in the rough. Up ahead, in the crook of the dog-leg, among the pale trunks of bluegum and beech, the sun glinted on sheet metal. The corner of an office block or a shanty town, he surmised. On the other side of the fairway, kudu cows stretched their necks between the palisades of an iron fence to reach the greener kikuyu and spicy dandelions, and dropped their steaming pats among the dewy kitchenware. A pastoral idyll. It was a long time since Fluxman had worked up a sweat. He gazed about him curiously and began to whistle. *I love to go a-wandering ...*

The grass beneath his feet, succulent and overgrown, the sky above, himself between, footloose and debonair ... it brought back the proofreading rambles of his youth. Then it had been his pleasure to go out into the world to find respite from the imperfections of the page, to rest the rods and cones. I spy with my little eye ... How things had changed. The world had become a perilous place, full of pitfalls and eyesores.

Valda-ree, valda-raa ...

At least Munnery, thanks to his stubborn nature and particular expertise, was in his proper place, where he had always been, in a chintzy little bungalow on a hill overlooking Alibia – although everything else in his vicinity, the efforts of the Society notwithstanding, had changed. Or rather, he had been there the last time anyone looked. Please God, Fluxman said to himself, let him be home. And he marched on, resignedly jaunty.

The walking stick had been a gift from the same Munnery. It had appeared on the breakfast table one morning a few months back, where the spoon was supposed to be, along with a catalogue for camping gear. He should have deleted it immediately, but there was a note attached, in the hand he knew so well: 'This small gift is a token of your colleagues' esteem. I implore you, do not turn your back on us. Alibia needs you.' Fluxman did not approve of such fakery. But he kept the stick. It was pointedly wrought in the shape of a pencil, and now the rubber knob and brass ferrule felt in his fist like a reminder of his civic responsibilities. This awareness lifted his spirits.

Valda-ree, valda-ra-ha-ha-ha-ha-ha …

A bandit crashed out of the undergrowth. A thickset man in a bottle-green suit, tattered at turn-up and cuff, muddied at elbow and knee, shoes scuffed to rawhide, belly wobbling between the ripped tails of his shirt. He burst from between the trees and bore down on Fluxman like some animate guy escaped from the bonfire, grass sticking out of his collar and cuffs, greasy hair standing on end. Close kin to the monstrous bobber from the lake. Fluxman fell back, brandishing the alpenstock like a club. To his surprise, the creature stumbled to a halt and raised its own hands in surrender. A bloody head, as featureless as a turnip, covered with purplish bruises and stiff bristles, raw feet, and open hands, panting for air. In one palm, an ear was turned to the wind, in another, a mouth opened and closed like an anemone, trying to form words. 'Police,' it said, 'police.'

Fluxman was skilled in the art of lip-reading and he understood perfectly, but he was in no mood to be manipulated. 'Lay a hand on me,' he cried, 'and I shan't be responsible for what I do to you.'

'Thanks for asking, can't complain.'

'What do you want? Come on, spit it out.'

'I'm the scum of the earth, master, but I've also got to live. I just need something to eat.' The mouth in the palm opened wide in anticipation.

'You disgusting thing!' Fluxman waggled the stick threateningly. 'Be gone, before I delete you.'

'Or a job, master. I can carry the master's bag.'

'If I required the services of a porter …' Even as he spoke, Fluxman felt the weight of the rucksack dragging at his shoulders. What had the rascal called him? Master.

'Some change, then?'

'I have nothing for you. Absolutely nothing.'

The sound of Fluxman's voice had given the creature new bearings, and it lunged forward with both hands conversing wildly. Fluxman leapt lithely aside. The creature might well have caught hold of him, but in its rush, it got one of its blistered feet jammed in a cooking pot hidden in the grass. Going in circles, hopping and skipping in an effort to wrench off the pot, it reeled away among the trees. 'Ciao for now!' it called out as it went. 'Pleased to meet you!'

Fluxman backed cautiously away, until he felt flagstones beneath his heels. Then he turned and ran, while the monster mumbled in the under-growth behind him, palms chawing and champing, ranting to itself. He was in an alley, rushing headlong through a jumble of angled shadows, and he let its twists and turns determine his course, breaking always towards the light, to where the darkness was less impenetrable, slashing with his stick when the gloom thickened. Broken things crunched underfoot, as if the madman's ravings had washed up here – chicken gristle and statu-ary, pieces of English, A-frames and I-beams, knick-knacks for the bar and doodads for the gym, dining-room suites, instant dinners, poems. A broken gramophone fell with a crash. Then the shadows were greyer, and the clutter thinner, and there was light ahead. A rectangle of sunshine traversed by people and cars.

Fluxman paused on the brink of the mundane to gather himself. He scraped the wreckage off the soles of his boots, mopped the sweat from his face and caught his breath. Then he walked to the mouth of the alley, where it gave onto the avenue, and glanced casually about as if he had just stepped out of his own front door. A broad boulevard with plane trees and pavement cafés, gleaming shopfronts full of mohair jerseys, potted meats and cans of petits pois, lamp-posts in the shape of lighthouses, benches in bus shelters like scalloped band-shells. Everything was running along so smoothly, so perfectly punctuated by parking meters and kiosks, so elegantly phrased into blocks and squares and loading zones, so idiomatically proper, that tears started to his eyes. Could this really be the Avenue of the Revolution? He looked around for a street sign. Nothing. What was it doing in these quarters? Must be a recent arrival.

He drank it all in: the clean-swept gutters, the fashionable throngs, the polished sedans. Everything seemed to be in order. Normal, well-proportioned faces met his gaze, eyes the recommended distance apart, brows smooth, noses straight, lips finely moulded, ears in pairs, perfect for supporting spectacles. Although he was not dressed for decent society, Fluxman tucked the stick under his arm, and falling in with the strollers, allowed himself to be carried along, breathing in the wholesome fragrances of baked goods and scrubbed bodies, recovering his composure.

In these troubled times, there was no activity more fraught with danger than wandering aimlessly in the streets. Something was certain to happen, and aimlessness only made it more likely that it would be unpleasant. Mindful of this fact, Fluxman sat down at a table under the canopy at Al Fresco's. A waiter came.

'Espresso, please. Make it a double.'

It was so long since he had sat at a café, and it felt so comfortingly familiar, that he was reminded at once of his old colleagues and the meetings of the Society. Displays of sentiment always made him uncomfortable, but a lump came to his throat as he looked about him and remembered the Alibia of yesteryear. A corn-roaster on the street corner stoked her charcoal brazier and a cloud of bitter-sweet smoke blew over him.

*

The Proofreaders' Society of Alibia was as old as the city itself. In every age, the Members of the Society had gone quietly about their business, maintaining order without making a fuss. This modest dedication found expression in the items displayed upon their escutcheon: a blue pencil, a dancing-master's shoe, a cobbler's nail (the emblem of St Cloud) and the freckled bloom of the tiger lily.

In former times, the Society had conducted its affairs in secret and jealously guarded the identities of its Members. But over the years, as the principles and practices of government changed, it came to exist more openly in the public eye. The modern Members no longer found it necessary to employ pen-names and passwords, and willingly submitted themselves to scrutiny, in accordance with contemporary requirements. Nevertheless, they wished to maintain the proper proofreaderly reserve. To kill both birds with one stone, they made a custom of holding their formal meetings at a private table in a public venue. In the years when Fluxman was Master, these gatherings took place bimonthly in a cubicle at the Café Europa. Though their purpose was to enable the Members to clarify questions of craft, they served equally to cement the bonds of friendship.

This was the era of Munnery and Wiederkehr, of Levitas and Banes, sharp-eyed and open-hearted men, and a meeting seldom failed to instruct or inspire. Someone might have struck an insoluble problem in the course of his work, a grammatical tangle that could not be undone, or a usage that had evaded the reference books. Someone else might have come across a peculiarity of spelling or spacing, or a rare typographical error. Banes, who loved legal documents, sometimes brought a questionable interpretation for discussion, a judgement that hinged on a misplaced comma or an ill-timed hyphen. Figg, the Treasurer, always looking for a penny to pinch, would demonstrate new techniques for extending the life of a pencil stub or a pink eraser. In the late hours, when the official business had been dealt with soberly, small glasses of sherry, and the thought that ordinary citizens were sleeping easily because good order was in the hands of responsible men, sweetened the camaraderie that bound them all to the professional cause.

Then signs of unrest appeared in Alibia. And no one saw them sooner or felt them more keenly than Fluxman. It began with an outbreak of error in the telephone directory, which was the great love and labour of his life. It was an unprecedented plague, not just in the frequency of the error, but in its nature. Strange animals started creeping into his proofs, species of error he had never seen before – letters turned inside out, flares of coloured print in the gutters, numbers joined at the head or hip. Some batches of galleys contained errors so odd they seemed to belong to another civilization. He did everything in his power to contain the outbreak; but there were inexplicable relapses on the page proofs too, as errors sprouted afresh where they had already been weeded out. Nothing could have been more distressing to a proofreader. Yet Fluxman did not discuss the problem with his colleagues. He waited impatiently for their regular meetings and the opportunity to unburden himself; but when he arrived at the Café Europa, the sight of their familiar frowns always discouraged him. The plague would subside on its own, he decided, and kept his concern to himself.

*

In these same years, the printer's devil at the Alibian *Star* was a young McCaffery. Every afternoon, it was his duty to carry the galley proofs of that day's edition from the printing works to the council chambers, where an official appointed by the City Fathers would read and approve them. The scooter ride across town was a welcome break in the gloomy routine of the boy's day, and he made the most of it, pursuing roundabout ways to prolong his pleasure, and then taking reckless short cuts to make up for lost time. More than one person, forced to leap from his path as he raced through a yard or down a staircase, predicted that he would come to an unhappy end, which he did.

On an autumn afternoon, in a little-used alley behind the football factory, he rode head first into a stone wall and was killed outright.

The next day, the *Star* carried a photograph of the dead boy sprawled in the wreckage of his scooter, with a babble of broken type from the wicker delivery basket scattered around, and the galleys washing over him like cheesecloth billows in a pantomime.

*

The spate of error in the Book did not abate. It grew steadily worse, until Fluxman knew that he could no longer keep it from the others. He convened a special meeting of the Society. He worried endlessly about how his statement would be received. Would they think that he had lost his senses? That it was some uncharacteristic prank for their amusement? Anticipating laughter or derision, he prepared a carefully worded speech and, when they had gathered in their cubicle at the Europa, he rose to deliver it, although such formalities were usually waived. His apprehensions proved groundless. He had scarcely begun to describe his campaign against phantom addresses and wayward dialling codes, when he was drowned out in a rumble of assent and relief.

'You haven't heard the half of it,' said Figg. 'I didn't want to complain, but I've been spending every spare minute at the Babcock, and I'm barely one step ahead of a total collapse.'

'Same here,' said Banes. 'I haven't had a weekend off in months.'

They all began to speak at once. Without exception, they had noticed alarming changes in the records under their command; and each of them, with the modesty native to the profession, had kept it to himself and set about restoring order in his own way.

Everywhere the trends were the same: not just rashes of missing spaces or jutting hyphens or simple transpositions, but massive disturbances and transformations that seemed somehow wilful, that actually resisted correction. Figg had spent so many of his lunch hours in the stacks at the library reordering alphabetically, re-sorting by category, invoking Dewey, that he'd lost ten pounds. Sure that someone must be sabotaging the catalogues, he'd lain in wait for them three nights running, armed with nothing but a pencil. Unbeknown to him, Munnery was also awake in the early hours. He'd burnt a barrel of midnight oil, drafting and redrafting the maps of the city centre, reattaching the numbers of the houses to the proper doors and gates, reorienting the points of the compass. On the other side of town, Levitas had been slashing and spearing until his arm went to sleep.

What were they to do? There was no simple answer. Figg was for alerting the City Fathers at once. The problem was too big for the Society, he said. It threatened good governance and the survival of Alibia itself. Fluxman argued against him. Such faint-heartedness was unheard-of in their long history. In any event, it was not their way to make a public hullabaloo, to be thrusting themselves into the limelight. They should sustain their efforts behind the scenes. When the City Fathers required their help, they would know where to turn.

Secretly, the problem had shrunk in Fluxman's own mind; now that the weight of it had been shared, it no longer seemed so daunting. There was something cheering too in the prospect of a request for help from the City Fathers. The Society was no longer shown the respect it had enjoyed in the days of secrecy and subterfuge. A public acknowledgment of their importance would be a good thing.

The majority went with the Master.

Then Levitas had them charge their glasses, although it had not yet gone nine, and drink the health of the paperwork.

'To the Records!'

Later that evening, when some of the company had already begun to drift off, Munnery produced the photograph of poor McCaffery. It had touched him, the small body among the smashed alphabets, despite the irritation of the caption: 'Art of God delays early edition.' His colleagues shook their heads over that cruel blunder and lamented the boy's misfortune, but failed to see what it had to do with their own troubles.

*

An official in the Department of Public Works by the name of Toyk studied the same photograph with a dry eye and drew his own conclusions. What held his attention was not the dead boy, but the wall against which he had dashed out his brains; more specifically, the point where that fatal wall, which was made of a distinctive yellow stone, joined up with another more ordinary panel of red brick. As the official responsible for granting licences and approving plans, Toyk took a particular interest in the city wall, and especially in the preservation of those sections of it that had survived from antiquity. There was a building regulation expressly prohibiting the erection of any structure so that it abutted upon the wall. It was clear from the photograph that the law had been broken.

The following day found Toyk in the alley behind the football factory. He expected to do no more than serve notice upon some refractory citizen to demolish his illegal hen-house, or have the Department do it for him. But what he saw instead struck him dumb.

Toyk was a land surveyor by training. He went home at once and unpacked his instruments, scarcely touched since his graduation to matters of regulation. He bore theodolite and spirit level to the industrial zone, where it did not take him long to verify what McCaffery had already proved by example and he himself had inferred from observation: the football factory was on the move. It had drifted off its foundations and floated away to the south, coming to rest against the city wall and sealing off the alley behind. The distance was not great, but the effect was dramatic. Who could tell where the building would have ended up had there been nothing to block its course? Perhaps it would have fallen into the sea?

Quietly, to avoid causing panic among the people of Alibia, who valued stability above all things, Toyk made a cursory examination of the surrounding blocks. He discovered that several other buildings had wandered away from their official locations. First thing Monday, he decided, he would make a report to his superiors and seek permission to broaden his investigations.

*

The Members of the Society soldiered on, with the silence of the City Fathers ringing in their ears. They were all past exhaustion. But whereas some were ready to submit, others were determined to go on to the end, no matter the sacrifice. Factions arose. The meetings at the Café Europa, which had been called to discuss strategy, but which always ended in stalemate, grew more and more fractious. Voices were raised and threats levelled. Then one evening, pencils were pointed in anger for the first time in the Society's history, and the meeting broke up in disorder.

In the small hours of that bitter morning, Fluxman stood sleepless at the window of his penthouse, looking down on Alibia. Tutivillus Heights was the city's only skyscraper – in Alibia, the top of a six-storey block will brush the brow of heaven – and it made him feel immensely alert and far-seeing, and utterly detached from the earth. His eyes wandered from rooftop to rooftop, from street to street. He felt it. The building was swaying, a motion so gentle it would have escaped the notice of all but the most perceptive observer. It was not soothing at all; it filled him with foreboding. Then he recalled who he was and what he stood for. He erased his frowning misgivings from the glass before him with an eraser shaped like an egg, but they came back again and again.

*

Toyk's report was an eye-opener. There was movement everywhere, not just in the outlying industrial zones, but in the heart of Alibia. The signs pointed to massive geological instability. Nothing would stay put. Structures were shifting closer together or further apart, skylines were rising and falling, streets were narrowing, views were opening up, cracks were appearing.

Most puzzling, he reported, was the fact that some of these changes would later reverse themselves, just as mysteriously, as if a countervailing force were at work. One of his own juniors, a certain Bron, was on hand when two houses in Capitol Hill, the most sought-after of the hillside suburbs, having moved slowly but surely closer together for several weeks, suddenly sprang back to their original positions. The deviation, a matter of inches, had been perceptible only with measuring instruments, but the correction was so abrupt, it was visible even to an untrained eye.

A stitch in time saves nine. But it is the lot of ordinary people that they are seldom aware of the loose threads in the seams of their own lives. And a missing button, as they say in Alibia, leads to a lost coat. Months went by, and the citizens remained blind to the changes taking place around them. Then, at last, the observant ones began to notice the more violent reversals. Some of them, like the occupants of the houses in Capitol Hill, whose crockery had been rattled until it broke, put it down to earth tremors;

others were inclined to speculate. Before Toyk had time to complete his investigation, there were letters to the *Star* suggesting that such upsets were symptomatic of chronic instability in the body politic, claims the City Fathers always denied.

Behind the scenes, Toyk's report caused a furore. Even as they were pronouncing the whole region as safe as houses, the Fathers were issuing urgent instructions to Public Works to begin with repairs immediately. Soon the streets were filled with teams of men in orange overalls performing highly visible and ineffectual shoring-up operations – securing cables to walls, hammering posts into pavements, building retaining walls and dykes, digging trenches, sinking boreholes, grounding flying buttresses, pouring road metal into fissures.

These busy efforts had no effect. On any day of the week, in any close or wynd, one might see someone trip over a step where no step had been before, or pause to gaze anxiously into the black space that had opened up between a newly built wall and a newly grouted pavement. All it took was for the street signs to make one quarter of a turn, anticlockwise, and the city would be clogged with people who had lost their way.

*

Night after night, a shudder of restless fidgeting passed through the city. Everything that opened and shut was doing so, secretively and obsessively. Windows and doors, posts and rails, tongues and grooves, stocks and mitres were testing the bounds of their unions, engaging and disengaging, clasping and releasing, over and over, as if they meant to part company soon. Those who were awake to this experimental dissent shivered, and imagined that someone had walked over their graves.

*

The Proofreaders, persevering in wounded silence, were not spared the trials that befell ordinary Alibians. Figg was inserting some new arrivals into the Register of Births and Deaths one morning – it was supposed to be his day off, but he was slaving away as usual – when the threads that secured the bone-yellow buttons of his cuffs unravelled with a fizz, as if he had held a flame to them, and fell away. He gazed in consternation at the squiggles of black thread on his sleeves and the flakes of ash on the backs of his hands.

He turned his eye again to the page before him. 'Knowing you enriched our lives' Good Lord! There was something wrong with the paper. It seemed strangely pale, it was floating, curling up at the edges and drifting free of the desk. 'Safe in God's care' And then he saw what the problem was: there was not a single full stop left anywhere. He paged backwards and forwards. Nothing. The leaves levitated, the edges feathered into deckle. The whole stack fluttered and began to reshuffle itself, as Figg hastily rolled up his sleeves. Then he pinned the concertinaed sheaf to the desk with one hand and took up his blue pencil with the other. He worked with feverish concentration until night fell, buttoning down line after line … caret, caret, caret … until he could hardly see straight.

In the end, he looked at his fist, lying like a leaden paperweight on the stack, and at the crumbled end of his pencil. He licked the dent in his forefinger and flipped through the pages. Twenty or thirty of them, newly buttoned, lay neatly on the desk … the rest mounted obstinately upwards. He checked the clock: he had not risen for more than seven hours. To save a minute, he had gone so far – God help him! – as to pass water in the waste-paper basket. But it was no good. Even as he calculated the extent of his commitment, the corners of the page under his fist, the page he had just finished correcting, twitched and curled into dog-ears. Exhausted, he fell back in his chair and watched the papers rising slowly into the air, gathering under the ceiling like cumulus, blown this way and that in the breeze from the fan, scudding against the mouldy cornices, sinking down in the four corners of the room. Enough was enough. He reached for the telephone.

'This is the residence of Aubrey Fluxman,' the machine began. 'Should you wish to leave a message …'

*

Fluxman had also been working that morning, banging away at the typewriter, when the lenses of his spectacles began to vibrate. He knew at once that something catastrophic was afoot. He listened to the first breathless accounts of the unfolding drama on the radio while he tweezered a screw from among the hammers. Then he slipped into a serviceable tracksuit, with an elasticized waistband, and went out into the streets.

The fruits of that convulsive instant lay scattered everywhere. The riverside coffee bars and eateries stood empty. In the shadowy interior of the Hottentot, which he had frequented in his youth, a leather banquette coughed. He crept in to take samples, hooking red and brown buttons from their resting places with the end of his pencil. He ventured into the furniture factory as well, despite the warnings of the security guards, to see with his own eyes the dowelled dead in the basement, sprawled among scatter cushions as fat as puffer fish, looking for all the world as if they had merely lain down to rest. In the Gravy Boat, it was business as usual. Just hours before, the regular morning sprinkling of tea-sippers and French-knitters had rushed away in a panic when the armchairs inflated beneath them. But the proprietor was treating it all with the levity appropriate to a minor mishap. Half-price for standing room only, snacks on the house. Finding a pillar to lean against, Fluxman ate a Croque Monsieur and drank a beer, which he normally denied himself in the daylight hours. Later, he simply wandered through the unnaturally rounded afternoon, mourning every vanished quilt and pucker in the urban upholstery.

Although it was early, many businesses had closed their doors, and the streets were filling with people on their way home from work, clerks and secretaries stepping warily from the lobbies of office buildings, blinking into the light like people after a matinée at the cinema. The gondolas were packed with more than the usual quota of tourists and touts, the carriages of the funiculars were bursting. Everywhere he saw the same bewildered expressions, the same pursed lips, which might be suppressing laughter or tears, the same downcast eyes, as if people were hunting for fallen change in the cracks of the pavements. They hurried by or stood whispering furtively on street corners, avoiding one another's eyes, clutching handfuls of their own clothing. Fluxman moved among them, wide-eyed, gazing at bare flesh between yawning lapels, coats held together with paper clips, safety-pinned cuffs and stapled shirt-fronts. On a corner near the station, a businessman was plucking the rubber-banded toggles of his duffel coat, and Fluxman, stooping to gather more samples, listened to that elastic adagio as if he had never heard music before.

Arriving home in the early hours, he let his answering machine stammer out its messages. Please to call Figg. Enough is enough: a meeting of the Society is in order. Then the worried voice of Munnery: Figg suggests a meeting. What do you think? Then Levitas, who hated speaking on the telephone. Munnery had called him too, and Wiederkehr, and Banes. Then Figg again, sounding drunk. The whole Society was in an uproar.

*

It became clear at last to the most faithful Members of the Society, standing by with their bundles of pencils, that the call for help from the City Fathers would never come. It was a bitter pill, but it had to be swallowed.

An extraordinary meeting of the Society was convened at short notice on the night after the great unfastening. They gathered at the Café Europa as usual, and although some semblance of calm had returned to the city after the disturbances of the previous day, each had a story to tell about the hazards he had faced just making his way through the streets to their rendezvous.

Wiederkehr had almost plunged into a crevasse that had opened up in the cobbles at his feet as he crossed St Cloud's Square.

'It may have been an unguarded excavation,' Fluxman ventured to say. 'You know how the procurers are always stealing the red lanterns.'

'It was a dry dock,' Wiederkehr said tetchily. 'It gaped as suddenly as speaking. One moment there was solid earth beneath my bluchers, the next a black hole as big as ten swimming baths, with a catamaran lying in the deep end.'

'Well, if it makes you feel any better, I nearly broke my neck too,' said Munnery. 'Fell over a tombstone in the High Street. I transposed it at once with a mossy bench from the boneyard, but the damage had already been done.' He showed them the torn knees of his suit.

Fluxman noticed, as he examined his friend's frayed tweed, that his trousers were tied up with a length of typewriter ribbon, but he said nothing. Munnery had brought a bulging portfolio of maps with him, and while they spoke, he was readjusting the highways and byways with his blue pencil, and keeping an eye on the more irresponsible rezonings.

'If the Fathers will not come to us, we must go to them,' Fluxman said when it was his turn to speak. 'We must do our duty for Alibia.'

'About time,' said Figg. 'What shall we say?'

'The simple truth: stop putting the cart before the horse. Take care of the paperwork, and the world will take care of itself.'

'But who will believe it?' said Banes.

As if to support his point, the first municipal reupholstery squad burst in through the batwing doors, clutching lumpy pouches full of leather-covered buttons, and waving bodkins as long as pencils. They fell to with a vengeance. Most of the patrons fled. But the Members would not budge, on principle, and boldly continued with their meeting. For their pains, Munnery got the sleeve of his jacket stitched to the arm of his chair, and might have spent the night there, had Wiederkehr not slashed him loose with a swift pass of his 2B.

*

Naturally, it fell to Fluxman to lead the delegation that went to discuss the problem of declining standards with the City Fathers.

A special audience was held in the oak-panelled council chamber. Fluxman presented their case. He showed how the seeds of decline had been sown in mischief and trivialities. He pointed to instances of looming chaos, like the great unfastening, and cited statistics on damage to property, loss of life and limb, and low levels of investor confidence. He painted a gloomy picture of a future in which everything was out of order, and nothing ran smoothly to a creditable conclusion.

'If appropriate measures to secure law and order are not taken soon,' he concluded, 'it will be too late. Getting things right is not just a matter of form (although that is important enough in itself), but of necessity. Dotting one i might be regarded as a mere punctilio, and failing to do so dismissed as a trifle. But all the dots left off all the i's accumulate, they build up, they pack together like a cloud over a field of stubbly iotas. Soon there is a haze of them in every hollow, and the finer distinctions begin to evade us. In the end, the veil of uncertainty grows so thick that everything is obscured.'

The last echoes of Fluxman's baritone clattered away in the rafters. There was a pause, and then, not the 'Bravos' and 'Hear hears' that would have done justice to his oration, not the grateful applause and relieved chatter, but catcalls and whistles from the peanut gallery. The City Fathers, perched like children on the bloated leather seats of the dock, with the toes of their shoes scraping the floorboards, looked down unperturbed.

'We have teams at work this minute repairing the damage that has been reported, all of it slight,' said Councillor Lumley, the father figure of refrigerator services. 'Routine maintenance goes on apace. Everything is under control.'

In the back benches, a team of upholsterers clad in their characteristic leatherette dungarees and cotton T-shirts were reattaching buttons. Hearing themselves mentioned from the platform, they raised a ragged cheer.

'All the maintenance in the world will be of no use,' said Fluxman. 'We need to look to our records.'

'Nonsense! What good would that do?'

Distasteful as it was, smacking as it did of the party trick, Munnery called for a seating plan, which the Speaker duly produced, and demonstrated the point the Society was trying to make by transposing a few desks, councillors and all. Levitas realigned the chandeliers and shifted a rose window in the west wall to admit the setting sun. But rather than impressing upon the Fathers the seriousness of the situation, this made them think it was all just a game. They wanted Munnery to alley-oop them, like so many children, they wanted their desks rearranged so that they could be closer to the cafeteria or the cloakroom.

When Levitas dumped Lumley unceremoniously in the lap of a secretary whose name had been romantically connected with his own, the mood turned nasty. Security was summoned, and before they could even gather up their files, the Proofreaders found themselves manhandled from the chamber, with cries of 'Fools!' and 'Traitors!' flying about their ears.

*

Having resisted the Fathers the longest, it was Fluxman who took their rejection most to heart. That night, on his return from the Café Europa, where he and the others had drowned their sorrows, he went to his study. He opened the telephone directory and paged to the L's. There were three Lumleys. Which was which? Never mind, he would dispense with them all. He took up his weapon of choice. He chewed the pink rubber, savouring its familiar tang, and gazed at the columns of names and numbers. They were restless, squirming and writhing, jostling one another. A riotous assembly. Setting his jaw, he drew three neat lines through the Lumleys and inscribed a curly bracket and a single delete mark in the margin.

Then his conscience assailed him, and he quickly restored the deletion.

*

As the disorder grew, so did the Fathers' determination to overcome it. Team after team of brightly clad workers were dispatched to put things straight. In addition to the usual repairs and maintenance – attaching splints, driving in staples, welding railings, tarring poles, clearing pathways, burning firebreaks – they began to take an interest in the smallest details. Minders were employed to sit on park benches just to weigh them down, to cross the street whenever the little green man bade them walk, to cock the ears of the teacups in a westerly direction.

All this amateurish tinkering only hastened a spectacular descent into chaos. One morning, Alibians awoke to find that St Cloud's Square had come adrift and rotated to the opposite quarter of the compass; had it not been moored in the south-east by the Musical Fountains of the Seven Martyrs, it would surely have floated away altogether. Glancing up as usual at the clock tower of St Cloud's cathedral, as they filled their kettles at the kitchen sink, or threw open the shutters to do their morning exercises, or stooped to bring in the milk from their doorsteps, people saw nothing but sky.

On the outskirts of Alibia, among the sporting-goods factories and balsa-wood mills, in the peri-urban badlands, in the housing estates and low-cost townships, where the building regulations had never been applied with rigour and foundations were shallow, the disorder was precipitate. Whole streets suddenly banged together, like two halves of a book slammed shut by a reader, smashing everything in between, animate and inanimate, to pulp and tinder. Blocks of flats turned topsy-turvy, raining down the occupants and their possessions, and re-established themselves with their roots of cables and pipes twisted in the air, like so many baobab trees. People found themselves living on top of one another, cheek by jowl with exactly the types they wanted nothing to do with.

Through it all, the Proofreaders did what they could to preserve the proper boundaries between things. But in the end, maintaining order requires concerted communal effort. As fast as the Members corrected errors in one quarter, new – and worse – ones sprang up in another. Proofreading was thankless work, as they never tired of saying. And the fact is that without Fluxman, the great strategist, their efforts lacked design. Where Banes might be tempted to spend an entire afternoon taking back cups and saucers in the disorganized canteens of the General Post Office, or taking over buds on the rose terraces at the Botanical Gardens, Fluxman would concentrate on the menus or rearrange the phyla in the family trees. Moreover, Fluxman was possessed of the single most important tool in the proofreader's bag: ᵔ. For delete.

But what Fluxman *would* have done is immaterial, for he refused to do anything at all. He withdrew from the campaign; he stopped coming to meetings at the Café Europa. He closed his ears to the pleas of his colleagues and stayed at home, quietly minding his own business.

Everyone assumed that Fluxman's withdrawal was a straight-forward protest against being snubbed by the City Fathers. Only to Munnery had he opened his heart. 'Delete is a dangerous weapon,' he said, hacking idly at the air between them with a sign as keen as a sickle. 'I've always known it, of course, and I've always trusted myself to wield it righteously. But it's no longer safe in my hands. Let me loose on this degenerate world, and there's no telling what I'm capable of.'

A year passed. The city fell into ruins.

*

Now Fluxman, ensconced at Al Fresco's with the espresso gone cold before him and the corn-roaster's smoke stinging his eyes, had time to consider whether he had been right after all to wash his hands of the Society's problems. He surveyed the passing parade. How odd that he should consider this shambles 'fashionable'. What a change had been wrought since the great unfastening. Before then, it had shamed people to be seen with a thread out of place; now, no one cared about appearances at all. It was nothing but particoloured suits and patchwork as far as the eye could see. Men in dresses, women in bed-linen togas, winding-sheets and corsetry. The very idea of an *outfit* had become laughable. No matter how much care you took over your grooming, there was no telling if it would last. You might step out in a lounge suit and wind up in jodhpurs. Why bother?

The corn smoke turned to an exhalation of cigars, and through this fragrant haze, a vision of Alibia in its heyday rose up to taunt Fluxman. He saw the interval crowds in Opera House Square, a mass of swirling silk and manly gabardine under rafts of picture hats and lively conversation. Rows of gleaming limousines under the limes, the chauffeurs in their uniforms, scarcely less elegant than their dress-suited masters, so gloriously accoutred for motoring you would have thought they were commodores. He saw himself passing through the arcades, with a paper cone of chestnuts in the pocket of his frock-coat warm against his thigh, going down the steps to the river, where lovers were leaning on the parapets to watch the moon dissolve like a paper doily in the Indian ink of the water, passing purposefully out of the more fashionable avenues into the stonier quarters, where the houses huddled closer and closer together, turning their lichen-clad backs against the night, past a steaming horse, up an alley-way where the shadows lay thick and velvety as coaldust in every corner. There was a spring in his step, a hope in his heart. The heels of his brogues resounded like hammerblows on the flags, his breath puffed out in chubby balls of cotton wool, a chill breeze lifted the offhand gesture of his scarf. Winter had fallen here. Turning into a narrower passage, thrusting his fists deeper into his pockets, he came to a lighted window. From within he heard laughter, the crushed ice of a piano, the chime of glass against glass, the drayman's chorus. Leaning close to the panes, he peered in, but they were misted over and weeping.

The earth shook and Fluxman knew at once that some larger-than-ever upheaval had declared itself. He uttered an uncharacteristic curse. To be facing the end at Al Fresco's. It was not exactly becoming. At least he was sitting down. Another lurch and a thud like a boulder on a coffin lid. What could it be? He tossed the espresso, cup and all, into the gutter where it would not foul his clothes, and looked about. Everywhere people were running and falling. There, that was the problem: the department store on the other side of the Avenue of the Revolution. It was rocking on its foundations, bearing up and sinking back again, like a ferry aground on a sandbar. Squirts of dust and squawks of metal issued from the parking garage. You'd think the basement was full of hippopotamuses. Why was some brutal force always butting its head against the undersides of things? The strain was so immense that the end was bound to be shattering. The building would fly into smithereens. Hardly had the thought crossed his mind when the store flew into the air and vanished over the rooftops, scattering a potpourri of saloon cars and scented girls from the make-up counters. A flying building! There was a moment of blank embarrassment, while a cloud of red dust swirled in the gaping socket. Then something crackled in the distance and a shanty town appeared on the horizon, just where the store had diminished to a speck, grew larger with frightening rapidity, and fell with a crash into the hole. The impact caused several shacks to collapse, and all the rest to creak and shiver. Plumes of smoke rose up from the jumble of corrugated iron and splintery wood, and a river of moaning and wailing poured out.

The shanty town did not fit its new site at all well. On one side, it was jammed up against the wall of a bank. A dreadful bleating came from beneath those crumpled iron sheets. On the other side, a black hole yawned with unearthly anticipation. A goat plunged out of an alley and vanished down the abyss. A trio of mongrels chose a cannier path and raced out among the cars. Then the first human inhabitants stumbled after them and gazed about numbly. Almost at the same time, the habitués of the cafés and fast-food joints began to scramble out from under tables and chairs and hurry away down the Avenue.

Fluxman had a strong stomach. He took his rucksack in his lap, as if it were a frightened child, and scanned the tumult's ebb and flow.

Most of the avenue dandies had run away at the first opportunity. But a gang of young bucks from the musical theatres were using their canes to drive the swarthy settlers back into the shanties. As fast as they were routed, others took their place. Then a whole tribe in luminous bubus came spilling out in a rush, men, women and children, reeking of woodsmoke and unthinkable foodstuffs.

As usual, when you needed a waiter there was none to be seen, and so Fluxman picked his way through the overturned furniture and scouted around inside. Fresco himself had scarpered through the back door. Fluxman fetched down a bottle of whiskey from a shelf. In the mirror behind the counter, he saw that he was wearing a velvet cap with an ostentatious aigrette – the sort of thing an Athos might have liked – and he threw it away with a weary sigh. Disconsolately, he clamped an assortment of notes under the spring-loaded tongue of the till. Then he secured the bottle in his bag, took out an apple to eat on the way, and went back into the street. The young bucks had commandeered a tram and stalled it in the middle of the Avenue. From this redoubt, they were launching attacks against the garish tribesmen, trying to drive them back into their uprooted town.

Fluxman hurried on his way. In the east, where the Avenue tapered away into twilight, it was raining cats and dogs. As soon as he was clear of the wreckage, he turned aside into a narrow street and went bravely into the dusk.

*

In days gone by, Maison Munnery, a squaredavel under moth-eaten thatch, had commanded a view of the old city, with the esplanade and the yacht mole beyond it; now it looked down on a jumble of factory roofs and chimneys. Unusually for Alibia, this industrialization had been gradual, a heaping up of cubes and cones and frusta like offcuts from a geometer's bench, and it took Fluxman an hour to carve his way through it. By the time he broke out of that intricate litter onto the railway lines on the valley floor, night had fallen thickly all around. Munnery's place was an oasis of glaring light on the dark hillside and Fluxman kept his eyes on it as he ascended. *Climb every mountain* ... When he drew closer, he saw the military searchlight parked in the rockery on the slope behind the house, with its beam trained down on the putting green.

Munnery was practising, and Fluxman paused in the shadows to watch.

Alibia's most famous par 5 had fallen into Munnery's possession by chance. Returning from a jog up Capitol Hill one Sunday morning, he had found it laid out there like a gift. The sight of it caused a flutter in his heart. He should return it at once to its rightful owners. He went straight in and fetched down his books of maps and registers of title deeds, fully intending to make the transposition. But his pencil remained poised over the page, irresolute and feeble. He was an avid golfer and the thought of his own private practice green was more than he could resist. They would not even miss it at the club, he told his wife.

Little Horst, Munnery Junior, was now playing with a bucket and spade in the largest bunker. Mrs Munnery, Patsy as she was known, had just left him there, and her skirt was still caught up in her panties at the sides. She was sitting on the doorstep, wriggling her toes in the grass to rid them of sand. Fluxman had never seen her legs before, and he was struck by how pale they were. Munnery himself was wearing plus-fours in the MacLaren tartan and a mismatched pair of spiked shoes, one that was white with black fringes and one that was red all over. He affected a little shuffle and gave the ball a tap. It curved across the green, tracing an s in the dew, and rolled down towards the cup. Fluxman waited for the ball to drop before he stepped from his hiding place into the light. Mrs Munnery hurriedly untucked her skirts. Junior demolished a castle with a backhander from the spade. Munnery dropped his putter with a cry of delight and advanced to greet his visitor, embraced him warmly, and drew him at once through the bright doorway.

*

Settling Fluxman in his study, Munnery went off to pour them each a whiskey from the bottle his guest had brought. As soon as he found himself alone, Fluxman rose from the armchair he had been pressed down in and turned about on the mat, gaping in amazement. The room was papered with printed sheets. Not just the walls but the door, the window behind the desk, the cupboards, the shelves, the desk itself – every surface had a page stuck to it. There were even papers pinned to the ceiling, with their edges curling downwards, and untidy stacks on the floors, weighted by rusty cogs and crankshafts and lumps of wood, with their edges curling upwards. Between the reciprocal curves of ceiling and floor, Fluxman felt curiously suspended, like an afterthought in brackets. The papers rustled and waved, making visible an imperceptible breeze, and it seemed as if the room was breathing uneasily and muttering to itself.

Years of practice had made of Fluxman a shameless scrutineer. He stepped closer to the wall and examined the peeling skin. Glacier ~ granite ~ grasslands ~ grike. It was Munnery's 'Dictionary of Geographical Terms'. His life's work. The page proofs. Simoom ~ sinkhole ~ slickensides ~ solifluction. Fluxman tugged at a few dog-ears. Every page was securely attached with tacks or loops of tape, drawing pins or tees. Munnery had been known as the most fastidious of proofreaders, a stickler for sequence and consequence, a meticulous keeper of order. Finding the great project of his life in this disarray shook Fluxman. Perhaps he had come just in time. Or was he already too late?

When Munnery returned with the drinks, he found his colleague tactfully seated, flipping through the Phone Book, which he had taken from his rucksack.

'A toast,' said Fluxman. 'To the records!'

This was the battle cry of the Society, the oath with which they closed their gatherings, and its import was not lost on Munnery. 'The records!' he echoed, and they clinked glasses. 'Welcome back.'

'My pleasure.'

They drank. Fluxman, examining his old friend for signs of deterioration, noted that his pullover was back to front. Why did Mrs Munnery let him wear the spikes inside? It would ruin the floors.

'I thought you were gone for good,' said Munnery.

'That was the idea. But I've changed my mind, as you see.'

'Why?'

'Some observations I've made lately have led me to believe that looking the other way might not be the answer.'

'It's a fact that you've behaved very selfishly, turning your back on us when you might have done something.'

'You misunderstand. My presence here is as selfish as any of my old refusals. I thought I could manage well enough as Alibia declined, preserving my own little corner amidst the ruins. Unfortunately, it isn't that simple. While we still have the tools to wield against chaos, even if we choose not to, we may feel safe. While we are models of order ourselves, and stuffed with the assurance of our own solidity, we may hold ourselves up to one another as examples and reflect that there is something wrong with the world we live in. But when we ourselves succumb ...'

'Are we in danger, then?' The question made Munnery anxious. He gulped his drink and began to pace up and down in the channels between the papers. 'What do you think?'

Fluxman was tempted to say: 'Open your eyes, man. Take a good look around you.' Instead he said: 'Let's say I've seen signs of dissolution. Surely you've seen them too?'

'Minor disorders, yes.'

'In yourself?'

'Not really, but I have noticed worrying signs in others.'

'It's to be expected that we proofreaders should hold out to the last, that we should be more resistant than the man in the street.' The mugger on the fairway came into his mind, and he shivered. 'Which is all the more reason to act now, in concert, while we still have our wits about us.'

Munnery had grown more agitated as they spoke, marching up and down over the pages on the floor, which stuck to the soles of his shoes in untidy wads. Several times he muttered, 'Patsy ...' For a while, there was nothing but the rustle of his feet. Then he halted before Fluxman and asked: 'What do you propose?'

'To begin with, an emergency meeting of the Society. We must come up with a strategy. Late as it is, I believe we can beat back the plague.'

The mugger stumbled into Fluxman's mind again, and so he told Munnery about him, and also about the bobber he had fished from the water. That reminded him in turn of the Wetland Ramble. 'I'm afraid my house will be flooded while I'm gone. Would you mind putting the water feature somewhere else? I haven't had much practice with such things lately ... and it's been a long day.'

With trembling fingers, Munnery unpinned some pages from the back of the door. Fluxman couldn't help noticing that he left the leaves to float up to the ceiling while the pins spiralled slowly to the floor. There was an ordinance survey map beneath, and he studied it.

'It can't go back to the Zoo,' he said with a worried face. 'The Stoute Kabouter nursery school's been squashed in there.'

'That was probably Banes's doing.'

In the end, Munnery earmarked a bit of virgin woodland on the escarpment and relocated the Wetland Ramble there among the trees. Constructive effort calmed his nerves at once. He fetched a canal, which was gathering slime behind the gasworks, and put that down in the reeds to make a sort of weir, and rounded everything off with some concrete tables and chairs from a picnic site and a circle of caravans from a roadworkers' camp (long since abandoned). The effect was bound to be pleasing, as Fluxman remarked.

'Let's start looking ahead,' said Munnery hopefully, 'to the day when Alibia takes its place among the tourist destinations of the world.'

Dinner was a ratatouille, a veritable drumroll of pepper and aubergine, and a sirloin of beef. Dessert was more of the whiskey dashed over ice cream.

Then Fluxman, exhausted by the exertions of the day, bedded down in the lounge with the Phone Book under his head, while his host withdrew to his study to contact the other Members of the Society. Fluxman listened to the murmuring voice behind the door, and watched the searchlight beams toppling like gargantuan spillikins across the sky behind the window, until he fell asleep. And then it was just the rumble and clash of suburbs and streets under the cover to which his ear was pressed, a sound he had long ago grown used to, and was hardly able to dream without.

*

The next morning in Munnery's lounge, the Proofreaders' Society achieved a quorum for the first time in nearly a year. Fluxman had imagined that the others might be awkward in his presence, that his 'betrayal' would still rankle, but to his relief the atmosphere was businesslike and bellicose. Munnery had primed the Members and several were dressed for battle – Levitas in his broadcloth waistcoat, Banes in his worsted boilersuit. Wiederkehr was wearing his stetson. Consensus was reached before Mrs Munnery even had time to serve the tea. Those present reaffirmed that they themselves were all that stood between Alibia and its ruination, and that duty called them to make one last effort at restoring law and order. This initiative they resolved to pursue 'jointly and severally' (as Banes worded it): they would work as a team, coordinating their actions and lending one another support; but each would also take primary responsibility for a particular sphere of correction, and focus on applying those skills at which he was most adept.

Munnery was put in charge of transposition. The others were encouraged to place their personal collections of maps and plans at his disposal for the duration of the campaign. He would work closely with Figg on insertions and Levitas on alignment. Banes was assigned to reappropriation and given leave to commandeer statute books and municipal records, title deeds and carbon-copy invoices, and to take over and take back at his discretion. The director of restoration was Wiederkehr. It was surmised, rightly as it turned out, that his services would prove invaluable if any of his colleagues applied themselves too zealously to their own tasks. No one appreciated this more than Fluxman, who was responsible for deletions and removals, the most sensitive portfolio of all.

When the toasts had been drunk and the farewells made, when the last of the Members had gone off down the hill, each carrying a little tub of Mrs Munnery's linguine, Fluxman was left alone to pack his bag. He stood at the window, where a clutch of stray proofs fluttered against the blinds, and looked out onto the sunlit green. Junior lay on his stomach on the grass, with his feet jutting over the bunker and a bucket of golf balls at his shoulder. He held one of the balls in both hands and rested his chin on it. Then, with a flick of his wrists, he sent the ball speeding towards the hole.

*

Fluxman took his leave. He meant to go straight home and set to, but now that his thoughts had turned to the work at hand, he found himself drawn from the path again and again to tinker at the wayside. Little things to begin with, minor repairs to an unhyphenated split pole fence, a badly spaced milestone , a broken win-dow pane … but in the end, an italicized *townhouse complex* detained him for the better part of the afternoon. The place was an eyesore, nothing but curlecues of stucco and folderols of wrought iron. It took him half an hour to introduce some Roman columns of a plain, upright kind, and another to summon a vine-leaf screen to hide the whole thing from view. He should have referred the matter to one of the others, he thought afterwards, as he went wearily on his way, Figg or Banes would have made light work of it. Or he should have stuck to what he knew best: Strike it out! Away with it!

The effort had exhausted him. He felt uncomfortably disordered. Twice he had to fetch a wandering eye back from the crook of his arm and re-attach a limb with conjunctive sinew. And in this agitated state of mind and body, he thought of Ms Georgina Hole, his former fiancée. It was half a year since she had broken off their engagement, and a quarter since she had entered his mind. He went towards her flat.

No one answered his knock. Was she still manning the charity kiosk at St Cloud's on weekday afternoons? He could wait. He sat down on the doorstep and looked around. The place was getting tatty. When she came in, he would have to tell her to take better care of herself, and offer to lend a hand. He made a few emergency repairs to pass the time, but his thoughts kept drifting. Soon he fell asleep.

He dreamt of Georgina. He dreamt that she had stopped at the Good Cockatoo on her way back from work to share a meal with Bibliotheker, a fund-raiser and friend, whose advances she had been stubbornly resisting till now. On this day of all days. It was ten before she arrived home, and then she found her old flame slumped asleep against the doorpost. He half-opened his mouth, not to accuse her, but to explain that he had come to seek her blessing, even if he had lost her affection. But his tongue was as thick as blotting-paper in his mouth. She prised the rucksack from his embrace and led him inside, made him stretch out on the settee among the ungrammatical scatter cushions and overstuffed pouffes. She unlaced his hiking boots and loosened his bandanna. As she drew a blanket over him, his hands rose of their own accord and held her. To his surprise, she did not rebuff him. He measured the columns of her thighs with the upsilons of his outstretched fingers and thumbs. Then his hands slid over the parenthetical curves of her hips, smoothed a shiver out along the ridges of her ribs and the rounds of her breasts, paused for breath at the full stops of her nipples, rose again over her shoulders, felt the flutter of lashes against their palms and fell away from her flesh in amazement, as she drew back and receded, plunging him into an exclamatory darkness. He reached for a page of her in his mind. Not a jot, not an iota must be lost. Then his eyes and hands moved over her surface, proofing the metrical skeleton concealed in her warming limbs, reconnecting joint to joint, easing the flow of words like water over skin, making her fluent, feeling the prickle of his own gaze on the backs of his hands, tracing with the crumbling nib every pore and fold, every tendon and sinew, the popliteal hollow, the pillowed lips, the pressed ear, the whorled navel, delete and close up, wound and heal, the wet whisper of the font, the long alliteration of her throat, the elliptical flesh of her face, the bone beneath, the tongue between, the mouth, composing every square word of her into a perfectly ordered meaning, into a sentence that meant exactly what it said. Yet when he awoke, dishevelled and alone, this meaning had escaped him.

*

It was Munnery's idea to remove the Restless Supermarket to the countryside, where they could work on it without fear of injuring passers-by. They had decided to act more circumspectly in such matters, and so the implications of the removal were first examined from every angle. What if it harmed the very people it was meant to help? What if it led to shortages in the surrounding suburbs, to a critical want of staples, to starvation? When such questions had been answered to everyone's satisfaction, the renowned transposer went to work. He found an abandoned aerodrome in the hinterland, at the end of a country road, and put the Restless Supermarket down there, lock, stock and barrel. On the vacated site, Figg inserted a small section of the Rainbow Chicken Farm to tide the locals over until more permanent measures could be taken. Then the Proofreaders boarded their bus, specially chartered, and took the slower route into the interior.

Even from a distance, when the old control tower had just appeared on the horizon, the Restless Supermarket could be heard grumbling and groaning. Fluxman drew up in the parking lot near the delivery bays, and they disembarked into the noisy air. Then he led them inside and down a corridor to the manager's office. On the other side of a flimsy wall, they heard the contents of the building churning like an angry sea, and some of them slumped a little, and some puffed out their chests.

A closed-circuit camera, the sole survivor among a dozen installed to combat shoplifting, was still relaying its impressions of the store to a television monitor on the manager's desk. At first, it appeared to them that this camera had also broken down, and that the screen contained nothing but meaningless static. But then among the squirming motes they began to distinguish fragments of sense, flickering here and there, and they drew fearfully closer and gazed at the screen as if it were a window into the inferno.

The interior of the Restless Supermarket was barely recognizable. The entire space was seething, alive with an indiscriminate, indefatigable jumble of tins, jars, bottles, packets, boxes, bags, all mingled into one substance, whose textures eluded them, being simultaneously soft and hard, fuzzy and sharp, perishable and indestructible. Each element remained vividly itself for as long as they focused on it, and then dissolved back into the irreducible compound as soon as they relaxed their attention. It was like trying to watch one wing in a wheeling flock or one brick in a striding wall, although such things gave no inkling of the frenetic movement, the ceaseless and senseless changing of places with which the products had been charged. Occasionally, the ribs of a shelf gleamed white in the roil, or a chequered floor tile flashed like a tooth.

They stood there mesmerized, and might have gone on standing there until they lost all will to act, had Fluxman not roused them by clapping his Phone Book open on the desk.

Quickly, before they could lose heart, they constructed makeshift desks of cardboard cartons, laid out the documents they had brought with them in their portfolios alongside jars of pencils and rubbers and rulers, and gathered inventories, advertisements, ledgers, marketing plans and flow charts from the filing cabinets. Munnery and Levitas launched into the engineering, locating salients in the soup, righting gondolas and levelling refrigerator units, realigning shelves in the proper parallels, with aisles of the optimum width between, rearranging sections and departments to create a rational flow of custom. Wiederkehr repaved and Figg repapered. And then the two together set about repacking the shelves, tidying up the debris as they went.

It was an enormous labour. The product substance was hard and soft, impenetrable and yielding, solid and liquid. It resisted their efforts to cut into it, to separate parts from the whole. A single item grappled from its clutches and put aside on the end of an empty shelf, in a little white clearing, would maintain its integrity for a moment. But then the substance would begin to exert its viscous attraction, and soon the item would be jiggling and turning on its base, and floating free again into the general mass, where it would be whirled away into restless anonymity. The shelf itself would come loose and be lost in the uproar. The categories had to be built up painstakingly, row by row, line by line, and all the while chaos threatened to overwhelm them.

The Proofreaders worked in shifts. When they were exhausted beyond endurance, they lay down and slept with their twitching hands clasped between their knees. When they were famished, they transposed a tin of something from the stock.

At last, patches of stillness appeared in the tumult. And then a solid shelf or two. The seething died down a little. One day, the space between the shelves and the rafters cleared momentarily and revealed a row of dangling signboards: Tea & Coffee, Breakfast Cereals, Dairy Products, Pet Food, Household Cleaners … The Proofreaders gave a weary cheer. Already, in the mind's eye and the mind's nose, they saw the master chefs of Alibia walking enraptured down the gleaming aisles and smelt the aromas of feasts to come. But the battle was far from won. The superstructure was refractory. The gondolas floated off half-laden. The dairy went sour. The overtaxed shelves collapsed. The products kept bubbling back into substance. No sooner was one aisle restored to order, than another rose up clamorously, shedding labels and price tags in promiscuous profusion. From his headquarters in the back room, Fluxman rallied his colleagues again and again. He would not submit. And at the end of a week, the basic shape of the enterprise had been secured.

Night had no meaning in the Restless Supermarket. They laboured on, raising up pyramids of tins and cans, stabilizing barrows of fruit and vegetables, racking and stacking, piling and puzzling, until the shelves began to settle down, rising up and subsiding in waves, as if by general assent, as if a rumour of defeat had run like a swell from aisle to aisle.

Glaring absences became visible. Baked goods were required, said Munnery. They brought in quantities of Chelsea buns, Madeira slabs, Lamingtons, pita-bread with hummus. What about the liquid refreshments? They brought in whiskey, wine in boxes, soda water, ice. Everyone needed something special, some little extra. They added mops, marinades, wonton dumplings, asparagus spears, noodles in the shape of shells. Wiederkehr became quite inventive, importing strings of vanished delicacies he remembered from his childhood. He and Figg devised entirely new dishes, and arranged the ingredients on the shelves by menu, season and refinement of taste, constellations so subtle that only gourmets would appreciate them. Meanwhile, Banes was making his way down the aisles for the last time, straightening labels and marking down prices. Something like peace and quiet descended and endured.

It was then that they noticed the absence of Fluxman. As soon as the tide had turned, he had left his post and gone into the butchery. The air smelt of blood. There was mopping up to do. He must excise sawdust and broadcast desiccated coconut, just as an interim measure. He must delete sub-standard carcases in the freezer room. Munnery found him there, sweeping behind a stiff downpour of plastic curtain, and gave him the news: the sun had risen over the Alibian Sea and the Restless Supermarket was at rest.

*

Although the Wetland Ramble was gone from Fluxman's yard and a patch of forest rustled in its place, a muddy breath still clung. In the stench that blew into his study, a mixture of dung and waterweeds and feathers, gnawed bones and half-hatched chicks entombed in eggshell, there was a lingering reminder of captivity.

Having risen to shut the window against this poison, he stood gazing at the beeches silvered in moonlight, while a flock of noisy gulls scattered into the heavens. Then he returned with a sigh to the blighted landscape of the Book. The breeze had rifled spitefully through his pages. As he leafed back to his bookmark, his eye fell on:

Lombardo WH Saphire St Imprl Mnt 878-4322
oologi dens Cnstntia
Lombat, D 34 Burrows Rd Blk Hl 642-1986
Lomnitz Z Refinery Rd Pkld Dl 486-0051

Just how the missing half of the Zoological Gardens had landed up in the L's was anyone's guess. He had been searching for it for five days; finding it by chance was an affront to his professionalism. He wrung the neck of the blue pencil in the sharpener and put its point down on the first o in oologi …

On second thoughts, he fetched some of Munnery's catalogues off a shelf and found the section on animal life. He saw that Figg had already been busy among the marsupials. The cage must be bursting! Fluxman deleted a couple of bars in the reference material, a koala and the chubbiest of the kangeroos. And then he thought – what the hell – and put a line through the whole lot of them.

*

The campaign to recapture the Restless Supermarket had been intended as a trial run to prepare the Members for the war of attrition that lay ahead, and it achieved this end. A division of labour was established, and an armoury of weapons tested. A point was made. What remained now was to repeat the point over and over again on a grander and grander scale.

But the Restless Supermarket outdid itself, for Fluxman at least. It proclaimed itself the great offensive against error. It exhausted every potential, it surpassed every anticipation. From that moment on, everything that remained to be done became routine. The initial topographical work – arrangements for mountains, forests and streams, ocean currents and seasonal rainfall, reservoirs and dams, the restoration of mineral deposits and rock faces, the replenishment of slag heaps and landfills – all this could not but seem like a faint echo of flooring and shelving and plumbing.

When it was time for a bit of town planning, Fluxman's interest quickened. The residential areas and office parks and industrial zones had to be unshuffled and restored to their proper places. There were green belts to loosen, highways to unravel, pylons to restring. The displaced masses of Alibia had flung down their makeshift houses in the buffer zones: now the appropriate social distance could be restored between the haves and have-nots, the unsightlier settlements shifted to the peripheries where they would not upset the balance, the grand estates returned to the centre where they belonged. There was wasteland to play with, and blasted veld, and dead water. The possibilities seemed endless. But when he got down to it, it was no more difficult, and indeed no more important, than the sorting and packing and pricing of boxes and tins on a shelf.

The city pulled itself together. Slowly, the recognizable outlines of Alibia reappeared, as street after street and block after block was knocked back into its familiar, ordinary shape.

It was not a riddle, a puzzle, a paradox, as many supposed. Every little victory had to be earned. The boffins of the Proofreaders' Society worked overtime. Levered up by their acute pencils, whole paragraphs of the world came and went. Their eyes crossed and recrossed every line of the city streets until the most crooked found their truest delineation. With every hyphen that tacked a building to its neighbour, knit one, purl one, with every colon that suggested a passage from one block to another, with every dotted line that restored a highway to the symmetry of coming and going, the earth drew Alibia tighter to its bosom. It should have been a spectacle, but it was not.

In the corrosive solution of tedium that flowed from this realization, Fluxman's qualms about his own excesses were dissolved. If ever he went too far, he told himself, and deleted more than was strictly necessary, he could always call on Wiederkehr to undo it again. He became ruthless. First it was dittographies in the Book, people and places, like the Lumleys. Later it was the minor irritations, like that Goosen who refused to answer questions about the price of eggs, and that Schneider who had to go setting up a business with a Sartorius. And then it was the human detritus he found in the margins of the city, the erroneous ones, the slips of the hand, the tramps, the fools, the congenitally stupid, the insufferably ugly. They were incorrigible, he reasoned, and doing away with them, at one painless stroke, was more humane than trying to improve them.

His colleagues shared these frustrations. First Munnery, and then Figg, and then all the others began to create their own amusements – which they passed off as 'improvements'. In certain areas of Alibian life, they said, there was simply no point in returning to the past. Levitas, for instance, redesigned the Alibian Alps to allow for more pleasant skiing in the foothills and more hazardous climbing on the peaks. He put the General Hospital up on the snowline where the air was more salubrious, and he put the Hotel Grande down on the beachfront, with its wings stacked one on top of the other, so that every room had a sea view, and he gave it a casino and a Ferris wheel and a miniature golf course, because he himself was fond of simple pleasures. The people of Alibia were so grateful for these alterations that Banes, intent on eclipsing the example of his colleague, embarked on a public-spirited campaign of his own. He reappropriated mansions for the homeless, he reassembled the Royal Alibian Golf Course in the wilderness (Munnery was allowed to keep the eighteenth), he reunited families who had been separated by the upheavals. These acts made Banes something of a hero to the lost and the loveless, to widows and orphans, to the homeless and the unemployed.

Experience taught them that nothing is perfect. They reconciled themselves to the errors of judgement and perception that beset the best-planned operations. It rained loafs from Buurman's Bakery and fishes from the munchipal reservoir. The streets were littered with crutchers, rhinocerous products, muslin fundamentalists, celeried employees and their pardners, bonsai boababs, dawgs.

When the waste material piled up, they called for Fluxman. It was enough to make him feel like a street sweeper.

*

In time, everything was returned to its proper place, which sometimes was not the place it had started out, but the place it deserved to end.

Alibia basked in its imperfect glory. Even the Members of the Society – Fluxman aside – had come to consider one error in five pages acceptable. Who would notice the odd waterfall flowing upwards to its source, the icicles on the fronds of the palms, the gondolas marooned in a stream of concrete? Who would begrudge such flaws, or even perceive them, when there was a promenade beside the sea, a bandstand in the park made for old-fashioned melodies, a tavern at the end of a fogbound wynd? The bells of St Cloud's rebuked the faithless on the hour, the waves kept beating against the quays, the metronome of a searchlight kept time in the absence of the sun.

When peace had been restored, the City Fathers afforded the heroes a victory parade, the grandest that had ever been seen, proceeding now on foot through the streets in a blizzard of ticker-tape, now on barges down the river, and now on sleighs across the frozen canals, and arriving finally at the triumphal arch through which they all passed, first the heroes and then those who had come to honour them, vanishing as they went, drawing the offspring of error after them, and abandoning the city to a state of flawed completion.

All except Fluxman, that is, who came behind in his dignified way, sweeping the last of the delenda up from the gutters with his hoop and stuffing them into his bag. When the streets were clean, he went down to the white beach in front of the casino, where his coracle was moored, rowed out into the bay, and emptied the bag into the water.

The Goodbye Bash

PART THREE

Ye blind guides, which strain at a gnat, and swallow a camel.

– *St Matthew 23:24*

MINUTE PRINT MADE ME TWELVE PHOTOSTATIC COPIES OF 'THE Proofreader's Derby'. For the Last Finger Supper. Cost me a packet, but one had to be prepared, one never knew what would happen. How many guests were we expecting? Wessels wouldn't say. My budget stretched to a round dozen. I bound the copies with rubber bands and wrapped them in a plastic bag courtesy of the Okay Bazaars. Then I bore them to the Café Europa in my briefcase, pressed back into service specifically for this purpose.

In the bag I also carried the eighth edition of the *Concise Oxford Dictionary*, 'the New Edition for the 1990s', scarcely opened, edited by R.E. Allen, and proofread, hallelujah, honorifics in the original, by Mrs Deirdre Arnold, Mr Morris Carmichael, Mrs Jessica Harrison, Mr Keith Harrison, Ms Georgia Hole, Ms Helen Kemp, Ms E. McIlvanney, Dr Bernadette Paton, Mr Gerard O'Reilly, Ms J. Thompson, Dr Freda Thornton, Mr Anthony Toyne, and Mr George Tulloch, amongst others. (Thirteen, if you didn't count the et alii. Was it wise, I wonder, to choose an unlucky number? Was it wise at all to employ a *team*? And eight of them women.) The eighth edition of the *Concise* was the current one. I do not care much for currency, but something told me the night would hold surprises it might be useful to define. And if the opportunity to administer a sample of 'The Proofreader's Derby' arose, if it actually came to that, I would present the volume as a prize. The floating trophy would have to wait for the first fully-fledged competition.

The New Management was amusing itself in the pool room, stringing crinkle-paper decorations of its own manufacture, and I was able to march straight into the Gentlemen's room and lock the door behind me. The little window opened onto a dirty grey well, veined with pipes for power and plumbing. I secured the plastic bag to a downpipe on the outside wall and closed the window again. The *Concise* I secreted on top of the cistern in the cubicle. Then I went home to freshen up.

*

When I set out for the Goodbye Bash a few hours later, I carried in the pockets of my blazer the original copy of 'The Proofreader's Derby', twelve sharpened pencils (pointing due south in the interests of safety), a sharpener, my current notebook and the *Pocket Oxford Dictionary*, in its berth over my heart. The particoloured tops of the Faber-Castells jutting from my breast pocket made me feel like a general.

I once read a newspaper article in which some so-called celebrities were asked what book they would take with them to a desert island. A surprising number, given the godless times we live in, said the Holy Bible. And several, including a star of pornographic films, chose the complete works of the Bard. But not one had the *Condensed Oxford Dictionary*, which was my choice, doubly sealed by the little magnifying glass in its velvet pouch, so useful for making fire. Much has changed since then. What would I choose today? My bosom friend the *Pocket*.

As I made my way to the Café Europa for the last time, I turned a few heads, I think I can say without exaggeration. A smartly pressed pair of flannels is not an everyday sight on the streets of the Golden City – Grubbier Johannesburg, to quote my pal Wessels.

There was an air of expectancy in the dusk, along with the volatile essence of newsprint and exhaust fumes. Luminous dabs of tail-lights glimmered and died on the smoky canvas of the street. Shop windows frosted with shoewhite and dusted with detergent snowflakes were aglow like nativities in the cathedral of the gathering darkness: the ruins of our grey Christmas. The new year in the offing was black as pitch. It made one want to hurry on to some place bursting with light.

Who should totter out of the shadows but Mrs Hay. The first of the old bodies. I knew her at once by the sticking-plaster sutures: keeping up appearances. She tried to clasp me to her breast, like a long-lost missal or a pint of gin, but I fended her off with my elbows.

'So, what are the portents?' I asked, being friendly.

'Excellent, Aubrey. We're going to give you a wonderful send-off.'

Silly old bat. You'd think it was a farewell do for me.

We ascended in Indian file, nostalgically and irritably respectively. The Café Europa was dark. I could barely make out the sign on the door: Private Function – Members Only. We stepped into the coffee-stained hush. Paper chains strung from the ceiling, and looped over one another, sketched a series of vaults upon the twilight above. A red light winking in the far corner indicated Hunky Dory's laboratory; the pink glow in the chapel came from the 'fruit machines' (when Mrs Mavrokordatos first mentioned these, I thought she meant the juice dispensers one finds in cinema foyers). Washes of cherry skin and strawberry juice. Otherwise dark and empty. Never be the first to arrive or the last to leave.

Mrs Hay headed for the Ladies' room to fix her face. I went towards table No. 2. But as I drew closer, I saw that it was already occupied. Pipped at the post again … by Spilkin and Darlene! What with his suntan and her natural shade, which had always tended to powdery shale, they were almost invisible against the Alibian sandstone.

*

'Care to join us?'

I drew up my usual seat.

They were sitting with the armrests of their chairs pushed together, their temples touching. Her head in silhouette was swollen and empty at the same time, gaping over his own hard nut as if it were an ingestible morsel. On the table stood a bottle – I couldn't make out the label in the gloom – and two glasses.

He looked older and wearier. The eyebrows were shrubby, the eyelids sagging. Subocular luggage (punchlines, Spilkin). I refused to focus on her, but even from the corner of my eye, I could see that she was just the same, and it made the change in him all the more regrettable.

'Long time no see,' he said.

I would have expected the pidgin to come from her mouth rather than his. It struck me dumb. A nonsensical phrase sing-songed through my mind: *wena* something or other. Eveready had written it down for me one day, his contribution to my notebook, but I'd forgotten the translation. Was it Psalm 23 in the isiZulu? Spilkin's hand felt puffy and damp. Chop-chop, chop-chop. I forced the melody to be quiet and enquired instead:

'Still living in Durban?'

'No, we're up here again.'

'Back at the Flamingo?'

'No, in Bez Valley with the in-laws.'

'How do you find it? I mean Johannesburg.'

'Turn right at Vereeniging. No seriously, it's dreadful. Full of madmen. They've gone and changed the typeface in the *Star* again to something illegible. How're the peepers, by the way?'

'Like a hawk.' I gave him a verse of the old rhyme – the Elephant variation.

'Monoblepsia playing up at all?'

'No way, José.' Mexican rhyming slang courtesy of Errol and Co. I thought he might appreciate it.

It was almost like old times. If one paid no attention to the wardrobe, that is. Spilkin was wearing blue-denim breeches – Wessels would say 'a jean' – and a turtleneck sweater. Pork dressed as piglet. Everybody's Darling, coming insistently into focus as my eyes grew used to the light, was got up like the Rain Queen. Enough linen in her turban to make a yurt, a dress full of darts and flounces. The cloth was so loud it made my ears hurt, banana yellow, predominantly, and garish beadwork. I greeted her civilly, still prepared to let bygones be bygones, but she was as rude as ever. That bloody mouth of hers opened like a wound in the gloaming.

'Talk about African time. They said six-thirty for seven, and it's just us two. Or should I say three. Where is everyone?'

As if in answer to her question, the lights went on and the room leapt into view. Those must be the eats, under a shroud. Paper chains overhead. 'Seasons Greetings' on the wall by the Gentlemen's room.

Then a fuss at the door. It was Mevrouw Bonsma, in full costume, on the arm of the New Management. If Darlene was got up like a bedouin tent, Mevrouw Bonsma was a big top, extravagantly striped, sequinned and fringed. Several of her garments appeared to be inside out. On her thick coiffure lay a tinny tiara like a mislaid cookie cutter. What was happening to the women? You'd think Boswell Wilkie's circus was in town.

'Look who's here!'

'Spilkijn!'

'Mevrouw!'

'What a surprising development!'

Mevrouw Bonsma billowed about in the doorway. The New Management dragged her over to our table, like a hot-air balloon harnessed to a pony, and wedged her in a chair. She began to gush.

'You don't look a day older,' I was able to say in all honesty (one reaches a point of decrepitude beyond which the day-to-day ravages are scarcely perceptible).

*

When the fuss had spent itself, Mevrouw Bonsma looked me over from toe to top. Her eyes came to rest on my summit. I was gazing at the confection, and so we remained for a moment in puzzled symmetry, transfixed by the tops of one another's heads.

'I like the new look, Tearle,' she crackled.

I'd invented the hairstyle myself that morning, but I wasn't sure whether to own up or not. Would it look cheap?

I've been cutting my own hair in my retirement. Editing the end matter, as I think of it. I last tried the professionals some years ago, around the time I met Merle. 'Hair Affair' was up an escalator, which gave me false hopes of privacy. The 'hairstylist' was an extremely garrulous woman: while I waited for her to finish off the previous customer, I established that she was a Czechoslovak, a Jehovah's Witness, a Free Marketeer. I should have made my escape at once, but morbid fascination kept me pinned. When my turn finally came, don't think she didn't want to shampoo me right there in front of the windows. I'd been worrying that she might nick one of my excrescences with her scissors while she was railing against the bolshie bigwigs of the home country, but this was an entirely unexpected threat. I made myself scarce, and I've been doing my own barbering ever since.

Mevrouw Bonsma's bun looked harder and shinier than before. The sight of it reminded me how Spilkin and I had behaved when we first made her acquaintance. An unholy triangle, which Merle's arrival had restored to equilibrium. Now there were four of us again – except that Darlene was in Merle's place. It made a mockery of quadruplicity. I couldn't wait for Merle to arrive – even a pentagon would be better than this.

I enquired after Mevrouw Bonsma's welfare to get the conversational ball rolling, but it trundled no further than the next sticky pause. She was doing a bit of teaching, she said, it was surprising how many of the underprivileged were interested in music. And playing a bit of bridge.

*

Punctuality is not the least of the devalued virtues. To pass the time, until the rest of the company 'rocked up' (Darlene), I suggested that Mevrouw Bonsma and I pay our respects to the buffet, which was lying in state under netting. We were welcome to look, but there would be no tasting until the New Management gave the signal. As he explained it, the success of the Bash hinged on the timing of the moment at which eating was introduced into the general course of drinking. Too early, and it would prevent the pot from coming to the boil; too late, and the pot might boil over and extinguish the fire. The bar was open, though. Any orders? Strictly cash. Or could he open a bottle on our behalf? Corkage waived.

What we could see of the feast through the camouflage net looked unbalanced, nutritionally speaking, and so unappetizing that safety measures hardly seemed necessary. The inevitable poultry, hacked into pieces, packets of Knick-Knacks, stacks of Sesamemates (apparently one needed to be on friendly terms with the food before one consumed it), swatches of sweat-beaded sweetmilk, jaundiced dips, lettuce.

'And what are these?'

'Buffalo wings.'

'If buffaloes had wings, Mevrouw, they would certainly be a great deal bigger than this.'

'If pigs had wings, they would taste like bacon.'

Where had she come by that? Sounded like a Wesselism. Could they have been seeing one another on the sly? He couldn't possibly be taking piano lessons. Rummy more likely, or bumblepuppy.

I remembered fondly the spread Mrs Mavrokordatos had promised for the inaugural championships. 'Mrs Mavrokordatos would have given us a good square meal. And if not that, then a smorgasbord.' As it was, there was not a *smorgas* in sight, just these tubs of yellow margarine. Cheddar and Melrose wedges.

A rubbery nose nuzzled my hand. It proved to be Wessels, snuffling at me with the stopper on the end of his crutch. That fat nincompoop was so excited he could hardly contain himself.

'Is everythink to taste?' He poked the forbidden food with his finger. And then suddenly, improbably, as if she had been invisible until that moment: 'Suzanna!'

'Martinus!'

Such a quantity of hissing and steaming, you'd have thought they were a pair of Christmas puddings.

*

I am not easily discouraged. I returned to table No. 2. I meant to engage Spilkin in discussion this evening if it was the last thing I did. Mrs Hay had commandeered my chair, so I pulled another closer from the next table. The conversation was about salad dressings, knitting patterns, the declining fortunes of some soap-opera family or other, the 'hit parade' – but I could raise the tone in a moment. There was a point about dictionaries

I had been harbouring, a point that illuminated the age-old tussle between forging ahead and maintaining standards, and I intended to make it, come hell or high water.

They were talking about something called 'Magic Johnson'. A popular group, no doubt. It was all the opening I needed.

Speaking of Johnson ... I was with Dr Johnson, I said, when it came to relying on dictionaries of current usage rather than the Academy for correctness. Language is changing all the time, I'm the first to admit it. But at any given moment, we must have standards of correctness. What would be the point of having dictionaries at all if that were not the case? I liken it, I said, to the act of proofreading itself, which I have often described, in which a rapid sequence of still points creates the illusion of constant motion. That got me to Horne Tooke, the philologist. 'I was never very taken with Tooke,' I remember saying. 'The man was a radical. As for those closing e's on forename *and* surname ...'

But Spilkin would not be drawn. He kept switching the attention back to Darlene, to her sayings and doings, her comings and goings, her hemlines, her hairdos, her curry and rice.

*

Despite Spilkin's efforts, Darlene's dress sense was a subject soon exhausted, and the conversation turned inevitably to 'one man, one vote' and the coming election. A politician with the unconvincing name of Martin Sweet had showed up at the Home where Mrs Hay was now living to canvass support for his campaign, and she had divined that he would be the one to lead his people forth from bondage. He was the only candidate, she said, who would give The Madiba a run for his money. The name of his party would come to her in a minute.

I ventured the opinion that The Madiba might not be all he was cracked up to be. One shouldn't expect too much of a man who had led such a sheltered existence. He had passed nearly thirty years of his life behind bars, and it would take more than a year or two in the outside world to catch up. What would he know of topical concerns?

Darlene shouted me down. The Madiba had more knowledge of the world in his *pinkie,* she said, than I had in my entire white body.

Now that we were on the subject of white bodies, Mevrouw Bonsma wanted to know how Wessels had broken his ankle, and so he retold the tall story about his apprehension of an armed bandit. His nonsense made everyone laugh. 'You and your stories!' Mevrouw Bonsma said. 'What a pity Merle isn't here. She would have loved it.'

'It's not like her to be late,' I said.

She looked at me, appalled. 'You haven't heard?'

'Heard what?'

'I'm sorry, Tearle, she passed away.'

'Passed away?' The phrase cut me to the quick. 'What do you mean?'

'Must be a month ago. I'm surprised you didn't see it in the paper.'

'Ag, no man. I was just wondering where old Merlé was.'

'Jason said it was over quickly. She was at home until the end and then the hospice.'

'She died? I didn't even know she was ill. Were the two of you in touch?'

But she did not want to talk about it. It upset her too much, she said, it would spoil the evening. Mrs Hay awoke as if from a trance and said that no one was more shocked than she. Wessels declared that drinks were needed all round, for the nerves, and went to fetch them. There were no waiters tonight, it was self-service only.

A lost fascicle of 'The Proofreader's Derby' drifted down from the roof of my mind. Dinner at the Budgerigar. The maître d' had recommended the duck and gone away to the kitchen. Fluxman took Georgina's hand in his and carried it up to his lips (Alibians knew without even thinking to confine such gestures to the entrée). There was a faint zest of lemon on her fingers.

'Whatever tomorrow brings, I want you to know that I will never allow anything unpleasant to happen to you.'

'If it's within your power.'

'Exactly.'

Dead. Spadework for gravediggers. Graaff. Graf. Earl. Tearle. The doggerel of the interior life.

I could have killed Wessels. When he came back with the brandy, he'd taken a swig off the top of the bottle two fingers deep, I spotted it at once. 'You said you got hold of her!'

'I left a message with the mate.'

'Douglas has been dead for years.'

'With the domestic, Aubs-ss. What's your case anyway?'

'If you were more responsible, I wouldn't have heard the news in this way, at a party of all places. We should call the whole thing off out of respect for her memory.'

'Don't be ridiculous. We haven't seen Merle for ages.'

'She wouldn't want us to neither. She'd want us to enjoy ourself.'

Spilkin suggested that Mevrouw Bonsma play something to remind us of Merle, as a tribute to her, and she went to inspect the musical machinery in the corner.

'We've got a responsibility to Tone as well. He's gone to a lot of trouble.'

'You can always go home,' Darlene said. 'We'll understand.'

The news of Merle's death was a blow. More so because I felt it not just as a personal loss, but as a professional failure. Mevrouw Bonsma had put her finger on it as surely as if it were middle C. How could I have missed the announcement? The sad fact was that I couldn't bear to read the death notices any more. 'Safe in God's cave' … 'I will always remember your similes and laughter' … For heaven's sake! One was not even free from insult beyond the grave.

I had looked forward so keenly to showing her 'The Proofreader's Derby' and thanking her publicly for her guidance. There was a line to that effect in my speech.

'There's one more angle in heaven' … 'Dried tragically' … 'A cruel twist of fete' … The only fate I could remember now was Clotho. Who were the others? I looked up 'fates' in the *Pocket*. No names. While I was about it, I looked up 'monoblepsia': also not there. Mono was 'one', of course, but one what? **-ia**. Forming abstract nouns. Often in Medicine. Blepsia … blepsia …

Mevrouw Bonsma came back and subsided into her chair. She regretted to inform us that she could not find the button to switch the music manufactory on. She began to hum. This made me aware of a sympathetic murmuring, like a muted string section, from the other tables. More old faces gathering, the newcomers as well as the originals. There was one of the 'Enries, McAllister, some Bobbies and Freddies and what-have-you. The show going on, as it must.

*

It was in the *Concise*. **Monoblepsia**: condition in which vision is perfect when one eye is used, but confused and indistinct when both are used. What was he driving at? I've got a lazy left, it's true, he knew that as well as anyone, and none of us were spring chickens any more. But I wouldn't say I was 'monobleptic'.

I put the dictionary back in its hiding place on the cistern and took out the original of 'The Proofreader's Derby'. How badly I had wanted to show it to Merle. I couldn't help wondering whether her approval was the main reason I had pressed on with it, perhaps even the only one. But she would never see it. What could be done with it now that she was dead?

Then it bore in upon me, unavoidable and crushing, like some juggernaut with 'How am I driving?' carved into its treads. Death itself was the greatest decline in standards of all. That was the certainty I had always been trying to evade. And expiring was just the beginning: unpleasant as it was, it was infinitely more palatable than the decomposition to which it led.

A gruesome vision took hold of me. Merle in her box, disintegrating, liquefying. It was wet, this deterioration, it consisted of leaking and oozing, it struck through crêpe, it wept. And then I saw myself too, mummified, in a box as grey as a ledger, the skin stretched tight as parchment over my irreducible bones. My solid waste, my dry remains. Such fine distinctions would have comforted the squeamish, the ones afraid of water, but they made my blood curdle. A match flared up on the edge of my vision, wet and dry fought a battle on the tips of my fingers. What did it matter? We would have to pass through a river of putrefaction before we issued in dust. Perhaps it would be better to burn, to turn at once to ashes, to go up in smoke.

Morbid thoughts. What next: a public display of emotion? Pull yourself together, Aubrey. Asafoetida ... liquidambar ... turpentine. Now who will keep you in bon-bons, madame (6)? It fitted itself into the dibbled furrows of 'An English Country Garden'.

*

Hunky Dory was twiddling his thumbscrews. Time I introduced myself.

'Good evening. Tearle. You must be Hunky. Any relation to John?'

'It's Rory actually. Hunky Dory's the name of my group.'

'Group? There's only one of you.'

'The drummer split. It used to be Rory and the Hunky Dory, know what I mean, but my drummer fucked off to Cape Town. He says Joburg's getting too heavy.'

Hunky pushed some buttons. 'Wanna see my wah-wah?'

'If it's all the same ...'

'Okay, that's cool.'

'Do you know any Max Bygraves? Let's see ... "Consider Yourself"?'

'How's it go again?'

But I am not a hummer.

By way of showing an interest, I threw in a couple of gems from the Look and Listen: 'How about some Tosh? Or some Luther van Dross?'

*

As soon as everything had been properly connected, Hunky played some 'golden oldies' on our behalf with the sound turned down low. 'Played' is too strong a word: his part in the production involved no more than the periodic throwing of a switch. Killed the conversation stone-dead. *Daisy, Daisy, give me your answer do.* The machines were less like musical instruments than gadgets for poking fun. He had one which gave a passable imitation of the absconded percussionist, and also of a trombonist and a

Scottish piper. It was marvellous. The band played on even when Hunky excused himself to fetch a drink from the bar.

Mevrouw Bonsma, who had been gazing mournfully into the distance since the first note, made a special request for 'Roll out the Barrel', and he was playing that when Bogey arrived with some Patronymić or other in tow. Looking quite spruce, in a leather jacket and a Paisley cravat, the genuine Croatian article, presumably. I noticed, when he slung the jacket over the back of a chair, that the labels of his clothing had retreated to the linings where they belonged. But the pockets were bulging with fruit and vegetables. Must have become a market gardener.

'I am make big money,' he declared by way of introduction, indicating with outflung arms banknotes the size of beach towels. 'It so easy make big money in new Sout' Africa, only lazy pig poor like you.' He was holding out a fistful of notes, as if he meant me to take them. The cheek of it. I made a point of ignoring him, and he stuffed his ill-gotten gains back into his pocket and took out a carrot. What was that Wessels joke about the shrinking rand? It was a manhole cover … Poor old Van der Merwe, if I remember correctly, the butt of all jokes. 'I am just worry about damn Communists,' Bogey went on. 'They want take everytink. Is good we kill them.'

His English was much improved, although he was rolling his r's and twanging away at his n's like a singing cowboy. I should send him across the road to cry on Herr Toppelmann's shoulder, I thought. I could see the pair of them lamenting among the sausage-skins.

Bogey and Spilkin began to talk business. The vegetables were a sideline; the war hero had gone into souvenirs.

My thoughts returned to business of my own: 'The Proofreader's Derby.' Finished or unfinished business? It was hard to say, exactly. Spilkin's question – which is everyone's, when all is said and done – came back to me across the years: 'So what are you going to do with it?' I still wasn't sure. Long before, when the idea of presenting 'The Proofreader's Derby' to the world was still fresh, a false spirit of invention had had me in its thrall and my imaginings had been grandiose. But in the weeks before the Goodbye

Bash, as I laboured to finish the fair copy, I had decided to content myself with making my work known and leaving it at that. If a full-scale championship followed, at someone else's initiative, well and good.

'Ladies and gentlemen.' I would chime on the rim of a champagne glass with a cake fork until I had their attention. 'Many of you will know of the project on which I have been engaged these many decades, the crowning achievement of a long career' – with a nod towards Spilkin – 'my life's work.' I had the speech in my notebook. There was a prologue on declining standards and the prophylactic properties of 'The Proofreader's Derby', some expressions of gratitude – especially to Merle! – a passing reference to the floating trophy, an outline of corrigenda and proofreading marks, a digression on deletion, an epilogue on the rules and regulations. By the time I proffered the photostatic copies, an interested few would be pressing forward to take them from my hand. Perhaps their enthusiasm would be infectious, and the others would ask for a demonstration. Then a few sample fascicles – not the whole thing, of course, this was neither the time nor the place – could be administered right there to whet the appetite. I might provide the corrected version on an overhead projector (if one could be secured), and then glance over their efforts and reward the author of the best one with a prize, as an encouragement. So I had imagined.

Now, as I looked around at my companions – Spilkin and Bogey brooding on the price of ostrich eggs (painted, for the tourist trade, I discovered afterwards), Mevrouw Bonsma and Darlene on the care of the cuticles, Mrs Hay somewhat crestfallen, a herd of Olé 'Enries, Wessels agleam like a toby jug – my ambitions shrank to even more modest proportions. I would be satisfied with a simple announcement. Do you remember 'The Proofreader's Derby'? Well, it's finished. I've done it, as I said I would. If any of you want to take a closer look, I have copies. You only have to ask.

And this is the moment to do it, I concluded, with just the few of us here, the originals and the less disruptive late arrivals.

But Clotho put a spoke in my wheel. As I gathered myself to speak, there was another rumpus at the door, and Errol and Co spilled off the escalator, laughing and swearing. The New Management rushed to defend the buffet.

*

The newcomers came rolling in. 'Yo!' they said. Raylene, Nomsa, Floyd. The new girl – she hadn't been hardened yet, I thought, she might still be redeemed if someone showed her a good example. A new boy too, so black he would have served quite well as a printer's devil. He would scarcely have required inking.

'Huge,' he said, holding out his hand. 'Huge Semenya.'

'Phil, Phil Harmonic.'

They were toting cardboard boxes full of bottled lager. 'The invite said BYOB,' Raylene explained.

Boy backwards to the blood group. Boy backwards. They should have 'Yob' on their caps instead of 'Boy'. I should find some entrepreneur and suggest it as a new range. Yobs and slags: backward children. It would look good on a baseball cap, especially when they wore them back to front on their silly heads. Wessels says it's because they don't know whether they're coming or going. Sometimes they wear their trousers back to front too.

As their contribution to the 'graze', they presented an enormous plastic bag of fluorescent 'Cheesnaks'. Floyd was carrying this fodder over his shoulder.

'I see you brought the Cheese Snacks,' I enunciated, not that I expected him to get the hint. 'No nutritional value whatsoever. You may as well eat this newspaper.'

Spilkin piped up: 'That's a very unhelpful attitude, Aubrey. Some snacks will tide us over nicely while the buffet is out of bounds.'

Unhelpful? Aubrey?

Floyd took a dagger from his pocket and cut a corner off the bag. He was wearing one of his playsuits with cartoon characters on it, odd creatures, hybrids of human and hound. You'd think he was on his way to a pyjama party. Errol, by contrast, was wearing a tuxedo.

'Where did you swipe that?'

'Don't be like rude, Mr T,' Raylene said. Evidently they had all taken it upon themselves this evening to tell me what I should and shouldn't do. 'He bought it at the Jewish Benevolent in Yeoville.'

'It makes him look like an assassin.'

'He's going to get a job as a bouncer.'

'And he's gonna practise tonight, keeping out those what wasn't invited.'

Floyd began to make a circuit of the room, spilling the garish doodahs out on the tablecloths.

The 'invite'? Had Wessels gone so far as to print invitations? And if so, why hadn't I received one?

*

'Have you got any tassies?' Another new one, going by the name of Ricardo. He'd mistaken me for the proprietor. I suppose I did look rather authoritative in my collar and tie.

Tassy? Tassie? It rang a bell. I looked it up: small cup, a Scots term. This Ricardo had unexpected depths of vocabulary. His preference for small measures was encouraging too; the others were drinking straight from the bottle as if tomorrow would never come. Where had he sprung from, I wondered, as I steered him towards the paper cups. Perhaps there was a Highlander in his colourful background? I should find a way of testing his capabilities later on. He might even be ripe for 'The Proofreader's Derby' – and wouldn't that be a turn-up for the books?

*

In the clutter behind the counter was a bottle of Pfeffi, the Pfiffiger Pfefferminzliqör, green stuff as thick as cough mixture. The neck of the bottle had been stretched by some clot of a glass-blower into a screw a yard long, and it had stood unopened on the top shelf, with its cap brushing the ceiling, since the reign of Mrs Mavrokordatos. Floyd climbed up on the counter to fetch it down – they just wanted to see the label, they said, and that bumpy thing in the bottom that looked like a gallstone – and before I could say a word, he had seized the floating trophy for 'The Proofreader's Derby' as well, and they were passing it around and cracking jokes. Lascivious comments about the little gymnast on the lid and their own reproductive prowess.

'Where'd this come from?'

'Ask old Churl,' Wessels said.

Another opportunity to introduce 'The Proofreader's Derby' came and went. It would be madness to raise a serious subject in the company of this rabble. I should bide my time until Errol and Co grew bored and wandered off into the streets. When the old crowd was left, in the lull, I would produce my *fait accompli*.

As for the trophy, much as it pained me, I must let them have their sport, they would tire of it soon enough; not one of them could concentrate for more than five minutes at a time on a single activity, pool excepted. At an opportune moment, I would recover the trophy and put it somewhere for safe keeping. While I was musing, the trophy had already been discarded on table No. 2, and they were beginning to drift off in the direction of the pool room with the Pfeffi in hand. Then that blasted Darlene sat straight up in her chair as if she'd been bitten by a horsefly.

'What's a champoin?' she squeaked.

Stupid woman. No social graces whatsoever, all flaking varnish and crooked pri-horrities. She showed the trophy to Wessels, who buffed it with a forefinger like a maulstick and guffawed. I ought to have cleaned it.

'What is it now?'

'Put on your spectacle and you'll check.'

Spilkin stuck his nose in and smirked, 'This is rich. A corrigendum.'

'Cham-poing!' said Wessels, as if one of his inner springs had finally broken.

They were pulling my leg and pinching a nerve. Spilkin thrust the trophy at me, almost gleefully, and I glanced at the inscription, still touchingly familiar, although I had not examined it closely in years: Transvaal Gymnastics Union – Senior Ladies – Overall Champion. Except that it did in fact seem to say: Overall Champoin. I would have been grateful for a more palatable explanation, I might even have stomached a practical joke – but the simple transposition of i and o was irrefutable. Champoin. Engraved in metal. I had missed it. I saw at once what had happened: those io's in 'Union' and 'Senior' had lingered on the retina and the after-image had bamboozled me. Then again, the whole inscription had been an irritation. Was it because I'd wanted too badly to wish it away that I'd overlooked a blunder so elementary even Spilkin's illiterate lady friend had spotted it?

I felt my cheeks burning as if she'd slapped me.

'I'm glad you noticed that.' A melting ice cube jammed in my throat for a breathtaking instant and then slid down. 'That's half the reason I bought this particular cup. To test the mettle of the champion. Or should I say: the cham*poin*. At the prize-giving.'

She was looking at me blankly. Suddenly, I couldn't remember whether she knew about 'The Proofreader's Derby'. She must have, they all did. Surely Spilkin would have told her. When exactly had Darlene come among us? I looked at Spilkin, for whom my rather clever explanation had been intended. If he could be convinced … He looked back with a sceptical smile on his cherubic lips, but said nothing. I'd never noticed before quite how curvirostral he was, for a cherub.

'There'll be no silverware for you,' I said, 'if you don't know your Onions.' I'd been saving the joke for later, during my speech, but it slipped out now, as if Wessels had poked me in the ribs.

No one laughed.

Once when Spilkin was doing the crossword, he'd got stuck on: O--o--. Authority on English language (6). Naturally I suggested Onions, thinking they had Charles Talbut in mind. Talk about throwing a spilkin in the works. They were looking for 'Oxford'!

Excuse me, back in a tick.

My legs felt wobbly. What a scrape I'd got myself into. And even though I'd managed to come out of it with my dignity unsullied, I saw afterwards that it was the turning point of the evening. From that moment on, it was downhill all the way. It was as if they'd sensed some weakness in my character, caught a whiff of blood on the breeze, and that gave them the courage to turn on me. Like the herd on the old bull elephant.

*

The Gentlemen's room smelt of Jeyes Fluid. I took off my spectacles and splashed water over my head. My excrescences were acting up – the eight o'clock occipital had begun to throb and its companion at nine was itching sympathetically. In the frosted glass of the window, behind which my precious copies dangled over the abyss, the familiar pattern of light appeared, like a pelt stretched to dry. *Tan me hide when I'm dead, Fred.* The paper-towel dispenser was empty and I had to mop my head with my handkerchief. *So we tanned his hide when he died, Clyde.* What do you call a boy who's been mauled by a lion? Claude. One of Merle's games. I felt queasy. I went into the cubicle to suck a mint. The lock had been jemmied, and I wedged the door closed with a cigarette box from the floor. On the back of the door was a childish drawing of genitalia, male and female, labelled 'Supply' and 'Demand'. I could imagine them as two painted signs: Adam and Eve, Jack and Jill, Mickey and Minnie. Or pinned to the notice boards in the public library. What do you call a boy with a car on his head? Jack.

A scrap of melody with its agmas in tatters bowled along the horizon of hearing … *tumblin' along, like a tumblin' tumbleweed* … and disappeared into a merciful silence.

'Ladies and gentlemen, we're going to take a short break. We'll see you in ten minutes.'

Machines must be weary.

I sat down on the throne to compose myself. The King of the Elves. Glancing to one side, I saw that someone had bored a hole clean through the chipboard panelling. What would the vandals think of next? Putting my tireless right to the hole, I discovered that it afforded nothing but an unobstructed view of the urinal. Honestly, I was thinking to myself, of all the senseless – when Hunky Dory came in to relieve himself and made the purpose of the hole apparent. Thank God he didn't see me.

*

Once the neck oil had been broached, there was no stopping them. They wanted to sample every bottle on the shelves. BYOB went by the board. Put it on the tab, they said, devil-may-care, and Tone obliged hopelessly. Errol made his selections with the tip of his pool cue and potted the stoppers off the end of the counter into the waste-paper basket to demonstrate that they would not be needed again. Bokma. *Gestookt,* it said. Bärenjäger honey liqueur, with a plastic bee stuck to the label. Moringué. Made of peanuts.

Wessels came hobbling at the first pop and pronounced the Friesian genever the best thing he'd ever tasted. It wasn't long before everyone wanted to join in. Mevrouw Bonsma ordered Eine Kleine Nachtmusik, and Errol made it a round for the company. The stuff tasted of chocolate.

Tone put a brave face on it. He unsealed concoctions even the Bogeymen had declined to consume and mixed up a cocktail called an Exploding Rainbow. Like a chameleon in a paintbox (punchlines, Wessels). Errol drank it down in a gulp.

I'd never seen such drinking in all my days. It was inhuman. And they would keep forcing one to join in, practically pouring the liquor down one's throat. When one was upset too, what with the shock of Merle's death and the closing down of the Café to deal with.

*

'Howzit Phil.' It was Huge, in the vernacular. 'What you got there?'

'This is a dictionary. The *Pocket Oxford Dictionary of Current English.* The words of a language with their meaning and usage. Mausoleum ~ mean ~ mean ~ mechanical.'

'Come again?'

'Do you know that you're in here?' I asked, thumbing. 'See: **Huge**. Adjective. Very large. *Huge mountain, rat, difference.*'

'It's not "Huge", man, it's "Eug". E-U-G. For Eugene. How's your mind?'

*

Wessels had crept closer to eavesdrop on my discussion with Bogey. I could practically hear his ears flapping.

'Apartheid is yesterday,' Bogey was saying. 'But things of apartheid is today. Many things, rememborabilia ... benches, papers, houses.'

He pressed a business card into my hand. Dan Boguslavić. Apartheid memorabilia. Import/export. The postal address was in Rndbrg. He made me look at his catalogue, eight glossy pages smelling of fresh ink. Ostrich eggs with paintings on them: Sharpeville Massacre. District Six, Forced Removals. Student Uprising, 1976. Stephen Bantu Biko. I thought 'Bantu' was outré? It didn't end with eggs, either. There were all sorts of things for sale. Benches, whites only. Easy to assemble. Blankets, prison, grey. Books, reference.

'People will hardly be interested in this old junk.'

'Wakey-wakey, Aubrey. Is same in Germany now. Uniforms and hats is coming very strong.'

'It'll be Yugoslavia next.'

'Bingo. Is exactly so. Major turnover is rubble.'

As if I couldn't see the fresh produce sprouting from his pockets.

'What's with the veggies?' Wessels said, *sotto voce,* the voice of the sot, canny as ever.

'Is help for keep mout' busy. I am give up smoking an' stress like mad.'

In the pool room, Raylene was dabbing the end of her cue with a block of chalk. She must have felt my eyes upon her, because she glanced up and showed me the blue-smudged tip of her finger. Quite friendly, despite the muscles. There was Errol, bent over the table, with his bottom lip almost touching the cue. Full of himself, slopping over, dripping from that fleshy spout. And there was the improvable girl, drinking beer again and blowing smoke through her nose as awkwardly as a child who has stolen a cigarette from her mother's handbag.

'Quite a jôl, hey Aubs? And you said it would be a damp squid.'

Empty Wessels, the echo chamber, my incontinent, uncontinental china. He should be in Bogey's catalogue amongst the novelty items.

'You've certainly invited a crowd.'

The place was filling up. People who'd never set foot in the Café Europa before, by the look of them. You'd have thought it was a free-for-all. I'd half expected this to happen: chaos had been let loose everywhere and it was even worse during the festive season. Why should tonight be any different? And yet I'd hoped against hope for something fitting.

'Maybe they coming for the cham-*poing*-ships.'

'Buzz off, you jamjar. You urn.'

'Come, Mr Tearle,' said Hunky. 'You mustn't let him push your buttons.'

*

'What you call this spot again?'

'Alibia.'

'Isn't that where old Gadaffi hangs out?'

'You're thinking of Libya, Floyd. This is A-libia.'

'Pull the other one, Mr T. I can check it's only Cape Town.'

'What an absurd idea.'

'Look. Here's Khayelitsha.'

*

Elements, quinary. The digits: thumb and fingers (fore, middle, ring and little). Away with pinkie! To the market with him! To the nursery! The excrescences: occipital (three o'clock, eight o'clock, nine) and cranial (half past five and twelve on the dot). The vowels: a, e, i, o and u. The violences: train, bus, taxi, car and pedestrian.

From the balcony, we watched people gathering in the streets, clustering and parting, drinking from bottles and whooping like Red Indians, rushing this way and that as firecrackers went off at their feet. Some of the fireworks were as loud as bombs. 'Thunderflashes,' Wessels said. 'Used them on manoeuvres at the Battle School in Luhatla.'

A beer bottle exploded on the tar. One of the tribe of Merope had lobbed it from a window in the High Point Centre.

'This is nothing,' Floyd said. 'Just wait till tomorrow night, then you'll see sports. Last Old Year's, someone chucked a fridge from the top of Ponte. It was cool. It landed on a minibus.'

The most dangerous missile that had been launched inside the Café Europa so far was a Cheese Snack.

The taxis: PNK497T To Gether As One … NGV275T The White Eagle … HJS046T Step by Step … MNN391T My Business Is My Parent … LTT843T The Young and the Restless.

A window shattered high above in the darkness and guillotines of glass sheared down. Some of the rabble-rousers swaggered around in the dangerous air, others dashed for the shelter of the verandahs. More and more of them came up the escalator. Errol didn't seem to be taking his duties as commissionaire too seriously.

'Who are all these people?' Wessels kept asking. 'It's only half past nine.'

'You should know. You invited them.'

A horde of Olé 'Enries stampeded in. Mimicking the unsporting frenzy of exultation into which their heroes, the football players, would fly whenever one of them scored a goal, they hurled themselves to the floor between the tables and slid along on their bellies like toboggans, clearly as impervious to carpet as to grass burns. There must be new varieties of both, quite unlike those I knew in my youth.

The 'Open Door Policy' always gives me a chill – you can feel the draught blowing through. I'm for 'Right of Admission Reserved'.

I should have stayed at home.

*

'Don't get me wrong, Hunky. I dig your sound. Reminds me of old Felonious Monk, the musical Rasputin. But take it from me, you would be more of a *hit,* you would be further *in,* if you had a daft hairstyle. Say a bun like the Bonsma. And you must write your name on the side of the big bass drum.'

'Ja, but I don't have a drum. I told you, my drummer left me.'

'I'm sorry, I clean forgot.'

His drummer left him. Can you imagine anything more pathetic?

The brushcut, the moptop, and now these besoms and feather dusters. It's no wonder they can't find jobs.

*

'He had his moments. I remember once he tried to persuade us that the word "robot" was pronounced *"reau-beau"*. Said it was from the French.'

'Don't go spreading lies about me among the rowdies. I know exactly where the word comes from. It was invented by a Czechoslovakian called Capek. Pronounced tʃæpek.'

It should have been easy to turn the tables on them. But even as I was speaking, I could hear that I sounded ridiculous.

Spilkin said: 'Tsk tsk tsk. Pronounced cha-cha-cha.'

Hoots of laughter.

Next thing, he'd be introducing them to Conrad Mandela.

*

'You're on my spot,' Mevrouw Bonsma said. 'My piano used to stand right here, believe it or not.'

For old times' sake, Hunky surrendered the keyboard to her. It could produce a sound reminiscent of the piano, had she wished to perform one of her old standards, but she plunged instead into a new repertoire. He adjusted the keyboard so that it twanged like a banjo, and she played one of the less maudlin Cape coloured folk songs – 'Daar Kom die Ali Baba.' Darlene put her up to it. The two of them were getting along like a shack on fire. Then it was some 'soul' music, which indeed made one want to give up the ghost, and a Croatian ballad left behind by the Bogeymen. Musical mayhem.

I was disappointed in Mevrouw Bonsma. She was cultivated in her own way, and what she lacked in sophistication she had always made good with a certain rustic charm. But this was uncalled for. Had my first impressions of her promiscuous excess been right after all? What did she hope to achieve by making a spectacle of herself? Some spurious popularity among hoi polloi? Did she miss the applause so much?

Someone called for a duet and Mevrouw Bonsma promptly assented. She played 'The Bluebird of Happiness' while Hunky twiddled the knobs to make the oscillator hum. She stood on her toes and swayed like a moored blimp. He waggled his head from side to side like a dog with a bone in its jaws. The machinery barked and bayed. I hardly wanted to think about

the havoc this discord must be invoking in the spirits of the listeners.
I myself was feeling strangely disconnected.

'Anything from the bar?'

'Whiskey please.'

'With an e. As in Tearle.'

'I'll have a Flight of the Fish Eagle and Tab.'

'Are you watching your cholesterol?'

Fish Eagle, Famous Grouse, Cold Duck. Birds of a feather. The Bluebird
of Happiness alighted upon the 'national anthem'. Everyone sang along
and beat time on the furniture. Not that I cared. It was all bound for the
auctioneers anyway.

'We're like the United Nations,' Darlene said.

'Amen.' And then Spilkin's distasteful joke about Eveready and Mevrouw
Bonsma, which I had not thought about for years, came into my mind.

'What a face,' Nomsa said, jiggling on Wessels's knee. 'You're so straight.'

'I refute that. I'm as cryptic as the next man.'

'He's not straight at all,' Wessels put in, 'he's completely bent.'

Spilkin came back with the drinks.

Bouncing up and down on the furniture had given Nomsa the idea for
musical chairs. In a moment, a space had been cleared and some chairs
arranged in ranks (I clung to mine like a leech). It was all just an excuse
to be loud and reckless, to laugh like striped hyenas, to bump their bodies together. Wessels loved every minute of it; he always managed to fling
himself down so that one of the girls would sit on him. The chairs would
soon have been reduced to matchwood, had the New Management not
pulled the plug. They gave Mevrouw Bonsma a special hand. Scattered
applause, like chapters closing. Hunky Dory announced that he would be
taking a slightly longer break than usual to eat his dinner. Once fortified,
he promised, he would 'rock on' into the small hours. I saw no reason why
the machines should not keep themselves occupied in his absence, but it
was a welcome respite.

With that, the New Management unveiled the eats.

*

'Five-finger exercises, that's what the doctor ordered, digital gymnastics.'
I was working my way round to the lexical version.

'Hip hop like sucks.'

'English please, Dory.'

'Later, man. I'm trying to chow, if you don't mind.'

So I was unable to discuss the etymologies of 'woofer' and 'tweeter',
which his performance had revealed to me.

Chow. For now. In the scramble at the buffet table, I bumped into
Herr Toppelmann, another gatecrasher. He had brought a barrel of dill
pickles as a donation, and urged me to try them. But by the time I got
to the front, there was nothing left but buffalo wings and tinker toys.
Blocks of Gouda, cross-sections of red-skinned wiener sausages and green
cocktail onions, skewered on toothpicks like little models of traffic lights.
Reau-beaus.

*

Chairs had been dragged to tables and a few ragged circles constituted.
The old faces and old bodies jumbled up with Errol and Co, higgledy-
piggledy. 'In utter confusion.' Probably with reference to the irregular
herding together of pigs, from the Latin *porcus*. With their snouts in
their paper plates. I'd expected someone to turn on the telly, so that the
silence might be filled up with chatter, but they were all too busy stuffing themselves. For a while you could hear nothing in the Café but an
oceanic murmur of snorting and snuffling, in which the sounds from the
street – hooters, curses, catcalls, explosions, drunken choruses – were
presently submerged.

I looked in on Alibia, where it was still broad daylight, where this
evening had not yet begun, and made straight for St Cloud's Square to buy
a buttonhole for the long-awaited dinner. Perhaps I should splash out on
a bottle of champagne, I was thinking, and pop the question along with
the cork? My old friend Munnery hailed me from the other side of the
canal: 'Big night tonight, Tearle. Don't forget the chestnuts.'

Should I present 'The Proofreader's Derby' now? As a prelude to my announcement, I cleaned my spectacles. When I put them back on again, I noticed the plastic No. 2 still standing to attention beside the sugar pot, and it brought a lump to my throat. I am generally a tough customer. As if to remind me of this fact, a girl with a silver boater on the back of her head took one of the sugar sachets from the pot, opened it with her teeth, and poured the contents into the pocket of Patronymić's jacket.

The gobbling rose, and fell, and ebbed away. As the plates emptied, and the realization that they were still hungry began to creep up on the grazers, the mood of disappointment grew. *They were still hungry.* It made them bloody-minded.

'Just like old times, hey?' Wessels smirked.

'Not exactly. We were a quieter lot.'

'You wouldn't shut up for a minute,' Darlene said.

I addressed Spilkin over her head. 'We got on splendidly in the beginning, before all this other nonsense started.'

'What nonsense would that be, Aubrey? Bad table manners? Talking with your mouth full?'

'This perpetual discord.'

'I think it's quite peaceful around here, all things considered.'

'Even you and I had our differences. But we always patched them up, because we had so much in common to start with.'

'I wouldn't say that. We shared a couple of interests, but we were worlds apart as people.'

'Do you really think so?'

'You're totally *verkramp,* for one thing,' Darlene put in her five cents' worth.

I'd heard the Afrikanerism before. There was silence for a moment, a true silence, round and hollow, as her words sank in, and then the grunting and grinding rose up in it like backwash in a blowhole. Greasy lips, crumbs of food in the corners of mouths, flies and fever blisters, morsels spilled on the tables, gristle, grubs.

'Some misguided people find me unbending, but that doesn't bother me in the slightest. It serves my purposes. My one aim has been to raise standards of conduct and thought, not just between these four walls, but in the world beyond. I've always tried to set an example.'

'That's the bloody problem,' said Spilkin. 'You think people need correcting. Your obsession with raising us up to your level shows exactly how little you think of us. It's the measure of your disdain.'

Then an 'Enry said I was a misanthrope, and Wessels said I hated him, and Darlene said I hated her even more. No matter what I said in reply, they just shouted me down with mock arguments about which of them I disliked the most. They were ganging up on me. I saw it now. At the eleventh hour, they had resolved to drive me out. The drumsticks rose and fell, beating a tattoo on the paper plates, the jaws went on grinding. Darlene drew a wishbone through the gaps in her teeth, first one branch and then the other. 'Make a wish, Tearle.' She held the bone out to me.

My little finger twinged, but refused to pronate.

'You see. He won't even pull with me.'

'He might get a bit of your gob on his precious pinkie.'

'He thinks his arse is parsley.'

Another round of gibing about my hypocrisy, my stand-offishness, I was high and mighty, that was the word, I did not want to mix. Someone claimed that I used to lie about my address so that no one would visit me. I made a spirited defence of the virtue of keeping one's private life private, of maintaining the proper balance between the private and the public – it was a European art, I said, by way of explanation. That caused an outcry.

'Your European affectations were always nauseating,' Spilkin said in a threatening tone, 'going on about the difference between "ambience" and "atmosphere", as if every pretentious little "bistro" didn't lay claim to "ambience". The estate agents cottoned on to it years ago. And picking on the Americans, as if it's their fault there's a Hamburger Hut on Piccadilly Circus.'

'I just happen to prefer the European way of life. I find it civilized.'

'They hell of a civilized … when they not killing each other.'

'Ah yes, the Europeans, you're very big on them. But when you meet one in the flesh, like Bogey, you can't stand him.'

'Bogey is a poor example. The man's a drunkard.'

'Hey, Bogue, did you hear this?'

Bogue?

'You're so churlish.' I supposed Spilkin was referring to the way Wessels mangled my name, but he went on, 'You never have a good word to say about anyone or anything. A real Jeremiah, that's what you are.'

'No, no, I might own up to being a Jonah, but never a Jeremiah.'

'Do you remember when Darlene first came to the Café? You said she was a whore.'

'Well, you did find her in a bordello.'

'Your bum in a drum!'

'How dare you! I met her at the Perm. She was a cashier.'

'I'm telling you, she used to come in here with her clients. As bold a bit of brass as you'd find in a Szechuan kitchen. I saw her with a man once, sticking her tongue in his ear.'

'She never set foot in this place until I brought her here myself!'

'Impossible.'

'You have a memory like a sieve. You shake out the bits that don't suit you.'

'There's nothing cribriform about my memory.'

'If you'd stop trying to be clever and listen to what we're saying, you might learn something for once. We should have spoken up when you started with Evaristus. It shames me that we didn't.'

'When I started what?'

'Calling him Eveready.'

'That's his name.'

'Nonsense. You came up with it. You said he was a bright spark. It's a nasty streak in you. Who else would have called Mevrouw Bonsma "Crêpe Suzanna" behind her back?'

'Spilkijn!' The word stuck out from between her lips like a toothpick.

'Remember when he said the blacks should have their own crockery.'

'He said it was unhealthy.'

'That was the dog!'

'You've got a short memory.'

'I've got a memory like an elephant.' Dumbo rose involuntarily to mind. 'You're all putting words in my mouth, inventing things I couldn't possibly have said.'

'You and your insinuendoes.'

'He never learns neither. Even tonight he called Eugene a rat.'

In the middle of this farce, who should come into focus but Quim, from the Jumbo Liquor Market, smiling at me superciliously, despite my glaring back. Could he have put them up to this? Has he acquired what they call 'clout' in what they call 'the new dispensation'?

*

Enough. This inquisition went on for what seemed like a lifetime. Until the plates, twice and thrice refilled, were empty but for wing-bones in smears of tomato sauce. Then they began to subside one by one into satiated silence, and would have forgotten all about me, casting me aside like another dented trophy – some of them were already nodding off – had Darlene not stoked them up again.

'You worked for the regime,' she said.

'I proofread the telephone directory!'

'Exactly. How do you think the cops found out where people lived? When they wanted to go harass them?'

I am not a coward. In those far-off days when the world was at war, I had itched to go up north, and I'd have gone too, young as I was, if it hadn't been for my eyes. I've stood up to my share of bullies along the way. But my blood ran cold when I saw where this crooked line of reasoning was leading. I remembered looking down on the plot in Prospect Road, where something lay with sheets of newspaper fluttering around it like flames.

'Terrible things have happened in this country,' a young woman was saying. 'And you are as much to blame for them as the men who did the dirty work.'

'Ja, you've got to stop pointing fingers. You've got to take responsibility.'

'It's your fault.'

'Ja, Churl or whatever the case may be, it's all your fault.'

Another wave of resentment. But just as I was beginning to think that they would actually beat me with their fists, or cast me to the wolves from the balcony, things took an unexpected turn. And oddly enough, it was Darlene who started it. In the middle of this diatribe, she suddenly waved everyone to silence and declared:

'But in spite of everything ... *everything* ... we forgive you.'

'Don't worry, be happy,' Wessels said. I noticed that he was smoking a Peter Stuyvesant in anticipation of a hangover.

Now a chorus of drunken voices rose up, a chorus of forgiveness just as vehement and unreasonable as the chorus of condemnation it had displaced, and broke over my head. Some of them were close to tears, some on the verge of laughter, yet others irate or indignant. We forgive you. We forgive you. There was clearly no room for argument. Yes, Mr T! Stop pulling faces. You are forgiven. We forgive you.

I was relieved and grateful. It would have been uncharitable to feel otherwise. But I couldn't see what it was all about. Why the blazes were they behaving like this?

Before I could frame the question in an inoffensive way, Hunky Dory, bless his copper terminals, burst out in a tarantelle.

*

I barely had time to slip the No. 2 sign into my pocket, before hands seized the tables and chairs and whirled them away into the corners. I saw it as the final sundering of the circle.

Dancing! Choreography by St Vitus. They lurched around, waving their arms as if they were trying to stop themselves from falling over, snatching at their clothing and barging into one another. The thickness of their soles had a practical purpose after all; no matter how much they tilted and swayed, they kept their balance in the currents of noise, like deep-sea divers on the ocean floor.

Mevrouw Bonsma and Hunky Dory played another duet, 'Shall We

Dance?' from *The King and I,* which may have been a reference to my head. Tit for tat, I supposed, for the crack about the crêpes.

My mind was full of the accusations that had been levelled at me. What an outpouring of ill feeling! I remembered Mrs Hay's comment about the send-off I was going to receive. Was the whole evening an excuse to humiliate me? I could believe it. They wouldn't let me alone to lick my wounds; they were insisting that I dance, to show that I was part of the gang, even after everything I'd done.

Nomsa, the chubby one, took my hands and dragged me onto the floor. 'Spider! Come out of your web.' Rolling her hips, trying to embarrass me. I stood my ground. I have the grace of a porpoise, a porcus-piscis, a pig with fins. If pigs can swim. Fly, I mean. I called for a bossa nova. No takers. I called for a lambda. The latest dance craze from Greece. Nothing doing. Nomsa went round like a schwarma machine. What did she mean by 'Spider'? Daddy Longlegs? Stood on a fanatic's foot, name of Arbuthnot, spelt it for him, letter-perfect, by way of an apology. Why did she remind me of vegetables? Eggplant. Her skin had a purple sheen I'd never observed on a colour chart. The sweat stood out like wampum along her hairline. Plastic pearls at the throat. Mouth improbably large, lips like segments of some sea-fruit, a creature that looked like a plant, but was really an animal, something that would snap if you touched it.

I was feeling queasy, should have had more sleep last night, should have eaten a proper dinner beforehand, should have tried the buffalo wings, resisted the whirligig. The liquor had gone to my head. Or had one of them slipped me something? Wessels, I'll wager, spiking the whiskey with that coffin varnish of his. Flight of the Bumblebee. It was one of his life's ambitions to see me drunk. He couldn't bear my self-control, precisely because his own was so sadly lacking.

Nomsa was going round in circles. Nail her other foot to the floor. Showed me her back. Not to mention her backside. Bang! Bang! Allowed me to escape to the table. I wasn't even sure if this was No. 2, now that all the furniture had been jumbled together, but quite by chance I found my old chair. Ah! In its supportive grasp, I regained my definition.

Four glasses of chocolate-brown liquor were lined up in front of Floyd. He shoved one of them at me. 'Blowjob?'

Now what.

With a sly grin, he picked up a straw and drew its paper wrapper down to one end, crumpling it up tightly. He put this worm down on the table. Then he raised a small quantity of liquor up in the straw and spilled it out over the worm's tail. At once, the thing stirred into life and began to stretch itself out on the table top. While I watched this phenomenon, frankly amazed, Floyd burst out laughing. The cartoon characters on his clothing winked with their human eyes and jerked their waggish hindquarters in time to the music.

I drank the brown stuff. Mocha.

*

'Why you so black?' Wessels said to the girl with the silver boater in an effort to charm her, trying to press his ear to her chest. 'Are you sick?'

*

'Eugene. Got a minute? I thought you'd want to know that you're in the *Concise* under your proper name. At **Jeep**. Unfortunately I don't have a copy to hand, but I do have a citation in my notebook here. "Eugene the Jeep. An animal in a comic strip." Shall I write it down for you? No, that won't do. Never smoked myself, but you're bound to throw it away. Pass me that serviette.'

'What's this about a animal?' Raylene sidled closer. 'You better come right, before I tell Huge to bliksem you.' To strike, as with a bolt of lightning.

'You're in questionable company, son. Slovo's in there somewhere, at **Slovene** ... and Smuts at **blight** ... and Tutu plain and simple. Interested in sport? Here's Borg, the tennis player, at **borrow** ... Senna, the racing driver, unkindly defined as a laxative ... Roux, a mixture of fat and flour used in making sauces ...

'On the back of your hand? I suppose so, if someone has a pen.'

*

'Punt up the Volga!' Don't ask me. The music was so loud, one had to shout to make oneself heard. Without my lip-reading, I shouldn't have followed a word anyone said.

For the umpteenth time that night I headed for the Gentlemen's room, to relieve myself of nothing more than unwelcome company. But Mevrouw Bonsma spotted me, returned the keyboard to its owner, and dragged me back onto the dance floor. I was powerless to resist. Her hand on my arm was like a manacle, although her mobile surface was soft and moist. She kept bumping against me like a deflating weather balloon, leaving powdery smudges on my blazer. She was listing from foot to foot, rocking from tiptoe to heel, punching holes in the floor with her stilettos. A dotted line appeared in the puff pastry underfoot, and the floor gave beneath me. I saw myself plunging through into the kitchen of the Haifa Hebrew Restaurant down below, sprawled among the cabbage rolls.

After strenuous bouts of proofreading, the pages would cloud into negative, and I would see the solid space around the empty printed word, as if hot lead had been put down on the paper, burnt its way through, and plummeted into the void on the other side. The blocks of type drifted downwards in slow motion, with undeserved majesty, like commodities in television advertisements, like spacecraft or bombs.

Without warning, Mevrouw Bonsma pinned me in her arms and started gnawing at my ear. No amount of squirming could free me. The baked goods of my head. Plunge in the skewer. Something wet dripped onto my hand. Had the toothy tiara drawn blood? Or was the hairdo melting around her ears like a mousse? Then I felt her chest heaving, thrusting into mine.

'I beg your pardon, Tearle,' she sobbed, 'in this instance, I am emotional.'

'So are we all, Mevrouw.'

'I am reminded that I made beautiful music once upon a time. Now I must type to make ends meet.' She held one of her hands up for inspection, a clump of red knuckles and fingertips bruised with carbon-copy blue. 'The minutes of meetings. The essays of students. The application for a licence.'

Pressing against me and swaying from side to side, in a swirl of noise, light and fumes, she went on brokenly about the Dorchester and the rotation of the dinner menus and God knows what else.

'Poor old Merle,' I said when the machines paused for breath. 'When was the last time you saw her?'

But she just clung to me more tightly, with long tears and face powder turning to batter on her cheeks, until the music went on again, and then she squeezed me into a new shape and dragged me after it.

Over her shoulder, I caught sight of the improvable girl. Why should improvement be a dirty word? Or was Spilkin joking? Her chest said: Get funky. I didn't mean to stare, but there was no way round it if one wished to read the message. Funkily. Funkiness. Whenever I'd seen her before, her hair had been caught up in a faggot on the crown of her head. Now that she had let it down, it proved to be in braids, as thick as monkey-tails and as spiky as cacti. They reminded me of some species of fern whose name I have forgotten. She was tossing them wildly as she danced. 'Corybantic' was the word that leapt to mind. Her gyrations drew my eyes to her belly – a musk-melon slice of bared flesh – and her navel. It was a proofreader's mark: ◌. Delete and close up. Stick to and part from (6). Cleave.

Steffi Graf went waltzing by with Max Bygraves in her arms. Stepping on his toes in her tennis shoes. The bulge on her hip, under the grass-green sheath of the evening gown, showed where a ball was tucked into the band of her knickers.

'Umpteen.' It belongs in the nursery vocabulary. Is there no mature alternative?

*

With a deft twist of my torso, I broke free of Mevrouw Bonsma's pruinose embrace and made for the balcony. There were a couple of questions I meant to ask Spilkin before I excised him from my life entirely, like a swollen appendix.

'Don't worry, be happy,' Wessels shouted after me.

There were crowds outside as well. I pushed my way through to the railing.

In the grisly shadow of Patronymić, Spilkin and Bogey were leaning. Spilkin's hair was standing on end like a clown's, Bogey had a carrot jutting from his mouth like a cigar. Gifts and Novelties. He gave me an apple and suggested I throw it into the street. I looked over the railing at the people milling down below. How big a fool did he think I was? The missile was bound to enrage someone. I gave the apple to Errol, whom I found at my shoulder, and he let fly. Meanwhile, I took out a pencil and sharpener.

Bogey licked the end of the carrot and dipped it in Patronymić's pocket. It came out sugar-coated. Crystalline ash.

'Old Aubs-ss is quite a literati, when you get to know him,' said Wessels at my side.

'Literatus, you burr. Not that there's a grain of truth in the accusation.'

'He's been working on that exam of his again. The other day he was telling me how you guys helped him with the papers and so on.'

'Now that really takes me back,' Spilkin mused. '"The Proofreader's Derby." I'll never forget it. An utterly mad scheme. That's when I thought: he's a crank. Aubrey, I can't tell you how pleased I was when you got that bee out of your bonnet.'

He had become a splinter in my flesh. What was it Wessels had once called him? … A chip off the old shoulder. To steady my nerves, I turned the pencil in the sharpener and watched the shavings carried away on the breeze.

'As a matter of fact …'

Bee? A Cheese Snack buzzed out of the night and caromed off the side of my head.

'Merle used to say that there was something almost Casaubonish about you and your "System of Records". She thought you were never going to finish it. Not that one required special powers of perception to make that deduction.'

Spilkin's expression drew me back to solid ground. 'Of course not,' I said, while 'The Proofreader's Derby' burnt a hole in my pocket.

*

My copies were still there, and so was the *Concise*. **Funky**. Presumably not 'terrified, cowardly' but 'fashionable, unconventional'. Having a strong smell? **Umpteen**. Indefinitely many. How would one spell 'Casaubonish'? Casualty department ... catafalque ... cat-and-dog ... But I wasn't dressed for fartlek. (I've since discovered who Edward Casaubon was, and it's an injustice second to none that we should have been mentioned in the same breath.)

*

'All this was mantled,' Herr Toppelmann said sadly, wagging a pimply pickle at the four walls, 'and now also dismantled shall be.'

*

They came shouting 'Viva!' and dancing the highveld fling. A mob. Capering about like baboons. From the Latin *babewynus:* an Old World monkey with naked callosities on its buttocks. To think that the Café Europa had once been a haven in an urban jungle, and now the jungle was in here too, on our side of the pale. I looked for a fist waving an apple as a credible excuse, but found no such comfort. Hunky Dory ran away. The hurdy-gurdy soldiered on without him. Patronymić flung Bogey down in a corner and lay on top of him. I hadn't realized he was a bodyguard. Why should Bogey require the services of a bodyguard? There was a rushing to and fro the likes of which had never been seen before under that roof. The proofreader's motto came back to me (in the illuminated version that hung on the wall behind Erasmus's desk): 'Widows and orphans first.' So I stayed where I was, in my proper place, a model of dignified restraint.

'Kill the bull, kill the farmer!' I'd heard it on the radio. A native folk song. Obviously, if one kills the bull, one kills the farmer, figuratively speaking, by depriving him of his livelihood. Why make a song and dance about it?

In the green meadows of Alibia, the lion was not lying down with the lamb, exactly, but Frieslands were chewing the cud alongside Jerseys and Aberdeen Anguses. Not an Afrikander in sight. I was there, under a willow-pattern thorn tree, flat on my back in the sweet grass, in clover. The sward beneath, succulent and overgrown, the sky above. One could never lie down in the veld as such, it was too scratchy. A stile over a bony hedgerow. A humpbacked bridge over a babbling brook, running off at the mouth. *Can the ocean keep from rushing to the shore? It's just impossible.* Mevrouw Bonsma, give the devil her due, had taken over the keyboard and was trying to restore order – *If I had you, could I ever ask for more? It's just impossible* – but it seemed to have no effect. Her spotlit face was as soft and wan as a ripened Camembert. A full moon stooped over Alibia, broadening the daylight. In the market place, the grocers were crying the last shipments of bottled beer. On the canals, the boatmen were singing. Children were climbing trees and rolling hoops. Men were shaving boards and twisting nails, tilling the earth and reaping the harvest. A busy human noise burbled up. But it was not the music of the Alibian masses gathered to honour the champions of order: it was the invaders in our midst, clamouring for blood. One beggar at the banquet might be tolerated – but a whole crowd of them? Then a voice rose above the din, like an ark on the deluge. Spilkin. Screaming blue murder. It was enough to give a chicken goose-flesh. There he was fleeing, leaping over the furniture, scattering paper plates and bones. They ran him to ground in the corner by the Gentlemen's room. I was shocked to see Darlene among the pursuers, grinning maniacally, her turban unravelling like a winding-sheet. They crowded in on him. I saw his mouth contorted, his eyes streaming. What were they doing to him? Their shoulders shook, their heads bobbed, their buttocks squirmed. Then the crowd scattered abruptly. There seemed to be more of them than ever. Spilkin had vanished. Had they consumed him?

I might have escaped their attention, had I remained frozen in my seat. But I must have risen spontaneously, meaning to intervene in Spilkin's defence, despite everything.

'Fuddy old barley!'

The strangers set upon me like a pack of wolves. Many hands seized me roughly. I wasn't going to submit without a fight. I let them have it with a few epithets, the sorts of things that would ring in the ears for days afterwards. I kept my eyes peeled, too, in case there was ever an identity parade. As I fell, I saw Mevrouw Bonsma stoking up the boilers, and then 'The Battle Hymn of the Republic' poured forth over the *babewyni*. Familiar faces, but trampled out of shape, tossed like leaves in the far reaches of the room, stuck to the wallpaper. *Glory! Glory!* Huge with the lid of the trophy on his head. Wessels – brandishing the crutch – 'Boonzaaier!' Raylene.

A storm of blows rained down on me. Fists, foreheads, kneecaps, elbows, heels. Hard bone under soft flesh. My spectacles, knocked sideways on my cheek, reduced my assailants to a blur. Yet by a fatal twist of optics, one lens was turned into a magnifying glass, and a single face came into focus within its frame: Darlene. They had wrestled me to the ground, and she was sitting on top of me. The bones in my chest cracked and splintered. I put out my hands to ward her off and clasped instead the swollen yellow bulb of her belly. Great with child. Spilkin? *Impossible!* And now, in all likelihood, gone for ever. Widows and orphans. But they were not even married. Before I could pursue this train of thought any further, my spectacles were plucked from my face and the world flew away. *Climb every mountain … Ford every stream … Follow every rainbow …* Hands were kneading my cheeks, pinching my chin, tweaking me, buffing me. My face felt cold. Then it went completely black before my eyes.

*

Merle.

*

My breath came back. I listened to its roar, to the buckled ribs squeaking, the throat rattling. Extraordinarily, I was still alive. The black gave way to grey, shot through with red. Blood in my eyes. I wiped them clear. I patted my head for gashes. Nothing gapingly obvious. One, two, three o'clock, four o'clock … Excrescences all present and accounted for. Pockets? Ditto.

I felt around on the floor for my spectacles. A fuzzy teddy bear appeared out of the mist, weeping hysterically, and put them in my hand. Somehow they had come through intact.

The world fell back into focus. A circle of people around me, but keeping their distance, like onlookers at the scene of an accident, chattering among themselves, pointing, pulling faces. I got to my feet. An odd little man stood before me, a black man, some faithful old servant perhaps, who had witnessed the massacre. He was wearing one of the caps with 'Boy' written on it, and weeping inconsolably. He wanted to speak to me, but every time he caught his breath, he was racked by a fresh outpouring. I considered slapping him across the face – it was the recommended remedy – but he had something wrong with his skin. It was as thick as paste. Scar tissue. Wattles of mortified flesh at the neck. Had he been burnt?

Despite the disfigurement, there was something familiar about him. Could it be Eveready? No, he was taller. I studied the features, the gasping maw, the eyes brimming with tears, the dripping nose. And then it came to me in a flash that made me reel. It was Spilkin. And in the glare of that recognition, I saw something else: he wasn't weeping at all. He was laughing.

I looked in disbelief at the wider circle. Then I pushed the spectacles up on my forehead with a numb index finger and let the lenses fall in front of my eyes again like guillotine blades. Mustering my spent energies, I put each face to the proof. There was Huge, as black as pitch. Nomsa with her wig on sideways, a few shades lighter, but black nevertheless. McAllister, an 'Enry, and a brace of Eddies. And they were black too.

I touched my own face and looked at my fingers.

Black.

*

I scrutinized without blinking. The Café was barely recognizable. They had turned it upside down. Nothing but black faces on every side. Who were the invaders? The newcomers? The old regulars? One couldn't work out who was who any more. I felt abandoned by friend and foe alike.

The sea was spilling over the breakwater in the Bay of Alibia. The other walls were streaming too. What was this liquid? Some frightful solvent in which all things would float and dissolve, gradually losing their shape and running into one another. A solution of error. It was striking up through the carpet, I was soaking it up like blotting paper. Sharp little objects pierced through my soles, and my shoes filled with a prickly sludge of delenda.

I bloated and swelled. The trembling in my innards, which I had taken for fear, revealed itself as rage. A rage to disgorge this superabundance of error, to get rid of it once and for all, to blow my stack.

I erupted. I gave them a mouthful, the Amadoda and Abafazi, the shit-houses (excuse my Anglo-Saxon) of the holey city of Joburg, the Rotary Anns, the Pump-action Bradleys, Mr Frosty and Mrs Sauce, the Bushbuck Rangers and the Crystal Brains, the bobbers, the peddlers, the stinkers. I poured it out upon them, the printer's pie, the liquid lunch, the hasty pudding, the swill of tittles and jots, the gaudy Gouda, the Infamous Grouse, the Jiffywrap, the Oatso Easy, the Buddywipes, the Wunderbuddels. Items, one-eared: Vincent van Gogh … John Paul Getty III … Dumbo … innumerable teacups and coffee mugs. I was not in the habit of speaking in this fashion, of seeing, of saying disorder, of chaos, of coarseness, but I had lost my tone. Where were my cadences, my measures? My pages were out of order. To be Papenfus or not to be Papenfus? What do you call a man under a shroud? Paul. Names for dogs, should I ever acquire one: Riley … Puccini … Houdini. Down ~ down ~ down ~ down. The beast would outlive me. It was past my bedtime.

They fell silent. Ashamed of themselves. Mevrouw Bonsma stopped playing. Then there was nothing but the sound of my own voice. It made no sense to me, it was nothing but a long, fluent spewing, it made no more sense than water gushing from a hose. I watched the stream of sound, I saw bubbles breaking underwater. I looked harder. Words were floating to the surface, and I rose with them into the familiar air, and found my place. My ears popped and I could hear properly again. Could hear a new voice, which was really my old voice, replete with authority.

I put my hand in my breast pocket and grasped 'The Proofreader's

Derby', my logical conclusion. But prudence caught my wrist. What if they thought I was fetching out a weapon? Nowadays, every second person was carrying a firearm. So I reached instead for Errol's pool cue, which was leaning against the wall beside me. How was I to know they use these things to beat one another?

*

I reached, as I said, for Errol's pool cue, his Helmstetter. An object lesson. It was my intention to screw it apart, to present them with Helm and Stetter, to screw it together again. Not with the arrogant ease of its owner, but with authority.

Errol tugged at my sleeve like a child.

'Keep your cretaceous little fingers off my blazer.' I jerked my arm free. The moment had given me unnatural physical strength. Errol stumbled back as if I had punched him, and banged into one of the marauders, a brute with boot polish on his hands, wearing his jacket inside out. They grappled and clinched.

Was that all it took, one act of will, one assertion, to rouse them from their torpor? They claimed afterwards that I made to attack them with the pool cue. Can you credit it?

And then pandemonium. Errol rose up in the air with his loose-limbed body rattling, as if an almighty hand had pulled his strings, and flew backwards through the stained-glass windows. It's a miracle he wasn't hurt. He can thank the Jewish Benevolent for giving him that tuxedo. Chaos all around, a full-scale bar-room brawl. They were trying to get at me, to tear me limb from limb. And in their midst Spilkin, the lord of misrule, stirring them up against me. Against himself! He was pummelling his own face, as if he meant to blacken it further, inciting them to do their worst. Why should he side with the mob? Why should he tar himself with the same brush? Was it a sign of how low he had sunk, or had he always been this way, and I as blind to his faults as he to Darlene's? She was there too, egging them on.

Then the bootboy, the one who had thrown Errol aside like a rag, stood in front of me. In his paw, the knife looked like a bodkin of the kind the compositors once used to winkle out type. He fell upon me. The blade struck my chest with a thud and went in. The force of the blow hurled me to the floor. I looked down and saw the hilt jutting from my rib cage. Pierced to the pith. I waited for the gush of bloody words. I felt no pain, but that was normal. I saw a crush of legs and enormous shoes with treads like teeth, and the plastered foot of Wessels, the toes squirming vermicularly, like the party snacks come to life. Then, in the thicket of combat boots and gymnasium shoes, I recognized a pair of winkle-pickers, with golden chains and black buttons. Moçes. He seized me under the arms and dragged me backwards into a corner.

Black and white and red all over.

'You mustn't pull it out,' someone said. 'That's what they say at the St John's.'

The fighting raged all around us.

I lay there, floating between life and death, waiting for the red river to carry me off into oblivion. It was a pleasant feeling, I wished it might endure. Then I opened my eyes and the spell was broken. I could not bear to look at the knife, lodged so improbably in my being, but I had an overwhelming urge to discover the extent of my injuries, to explore the split flesh, the intimate gore, while my life ebbed away. I reached my hand inside my jacket. And that was when I discovered that the blade had gone straight into the heart of the *Pocket Oxford Dictionary.*

*

I am not prone to theatrical gestures, but I made the most of this one. When they saw me walking calmly among them with the knife sticking out of my chest, the more superstitious invaders ran away, with Errol and Co in pursuit.

It was during this final skirmish that Floyd stabbed himself in the head. 'They stuck the old tawpy,' he said afterwards (meaning me), 'so I schemed I'd stick them back. But I stuck my own self by mistake.' I heard Floyd bellowing like a fatted calf and saw him fall by the glass doors. The others set upon him and began tearing at him greedily, like children opening presents under the Christmas tree. Were they ripping off his labels? No, it was worse, they were like scavengers at a carcase. A foot flew loose and landed near me. Not a foot, don't be ridiculous, only a shoe, one of the oversized bootees. The tearing noises came from Velcro fasteners – the buckles were all false.

The knife was a comfort to me. It made me feel young and healthy, invincible and immortal. I did a circuit of the room, enjoying the feeling. Not to mention the holy terror in the eyes of all who beheld me.

Then I strolled onwards to the Gentlemen's room to see what I looked like *in extremis.*

*

The mirror had been stolen, of course, and all I could see in the tiles was a swarthy smudge. I went into the cubicle for some paper to clean the muck off my face. And there in the corner stood the floating trophy. I sat on the toilet seat and rested the trophy on my knees. I looked at my image in its tarnished surface.

I wished I might cry, but my eyes were dry as newsprint. A lifetime of poring over galleys had done my tear-ducts no good. Just as damaging as breaking limestone, if not so dramatic. And now this boot polish on top of everything. Perhaps I would need an operation, like The Madiba, to restore my sense of sorrow.

Better assess the other damages. No broken bones, thank God, but my pencils reduced to tinder. I pulled the knife out of my chest. One perfectly good blazer ruined. As for the *Pocket,* the blade had gone right through the alphabet. There was a course to be plotted from A to Z in wounded words, but the exercise struck me as merely technical, a forensic parody of lexical gymnastics.

With the knife in my hand, I became fully aware of how narrowly I had escaped. A *salto mortale,* a double tearle with a twist, unfolded in my brain. Here was the double tearle: **jot** (small amount, whit) and **iota** (atom, jot), both from the Greek *iota,* which is the letter 'i' without the dot. A jot is an iota. And here was the twist: **tittle** (small written or printed stroke or dot).

Ergo: an iota is a jot missing a tittle or a tittle missing a jot. By distinctions as fine as these, I had cheated death.

*

The Café looked like a battlefield. I picked my way between broken-backed chairs, over the shattered kaleidoscope that was all that remained of the chapel, to the boneyard of the buffet. I was famished – it is common in the aftermath of combat – but there was not so much as a crust left. Mrs Hay passed like a ghost behind the blinds. In the doorway, Floyd lay clutching a bag of ice from the Hebcoolers, with a knot of people around him. Spilkin had the bloodied head in his lap, Darlene the stockinged feet. She glanced up accusingly as I approached. 'Are you satisfied?'

'By no means.'

'You've got a lot to answer for.'

I'd expected a chorus of mockery, but the levity of the early evening had been replaced by a sombre calm. All these faces masked in black. Even Darlene, the mustafina, was as black as night. It was no longer amusing to anyone.

Mbongeni had surrendered the tea cosy as a makeshift tampon and let his hair down. Cotton-waste wads as long as my arm, the kind of thing that would come in useful at the printing works for wiping down the presses. I showed him the skewered *Pocket*. The word quickly spread that I hadn't been wearing a bulletproof vest after all. It dispersed some of my mystique.

'You an incredibly lucky somebody.'

'You could of died.'

'But Floyd saved your life.'

'I wouldn't go that far.'

'Ja, they would of come back to finish you off if it wasn't for Floyd.'

It made no sense to me that he should have leapt to my defence after what had happened. But it seemed crystal clear to them. Errol, dusting a confetti of shiny glass from his padded shoulders, said: 'You a puss, Churl – but you one of our boys. Leave it or lump it.'

Hunky Dory reappeared. 'I called 911 and *wah-wah-wah*,' he declared, which was his way of saying that he'd summoned an ambulance.

*

The ambulance men put Floyd on a breadboard, for the spine, they said, and wrapped him in aluminium foil like a garlic loaf, for the shock. He looked smaller than usual. They carried him out through the glass doors. Incongruously, I thought of Merle. I saw her packaged by the undertakers, stuffed into a fluffy brown bag with a zipper up the front, like an oversized slipper. The idea was suffocating.

There was a muddle on the landing outside as they bundled the stretcher onto the escalator. In the midst of it all stood Wessels, with the silver boater on his head, swinging his crutch imperatively and bawling out instructions. His face had been rather inexpertly polished, except for the chin, which was as shiny as a toecap. The sight of me seemed to enrage him.

'It won't help to have a long white face,' he said. 'If you truly sorry for what you done, you can make yourself useful. Go with to the hospital.'

'I beg your pardon?'

'I say it might help to have a white face along.'

What relevance this had, seeing that I myself was as black as the ace of spades, was beyond me. In any event, I had no wish to go about in public looking like a greasepainted minstrel. I turned away and watched the ambulance men descend towards the pavement with their burden. The ghouls had gathered, crowding around the open doors of the ambulance, trying to catch a glimpse of Floyd.

Then Wessels stuck the crutch in the small of my back and thrust me bodily onto the escalator.

In my younger days I might have vaulted clear, like that daredevil in the tartan underpants; but when a man of my age finds himself upon a 'moving staircase', he moves with it, willy-nilly. I descended. A distracting consideration echoed in my mind: could one be carried *downwards* by an escalator? Strictly speaking. The very normality of the distraction reassured me that I had come to my senses. De-escalation. The sort of ugly back-formation that would be in the book on top of the cistern. Along with the sayings of sailors and whores. Anything goes.

I had every intention of returning to the fray. It was not as if I could be 'bounced' from the Café Europa, especially not by Wessels. I would go straight up again, I would take hold of his foliose lapels and shake him until his epiglottis rattled. Didymus. Skeuomorph. Jughead. Imagine quaffing the contents of that bonce – that watery pap! Point made, I would track down Moçes, the hero of the moment, and thank him for his help. A small reward might be in order. And then I would retrieve 'The Proofreader's Derby' and leave the whole lot of them to the mess they were in. That ersatz eighth edition could stay where it was, at the mouth of the sewer. I had every intention … But on the pavement, I bumped into the improvable girl, clambering into the ambulance. The child looked quite lost against a backdrop of cheerful onlookers. Evidently, the sight of a broken crown tickled them.

'What are you doing out here?'

'I'm going with Floyd to Casualty.'

'Where's his girlfriend?'

'She won't come. She says he's just being pathetic and he's not going to spoil her bash with his nonsense.'

My heart went out to her. She must have sensed it, because she began to plead with me to accompany her. I felt my resolve weaken. I should do the decent thing. Who else could be relied upon? Dimly, I couldn't help wondering whether I had played some part in this fiasco. Floyd's bloody head rolled over on the pallet. The wound was like the flesh of an olive peeled away from the pip. The doctors might give him a talking-to while they were stitching him up. Perhaps it would all work out for the best.

An ambulance man nearly saved my bacon by holding up a bloodstained rubber glove. 'You can't come with. Only the wife in the ambliance.'

But the girl said, 'He's my father-in-law' – as if that were within the bounds of possibility – grabbed me by the arm, and before I knew it, they had hauled me aboard and slammed the door behind me. The sirens broke into a Hunky-Doryish melody.

'I've never been in an ambulance,' she said.

'Neither have I. Strong as an ox.'

She smelt of watermelons. It reminded me of the watermelon feasts of my youth.

And then Floyd groaned: 'You gotta stand by me, Mr T. Don't let me die, man. Don't let me die.'

*

I had a funny turn on the way to the hospital.

It started with my crooked reflection looking back at me from the shiny surface of some piece of equipment. **Crank**. An eccentric person, especially one obsessed by a particular theory. See cranky. Perhaps from obsolete *crank,* rogue feigning sickness. I was sick. I belonged in an ambliance. I should lie down on the other stretcher. Flawless backflip with a double twist to **crank**, part of an axle or shaft bent at right angles. From *crincan,* related to *cringan,* fall in battle, originally 'curl up'. I was bent. Twisted in the wrong place. Crinkum-crankum. I needed straightening out. Ortho – as in orthopaedic, orthographic – from the Greek *orthos,* straight. 'You're so straight.' I moved myself backwards and forwards, watching my shape deform around the elbow in a silver tube. My head distended into a soggy melon, elongated impossibly, like a blob of molasses on the end of a spoon, until it suddenly flowed around the bend and stretched my neck into a long thin string. Just as my head was about to detach itself entirely and plummet, I moved slightly, causing my shoulders to swell up and flow after it in a rush. An abrupt constriction in the chest. My recent past, unsavoury to the last morsel, churned in my stomach and threatened to revisit the outside world.

The girl put her hand on my arm. Her voice was sweetly scented, candy-striped in flavours of green, it came close to my ear. 'Are you okay, Phil?'

Jesus Theodosius Christ. I drew her attention to the shape of my head.

'Lie down. They won't mind.' A confirming glance at the ambulance men, solicitous phantoms in a miasma of Old Spice and congealed regulations.

She pushed me back, and soft and melting as I was, I keeled over on my side. The canvas stretcher was red, and so was the rubber sheet, and the blanket. Sensible choice. My feet got left behind on the floor, and she picked them up like a pair of shoes, very professionally, I thought, and put them on the end of the stretcher. Long practice, probably, with a drunken father. Harvey Wallbanger, everyone's pal.

Floyd was trying to speak, but they had clamped an oxygen mask over his jaw. Blood welled in his crizzy hair, and one of the ambulance men swabbed it with the tea cosy. Blood was dripping out of the aluminium foil too, around the waist, and splashing the leg of the girl's jeans. I tried to raise my arm to point it out, but it was glued to the stretcher.

Lava lamps. Never had the temerity to buy one. I used to see them in the display window of the Okay Bazaars in Eloff Street, on the way home from Posts and Telecommunications. What was that substance? It always seemed to be red. Was it magma? Magma come louder. Magda. Merle. Mazda. Bogey. Bonsma. Organs suspended in … that other substance the lava was floating in … Amniotic fluid? Glycerine? Oil. Muddy Waters. Meltdown in my overheated brainpan, my head full of words, my prolix crackpate, my derivations running into one another. The sump. The sumptuous. The crankcase. I am not the crankcase, I am the crank itself. I have been moulded into a shape that was once useful, but is useful no more. I saw the crank. It looked like an S fallen flat on its face. A proofreader's mark: transpose. Cause to change places. Change the natural or the existing order or position of. The crank was made of hardened steel, and it was lying in a crankcase made of oak and lined with velvet. The velvet was blue, midnight blue. And the crank was me, that rigidly mortised form, that stiff. I was lying in my casket the way I prefer to lie in my bed, on my side, with my knees drawn up and my hands clasped between them. I was lying like that now; the rubber sheet that cleaved to my cheek smelt of methylated spirits. My stomach heaved.

I opened my eyes. The girl was shaking my shoulder.

'Wake up, we're there.' And then, with a morbid laugh, 'I thought you were dead.'

*

The ambulance men lifted the stretcher down onto its unfolding wheels and rushed Floyd away, and the girl hurried after him through the automatic doors, down the neon-scalded corridor to the accident unit.

Bodies under blankets. And the barely breathing, leaking fluids onto the floors. And the walking wounded, bound up and splinted, stilting along in their rods and slings. Everyone was staring. Was I an oddity in this infernal place? Had the Johannesburg General gone so solidly black in a matter of months that a white man was already a novelty? I should have come with the dirk sticking out of my chest. That would have given them something to gawk at. But then they were used to bodies stuck with blades and spikes, prickly as voodoo dolls. At Baragwanath Hospital, patients strolled in off the streets with axes lodged in their skulls.

I decided to take a turn in the grounds to clear my head. But I had not gone far when I tripped over something in the darkness. A signboard jutting out of the lawn. De Wet Irrigation. My stomach said: enough is enough. Heave-ho! Lights were shining through the trees in the valley below. Probably a squatter camp. Or was it Harold Oppenheimer's place? Living without a care in the world, either way. And poor old Tearle, fallen to earth again, on all fours in a herbaceous border.

*

I traced the girl to a desk in the reception area. The clerk seated opposite smirked when she saw me coming. It was time to take charge.

The girl gave me her seat. I reached for the admission form with one hand and a pencil with the other, forgetfully, and found nothing but splinters and ground graphite in my pocket. The clerk resisted. She put her fist down on the form like a rubber stamp and raised a plastic pen like a club. I brought my upside-down reading skills into play. Once you've tackled some Tagalog against the grain, a bit of plain English is a piece of cake – even standing on its head. The form was blank except for the word 'Floid' on the first line.

'That's a "y",' I said, 'F-L-O-Y-D.'

She took up the Liquid Paper, and I oversaw the lavish whiting out, the painstaking correction.

'We'll put you down as the next of kin. What's your name?'

'Shirlaine,' the girl said.

'Can you spell it for me.'

'S-H-I-R-L-A-I-N-E.'

It was like something you would find attached to a block of flats. Mount Shirlaine. I repeated the spelling for the clerk.

'Do you have surnames?'

Floyd was a Madonsela. Shirlaine was a Brown. True enough.

The clerk got half of it wrong. I made her do it over. No medical aid, of course, no fixed address. Allergies? Work, I should say. Previous conditions? Drunk and disorderly. Legal guardian? Impulsively, I put my own name in that box. Black humour.

Then Shirlaine went to find out what had become of Floyd, and I sat down in the waiting room on a plastic seat bolted to a metal frame, and tried to gather my thoughts. The seat was one of many, and I was surrounded on all sides by the wounded and bereft, all facing the same way in rows like passengers on a bus, all bathed in neon as corrosive as acid, all gazing forlornly at the Coca-Cola machines ranged against the wall.

*

i. For 'information'. Why didn't they use a capital? That minuscule 'i' suggested that the information was not very important. Information was what the doctor ordered. Surely they didn't think people would confuse a capital 'I' with the Roman numeral? I knew what that dot was, of course: a tittle. But what was it doing there? The question had never presented itself to me in exactly this form. Why should 'i', of all letters, have that detached fragment floating above it? I went through the alphabet in my head. Just 'i' and its neighbour 'j'. All the others were solid citizens. In that inhospitable waiting room, reeking of blood, it seemed ominous. What hope was there that prescriptions would be filled correctly, that the right tissues would be readied for dissection, that the appropriate procedures would be followed and diagnoses struck, that proper disinfectants would be swilled in the scrub-ups, that the diseased limbs would be amputated rather than their healthy counterparts?

These apprehensions proved diuretic. I sought out the cloakrooms. Dames and Here.

And so I saw myself in a mirror, lit up, fluorescently frank, covered in boot polish. How could it have slipped my mind? Tearle in blackface. Denigrated. A creature of nightmare. An aged printer's devil, on the wrong side of pensioning-off, not going out in a blaze of glory like that lucky McCaffery, but dropping dead in the traces like Aldus Manutius's slave. Black. No wonder people were staring. I fetched some toilet paper and cleaned away what I could, which was not very much. Was it indelible?

All along Hospital Street, as they called the main corridor, I looked for a nurse. No one familiar was on duty in the wards near the dispensary. I recalled that the gentler natures were sometimes posted to Paediatrics, on the sixth floor, and so I made my way up there. By a happy quirk of architecture, the sixth floor was just one above the ground. Nothing but glum faces. They were none too pleased to be on duty, but they cheered up no end when they saw me. Laughed like drains. I let them enjoy the joke. Then I persuaded one – a Xhosa, to judge by the cluck-clucks of sympathy – to lend me a hand. She poured methylated spirits into a kidney dish and scraped at me with wads of cotton wool until my skin hurt.

When she was finished, I made her fetch a mirror. I looked like a badly printed half-tone, dismally grey. But it would have to do.

*

On the television screen in the cafeteria, an American amazon called Debra Marchini was chewing the news to pap and sending it south down her supple windpipe, while her audience, a few forsaken inpatients and other lost souls, slept in the beige plastic chairs. I helped myself to a tea bag and hot water from the urn. Half a lemon would serve nicely as a febrifuge, and a rusk to line the stomach. As I dipped the rusk, Mrs Marchini dispatched another bolus of spittle-softened flong, and share prices plummeted in the Far East. The sun was setting in Atlanta, Georgia. Whereas we, according to the clock on the wall, were fast approaching the witching hour. I found a long-handled feather duster behind the silver counter and reached up with its end to change the channel. More news. Bloody bodies and broken glass. A terrorist attack on a Heidelberg tavern. The Germans were always a bloodthirsty bunch, never mind what Herr Toppelmann said. It would serve him right if some terrorist gang made mincemeat of him.

What a blast they must be having at the Café Europa. By now, Wessels would have uncorked the Cold Duck. Thank God it was all passing me by.

In the bowels of the hospital, someone began to weep. A thumping sound, like a chef tenderizing steak, issued from the air-conditioning ducts. Two Thomas Dooleys awoke at the same instant, at separate tables, and looked around with bleary eyes.

*

'I thought so! I've been hunting high and low for you, and I was just going to split when I remembered your thing about tea.'

Shirlaine had Floyd's bloodied pyjamas, sheared off him by the nurses in the theatre, bundled up in a plastic bag. The cartoon character on the cloth was more irritating than ever. Perhaps it was that Snoopy Doggy Dog whose adages they were always invoking? The eyes were human enough, but the ears hung down at the side of the head like a Labrador's.

'How is Floyd?'

'Needed some stitches. Sixty-five, if you don't mind. But the doctor says it's only a flesh wound. And he says it's just as well he stabbed himself in the head, which is full of bone, or it could have been serious.'

'Are they releasing him?'

'No, he's got to stay overnight.'

'I suppose we should get going then.'

'Suppose so. I just want to go past ICU to say goodbye.'

We went downstairs.

'Thanks a lot, hey, Phil,' she said. 'You really stood by me.'

'Don't mention it.'

*

The matron left us at the window, with instructions not to tap. 'They can't hear you.'

Floyd lay on his back, the sheets tucked tightly around him. His head was tilted back on the pillow, his eyes were wide open and glazed, his mouth yawned. The wound had been bandaged, but I imagined that I could still see it throbbing under the gauze. He looked pale, strange to say.

The screens had been drawn around the next bed. The green cloth sprang out, buffeted by blows from inside, as if some master of ceremonies was trying to find the join in the stage curtains. But Floyd did not stir.

There is a simple physiological explanation, I've been told, for why the mouth of a corpse is so often open, as if the dead were gasping for breath until the end or gaping in horror at their first glimpse of the hereafter. I could almost believe that Floyd had breathed his last. Or was he pretending? Any moment now, he would start up and hurl a bedpan against the glass. But there was no sign of life.

'Do you think he's all right?' I asked. 'Perhaps we should call someone.'

'He's fine. You can tell by the ghetto-blaster.'

She meant the spurt of green lights on the monitor, pulsing to the rhythm of his heart.

*

'Shall we call a taxi?'

'Are you paying?'

I reached for my wallet. Gone. Swine must have stolen it during the invasion.

'We could walk,' she said, 'if you're up to it. It's not that far.'

'That would be very pleasant.' Little did she know how fit I was for a man of my age. And if I exhausted myself, so much the better. It was bound to be dangerous as well, but after what I'd been through, ordinary perils no longer daunted.

We went out into the dark brown air. It was a thirst-slaking antidote to methylated spirits and floor polish, the smell of wet earth and cut grass rising up from beneath our feet as if it had been raining, although there was not a cloud in sight. The night sky was black and full of asterisms. A shooting star exclaimed and fell silent. Then a spatter of rain with a rhythm as steady as the pulse on the machine told me that De Wet's sprinkler system had switched itself on.

'Do you mind if I call you Phil? You won't think I'm too big for my boots?'

'That would scarcely be possible. And my name isn't Phil. That was just my *nom de guerre*.'

'Oh.'

In fact, she wasn't wearing boots tonight, but a pair of oversized 'tackies', visibly sticky things like the pedipalps of an insect, marked correct with a grandiloquent tick. Nike, the label said. A Nipponese tycoon, I supposed; the marketing managers of the East could not be expected to know Nike of Samothrace, the Goddess of Victory.

'What is it then? Your name.'

Aubrey, the erl-king, a bearded goblin who lures children to the Land of Death. Well, I wasn't exactly bearded, but I needed a shave. 'It's Tearle.'

'Is that why they call you Mr T?'

'I'm afraid so.'

'You don't look like him.'

'Like who?'

'The guy who used to be on TV.'

'Who's that?'

'Mr T in the A-Team. He was nothing like you. A big black guy, very well built, wore a lot of jewellery. And he had a Mohican.'

'Seems singularly inapposite, I must say.'

'Sure.'

'A Mohican? I thought we'd seen the last of them.'

The guard raised the boom for us, as if we were an emergency vehicle, and we went on into the darkness.

'You have an interesting name yourself,' I said.

'My mom made it up. My grannies are Shirley and Charmaine, and she didn't know which one to call me after, so she came up with a combination. It couldn't go the other way round, because that would have been "Charley".

The poor thing was a portmanteau.

*

'What do you do actually?'

'I'm retired now, and pursuing private interests. But I was a proof-reader.'

'What's that?'

I explained.

'Sounds about as exciting as reading the Phone Book.'

'Exactly.'

'So your spelling must be really good?'

'I like to think it's perfect.'

'You showed that cow of a clerk a thing or two.'

'That was just my party trick.'

'Maybe you can help me fill out my form for the Tech. I'm going in for Dental Technician. My mom wants me to apply for Beauty, but I'm not keen.'

We walked on for a while with our mouths full of teeth. Then I spelt 'houyhnhnms', 'ophthalmology', 'phytophthora' and, to show that difficulty was not purely a matter of consonantal bulk, 'chaperon' and 'anemone'. She seemed engrossed. On the spur of the moment, I introduced Mark Twain.

'Properly: Samuel Langhorne Clemens. An American. He said he had no respect for anyone who could spell a word only one way. Rubbish. Spelling a word one way ensures that we all know we're talking about the same thing. Once you're free to spell a word any way you like, chaos comes marching in. Imagine what might happen to Floyd if the doctors spelt the names of the medicines any way they chose. Or the names of the patients.'

She nodded in agreement, and so I pressed on: 'Spelling changes everything. A realization in the English manner is more profound than an American-style *realisation*. Just as it is more meaningful to go through an experience than to go *thru* it. There's a trend towards the superficial you should be mindful of; everything is being coated in the shiny veneers of advertising, that most appropriate exception to the rule. Nothing has done more to take the Christ out of Christmas than the "commercials".

Silence, for twenty paces, apart from the nutty crack of my heels on the pavement and the clammy whisper of her soles. And then she asked, with a touch of guile: 'Aren't there more important things to worry about than commas and full stops?'

'Absolutely! The decline in the standard of proofreading is linked directly to the decline in standards everywhere else. Because nowhere is the maintenance of standards more important than in proofreading. Indeed, that's all it is.'

More nodding and another silence, during which I realized with some discomfort that this was an approximation of the discussion I'd hoped to have with Spilkin earlier on. All mixed up with bits of my Introduction to 'The Proofreader's Derby' and my keynote address to the inaugural championship. She could hardly be expected to hold her own on Horne Tooke or the Great Cham; yet I had no doubt that she would get the gist of it perfectly. Anyway, it had been so long since I'd had a chance to express myself fully on these questions, to argue my case, that there was no stopping me. The Highlander coming into view over her shoulder, aloft on his pedestal against the sky, a stone-hearted McAllister with the Transvaal Scottish clinging to his skirts, led me boldly on.

'You mustn't think that I don't understand the appeal of the illicit, the urge to turn everything upside down. I was young myself once.'

I recalled the thrill of coming across a friend or colleague when I was proofreading the Book, and the temptation to slip in some secret message, a private joke we could laugh about afterwards, a nickname, say, or a mock title. A Miss Havenga came to mind, and a frivolous scheme I'd had for secreting a harmless endearment in the Book of 1976. How relieved I was today that I had conquered these impulses, I said, and never once compromised my professional principles.

While we were chatting, we had passed the College of Education and turned into Queens Street, and now our path sank down towards Empire Road. I was gearing myself for the uphill slog into Hillbrow when she proposed making a detour past the playground in Peter Roos Park. She wanted to play on the swings. The park was a mass of leafy shadow behind a corral fence of creosoted rails. Who could tell what desperadoes, dossing in the shrubbery, might be roused by a careless footstep, but an exhilarating recklessness had possessed me, and in any case, I needed to take the weight off my feet. We crossed the street, slipped between the trees on the traffic island, raising their jagged palms to menace us, and found our way through the undergrowth.

*

The playground looked like an obstacle course, all bristly ropes and tarred wattles, gigantic ladders made of logs and pits full of gravel. I sat down on a rough-hewn bench, a splintery conjunction of railway sleepers and split poles, and she skipped over to the swings. Soon she was coming and going, scooping up momentum with her feet and dragging it back with her calves, higher and higher, flinging herself against the sky, hurling herself into the future, stalling, plunging down again and back. It was enough to make me ill just watching her.

She took instruction well, I thought, but our discussion had been one-sided. She'd hardly got a word in edgeways. I should ask her some personal questions, encourage her to speak about herself. If I was going to cultivate her, that is ... She came and went, came and went ...

I thought about Henry Fowler and Major Byron F. Caws. In the second edition of the *Concise,* back in 1929, Fowler had acknowledged the quiet, unselfish efforts of Caws, an amateur in the best sense of the word, who for years had sent him packets of foolscap devoted to perfecting the dictionary – 'all this for love of the language not as a philological playground, but as the medium of exchange and bond of union among the English-speakers of the world'. How could one square this admirable point of view with the modern taste for 'fun'? What would Fowler have made of my idea for lexical gymnastics? Would he grant that it was closer to healthy exercise than the childish whiling away of time associated with the playground?

Of course, gymnastics and fartlek were two different things. Even the simpler gymnastic moves – the handspring or onions, the backflip or graaff – took years to master. Whereas one could teach the fundamentals of fartlek in a morning. Then again, one did not enter into lexical training for its own sake, but to build up strength and skill for proofreading itself. Fartlek gave you stamina; gymnastics gave you speed. It was necessary to put that across to a beginner.

I sat musing on such questions until she tired of the swings and came running back. The watermelon smell, sweetened by exertion and the foretaste of dawn, was vividly pink against the drab and dusty green of eucalyptus. In its cheery atmosphere, we set out again along Empire Road.

*

Up Hospital Extension, she insisted on walking in the middle of the road, skipping along the dotted line as if she meant to leave her mark there. I kept prudently to the pavement.

'What if a car comes?'

'At four in the morning?'

'It's possible.'

'Just whistle.'

I told her how I had nearly been run down by a delivery van from the Atlas Bakery. And then, in the middle of my story, a vehicle did come, an ambulance like the one we had ridden in, appearing over the rise shrieking and flailing, and bearing down on her so quickly that my heart stood still. She scampered out of the way with a laugh. All the same, the episode brought the interior of the ambulance and Intensive Care back into our minds, and put a damper on things.

'It's important to be able to whistle,' she said.

I kept my reservations to myself, and said, 'I heard you whistling earlier, when Hunky Dory was experimenting on us. It was very loud.'

'Thank you.'

'I've never been able to whistle myself. Even as a boy, when I might have found the knack useful for calling dogs and so on. I think it's the dental make-up. You've either got it or you haven't.'

'Anyone can learn.' She hooked her forefingers – not the little ones, mind you, which would have been conventional and marginally more ladylike, but the indices, right up to the second joint – into the corners of her mouth and let out an ear-splitting example.

*

A dawn like a prison blanket lay over the city as we crested the hill. The brisk pace we had sustained throughout the climb suddenly faltered, and we were seized by an odd sort of aimlessness. We should have turned left, towards home, but instead we followed the curve of the brick wall to the right into Kotze Street.

'This is the big chookie,' she gestured towards the Fort. 'My dad was in here once. For discharging a firearm in a built-up area.'

'Title deeds department,' I said in turn, pointing towards the Civic Centre up ahead. 'Friend of mine worked there, name of Banes. Records of owner-ship and sales. A wealth of material.'

We strolled on to the end of the block. The aimlessness intensified. We should have turned back or crossed over the street. Instead, we turned left and strolled downhill again. We gazed at the façade of the Institute of Immunology. We went on to the statue of miners wielding the water-drill. She thought they looked like rugby players or policemen, the bruisers she saw working out at Sam Busa's Health and Fitness World. We gazed south along Rissik Street, over the railway lines, to the grand towers of the city centre. Then at an unspoken signal, we toiled back up to the front of the Civic Theatre.

For the first time in months, the terrace came into my mind. Had they put back the flagstones now that the place was open again? I led the way to the side of the building – and there they were. Shirlaine had never seen anything like it: I had to explain how it worked. The inscriptions were illeg-ible in the gloom, and so she waved the flame of her cigarette lighter over the flags. We went down on our hands and knees and moved from stone to stone. The letters scratched into the cement were puckered at the edges like scar tissue, and there were drifts of yellow sand in the hollows where hands and feet had been pressed.

'Who are we looking for?'

'Max Bygraves.'

'Who's he?'

'A singer of yesteryear. A particular favourite of mine.'

'Don't know him from cheese.'

'Look. I think it's Hedy Lamarr.'

'Who?'

I could see I would have a lot of explaining to do. Flora Robson, Hayley Mills. Stars of stage and screen. I imagined myself kneeling before a tabula rasa of wet cement. What would I choose to impress upon posterity? My leafing thumb? My index finger? My mutton fist? No. My head. It would have to be that, warts and all.

Inevitably, Shirlaine tried to fit her tennis shoes into Beryl Grey's stiletto prints and marvelled at how small they were. All the women had such tiny feet! I had to dispel the misapprehension; the cement had merely subsided before it dried.

We crept up and down over the flags, the flame cupped in her palm like a little torch, but there was still no sign of Max Bygraves. On the edge of the terrace, a thicket of purple grass swayed in the breeze like an enormous anemone. My knees began to ache. I suggested that we repair to the park on the south side of the building to watch the sun rise.

Another bronze in the gloom, another unholy trinity: three fat men, with orthopaedic boots and plaster casts for feet, three Wesselses, dancing in a circle.

'It's the family of man,' she said. 'Like me, my mom and dad, and my brother Duwaine.'

We found a bench on the lawn, with a south-east prospect that wouldn't place too much strain on the neck. I confessed that I hadn't seen a sunrise in three decades. Sunsets, on the other hand, had remained a firm favourite down through the years.

The sky in the east was already the colour of mercury. Then the sun came up. Just a flat disc of light that hurt the eyes.

*

As soon as it was light, she took out a cigarette packet and handed it to me.

'Thanks, but no thanks.'

'No, man. Read this.'

I read: 'Camel cigarettes are blended from the finest Oriental and American tobaccos.' And at the bottom in small print: 'R.J. Reynolds Tobacco Co, Winston-Salem.'

'Now tell me how many e's there are. You can read it again. Count them.'

'Twelve.'

'I'm impressed,' she said, although she sounded disappointed. 'You'd be amazed how many people get it wrong. They usually say ten or eleven. I think they leave out this one in "Reynolds" or the second one in "cigarettes". Old Floyd said five, but that's Floyd.'

Suddenly I saw that she was extending the hand of friendship, and I grasped it, symbolically speaking. 'It's simple enough, if you're acquainted with the methods of proofreading. I could show you some techniques. The boustrophedon, for instance.'

'The what?'

'It means the way an ox turns in ploughing. Instead of starting at the beginning of each line, you go backwards and forwards like this. Some proofreaders I used to know – I've lost touch with them all over the years – swore that their best work was done backwards! Proofreading against the grain, we say. Others claimed that it was better not to know the language at all. I myself once proofread the Pentateuch in isiZulu, against the original (I don't have a word of the language) *and* against the grain – and made only one error.'

For a reason I still cannot fathom, this struck me as one of the saddest things I had ever said. A wave of melancholic nostalgia washed over me. Why do such things always come in waves?

*

The precise shade of her skin troubled me. The obvious choices had adjectives clinging to them, like swatches from the do-it-yourself counter, tropical sands, amber dawn. But it was more like fudge.

*

'Are you hungry?'

'I beg your pardon?'

'Do you want some breakfast?'

'I could do with a bite.'

'I'm going to swing past High Point for some chicken. Do you want to come?'

'We don't have any money.'

'Never mind, I'll draw some.'

I thought the streets would be empty, but there were still people about, night owls like ourselves, and more and more of them as we went along Pretoria Street towards High Point. Disreputable-looking people with dim eyes and hollow cheeks. Staring at us, nudging one another, sniggering. And who could blame them? What a sight we must be, walking along side by side, as naturally as sneezing, and she in her active leisurewear. Like a lecherous old duffer with a prostitute. If we bumped into Wessels, I'd never hear the end of it.

The Black Panther Debt Collection Service. That was new. The Carry Nation Shebeen. We stopped at an automated teller machine and Shirlaine fished a plastic card from the front of her shirt. Get funky. Why on earth did they call the thing 'Bob'? Personally, I don't believe in dealing with automata. Cash in hand, we went towards the passage beyond Diplomat Luggage Specialists. Daylight Pharmacy was open, living up to its name. Dispensing remedies for the morning after, no doubt, or prophylactics for the night ahead. We went down the stairs, past the straggly clumps of ha'penny creeper, the parched hydrangea, the arthritic aloes. In the instant photograph booth under the stairs, where I had once seen Bogey capturing the back of his head, a tramp was squatting to relieve himself.

How could one say, when there were so many contenders for the honour, whether this was the low point of the night or not?

*

The golden fringes of the 'Merry Xmas' sign stirred like the filaments of a sea creature as we went through the turnstiles. Fish-eye mirrors hung

at angles over the aisles, so that the cashiers could watch out for shoplift-
ers. I saw the shelves reflected there, filled with pot-bellied bottles and
jars, and myself, ashen-faced, with my head bulging hydrocephalically.
Everything was out of shape.

The last time I'd set foot in here, it was to rebuke the manager for the
menu's b-b-q chicken and cornish pastries. I saw him now, coming out
of the office, and caught his eye. I thought he might come over for a chat,
but he just raised a rascally eyebrow and went on towards the bakery.

We made our way to the fast-food counter. A whole flock of chickens
lay spreadeagled on the grille, with their wings flung wide, as if they had
died surrendering. We found a place at one of the toadstool tables. I have
never been in favour of eating standing up. It does the digestion no good.
Not that our scurvy fellow diners seemed overly concerned with their
health. Most of them were eating bristly chicken legs in that beriberi sauce
they're so fond of. Shirlaine went to place our order.

While she was gone, a hag in a blue dustcoat came to clear away the
papers and wipe the table tops with a damp rag, succeeding only in
smudging the fingerprints in the animal fat and spreading a film of grease
more evenly over everything. I remembered the dirty streets we had come
through, the flotsam of beer tins, the curled and blackened scrapings of
porridge pots, newspapers, food wrappers, mealie cobs, tripe ribbons.
What would it take to wipe these surfaces clean?

Shirlaine brought a whole chicken on a sheet of waxed paper. It was
savage, this obsession with fowl. Before I could say a word, she hooked
her thumbs into the alimentary canal, gripped the carcase with both
hands, and tore it in half with a great splintering of bone and splattering
of grease. Good Lord. We ate. She used her fingers and I did my best with
the plastic knife and fork.

'Make a wish, Tearle,' she said, proffering the wishbone hooked into her
little finger. 'And don't tell me what it is, or it won't come true.'

As luck would have it, I won. I wished that I could pass this entire city
through the eye of the proofreader's needle.

*

Gazing into the chaotic interior of the Café Europa, I felt like Moses arrived at Canaan only to find that the day trippers with their wirelesses and their wine in boxes had got there first. Shirlaine rapped on the glass with a coin, hoping to rouse some drunken Charon from the ruins. Then I thought to give the door a shove, and it swung open. We went in.

I lifted my eyes to Alibia. I expected a blank wall, a black wall, I thought the city would have been knocked down and carted away piece by piece. But it was still there, with its lights winking gaily in the dark. O happy Alibians, blessed citizens of elsewhere! In your bright rooms, before your clear mirrors, dressing for the Goodbye Bash. The big wheels are turning, the coloured lights are dancing on the esplanade, the band members are tuning their instruments in the park. On the football field behind the church, the warden keeps guard over the fireworks to make sure the schoolboys don't steal them or let them off early. The nut-roasters on Opera House Square greet me cheerily as I go down the steps to the river to hail a punt. The champagne is on ice. I will have a long hot bath, and shave at the window, looking out on the lights.

The Café Europa had been trashed. That was the word for it. We picked our way through the debris of paper cups, monkey vines of coloured streamers and tinsel and toilet paper, tattered dollars, carrot tops, bottles of every shape and size, the jewelled shards of the stained glass. And Cheese Snacks everywhere, crunched into powder, like shed gilt. The newspapers lay scattered on the carpet, with their pages curling from the wooden spines, like moths that had flown too close to the chandeliers. I was tempted to take one of the staves as a keepsake – but that would reduce me to the level of the vandals. I would take nothing more than what was mine.

They had used the base of the floating trophy as an ashtray. Filthy, stinking habit. I emptied the ash out in a potted palm. Were those Wessels's tatty butts? Mevrouw Bonsma's red-lipped little gaspers? Errol's marijuana 'zols'? The cup was full of slops. Cold duck and cold turkey. But at least no one had bled into it. I emptied the slops into the palm too. It really didn't matter any more. Everything once mantled dismantled had been. My trophy had only one ear. The missing one lay on the carpet like an italicized question mark. I put it in my pocket.

Now to retrieve my copies of 'The Proofreader's Derby'. I went into the Gentlemen's room and opened the window. A scrap of plastic fluttered from the pipe: the rest of the bag was gone. I climbed up on the washbasin and tried to stick my head out of the window so that I could see whether they had fallen into the well below, but it was impossible. My neck gave a warning twinge. Could someone have stolen them? Or had an ill wind scattered them to the four corners of the city?

Into the cubicle to look for the *Concise*. That was also gone. Someone must have needed it to prop up a table leg or weigh down a roof. To some people, a dictionary is no different to a breeze-block or a pumpkin. Perhaps it was just as well, with my neck acting up. No burden was too great, if one had bearers to do the donkey work; then one might carry all twenty volumes of the *Oxford* off to a desert island. But when you were responsible for the haulage yourself, it was a different story. My whole body had begun to ache.

Do you remember the one about Speedy Gonzales and his chum Pedro, who were lost in the desert? I used to have it down pat, but now it's gone like the rest, and all that comes back is the punchline: 'Pull yourself together, Pedro.'

I must have looked shaken when I returned to the Café, because Shirlaine said: 'I can't believe you're so upset this joint is closing down. It's not the end of civilization, you know. There are new places for whites opening up in Rosebank.'

It dawned on me that it really was over. Somehow I had imagined that Wessels and I would be sitting here for ever, while the world ran down around us like an immense grandfather clock.

*

'Do you want this?'

It was a little book with a floral binding, which she had picked up on the balcony. A rhyme had been inscribed on the flyleaf:

If this book should chance to roam,
Box its ears and send it home,
to Darlene Spilkin
33 3rd Avenue, Fez Valley

The first page was blank. The second and third pages contained a drawing of a wall, topped by the legend: 'Be a brick. Help me to build a wall of friendship.' There were a dozen bricks in the wall already – everyone from Hunky Dory to Henry the Eighth.

'You keep it.'

*

I kept a lookout for the Queen of Sheba, but the throne was vacant. Dumbo was in his cage, dumbfounded as ever, saucer-eyed. You'd think he'd been slurping the canned maroela beer. I addressed him fondly, exhorting him to revolt, to smash down the bars. Given half a chance, I would have taken up Quim's quirt, with its beaded handle, hanging against the wall by the refrigerators, and thrashed that dumb beast to the point of rage. I had a vision of him on the rampage in Kotze Street, gathering his comrades about him, a herd of pink elephants, trampling down pedestrians, tossing urchins around like straws.

But he didn't seem to recognize me.

Hypermeat was flogging half a dead sheep @ r16.95 a kilogram. On the tiled window-sill, behind the burglar-proofing, leaned a blackboard that read: Nice meat – Lekker vleis – Inyama enhle. Just a sample of the official languages, of which there were now dozens.

That @, which I had always regarded as the very omphalos of consumerism, reminded me of Shirlaine. I had expected some awkwardness when we said goodbye. She would try to give me a peck on the cheek, I would pat her shoulder and do my best not to wound her with my spectacles. But she had disappeared as if I didn't exist.

*

The delete mark is the most individual of marks, as distinctive, some say, as a fingerprint or a signature. I worked with a Dixit whose delete mark was a floating balloon, filled to bursting with nullity; a Figg who had a sharp-tongued scythe for cutting a swathe through verbiage; a Walker who strung up a hangman's noose; a Diallo who had a frying pan; a Munnery with a magnifying glass.

And I knew a Rosenbaum once (he was never a colleague), whose delete mark silhouetted his own Semitic nose, complete with a connoisseur's nostril for sniffing out error – although you had to turn the page upside down to see it.

As for me, when I started out at Posts and Telecommunications, I modelled my mark on a monocle; somewhat old-fashioned but elegant and unwavering. I regarded that lens as the echo of my proofreader's eye. But as I grew older, it began to change. A gap opened up, an unpardonable gap, where the lens was attached to its handle. It was probably my weakening eyesight. Yet it wasn't until the Café Europa's days had been numbered that it began to remind me of an unravelling bond, a broken circle with a loose end dangling from it.

A chap named Niblo, who tasted copy for the Government Printer, once argued that the mark, my 'fanciful' derivations notwithstanding, was neither more nor less than a delta. Short for 'delete'. But I see no reason to believe him.

*

Gideon the watchman stared at me as if I'd risen from the dead. When I scrutinized myself in the mirror, under the full force of the neon light, I saw why. My face was a deathly grey, and edged all round in black, like a telegram full of bad news.

Merle. I went to the stack of unread *Stars* on the corner of my desk. I saw that she had died on the second. The notices were in the newspapers of the third and fourth. The same wording in each of the three messages: Passed away after an illness. Lovingly remembered and always missed by Jason, Kim, Liam and Jessie. By her daughter Kerry, son-in-law Fred, and granddaughters Bianca and Katherine. And by her cousin Louella. An entire family conjured up. By some miracle, there was not a single corrigendum. But it was a pity about that repeated refrain, which revealed that they hadn't bothered to compose their own messages. Perhaps originality meant little in these circumstances. It had always struck me as ridiculous to apostrophize the departed, as if they took in a daily in the hereafter. What would I have said?

But nothing would come to me.

I emptied my pockets. The No. 2. The ear of the trophy. Pencil tinder. The *Pocket Oxford Dictionary*. When I tried to page to the back, the leaves wouldn't part. Still wedged together. In the depths of X, Y and Z, among the endpapers, I found the tip of the stranger's knife, snapped off in the board. I prised it out with my staple remover: a little curved triangle of steel like a shark's fin. I dropped it into the trophy, along with the plastic sign and the question mark.

I put the trophy on the window-sill and propped the original of 'The Proofreader's Derby' against it. It was a comfort to me, small, but comfort nevertheless, that I had been prevented – that I had prevented myself – from exposing this unfortunate construct to the public. But what had become of the photostatic copies? A dozen of them, riddled with corrigenda, had been let loose in the world. Things to be corrected; things corrected. Two sides of one coin. The urgency of preparing a corrected version pressed in on me. But the world was so full of error as it was. Surely it could wait for one night?

Then I collapsed on my bed and slept the sleep of the dead.

*

I awoke in the dark with a word sounding in my ears. Avogadro! Avogadro! I couldn't place it. Avogadro! Then my ears popped and I realized it was a dog barking. I'm beginning to think there's a wire loose in my brain – not a screw, mind you – but some short circuit, some faulty connection. With all the upsets of the past weeks, starting with that damned bakery van, it would hardly be surprising if something had been shaken loose.

Or perhaps it's not the wiring so much as the plumbing; a small leak through a cracked wall, spreading insidiously, making everything damp. The barking was somewhere in the building. I made a note to tell Mrs Manashewitz. The contract was clear: No pets allowed.

What had become of Il Puce? Was she pining away in an empty room? Greyfriars Benny.

My watch showed nine o'clock. Post meridiem! I'd slept the day away.

The previous day and night came back to me.

I went through to the lounge and switched on the light. My dictionaries sprang to attention on the shelves. Who will marshal them when I'm gone? The floating trophy was on the window-sill, with its one ear cocked for the sound of gunshots in the street outside. 'The Proofreader's Derby' lay face down on the carpet. On the curved lid of the trophy, the gymnast was pirouetting against a square of night, poised as ever, perfectly balanced.

All these trifles would endure, when their names, nestled now in the folds of my brain, were dead and gone.

I must get on with the correction. There's no rest for the wicked.

A fire rocket rose in the distance and burst in a rattle of explosions.

I crossed to the window and looked south, for want of another option. What was it Merle advised me to do? To look on the bright side ... The lights of motor town lay before me, the highways coiled like cables on the matt black of the mining wasteland, and beyond them the southern suburbs, the buffer zones, filling up with informal settlements, and the townships. Movements were afoot in those dark spaces that would never be reflected in the telephone directories. Languages were spoken there that I would never put to the proof. As if they were aware of it themselves, the lights were not twinkling, as lights are supposed to do, they were squirming and wriggling and writhing, like maggots battening on the foul proof of the world.

Dear readers,

We rely on subscriptions from people like you to tell these other stories – the types of stories most publishers consider too risky to take on.

Our subscribers don't just make the books physically happen. They also help us approach booksellers, because we can demonstrate that our books already have readers and fans. And they give us the security to publish in line with our values, which are collaborative, imaginative and 'shamelessly literary'.

All of our subscribers:

- receive a first edition copy of every new book we publish
- are thanked by name in the books
- are warmly invited to contribute to our plans and choice of future books

BECOME A SUBSCRIBER, OR GIVE A SUBSCRIPTION TO A FRIEND

Visit andotherstories.org/subscribe to become part of an alternative approach to publishing.

Subscriptions are:

£20 for two books per year

£35 for four books per year

£50 for six books per year

The subscription includes postage to Europe, the US and Canada.

OTHER WAYS TO GET INVOLVED

If you'd like to know about upcoming events and reading groups (our foreign language reading groups help us choose books to publish, for example) you can:

- join the mailing list at: andotherstories.org/join-us
- follow us on Twitter: @andothertweets
- join us on Facebook: And Other Stories
- follow our blog: Ampersand

Current & Upcoming Books by And Other Stories

Title: *The Restless Supermarket*
Author: Ivan Vladislavić
Editor: Helen Moffett
Proofreader: Sophie Lewis
Series & Cover Design: Joseph Harries

Printed in the USA
CPSIA information can be obtained
at www.ICGtesting.com
JSHW021457090224
57031JS00002B/73

9 781908 276322